THE BLUE PENDANT

VALERIE DUNCAN

The Book Guild Ltd

First published in Great Britain in 2016 by
The Book Guild Ltd
9 Priory Business Park
Wistow Road, Kibworth
Leicestershire, LE8 0RX
Freephone: 0800 999 2982
www.bookguild.co.uk
Email: info@bookguild.co.uk
Twitter: @bookguild

Typeset in Adobe Garamond Pro

Printed and bound in the UK by TJ International, Padstow, Cornwall

ISBN 978 1 91087 850 7

British Library Cataloguing in Publication Data.
A catalogue record for this book is available from the British Library.

For Maggie – 5-8-74
Alpha – Omega

And for
my family and friends for their
unconditional love and support

Preface

Could she breathe? No, she couldn't! Could she speak? No, she couldn't! All she could do was to stare bleakly at Sally.

Sally thought Jo was behaving strangely. She couldn't understand it.

'Jo? Did you hear what I said?'

Jo reached into the back of her mind and forced a monosyllable into the front. 'Yes.'

'It's Miss Standford, Jo. She's in reception.'

'Yes, yes, I heard you. What does she want?'

'I don't know, she asked to see you.' Sally was becoming increasingly irritated. 'Shall I show her up? Or ...' – she hesitated – 'shall I tell her you're busy?'

'No, no,' Jo responded, silently berating herself for her outward stupidity. 'Sorry, Sal, my mind was elsewhere. Yes, show her up.'

'Right,' replied Sally. But things were not right, she didn't understand Jo's hesitancy. She had expected enthusiasm. After all, not only was Jennifer Standford one of their most prestigious celebrities (whose article was instrumental in their magazine's triumph, so many years ago), but also an old college friend.

'I'll show her up then, shall I?'

'Yes.' Yet another monosyllable.

Jo stared at the door as it closed behind Sally. Her heart raced, as tiny droplets of perspiration began to form beneath her hairline.

It had been almost thirteen years since the name of Jennifer Standford had passed her lips. It had been carved on her heart, suppressed in her psyche, but never vocalized.

Questions came, evocative yet unanswerable. Why had she come? What did she want? And then suddenly she was there, standing in the doorway!

No more time for wondering. Jo hardly heard Sally announce her visitor, as the walls of her office closed in around her. She should move. Stretch out her hand in welcome, but nothing worked, her paralysis complete.

Sally left the office muttering something about coffee, leaving the two women to stand facing one another.

'Hello Jo.' The words were softly spoken.

Jo was inclined to ask the woman what she wanted, but good manners prevailed. 'Won't you sit down?'

'Yes, thank you.'

Good manners from both of them, then.

Jo smiled wryly at the stranger before her. For that was all she was. A stranger with just a hint of familiarity. Yet this stranger, dressed in a cool cream suit, pink open-necked blouse, which complimented her curly light brown hair and azure blue eyes, still wore the pendant.

Ah! The blue pendant. A symbol of a time when love was new, and all things were possible.

Part One

Part One

Chapter One

Jennifer Standford had been cosseted from young. Brought up with every advantage. Her father gave her everything his money could buy. She had no mother, but felt no emptiness, as she had been without her since birth.

Frederick Standford had never remarried after his wife's death, and lived his life through his daughter, leaving her only on the rarest of occasions. In latter years, however, his job had demanded long absences, so Jennifer was placed securely into a private school, and encouraged to learn all the social graces befitting a lady of her financial standing.

It was, therefore, a complete shock to her father to learn that his daughter had won an art scholarship. The battle was bitterly fought, will against need, determination against want, until finally love wore him down and Jennifer was allowed to leave the safety of private tuition and commence her career at the London College of Art and Media Studies. The stipulation, however, was that Jennifer was not to live in a garret, but in a house provided for her. 'After all my darling,' he had said, 'if you have talent it will grow no matter where you live.'

Chapter Two

1962

Looking back, it now seemed years ago when Jo found Jennifer (now to be known as Jenny, a shortened version Jo had given her) shivering in the uninviting college halls. The walls stood tall under ceilings which towered high above. Flakes of plaster hung perilously, just waiting for a breeze to shift them from their ancient positions. The acrid smell of turpentine, and mediocre staleness, tinged her nostrils.

Jenny had arrived too early, and as she stood by the closed shutters of the porter's office, hoped that she would not look too obviously like a new girl. A telephone rang in the distance, followed quickly by the slamming of a door. Jenny waited for the sound of footsteps to bring someone near, but none came. She wanted a cigarette, and wondered whether this was permitted. She lit one, deciding that if caught they could always say no. As she inhaled deeply she began to feel a little braver.

This was Jo's second term at college, and through her eagerness to get started again, she too had arrived early that morning. By the time Jenny appeared she had returned from the library, having collated her reading matter, and organized her timetable. She was about to head off for a coffee when she encountered this trim, elegant figure, nervously puffing on a cigarette.

It was a moment before she spoke. 'Well, well, well, calming the old nerves are we?'

Jenny visibly jumped at Jo's unexpected voice, turning abruptly, and coughing as the smoke caught in her throat.

Jo felt a little ashamed and apologized. 'Sorry, I didn't mean to frighten you.' And she stretched out her hand towards Jenny. 'My name's Jo, Jo Dawson. You must be new?'

'Yes, I'm, er, I'm Jennifer Standford, pleased to meet you,' Jenny replied, releasing her grasp from Jo's hand, averting her eyes, conscious that she was staring.

Jo was also staring, however more surreptitiously. Jenny's elegance was confirmed. Her clothes, obviously expensive, fitted snugly over her slim frame and her light brown hair fell in natural curls around her oval face.

Jo was conscious of feeling a little shabby in her blue jeans, sloppy jumper and white plimsolls. This, however, was nothing compared to the strange feeling she felt as she looked into this stranger's blue eyes. She found them deep and dark, like shadowy tunnels that held no light, no betrayal of thought. Jo hid her embarrassment by placing her hands resolutely into her jeans pockets.

Deciding to take command of her momentary blip she told Jenny that she was a wee bit early, as nobody did anything the first day back. She winked. 'The porter won't arrive until gone two. How about a cup of coffee?'

Jenny smiled at Jo and felt quite glad that her early arrival had produced this meeting.

Chatting informally, they walked out from the college, into the High Street and onwards to the Lyons Corner House. With the tray of coffees paid for, they chose a table by the window and sat down. Jenny had black coffee, whilst Jo had a 'milk and a dash'.

It wasn't long before they realized that they both shared a love of music and the theatre, and regaled each other on art and poetry.

Chapter Three

The following months nurtured their friendship, and studying became a delight. Although they took different subjects, which kept them apart during college classes, they met regularly for lunch every day, keeping each other up to date with their progress. As Jo had started her four-year course earlier than Jenny, it meant that as Jenny's was only a three-year course they would happily finish college together. They soon became inseparable, delighting in their shared fantasies and ambitions.

The first two terms flew by, and it became distinctly apparent that Jenny's talent was undeniable. She mastered quickly the concepts of colour, texture, perception and dimension, developing a keen sense of imagination and architectural foresight. Yet she never seemed to lose sight of the old masters' traditional and inherent passion.

Jo, on the other hand continued to write prolifically. Words inspired her, poetry besotted her. *One day,* she thought, *one day …*

Jo had already made plans for the Easter break. She would return home to Pen Marig and stay with her Aunt Doll and Uncle Tom. Although she had corresponded regularly since she left for college, there was no substitute for the warmth and security of going home.

The Easter term ended mid-morning and Jenny and Jo took themselves off to the park to spend the time eating lunch and feeding the ducks on the pond, and it was then that Jo told Jenny of her decision to go to Wales for the Easter holiday. She would catch the early morning train and arrive home just before the evening milking. She smiled as she remembered all the happy times she had spent at Pen Marig.

'What are you smiling at?' Jenny asked.

Jo half-laughed, and told her about her plans.

'Oh,' was all Jenny replied.

After a moment's silence Jo asked Jenny about her plans for Easter, and was told that she would spend it alone. Guilt overshadowed Jo's recent enthusiasm. Should she stay or should she go? Then the decision was made for her.

'Is it definite about Wales?' Jenny asked.

'Well no –' before Jo could finish her sentence, Jenny rushed on.

'Well then, why don't you stay with me for a couple of days and then go to Wales later in the week?'

Jo felt excited by the idea and replied, 'Well, I suppose I could.'

'That's settled then,' Jenny responded, not allowing Jo any change of mind. 'You go home, get your things, and I'll get us something to eat.'

On her way back to her digs Jo worried. Had she done the right thing? She felt slightly nauseous. Was it hunger or nerves? She did not quite understand the slight palpitation that seemed to increase her heartbeats. Although she had previously experienced these physical nuances when in Jenny's company, they were never as strong as they were that day. She told herself not to be stupid and put it down to her unexpected change of plans.

Finally she packed her one and only suitcase, a small overnight bag, and arrived at Jenny's a couple of hours later.

Jenny's house lay within a long thin mews, lazily sprawled along a cobblestone avenue. Each house was individually decorated with antique coach lights and ornamental window boxes, nestling cosily against one another.

Jo heard Jenny call her name, and looked up to see her hanging out of the window, frantically waving.

Those physical nuances, she had calmed during her packing were back again. *What is going on?* she wondered.

The inside of Jenny's house was warm, cosy and welcoming. Miniature pictures dotted the gold-papered walls, and deep burgundy drapes hung from the window pelmets. The living room was circular, with the kitchen leading off through a stuccoed archway. One side of the circle was completely encased with books and records, whilst the other held leaded light cabinets housing ornaments, glasses and bottles of wine.

Jenny took Jo's bags and walked towards the stairs. 'I've tidied the spare room and put a bottle in the bed to air it, so it should be alright. And,' she added, after a well-designed pause, 'I'll cook us something special.'

'Oh yes, what would that be?' laughed Jo.

'Beans on toast,' Jenny replied, holding up her arms and shrieking with laughter.

After Jo had settled in, they went back downstairs.

'Help yourself to a glass of wine,' Jenny called from the kitchen.

A glass of wine, Jo thought. The nearest she had ever come to alcohol was the traditional glass of Christmas home-made elderberry wine her aunty gave her.

She sipped the red liquid. The taste was strangely akin to burnt cork. This was definitely not the elderberry flower. She took another sip and began to feel rather decadent.

Jenny arrived from the kitchen and placed two plates of beans on toast onto a coffee table. She poured herself a glass of wine and turned towards Jo.

'Well how's the wine? Nice isn't it? Father brings it from France. He does like a glass or two when he visits me.'

Jo wondered whether he would mind his wine being drunk by a philistine, but kept this thought to herself and replied in affirmation.

With cold beans on toast left half-eaten on their plates, Jo's timidity began to dissipate as she drank her second glass of wine. Together they drank wine, listened to music, chatted and laughed, each of them happy in the company of the other. They were both extremely tipsy as they drank the last dregs from the first bottle, and languished comfortably on the floor in front of the fire. They had no inclination to move.

As the night drew on, Jo wondered whether she should produce the zircon pendant she had bought for Jenny as an Easter present. She had seen it in a second-hand jewellery shop, each time she passed. She had saved the money from the allowance that Tom sent her each month. Every day she would glance into the shop window, hoping it had not been sold, and purchased it the week before Easter.

The blue pendant, teardrop shaped, hung from a gold chain. As soon as she saw it Jo knew that it would complement Jenny's eyes exactly. But now she became embarrassed by the gift. *Oh well,* she thought, *nothing ventured, nothing gained.* And reached into her bag from which, rather hesitantly, she took the wrapped box.

'Um, I – I thought you might like this.' And then feeling that embarrassment again, very quickly added, 'Just a little something for Easter.'

Jenny looked up at Jo and smiled. 'Well, great minds do think alike, I also have something for you.' And she jumped up from the floor, ran up the stairs to her bedroom and returned with a neatly wrapped package.

She handed it to Jo and they unwrapped their presents together.

Jo's was a leather-bound edition of Wordsworth's poems. 'Oh gosh,' was all she could say, as she opened the book and read the words written on the flyleaf.

> *'True beauty dwells in deep retreats,*
> *Whose veil is unremoved*
> *Till heart with heart in concord beats,*
> *And the lover is beloved.*
> (Wordsworth, 'A Complaint')

Jo felt disconcerted by the words. Why were these chosen? Was it because Jenny had extracted them without thought, from a favourite poem, or was there a certain ambiguity in their meaning? Again, she told herself not to be stupid. The wine had enhanced her imaginings. Jenny's squeal of delight interrupted any additional thought.

'Oh Jo this is lovely. Quick, put it on for me.'

Jo gently placed the book beside her and moved around to the back of Jenny and began to fasten the clasp of the gold chain around her neck. She found the task difficult as her hands shook uncontrollably. Three times she tried, but failure was complete when she finally dropped the chain.

'Haven't you done it yet?' Jenny asked with slight irritation.

'No, sorry, the clasp is a bit small. I'll try again.' Silently berating herself, *stupid, stupid woman.* Finally, she managed to unfumble her fingers and close the clasp over its gold ring. 'There,' she sighed, 'all done.'

Jenny cupped the pendant between her thumb and index finger, raised it to her lips and gently kissed it. 'There you are Jo, I will wear it forever.'

They both half-laughed and fell into an embarrassed silence.

As they quietly sipped wine from a second opened bottle, Jo watched Jenny's neatly manicured fingers thread their way through the tufts of the carpet. She knew, with the enormity of realization, that she wanted to reach out and touch them. In that moment Jo felt ashamed of her thoughts and cast them away quickly under the camouflage of another sip of wine.

'I suppose we ought to make a move,' she said presently, not really wanting the evening to end.

'Oh no, not yet,' Jenny replied. 'I'm quite comfortable here and I'm not a bit tired.'

Jo's new-found realization had backed her into a corner, from which she needed to escape. No longer could she look at Jenny without fear of becoming exposed. The only thing she could do was to scuttle off to bed. She half-turned to get up.

Jenny reached out to stop her, placing the palm of her hand gently upon Jo's face. Her touch threw a bolt of electricity through Jo's veins, and as she jumped back she cried, 'Don't! Don't!'

'Jo, Jo, what's the matter? Are you ill?'

All Jo could muster was a faint 'No,' as Jenny once again gently placed her hand on Jo's cheek, at which Jo's fragile composure dissipated, leaving her bereft of all defences.

'I'm sorry Jen, but I can't do this.'

'Do what?' Jenny asked.

Jo sighed, resigned to her fate.

'I can't ...' she searched for words, 'I mean I can't ... we can't. We can't be friends any more!'

'And why not?' Jenny replied with a laugh that made Jo angry.

'Don't play games Jen, you know why not!'

'Games? What games Jo? Aren't you the one playing games? Don't you know by now how I feel about you?'

Jo was surprised and quite afraid at the passion she saw in Jenny's eyes – no longer the cultured refined young woman. Was this the same passion that drove her to paint? But she said nothing. This one moment could be lost to misinterpretation.

Jenny placed her hands on Jo's shoulders and gently shook her.

The wine had made a heroine of her. 'For God's sake Jo, don't you know that I'm in love with you?'

There, the words were said, it was out in the open. No taking back. Bridges burnt, boats sunk. The die was cast.

Suddenly Jo felt a cacophony of fear, excitement and anticipation swirl around her brain, threatening to erupt into manic insensibility. She could say nothing, only stare at Jenny, who now realized she may have been too forthright, too quick with her assumptions.

'Oh, Jo, I am sorry. I've embarrassed you. I –'

'No, no Jen, you haven't. It's just …'

'It's just what Jo?'

If Jo didn't own up now, didn't vocalize her true feelings for Jenny, she knew nothing would ever be the same again.

Just what? Yes it was just what, as Jo poured out all those secretly kept feelings. All the personal admonishments that swung like a pendulum from guilt, possibility and then back to guilt. When her rhetoric was over, a stillness engulfed them as they sat holding hands. Neither knowing what to say or what to do.

Finally, they resigned themselves to the inevitable. In one magical moment they were in each other's arms, with Jenny's hair brushing gently against Jo's face. Both hearts beating thunderously against the other. Jo lifted Jenny's face towards hers until their lips were just a kiss away.

It was a beautiful kiss, timid at first with a reluctance at being discovered, and then strong and courageous, burning with all the desire for fulfilment. In that moment they were oblivious to the world, and time became an irrelevant bystander. Their lips met again and again, not wanting a space between them. They were locked in a prison, shackled by unfamiliar boundaries. Boundaries that would outlaw them from society.

They rushed in like fools. Treading where no angel had dared to tread, going where no mortal had dared to go, and loving where no woman had dared to love. They were hesitant lovers, unsure within their naivety, and yet instinctively surrendering to each touch, each unfettered desire.

The morning came, with the previous night's revelations stored secretly within their hearts. There was no turning back for they had set their sails by a wind that blew only in one direction.

Yet they had sailed their ship through uncharted waters. They had no map to follow, no sonar to warn them of the hazards that lay beneath the depths. Their love had given them no place to go, and the enormity of it paid homage to a lost appetite at breakfast.

Jo had decided that her trip to Pen Marig could wait, and they spent the rest of the Easter break together. They ventured out of Jenny's house only to buy food and take long walks along the Embankment. They were, to all intents and purposes, just good friends, but when alone behind closed doors, they were just two people discovering the passion of their love for each other. A love that must be kept secret.

And so it was all through the next two years, and only realized in their separate thoughts during the day, and their time together at night. For as certain they were of their love, the lack of propriety for its existence gave slender hope for its future. As a back street mistress would obtain security from the vacuum of anonymity, their moments of happiness relied solely upon the public transition from lovers to friends.

Finally, after the long wait to finals day, Jenny and Jo were both rewarded with first-class honours degrees, and after much thought they decided to take a couple of weeks off and make that promised trip to Pen Marig.

Jo had obtained a post as junior editor for a woman's magazine, and Jenny was to pursue her own career, with a possibility of studying at the Slade School of Fine Art in London, although her father had wanted her to join him in Paris, where she would be able to study at the Sorbonne. Now she was not too sure whether she wanted to do this, as it would mean leaving Jo for a year. Still, time would tell, and Jenny decided to mull this over during their trip to Wales.

Chapter Four

But, what was Wales to Jo? A homecoming from the wars of deprivation? A sanctuary from the ravages of living? No – it was her soul. It had held her in its arms when she needed comfort, and found her when she was lost.

Jo had come to Wales by default when her mother grew too sick to look after her. Mrs Dawson had been a very fragile person, with her fragility heightened by Jo's father's infidelities. When the years of loneliness had taken their toll, and were too much for her to bear, Mrs Dawson found her final solace in the quiet surrender of a gas-fumed sleep.

The funeral passed by as uneventfully as did Mrs Dawson's life. Without pomp or circumstance. An affair to be recalled to mind only briefly. Jo was taken to the church, in the absence of her father, by her Aunt Doll (Jo's father's estranged sister) and Uncle Thomas (Doll's husband), who were to become her guardians.

Jo's mother's body was laid to rest in unconsecrated ground, and as Jo looked dry-eyed at the flowerless mound, she remembered thinking how lonely her mother must have been without the company of other souls.

There was no reception, as none felt the need to either celebrate Mrs Dawson's life or mourn her passing, and on a cold November morning Jo began her journey to North Wales.

Sandwiches for the trip were placed into a basket, cases were stowed away in the small boot, and the tank of her uncle's Ford was filled with petrol.

The drive was a long one, and it seemed an eternity before they arrived at the gate leading to Pen Marig. As the motor car chugged and coughed up the hill to the farmhouse, Jo felt a sense of relief that this journey would at least soon be over.

As it was late, Jo was given supper, bathed and shown to her bed. No time therefore to survey her new home, and she fell asleep wondering what the next day would bring.

What it did bring was truly magical. Dawn broke to a Mozart symphony, clatterings from downstairs, muffled voices and the distant barking of dogs. Jo got up from her bed, ran to the window, and saw a landscape that took her breath away.

Everything was green. Instead of grey buildings packed together like badly thrown clay on a potter's wheel, there was grass as far as her eyes could see. She had never seen so many different shades of green. Bright and glowing, soft and subdued. Jo rubbed her eyes, for she could not take in so much colour all at once.

Suddenly there was movement and she looked down to see her uncle walking up towards a solitary tree which stood proud upon a hilltop. In front of him were two black and white dogs running here and there, barking all the time. Jo watched him until he disappeared down the other side of the hill, and thought she might go there one day.

All reveries were interrupted by Aunty Doll.

'Jo, are you up yet?'

'Yes. Yes I am,' she called.

'Well hurry up, wash and dress, breakfast is almost ready.'

Jo did as she was asked, and raced down the stairs to the kitchen.

Breakfast was a grand affair. She had never seen so much food on one plate. Bacon, sausage, egg. Freshly made bread and butter and a large mug of tea. Jo ate with relish, eager to escape the house and run up the hill to follow the footsteps of her uncle.

With breakfast eaten and washing up done, Aunt Doll turned to Jo. 'Now, child, we shall be going to the village today, to see the schoolmaster. Can't have you falling behind with your schooling.'

Jo felt bitterly disappointed, but Doll was not to be moved.

'No time to play, school first.'

And so it was, Jo divided her time between studying at the Cymgurig School for girls, and helping her uncle on the farm. No prizes for knowing which activity she preferred.

Tom and Doll Davies spoke long about Jo's future. It was apparent that Bert, Jo's father, would have no part of her.

'Can't let her go back to that place,' Doll had said. 'She needs fattening up, the poor little thing.' Food was Doll's universal panacea.

Tom felt softer about it all. Jo would soon blossom. Fresh air and home-cooked food would see to that.

'Trouble with you, Thomas' – she always called him Thomas when she had a point to make – 'you just want her with you on the farm. But she's bright and needs a good education.'

'Yes, yes, I know Doll, she can do both,' he grumbled in reply.

Doll retorted, 'You'll just turn her into a tomboy, that's what you'll do!'

Tom smiled inwardly. Poor Doll, couldn't she see Jo was already a tomboy?

As the years passed, Jo's schooling was a hit and miss affair. She found no aptitude for anything but English. She therefore decided to concentrate her studies in this area, expertly guided by Miss Griffiths, her English teacher. Soon she became a prolific story writer, and would sit for hours underneath the tree on the hill, which she now knew as Marling Rock.

Much to her aunty's pleasure she agreed to stay on at school until the sixth form, and after much persuasion took a college entrance exam.

'My Jo will be a writer one day,' Doll would say to the villagers, boring them rigid with recitals from the letter of acceptance from the London College of Art and Media Studies. 'There you are, didn't I tell you how clever she was?' And the villagers nodded respectfully, as if it was the first time she had ever uttered that sentence.

Paradoxically there was always a price to pay for good fortune. Pride vied with Aunt Doll's disappointment.

'Why couldn't she have gone to Aber? There's a good college there. Why did it have to be London?' she grumbled discontentedly at Tom.

'Be careful what you wish for,' was all Tom could answer. He kept his sadness deep inside him. He had wanted Jo to stay and work the farm with him. Yes he was sad, and yes he grudgingly admitted that he would miss her a great deal.

Tom and Doll did not have the monopoly on sadness. Jo's heart deadened at the thought of leaving Pen Marig. She had always viewed the green hills and the valley as her security, the early morning light as her rainbow, and the subtle stirrings of the animals and birds as her music. To leave this place, this harbour, where she was happiest was a torment that almost broke her heart. But leave it she must, if she was to find her way and her career. She consoled herself with the knowledge that this was where her life had truly started. Loving the beauty and the peace of it. She realized then that she would always be a part of it and knew that she would always keep her promise to return. And return she did.

Chapter Five

1966

Jo and Jenny caught the early morning train to Aberystwyth (known as Aber) from where they would travel by bus to Cymgurig. Aunty Doll had been telephoned that morning.

'Yes, my dear,' she had said. 'Of course your friend will be very welcome.'

Jo calmed Jenny's nerves. 'They will love you. After all, who wouldn't?'

The length of the journey seemed to shorten as they watched the grey urbanity of the matchbox buildings change to green countryside. Jo hummed quietly to the tune of the wheels rolling along the track, and drew faces in the clouds as they scurried by. She glanced fleetingly at Jenny, who had been rocked to sleep by the motion of the train, then looked back to the window and her reveries.

The train pulled into the station. 'Are we there?' Jenny asked sleepily.

The porter, with all due courtesy, took their cases to the waiting bus. With cases safely stowed, they made themselves comfortable at the front of the bus. It took almost an hour to cover the twenty-five miles from Aber to Cymgurig and it was six o'clock when they arrived in the village.

Guy Evans ran both the only taxi service and the garage, and as Jo approached the forecourt she wondered whether he would remember her. After all it was almost four years since she had been back. She found him leaning under the bonnet of a car.

'Hello Mr Evans, any chance of a lift to Pen Marig?'

He turned round sharply. 'Well I'll be ... If it isn't young Jo!' And then, as he wiped his hands on an oily rag, 'Thomas told me you were coming. Won't be long … just wash up.' He wiped his hands on his trousers and headed off to the washroom.

Jo was glad to be home and felt an inner excitement at the prospect of seeing Tom and Doll again. Evans returned, locked up the garage and walked towards them. He nodded in acknowledgment as Jo introduced him to Jenny.

Pen Marig was situated about two miles from the village, over a hump-backed bridge and along a narrow lane, bordered on each side by fields and hills, scattered with buttercups, daisies and of course the obligatory sheep and cows.

The car was halted outside the bottom gate to the right of the lane. Mr Evans got out, unlocked the gate, got back in and drove onto a rutted path. Got out again to relock the gate. This was the never-ending ritual of the countryside, Jo explained to Jenny, who was highly amused by it all.

As Jo peered out of the window, she could just about see the roof of the farmhouse appearing over the brow of the hill. It was a bumpy ride as the path had become well worn with ruts made by the frequency of both tractor and motor car. Jo didn't care, though, for she knew in a few moments she would see her Aunt Doll standing in the doorway of the farmhouse.

The car drew up and there she was, arms outstretched, hair all tousled and apron coated with flour. Her round red face beamed and her shrill Welsh voice cried 'Hello *cariad*' in her old familiar welcome.

Guy placed the cases in the boot room, waved a cheery goodbye, and with 'I expect I'll see you in the village sometime', got back into his car.

Jenny looked anxiously at Jo.

'Don't worry, it will be fine,' Jo whispered, squeezing her arm as they followed Aunt Doll into the house.

Jo was excited, as she always was, by her return to her childhood haven. She was eight years old again, smelling the odour of freshly baked bread which wafted through the house. She remembered sitting underneath her favourite tree up on the Marling Rock, watching her uncle train the young collie pups to herd sheep. It was always a magical time. She never felt alone, but surrounded by noise and smells which emanated from the farm. She wondered then whether Wordsworth had sat under a similar tree, watched a similar view, and had substituted the white fluffiness of the sheep for the yellow heads of his daffodils. Jo again remembered how her heart soared with the power of nature, and her ears filled with the music of that symphonic symbolism.

Coming back from her thoughts she followed Aunt Doll into the kitchen and introduced her to Jenny.

Doll stretched out her hand and shook Jenny's in welcome.

Doll already felt acquainted with Jenny through the numerous letters from Jo. 'You know, Thomas,' she had said, 'Jo seems really taken with this, this Jenny.'

Tom ignored her undertone. 'Well that's good, isn't it?'

'Yes, but don't you think –'

'No, I don't think Doll. There's too much thinking going on if you ask me. You read too much into things. You should be happy for Jo.'

'Well, yes, I am. But –'

'Well, let that be an end to it.' stopping Doll mid-sentence, impatiently throwing his jacket over his shoulder. 'I'm off to the top field.'

Doll knew better than to labour the point, and set about baking scones and cakes ready for Jo's arrival.

Now, as she held Jenny's hand in hers, Doll pondered on the strangeness of it all. *Chalk and cheese, chalk and cheese,* she thought.

They were in the middle of tea when Jo heard the sound of footsteps. She turned in her chair and smiled a greeting at Uncle Tom. This sent a tinge of red to darken his already weather-beaten face. He winked at her. He had picked up the cases Guy had left in the boot room.

'I'll take these up to the girls' rooms, shall I?'

'Yes,' was all Doll replied, her attention taken by the all-consuming business of buttering yet more scones.

Thomas strode up the white scrubbed stairs, effortlessly carrying a case under each arm. He was so pleased to see Jo back home. He had kept new puppies for her to see. *We'll train them together,* he thought, forgetting that Jo was staying only for a week. *But what,* he thought, *can we do with her friend?* He felt slightly mystified, and yet amused at the thought of Jo's friend tripping about in gum boots.

'Jo, I've got some pups for you to see,' he said as he strode back into the kitchen, to Doll's exclamation of 'Oh no you don't, Thomas, the girls need to wash up. Plenty of time for that tomorrow.' Doll dismissed him with a wave of her hand, ignoring his mutterings as he walked out to the yard.

Jo had to agree with her aunty, and taking Jenny by the arm guided her towards the stairs. Not surprisingly they were still as white as they always were, and she remembered with amusement the hours she had spent on her knees scrubbing them until they were as smooth and white as marble. The wooden door to Jo's bedroom still had her name engraved on a wooden plaque, and as she turned the handle she felt a deep sense of nostalgia. If there was ever a place she could wish to end her days, it would be here, amongst the antiquated, uncultivated goodness, devoid of all material baggage.

Jenny, instinctively feeling Jo's need for privacy, stood back while she entered her room alone, and thus into yesterday. Jo was small again, with the looming presence of the walls and oak-beamed ceiling. She could almost smell the burning wick of the gas lamp and the aroma of polished beeswax. She turned and saw Jenny looking at her, and with one hand pulled her inside the room and closed the door with the other.

This was all that Jo wanted, Jenny and the peacefulness of quiet solitude. The toy farmyard with wooden animals, and the rusted train set stood on a table underneath a window. Framed pictures of Welsh border collies hung from the walls.

Jenny laughed. 'No dolls then?'

'No,' replied Jo. 'No dolls.'

Sensing that Jenny had had enough of her childish reminiscences, Jo showed her into the room across the landing which Aunt Doll had made up for Jenny. It was full of freshly grown lavender, the smell of which filled the air, and was complemented by the crisp fragrance of recently washed linen. Jo left Jenny to unpack, and then returned to her room, and also became engaged in the business of unpacking.

Supper was accompanied by farmyard anecdotes expertly rendered by Thomas. He enjoyed the youthful laughter that resonated around the whitewashed walls of the kitchen.

Finally when supper was over, the table cleared and the washing up done. Stifled yawns dictated retirement to bed. They both said their goodnights and went up the stairs.

They stood silently outside Jenny's door.

'I want to kiss you,' Jo whispered, cupping Jenny's face in her hands. 'I've been wanting to kiss you all night.'

'Me too,' Jenny giggled.

But kiss they didn't, as voices from the bottom of the stairs shattered their moment. They, still giggling, scuttled off to their respective rooms.

Doll felt an uneasiness that seemed to grip her heart with dread. 'What do you think Tom?'

'What do I think? What are you talking about, woman?'

'Something ain't right Tom. Something ain't –'

'Oh go to bed, woman.'

However, roaming the hills the next day, Tom had to silently admit to a slight foreboding, but couldn't quite put his finger on what bothered him. 'Stuff and nonsense, stuff and nonsense!' he said quietly to himself.

Unaware of Tom and Doll's misgivings, Jo and Jenny spent the next day walking along the stream that rolled down from the hills, and finally rested below Marling Rock. They laughed incessantly, happily sharing Jo's youthful nostalgia. Jenny said everything was delightful, and carried her easel and paints wherever she went, stopping frequently to catch the mood of the day on her canvas.

Both God and the weather were kind to them that week, perhaps realizing that there may be a price to pay for these shared moments. With tokens of love as treasure stored within the confines of their memories, they slowly drifted into a spiritual world where nobody could reach them. Their thoughts, words and laughter shielded them from the prospect of any exterior bombardment. Each knowing, perhaps, that reality would soon march against them.

Time went quickly by and on their final day Aunt Doll packed a picnic basket, as Jenny and Jo were to spend the day together, walking and then, finally, picnicking under the tree at Marling Rock.

It was almost one and lunch was already on the table when Tom arrived back from the fields. He washed in the butler sink and sat down opposite Doll. She was unusually quiet. No gossip, no chatterings about her morning's domestic adventures. He dipped his bread in his soup and peered at Doll from under his eyelids. She was nibbling on a crust, staring bleakly at her bowl.

'What's up, *cariad*?'

Still she didn't speak.

'Ugh,' he groaned. 'Silence, is it?'

She nibbled once more at her bread. Tom continued with his soup.

'It's not right Tom, it's not right,' she whispered as if talking to herself.

'What's not right, Doll?'

'That … that friendship. I've seen them together Tom.'

'And seen what, Doll? Two girls who are fond of each other. Nothing more, nothing less.'

'You're a fool Thomas if you think that's all there is.'

Tom felt exasperated, not at Doll's words, but at the fact that they nurtured his own misgivings. He had not seen much of Jo this week, and disappointment irked him.

'So?'

'So, Tom, you'll have to speak to Jennifer and I'll have to speak to Jo.'

'And say what?' he answered, feeling cornered. 'And say what?'

She put down her half-eaten crust and wiped her hands on her apron. 'I don't know. Thomas. I don't know.'

The subject was dropped, and Tom's appetite had gone. He stood up from the table and without speaking strode off to the yard. He whistled for Cass his collie and tramped up the hill towards Marling Rock. He'd lived with Doll long enough to know she wouldn't let the subject go.

In the distance he saw Jo and Jenny sitting under the tree, their closeness apparent, and he was reminded of Syd and David. Syd and David ran a linen stall in Llanidros, which Tom had often passed on his way to market. Syd was the exact opposite to David, slim and short with a close gait which left no space between his legs as he walked. Whereas David was a tall and thickset man with a farmer's gait. But their physical differences seemed to bind them together with a closeness that appeared out of step with nature.

'Queer combination,' Tom had remarked to his friend Dai.

'Um' was all Dai could manage, not wanting to elaborate upon the queerness of it all.

By this time Tom had moved over the brow of the hill and away to the flock of sheep grazing in the valley. He patted his thigh. 'Come, Cass, let's go to work.'

Doll polished and repolished the sideboard. She wished Jo hadn't brought her friend. She wished … but then stopped the thought. She would approach the subject with subtlety, and consoled herself with this thought. But when was she ever subtle? She always spoke plain and to the point. She didn't know how to be subtle. She put the polish away and went to the kitchen to prepare tea.

With chicken sandwiches eaten and coffee drunk, Jo and Jenny leaned against the tree and quietly smoked a cigarette.

'I don't know how you could ever leave this place Jo, it's so beautiful.'

'Yes, I know Jen. I will always consider Pen Marig my home, but if I'd stayed, I would never have met you!'

Jenny lifted Jo's hand to her lips and kissed it. 'I'm so glad you did, so glad. Now' – letting Jo's hand fall to her lap – 'go away Jo. I want to sketch and can't concentrate with you beside me.'

They both laughed.

'Alright, alright, I'm going.' Jo jumped to her feet, picked up the repacked picnic basket, and ran down the hill, stopping halfway to turn back and blow a kiss. She had never felt so happy.

'Is that you Jo?' Aunt Doll called from the kitchen. Her question was superfluous as, watching through her kitchen window, she had already seen Jo run down the hill. 'Wash up and come and have some tea.'

Tea was poured and scones buttered.

'Shame you have to go back Jo. We've loved having you here.'

Jo sighed. 'Yes it is, but I have to get things ready to start my job at the magazine Monday week.'

'Oh yes, the magazine. And what about your friend? What will she do?'

'Off to Paris for a year I think,' Jo replied, and then almost inaudibly, 'I shall miss her dreadfully.'

23

Aunt Doll internalized a sigh of relief. Did she really have to say something now?

'Yes I know, dear, but don't you think that's a good thing?' Doll had started and Jo's raised eyebrows were not going to stop her midflow. 'After all, you'll meet new friends at work and perhaps a –'

'A what, Aunty?'

'Er, a nice young man'.

Jo, suddenly feeling defensive, jumped up from the table. 'Not for me, Aunty, I'm quite happy as I am!'

Aunt Doll stretched out her arms. 'Come here child.' Once Jo was in them she felt she did not want to let her go, and as she patted Jo's back a tear formed in her eye.

'I know you are, child, but is it right? You seem to set such store by your friend. Too much store I think'

'I don't know what you mean, Aunty. Jenny is my best friend.'

'Very well Jo, I'll say no more.' But as she remembered Tom's words, she added, 'Just be careful what you wish for.'

The matter was closed and Jo walked into the yard, and sat on the wooden bench to await Jenny's return.

As Tom whistled directions to Cass, he thought how simple life was, simple and uncomplicated. Cass knew what to do – his sheep knew where to go. He couldn't deal with complications; he was pragmatic in deed and unemotional in thought. He was annoyed at Doll, why couldn't she let matters be? And then as an afterthought: none of this would be happening if Jo had stayed on the farm. So this is what education does for you. But she hadn't, and a task had to be done. If not he had to look forward only to silence, punctuated by monosyllabic answers from Doll.

With sheep safely herded to the lower field, Tom returned to Marling Rock. As she saw him approach, Jenny stopped sketching, looked up and smiled. She could see why Jo loved him so much.

Tom took out his pipe and matches. 'Do you mind?'

'No, of course not.'

He sat down beside her and bade Cass to sit and stay.

'She's a lovely dog, Tom.'

'Yes she is, she's my best friend. It's good to have a best friend.'

'Yes it is,' replied Jenny.

'You and my Jo seem very close.'

'Yes, I suppose we are.' Why was it Jenny began to feel a little uncomfortable?

Tom puffed avidly on his pipe, keeping the stem between his lips as he carefully chose his next words. 'Used to think her heart was Pen Marig. But it seems her heart is somewhere else nowadays.' He hurried on. 'I wanted her to stay on the farm you know, but Doll set a lot of store by education. Let's hope she comes to no harm!'

'I think she'll be alright, Tom. London's not a bad place.'

'Probably not, but their ways are different to ours, more … untraditional.'

Jenny decided to take the bull by the horns. 'Tom, don't worry about Jo. I'll –'

'Yes I know,' interrupted Tom. 'As I said, her heart is somewhere else nowadays.'

With a sudden movement, Tom leapt to his feet. The matter, as far as he was concerned, was closed. 'Well, I'll leave you now. Supper won't be too long.'

Not quite certain what had transpired, Jenny returned to her sketch, but concentration was lost after Tom's words. She put the pad and charcoal in her case and laid it beside her unopened easel. She had wanted to add some watercolour to catch the hues that changed with the dimming light, but had lost her enthusiasm for it. She sat back and lit a cigarette.

The light had almost faded when Jenny appeared in the yard. Jo's heart leapt as it always did at the sight of her. She felt glad this was their last day at Pen Marig. Aunt Doll was acting very strangely. She couldn't wait to be back alone with Jenny, cloistered within the confines of Jenny's house.

Jenny grabbed Jo's arm and whispered, 'We have to talk.'

Jo placed Jenny's things in the boot room. 'Aunty,' she called, 'won't be long, just popping to the village.'

Doll was put out. Supper was almost ready. Keeping the irritation out of her voice she requested them not to be long.

'What's going on?' Jo asked as they reached the gate.

'I don't know, but your uncle seemed a bit strange.'

'How do you mean, strange?'

'Well he seemed to be saying – whilst trying not to say – that he thought you were too fond of me.'

'You're right Jenny, Aunt Doll acted just the same. I think they've guessed.'

'Guessed what?' replied Jenny, whilst already knowing the answer.

'About us.' Jo shrugged. 'Well, it doesn't matter, we'll be back in London tomorrow.'

'I know,' Jenny sighed wistfully.

She had been shaken by Tom's words, and added, 'But what if the same judgements are made? You'll be working for a woman's magazine, whose agenda is fashioned in propriety. What if –'

'What if what, Jen? If you are thinking of going to Paris, surely they can't suspect our relationship from across the Channel.' And then she laughed, 'Unless they're clairvoyant.'

Jenny was not comforted by Jo's words. Making light of the situation did not make it go away.

Supper was a quiet affair. Everyone lost in their own thoughts. Parting was perhaps not such a sweet sorrow after all.

Aunt Doll busied herself clearing away and washing up, whilst Tom retired to the front room to smoke his pipe. The girls had decided to retire early and finish packing ready for tomorrow's early start.

The next day, kisses and hugs were given whilst Guy stowed their cases into the car.

'Don't be a stranger,' Doll's voice shrilled out as they moved off down the lane away from Pen Marig.

As Jo glanced back, she wondered whether she would ever return.

Jenny squeezed Jo's hand. 'Don't worry darling, you'll soon be back.'

Chapter Six

It was cold and damp when they finally arrived at Jenny's.

'Oh, let's unpack tomorrow Jo,' Jenny said as they dumped their cases in the hall.

'Oh yes, let's.'

Jenny walked to the kitchen. 'Cup of tea?'

'No, don't think so.'

'Glass of wine then?'

'Yes, please.'

It was too late to light a real fire, so they sat huddled together on the floor in front of a two-bar electric one.

Jo watched as Jenny sipped her wine and fiddled with the blue pendant around her neck.

'Gosh, Jen, I do love you so.'

Jenny turned and smiled. 'Ditto.'

As they kissed away all previous misgivings, it seemed that they were the only two people left in the world. How could anyone say that this was wrong? Different, certainly, but wrong? No. There was a kind of completeness that welded them together. Each breath capturing that of the other. Each synchronized heartbeat pounding out a single existence. Different, certainly, but wrong? No!

'In the primal sympathy
which having been must ever be;

Thanks to the human heart by which we live,.
Thanks to its tenderness, its joys, its hopes, its fears,.
To me the meanest flower that blows can give
Thoughts that do often lie too deep for tears.'
(Wordsworth, 'Imitations of Immortality')

This was to be the final week they would spend together, and still Jenny was undecided whether to go to Paris.

'If I did go, Jo, it's only for a year. I'll write constantly. And if you can, perhaps come for a visit?'

Jo was not convinced. Before their visit to Wales, Jenny had thought of staying in London and studying at the Slade. Why was she so hesitant now?

'Where would you stay?'

'Oh I don't know, Father would find me something, and then I'll write to you and send the address. But if I do go, darling, I would want you to stay here at Flaxman Square.'

Jo hated the thought: stay in Jenny's house without Jenny?

'No Jen, I'll be OK in my digs until I can find something else.'

Jenny was dismayed. 'But how would I know where you were?'

Jo kissed her. 'Silly goose, I won't move until I hear from you. Then if you do go to Paris I'll write and let you know the new address.'

'All right darling we'll leave it at that. If I do go, I mean.'

A passing remark changed everything. On the day before Jenny's departure they had decided to go out for a meal. This was to be paid for by Jenny's father who had sent her money, a present for graduating. It was to be their last night together, before Jo started work and Jenny pursued her own career in the art that she loved, and they wanted to make the most of it.

Jo wore a tailored trouser suit, which she and Jenny had picked out for her first day at the magazine, and an open-necked blouse. Her short dark hair was combed back into a V shape which nestled close against the back of her neck. Jenny wore a primrose-coloured dress which flared out under her breasts into a long flowing skirt. Her oval face was framed by golden curls in which she had pinned a silver clip. Satisfied with their appearance they left the house and ordered a taxi to the restaurant.

They sat down at the table and ordered two glasses of house wine. This came and was drunk in happy solicitude. They peered at each other across the table, sending secret messages under their half-closed eyelids.

Prawn cocktail was brought and eaten. Lamb chops were brought and eaten. Two more glasses of wine were brought and drunk. Dessert was substituted by another two glasses of wine. With the meal finished, complemented by intoxicated high spirits, Jo requested the bill.

She was aware of the odd glances made in their direction. As she looked over to the next table she saw a man surreptitiously nudge his lady friend. 'Bit queer, not really the kind of people you'd expect to see in a place like this!'

Jo glanced quickly at Jenny, only to see her face colour with the deep red of embarrassment.

Jenny rose from her chair. 'Jo let's go, please. Let's go.'

Jo left the payment for the bill on the plate for collection, and taking Jenny's arm walked out of the restaurant.

Jenny was mortified by the incident. She huddled in the corner of the taxi as if trying to make herself invisible. She shunned Jo's affectionate pat on her arm. She felt wounded, and without a plaster, open to infectious innuendo.

Jo paid the cab driver and followed Jenny to the front door. Tears fell from Jenny's eyes in tumultuous ferocity. Jo took the key from her shaking hand and unlocked the door. Jenny, half stumbling, half running, went into the living room and collapsed on the sofa. Jo had not seen her like this before, all sense and sensibility spent.

She sat beside Jenny and gently pulled her close. She held her until the crying had subsided into breathlessness.

Jo's hand moved against Jenny's back in gentle pats. 'Don't cry darling, it doesn't matter what people think, it's just … just ignorance.' And then with a scoff, 'You'd think they had something better to do.'

Jenny was not to be dissuaded, as she moved away from Jo's arms. 'It may not matter to you Jo, but it does to me.'

Jo became angry. 'Why, Jen, are you ashamed of me? Ashamed of us?'

'No, but …'

'No, but what?' A sinking feeling gripped Jo as a chasm began to open up deep within her stomach. 'But what, Jen?' she reiterated.

'Those people are right. What we have, what we do, is wrong. It's alien, it's not normal.' Jo tried to make light of it. 'Nout so queer as normal folk, you know.'

But Jenny was having none of it.

Jo tried not to ask the question, but she did. 'So what are you saying, Jen?'

'I don't know Jo. I don't know what I'm saying. It's all too … too horrible.'

The chasm in Jo's stomach opened wider, and into it fell all her hopes and dreams. She stood up from the sofa. Her hands were clenched by her sides. Angry words came from the thin line where once her lips had been.

'I see,' she said, in a voice which meant she didn't see at all. She shrugged her shoulders, held out a hand to Jenny. 'Look, we're both tired, Jen. Let's sleep on it, you'll feel better in the morning.'

Jenny ignored the outstretched hand. 'You go, Jo. I think I'll stay here for a while.'

Jenny did not go to bed that night. She wanted to. Wanted to tell Jo it was alright. But she couldn't, for it was not alright, it would never be alright.

Jo tossed and turned, drifting in and out of sleep, awaking periodically to glance at, and then with resignation pat the empty space beside her.

She rose at half past five and found Jenny asleep on the sofa. Quietly she made some tea and sat at the kitchen table smoking a cigarette.

'Did you make a pot?' a voice called from the front room.

'Yes,' was all Jo could reply.

Jenny's entrance, as it always did, took Jo's breath away. Her dress was crumpled, her hair flattened on the side where she had lain. Mascara ran down like black streams and gravitated to the smudged blusher on her cheeks. But Jo had never seen her more beautiful, so untouched by the ravages of dreamless sleep.

She poured tea into a cup and handed it to Jenny. *Forget last night,* she thought, *pretend it didn't happen. Let today be the first day of the rest of their lives.*

She smiled and winked at Jenny, who responded bleakly. *Not the first day, then,* Jo thought.

'What shall we do today, darling?' Jo asked, trying to dismiss Jenny's coldness.

Jenny inhaled deeply, and then answered quietly. 'I think you should go home Jo.' And then, not allowing any rebuttal, 'I have to phone Father and arrange things for Paris.'

'Oh, so you've made up your mind to go, then?' was all Jo could say.

'Yes, I think it's for the best Jo. Perhaps –'

'Perhaps what?' Irritation and anger snatched at her words. 'Well, yes, I suppose you would think it for the best. Rich daddy, driving ambition, how could anything compete with all that? Not our love, for sure!' There. It was out. Hurting, cutting succinctly to the quick.

'Yet each man kills the thing he loves ...'
(Oscar Wilde, 'Ballad of Reading gaol')

'I think you'd better go Jo,' was all that Jenny replied. Jo packed hastily. The back of her throat burned with the ferocity of uncried tears. It was half past seven when she stood in the hall, bags held in leaden arms.

'I'll phone for a taxi, Jo.'

'Don't worry yourself, Jen, I'll walk.'

'But it's too far!'

'So?'

'Jo, I ...' Jo turned round hoping for salvation, but there was none. 'I'll ... I'll keep in touch.'

The 'Don't bother' floated on the cold, fruitless morning air. Where had the love gone? Was it so feeble it could be shattered by one malicious remark? If that was true, could it really have been love? Was it just a dalliance? An exploratory probe into an untapped universe? No, no, no, Jo would not believe that. What they had shared was real. *Well for me it was,* she thought bitterly.

When Jo finally arrived at her digs, she dropped her case and bag in the bedroom, rubbed her aching arms and then sat in her cold empty room. She waited for the public telephone to ring. But it didn't. Hurt pride came before the fall. She would not lift the receiver and dial Jenny's number.

Chapter Seven

Jenny Standford was born at half past eleven in the morning on the 23rd September 1944, after a difficult and tragic labour. Her mother's heart, weakened from a sickly confinement and four previous miscarriages, gave out almost immediately after Jenny's birth. She was left in the sole care of her father.

To say he doted on her would have been an understatement, for she was his very existence. He felt no need to remarry, and was content to have Jenny the centre of his universe, and indeed as he was to her.

She grew up both spoilt by her father, and disciplined by a governess. When of an age, she was sent to a girl's boarding school in Sussex. Here she would have her academic training, and learn all the social skills befitting a woman of her privileged background.

Of her father's business she knew nothing. He was something in banking, she had been told. 'Nothing to bother your pretty head with,' he would say. So she didn't.

Instead, when the day's classes had ended, she would sit on the beach opposite the school, sketching ships as they sailed on the horizon, and then wander down to the harbour and draw fishermen as they sorted their catch of fish and crabs.

Art became her obsession. It was something she could do all by herself without input from anyone. She studied hard, balancing her time between the mediocrity of academic lectures and the blissful exploration of art books from the library. Her appetite was voracious and was soon rewarded with a scholarship to the London College of Art and Media Studies. Persuading her father that art was the road she wanted to follow, would be no mean feat. Art for him was a frivolous journey of make-believe, with no money to be gained, no reputation to be had. His mind was filled with a vision of starving, unkempt souls, living in squalid garrets. No, this was not a path he wanted his daughter to follow.

However, common sense prevailed. He did not want his obstinacy to drive a wedge between them, for this would be even worse than mere capitulation. Procrastination he knew to be the thief of time, and therefore he conceded. He hoped that she may grow weary of it all and do something more sensible, something more befitting a woman of her upbringing. She was not to live in a garret, however, and so a rented house near the college was procured.

Jenny rose early that first Monday morning. She looked at the little piles of clothes on her bed. What does one wear? This would be her first day at college and she was filled with anxiety. She decided on a plain, navy suit, white blouse and navy shoes. She had brushed her hair until it shone and curled effortlessly around her pale oval face. Her long mascaraed eyelashes framed her bright blue eyes in ebony shadows. She looked into the mirror and thought, *that will do.*

She arrived to a vacant hall of residence and a shuttered porter's window. Panic overtook her. Was she too early? Was she too late? Did she have the right day? She lit a cigarette, drawing the smoke in deeply.

'Well, well, well,' a voice proclaimed behind her. 'Calming the old nerves are we?'

She spun round, almost choking as the inhaled smoke caught in her throat.

'Hello, my name's Jo, Jo Dawson. You must be new.'

Jenny saw the twinkle in the girl's eye. Was she poking fun? She said something like 'Yes', and 'Pleased to meet you', but everything else was lost as she looked at the figure before her. She saw dark brown eyes that looked straight through her, and shivered a little as if an exposed nerve had been lightly touched.

She hid a smile of amusement as she looked at the woman's hands, trying to seek anonymity inside her jeans' pockets. What a complexion, she mused, and was reminded of the weather-beaten fishermen on the Sussex coast. She wondered why she was affected so by this person's presence, and timidly accepted the invitation for coffee.

To her surprise she found their conversation fluid, delighting in Jo's stories of Wales. She made no apology for her own insular upbringing, for she knew that this had no bearing upon the friendship that was slowly forming between them.

Each day became an addiction. Lunch times were a necessity for her to meet Jo. To walk arm in arm with her along the embankment. To find an empty seat and eat sandwiches. She was both disconcerted and intoxicated by the deep feeling of affection she felt for her friend, an intoxication that fell flat when she wasn't with her. She constantly rebuked herself for such thoughts and remembered the stories relayed to her by her contemporaries in Sussex about school girl crushes. Yes, yes that's what it was! She had no reconciliation to the fact that she was no longer a school girl.

Easter came, and with it the close of the college term. She had heard Jo mention a visit to Wales, and felt disappointed. Should she invite her to stay with her for a couple of days? Yes she would. After all, Jo only had to say no. *Please say yes,* she inwardly pleaded. Jo said yes.

Excitement overwhelmed Jenny as she tidied the house. Search of her kitchen cupboards revealed a tin of baked beans. She hoped that Jo wasn't hungry. She was tired of clock watching. She could wait no longer for the bell to ring. 'No harm in looking out of the bedroom window,' she kidded herself. Nonchalance was not the order of the day.

When she saw Jo walking towards the door, carrying one suitcase and an overnight bag, she almost fell out of the window. 'Jo! Jo, I'm up here. Wait, I'll come down and open the door'

In that instance, she knew then that this was no school girl crush!

She showed Jo into the front room and told her to pour herself a glass of wine. All the while, in the kitchen, she was panicking. Beans on toast? Oh God, why didn't I get something more exotic?

She need not have worried. The evening was a delight. Her tangled nerves dissipated as the wine steadied them. She sat on the floor beside Jo, feeling heady and intoxicated. Her thoughts scrambled around her brain, disorientated and uninhibited. She longed to reach out and trace Jo's lips with her finger, but lit a cigarette instead.

She had bought Jo an Easter present. Should she give it to her now? She was in two minds when she saw Jo retrieve a wrapped packet from her bag.

'Thought you might like this,' she heard her say. 'Just a little something for Easter.'

She muttered something about 'great minds' when she rose to fetch her gift. Knowing Wordsworth was Jo's favourite poet, she had purchased a volume of his works. She had spent hours looking for a passage that would replicate her now secretly acknowledged feelings for Jo.

> *'True beauty dwells in deep retreats,*
> *Whose veil is unremoved.*
> *Till heart with heart in concord beats,*
> *And the lover is beloved'*

Jenny did not dare to look at Jo, as she read the lines written on the flyleaf. Instead she busied herself by opening the parcel on her lap. When she saw the gold chain upon which hung a delicately crafted blue zircon pendant, she squealed with delight. She couldn't believe how beautiful it was, and called to Jo to fasten it around her neck.

The warmth of Jo's breath on the back of her neck made her feel giddy. Her giddiness transcended into irritation. 'Haven't you done it yet?' she scolded. But she didn't mean that at all. All she wanted to do was to turn around and kiss the lips she had secretly traced with her finger. She felt afraid. Vulnerability overwhelmed her, so she drew the pendant to her lips and kissed that instead.

'There you are Jo, I will wear it forever.'

Suddenly the moment was gone, and she sat back down beside Jo and they finished the last of the wine. The anticlimax was unbearable for her, and when Jo suggested the evening should end, she thought her heart would break.

She decided then that this was too precious a moment to lose to unspoken words. She wanted to touch Jo, and she would. The wine had given her a heroine's courage. She reached out and gently touched the side of Jo's face, ignoring her cries of 'Don't! Don't!' She could put off the moment no longer, and gently shook Jo by the shoulders.

Time is such an oddity on these occasions. Did it stand still or move with the speed of light? She didn't know. She couldn't fathom it. Jo was in her arms, and time was irrelevant.

Chapter Eight

It was eleven o'clock. Jenny had enough time to ring the train station and book a boat train to France. After booking a seat for six o'clock that evening, she rang her father.

'Father, I'm coming to Paris. Can you rent me something? Nothing too grand, one room will do.'

Frederick Standford viewed his daughter's request with delight, and arranged for a car to meet her at the train station. In a matter of two hours he had found an apartment three streets away from the Sorbonne, and felt very pleased with his choice. He had missed his daughter these past three years and was glad to have her back in his life.

Jenny looked out of the carriage window. What had she done? How cowardly was she? She'd hurt Jo so badly. 'Oh Jo!' she cried as she lifted the pendant to her lips. As the wheels clattered along the track, they seemed to take all her dreams with them. She felt alone and utterly miserable.

The night Jo had left, she had wished for bravery. She had wished that her love for Jo could have been all-consuming, all-protective. Instead of her cowardly repackaging in the wrapping of wagging fingers and angry voices.

She felt disadvantaged by her father's cocoon that had shielded her from harm's way. She was now alone, denuded of the love she had abandoned. Her thoughts taunted her. She felt ridiculed by her own selfishness. Would she ever see her Jo again? *I know,* she thought, *I'll write to her as soon as I arrive in Paris.* She found a little comfort in the thought, and settled back into her seat, allowing a small tear to drop silently on to her cheek.

She finally arrived at the apartment her father had rented for her. The concierge carried her luggage up to the top floor and handed her a key. She unlocked the door, which opened into a large wooden-floored room. Shafts of coloured lights danced their way through the partially stained, unshuttered glass windows that rose from floor to ceiling.

As she surveyed the room she felt pleased that her father had taken her literally, and not rented a chic, expensively furnished pied-à-terre, which would not have afforded the authenticity she wanted. Authenticity which had been an inspiration to the Great Masters. To the left of the room were steps leading up to a mezzanine where the bed, washstand, oak wardrobe and dressing table stood.

Her eyes fell back to the main room. Although large, it evoked a kind of homeliness that seemed to surround her. A stone sink, accompanied by a frequently scrubbed wooden drainer, stood below a window. Two brass taps sat proud out of the wall. It was obvious from the double-ringed gas appliance that not a lot of cooking had been done, but it would, from her limited expertise, serve her well. A pot-bellied wood burning stove stood in the middle of the room, from which its chimney curled up towards the ceiling and disappeared. It had been previously lit, hence the warmth of the room that had greeted her arrival. A large oak dresser stood against the wall to the left of the door, and a large sofa to the right. A wooden table, covered in oilcloth, and two wooden chairs rested under the mezzanine.

As her eyes wandered around the room that was to be her home for the next year, her thoughts turned to Jo. She spoke in a half-whisper, 'Well Jo, I'm here in Paris. I wish … I wish …' but her voice trailed off as it guttered under the high ceiling. If wishes were dreams, she knew that these had been crushed the day she had let Jo walk out of the door.

She decided to have a shower and wondered whether the antiquated plumbing would allow such a luxury. Fortunately, although very hesitantly, the hot water gurgled from the lime-scaled shower head in concert with the rat-a-tat as air bubbled through the lead piping.

Once showered she felt more at ease, and unpacked her clothes, awaiting her father's visit. He had left a message with the concierge, and was to arrive about seven that evening. For Mr Standford, punctuality was an inherent condition, and he arrived promptly at 7 'o'clock.

'Hello Jennifer,' he gasped, his breath nearly exhausted from the climb up the stairs.

She went to him and kissed him affectionately on both cheeks. 'Hello Father, do sit down and catch your breath.'

He smiled, thankful for the invitation. As he plonked down on the well-worn brocaded sofa, Jenny took from him the bottle of wine he had brought, and busied herself with the corkscrew.

Finally, with wine poured, and breath regained, her father looked up at her. 'Well, Jennifer, you said you didn't want anything too grand.' And then with a little laugh, 'Not sure whether I will be visiting that often, unless they install a lift in the building.'

She joined in with his humour, and felt a lot happier than she had done a few hours before. She grabbed his hand and pulled him off the sofa. 'I love it, Father. Come, quick, see where I've put my easel. See how I have all the light from the windows? I shall be able to paint all day.'

He joined in with her exuberance, and laughed, 'Don't forget your studies at the Sorbonne. You'll be spending most of your time there.'

'Oh well,' she sighed, with slight irritation. 'I'll have the early evenings and weekends.'

He smiled. 'Come, Jennifer' – no abbreviated name from him – 'we'll go out for something to eat and then tomorrow, we'll buy some provisions.'

'And canvasses,' she interrupted.

'Yes Jennifer, and canvasses.'

The next day they shopped and shopped, and after making two torturous journeys up the stairs, even Jenny would have been glad of a lift. They spent one more evening together before her father flew off to Milan on business. This meant she had four more days to organize herself before commencing at the Sorbonne. There was no talk of London. Jenny had never spoken of Jo to her father. Primarily because she had not known what to say, how to explain her deep feelings; *best left unspoken,* she thought.

The following morning she opened up her sketch folder and took out each sketch, laying them gently on the floor around her. A gasp rose in her throat as she looked at them. Each page seemed to link together like a jigsaw, producing a retrospective picture of the life she had left behind.

She sank back on her haunches and just stared at the charcoal drawings. There was the lake where she had sat with Jo that first

Easter. Marling Rock, Pen Marig, the Cymgurig village post office and numerous other shared landscapes. All their days together, lovingly captured in her sketches.

As she gazed at the pages before her, her thoughts drew upon the promise she had made on the train. She got up from the floor, took pen and paper from the dresser drawer, sat down at the table and began to write.

> *My darling Jo,*
>
> *I don't know how to start this. What can I say to you? I could make promises, but would they be kept? The only thing I do know is that I love you with all my heart. Yes I know what you will say, if I loved you that much I would have stayed. Oh Jo, why could not my courage be as great as the love that I feel for you? I want to be brave Jo. I want to make things better between us. To love you, hold you, walk, talk and lie with you. I want to wake up in the morning and find you there. I want to fill my days with you and go to sleep with you. I want all these things Jo, but the wanting is lost inside my own weaknesses.*
>
> *I hate myself for hurting you so, but your honesty would not have allowed you to live with my pretension, my denial of what we are. So it is my secret to keep, and I shall keep it within my heart alongside my love for you. Will you ever forgive me?*
>
> *My love forever, Jen*

She folded the letter, tucked it into an envelope and put it away in the dresser drawer. She had meant to send it, but never did, and there it lay alongside all the other letters she wrote but never sent.

Her year at the Sorbonne was a complete success. With her technique nurtured and her talent undeniable, she was given her first exhibition.

Chapter Nine

Jo dressed wearily that Monday morning. This was supposed to have been a happy, exciting time for her. She had been pleased to obtain the post as junior editor, but pleasure seemed inappropriate now. She should have telephoned Jenny. But she hadn't, so that was that. She felt bitter and uncommonly resigned. As she caught the Tube to work, her heart closed ranks within itself. She opened its imaginary box and tucked Jenny inside.

Days turned into weeks, weeks into months, as Jo threw herself into her work. She became passionate and obsessive, until work became her nemesis. She rose quickly from junior to deputy editor, and when Susan Brown was asked to leave she was shortlisted to succeed her as editor.

Much to everyone's relief, Jo was chosen. She was a shrewd advocate and treated all her staff with respect. 'Firm but fair,' Sally her secretary had remarked.

Sally admired Jo deeply, but although obligated to Susan she didn't much care for her. She found her gregarious. A socialite but with all the social graces of a pariah. It was she who would select the celebrities to be profiled, the subjects to be written, each according to her own preferential tastes. Her choices were mediocre, and unfashionable, sending the magazine spiralling into decline.

Jo was briefed to pull the magazine up by its boot strings and into the twentieth century. The new age had begun. Banks had become mechanized, comptometers replaced by calculators and the silicon chip discovered. The time was ripe for Jo to move up to the plate.

On the day of her appointment she called all her department heads together. She explored each individual's thought processes. She wanted their ideas, and they didn't disappoint. The first change to be made was the name of the magazine. It needed to be both evocative and representative of its content. 'I'll leave it up to you.'

That was all that they needed. And left her office buzzing with excitement. It had been such a long time since they had felt motivated. Gradually *Millennium* was born, and within six months, with its format revamped, it became a flagship for its contemporaries.

Sally Bishop was no slouch when it came to work. What she lacked in academic ability she made up with enthusiasm. Having failed her 11 Plus, she had galvanized her efforts into passing her RSA Certificates 1 and 2 in Commercial Studies and left secondary school proficient in shorthand and typing. She joined the magazine at the age of sixteen, starting in the typing pool and worked her way up to become secretary to the editor. Admonishments from Susan Brown were disregarded. Her backbone stiffened by the support of her mother and father.

'Don't need to be clever,' her father had said as he turned wood for the legs of a table he was making in his carpentry shop. 'Just need to be better. If you put your mind to it, girl, you can do anything.'

It seemed such a long time ago now, but she had run the gauntlet of Susan Brown's pomposity, without malice or efficacy. As she extolled the virtues of her new boss, she felt rewarded for not having risen to the patronization of her predecessor. Yes, she admired Jo deeply, and thought herself more a friend rather than a mere colleague.

It was her friendship that made her concerned for Jo. Her obsession for work never seemed to tire, or leave her time for any extra-curricular activities. Sally's invitations for Jo to join the team on evenings out were met with polite refusal. Even when the final quarterly run was completed, she would join the team for one congratulatory drink and then leave money behind the bar before departing for home.

Sally worried about Jo. The six years she had been her secretary revealed no personal conversation between them. 'Surely,' she had confided to Brian, the magazine's star photographer, 'she must have a private life?'

'Not our concern,' Brian had rebuked. He was not one to become embroiled in salacious gossip, however harmless. He knew to his detriment what that could do.

As Brian's interest was conspicuous by its absence, Sally let the matter drop.

It was early August morning when Joan, the features editor, burst into Jo's office. 'Jo, you'll never guess what!

'What?' asked Jo, smiling. By now she was used to Joan's ebullient ways.

'Jenny Standford is showing at the Whitechapel! You know, the famous artist!' And not letting Jo speak, she rushed on. 'What a coup, Jo! No one's ever been able to interview her. Anyway just on the off-chance, I sent her an invitation, or rather a request, for us to profile her, and guess what?' Again she didn't wait for an answer. 'She's said yes!'

Joan's words flowed unheeded. Jo heard nothing after Jenny's name. The shutters came down, closing out the daylight. Ten years of confinement had isolated her consciousness. If Joan had offered her parole, could she take it? She laboured back to coherence.

'Jennifer Standford? Well yes, Joan, quite a coup!'

Joan was thrilled, and went off oblivious of Jo's discomfort. It would be three weeks before the interview, and Joan and Brian had their differences of opinion.

'Don't you think,' Brian asked, 'that Jo should be involved? After all, we've never had such a prestigious celebrity.'

Joan was slightly put out. 'Well, I suppose so …'

No more was said about it.

That evening, Jo returned to her apartment, an upgraded two-bedroomed affair she had moved into in 1969. The space it had once presented seemed to close in around her. Thoughts bounced off the walls, reverberating into simultaneous echoes of "Jennifer Standford". Jo never thought to hear that name resound on someone's lips. Although hers had touched it briefly, it had been lost in a ghostly whisper. She laughed, a humourless laugh, which rose deep from within the bowels of a defunct volcano, and erupted explosively.

She poured some wine and gave way to reminiscence. Jo's reminiscences were hollow – she had nothing with which to fill them. Ten years of work had controlled her emotions. Brick by brick she had built her wall, with competence and dedication her foundation. She felt proud that the mortar had left no chink in her defences.

But love? No! She would never love again. Hope did not spring eternal but remained a stagnant pool of wasted emotion. Time had been the plaster to heal her wound, but the sound of Jenny's name promised to reopen it. Could this force her out of her enforced wilderness? She thought of Jenny's eyes, and wondered if she would see a look, a passion or a recognition, should they meet again.

Chapter Ten

Jenny's heart ached for Jo, an ache that would only leave her when she immersed herself in her painting. She became prolific, with an obsessional madness, until nothing else mattered. Her thoughts of Jo were submerged in oil and turpentine. She spent her days quaffing down every last drop of the essence of her tutorials, and spent her nights compulsively transferring her soul on to canvas until her work became her aphrodisiac.

Frederick Standford was a worried man. He had never seen such obsession in his daughter. Jenny seemed to have no time for anything, and his invitations to dinner remained unanswered, as did his telephone calls. He had had enough! It was time to call a halt to this madness.

It was a warm Sunday morning when he arrived at Jenny's apartment. The summer term had ended so there would be no excuses, no avoidance. Confrontation was all that Frederick Stanford had in mind.

The door opened, to his disbelief. Was this his daughter? No! A replacement. Where was the young, fair-skinned blue-eyed woman? Whose was this sallow, gaunt face before him? The dishevelled hair and paint-stained overalls? Mohammed and mountains came to mind, but this was no time for philosophizing. He followed her up those interminable stairs, his breath almost failing him as he reached the top.

Chaos confronted him as he opened the door. Every available surface was covered with paints, brushes, canvases, half-eaten food congealing on unwashed plates, wine glasses misty with oil-painted fingerprints. He gasped, not from lack of breath, but from the sheer magnitude of the squalor that confronted him. In his anxiety and concern, he ordered her to shower and dress whilst he tried to tidy up. He left no room for protestation.

After awhile Jenny appeared, looking almost like his daughter again. They caught a taxi to the Coq D'Or, Frederick's favourite restaurant, and chose a table by the window.

An aperitif diffused the tension, and soon they were chatting, almost like old times. Lunch was a Parisian affair, each course punctuated with a glass of wine. A mellow Frederick decided it was time to talk.

'I think, Jennifer, that all this art is having a bad effect on you.' He raised his hand, forbidding interruption. 'Perhaps a holiday would benefit? Henri St Clair, a very good friend of mine has a chateau in the Rhone Valley. I will telephone him and make the arrangements.'

Jenny knew it was fruitless to object, so she shrugged her shoulders in hollow resignation.

Henri St Clair was aristocracy personified. His family, raised from the "old guard", oozed pomp and circumstance. *He would,* Frederick pondered, *be a good catch for his daughter.*

Henri greeted them on the front steps of the chateau. Jenny thought his smile disarming, his manner gallant, as he stooped to kiss her hand. *Perhaps,* she thought, *this was not such a bad idea after all.*

The holiday raced by with tours of vineyards, chateaux, and picnics by the river. Memories of Jo softly brushed her mind and then melted away like a snowflake on dampened ground. Jenny became flattered by Henri's attentions, and yet felt this to be a half-truth. Was this how Alice felt when she fell into the rabbit's hole? What would happen if she clicked her red shoes, would she be transported back to Marling Rock?

'What are you thinking about Jennifer? I've been talking to you for hours.'

'I'm sorry Henri, I was miles away.'

'So it seems,' he answered, a little disgruntled.

They were sitting on the veranda overlooking the valley. A breeze gently brushed the tips of the distant vines, the warm air permeated with the fragrance of vineyard blossoms.

Henri poured some wine, and handed a glass to Jenny.

'Jennifer ...' he hesitated. 'You must know that I'm falling in love with you!'

'Oh,' Jenny replied, startled at the outburst. 'Are you?'

She sipped her wine. Shouldn't she feel something? Wasn't this the way it should be? Again Jo slipped uninvited into her mind, and she remembered the glory of it all.

'Well, is that all you can say?'

'I'm sorry Henri, I didn't mean to be rude, and you know I'm very fond of you. It's been so lovely here.'

His voice softened as he reached for her hand. 'You're so lovely, Jennifer. Do you not love me just a little?'

If she were to love a man she could have no better choice than Henri. 'Perhaps,' she whispered.

He took the glass from her and kissed her gently. She closed her eyes, hoping to discover an absent emotion within the unfamiliar.

She spent the next few days enmeshed in her secret, ambiguous feelings. She felt ashamed at how easy deception became her. Fear of discovery heightened her senses as she lulled Henri into the mutuality of a loving union.

With the holiday over, Henri escorted Frederick and Jenny back to Paris. They had made plans, much to Frederick's pleasure, to continue their relationship. Jenny had no desire to continue at the Sorbonne, but would resume her painting, and with Henri's help exhibit at the Gallerie Tolouse.

Fate played its hand, and Jenny discovered she was pregnant. Henri's marriage proposal brought the emphatic realization that their relationship had been merely a dress rehearsal for the charade she was proposing to perform with him. She could play this part no longer. Her rejection of Henri astounded him, and despite both his and her father's pleas for rationality, she would not capitulate.

Finally, as a fait accompli, she realized the true nature of her existence. She viewed her pregnancy as stoically as she viewed her future, and when her baby girl was born she loved her with an unbridled passion. Whether it was a result of the trauma of the birth or the sweetness of its outcome, she would never know. What she did know was the overwhelming need she had to be with Jo. Did this tiny bundle she cradled in her arms represent her accomplishments, or her failures? She had no answer to that.

"*I'm going to call her Josey*", she wrote to Jo in yet another letter to be kept in her dresser alongside all the other unposted ones, "*for when I look at her I will think of you, and by saying her name I will keep a part of you close to me.*"

Henri St Clair was a bitterly unhappy, but determined man. He had lost in love, but he would not lose in paternity. Suddenly the battle lines were drawn, and although Frederick Standford hired a prestigious team of lawyers, custody of Josey was awarded to Henri, in whose established French family, the advocate ruled Josey would be better served. Jenny was granted limited access, with the proviso that she could not take Josey out of France.

Her devastation at losing custody of Josey in fact served her well, though this was unapparent at the time. She moved from the Paris apartment to a cottage near Reims, to live as close to Josey as she could. And thus, she went on painting, with both a maniacal passion and an infinite maturity. Fame and fortune ensued, shaped by the entrance of George Slingsbury.

He was looking for a "new age" artist to manage, and had heard good things about Jennifer Standford. Meeting her for the first time only enhanced his enthusiasm. She was as beautiful as her work was magnificent. Upon reflection, he knew that he would keep her permanently under his wing.

When Frederick Stanford died suddenly of a heart attack, Jenny was left with a vast chasm that nothing seemed to fill. She could have reconciled the loss if his illness had been a protracted affair, but the suddenness of it all was too much for her to bear. Her reliance on George grew stronger, but she continued to remain aloof from any other emotional contact. She worked frantically in her studio, locking herself away for days, appearing only when it was time for her to have Josey.

Three years went by unnoticed, but the pain of her father's loss, although less intense, remained. She spent many hours writing to Jo, and although these letters joined all the others, she found a certain salvation in the writing.

It was late August when the letter from *Millennium* arrived. They had heard she was showing at the Whitechapel Gallery in London, and wondered whether she would consent to having a profile written. Knowing that Jenny had avoided such interviews, George screwed up the letter and threw it on his desk, with a 'Don't think you'll want to do this.'

'Do what?'

'Have an interview with that *Millennium* magazine.'

'Let me see.'

George unscrewed the letter and handed it to Jenny.

As casually as she could, she placed the letter on her desk and flattened her hand against its creases. She looked up at George. 'Well, it might be interesting.' And then, 'It would be more publicity for the gallery.'

George nodded. 'OK, if you are sure, I'll ring them tomorrow.' And then, 'Wouldn't it be funny if the editor was the same Jo Dawson you met at college? Don't you remember, wasn't that the girl you told me about?'

'Yes, wouldn't it,' Jenny said, in a half-whisper.

Sleep was elusive that night. Thoughts of Jo flew rampantly around her mind. Would she ever have the courage to see Jo? And if so, what would she say? Ten years had gone by. She had made no contact except in the secret content of her letters. Letters that she had never sent. How could she ever explain this to Jo?

Anxiety and excitement are not a palatable mixture, are not a panacea of ills, but a catalyst. But could she be catapulted by her emotions into a realm of possibility? Time would tell, and she had three weeks in London before she had to return to France for Josey's next visit.

Chapter Eleven

Jo stood firm. She would not be seen as an interloper at Joan's interview. After all this time she could not alienate Joan's loyalty by presenting the assumption that her professionalism was in question. However, Brian was adamant that Jo's presence, even if only to meet and greet the renowned artist, was imperative. Jo decided to talk to Joan.

Brian had felt perturbed at Joan's decision to go it alone with her interview. He, like Sally, deeply admired Jo, and felt there was an inconspicuous empathy between them. He knew that Jo would never steal Joan's thunder, as Joan might have thought. She was not that kind of person. Brian had an instinct regarding people that had grown with him through the experience of his childhood. It had always seemed that Brian's roots were as fragile as a sapling's, blown down by a wind to rest precariously onto the forest floor.

From an early age he lived at the mercy of passing strangers who moved him from one unknown destination to another, never allowing any establishment of roots. It seemed to him that he would fade into obscurity as he moved from one children's home to another.

Children's homes by their very nature were an ambiguity. Not catering for children, but spawning young adults; not homes, but inanimate bricks and mortar. There was no welcome to be found there, just cold green and white corporation-painted walls. Tiled-floored corridors to which there appeared to be no end. Dormitories with "hospital-cornered" beds, and cheerless wooden furniture, uniformly separated like soldiers on parade. Each corridor patrolled by the obligatory matron, whose rubber-soled shoes squeaked like unoiled bicycle wheels on cobbled streets, and whose overstarched apron swished to the rhythmic urgency of her steps.

Brian had no appetite. Eating for him was a chore best left

alone, yet the same plate of macaroni cheese appeared in front of him day after day. His stubbornness not to eat this food only succeeded when the rancid meal was finally thrown away. But then, there was his punishment: no sleep for him until allowed by matron. Each night as his bottom grew numb on the tiled floor outside matron's office, he would retreat inside himself and dream of escape. One day, he dreamt, I will run away. One day I will be somebody! And as each new daydream came, he would open up a little box in his heart and tuck it away until it was time to reclaim it during his long hours outside matron's office.

Gradually he found he had no need of friends, for they would interrupt his singular world. He was an island, and yet happy within his own skin. Deprivation had strengthened his will. Solitude had honed his independence. Dreams had heightened his imagination.

So, when at the age of eighteen his incarceration ended he took the gambit of the outside world as a challenge. Relationships, however, were never accomplished. His inability to communicate left him bereft of the social niceties of conversation. So much so, that his introversion left him suspicious of any human contact, especially of the female gender, of which, he quietly admitted he was afraid.

His occupational choices were therefore somewhat limited, until he joined a printing firm as an apprentice in the litho print shop. Almost immediately he was captivated by the variety of colour as each print run metamorphosed itself into translucent life.

He pondered briefly upon his past, and when ghosts threatened to haunt his consciousness he would turn, as he always did, into his world of fantasy. His emotional life was non-existent, and when, unwittingly, he was drawn to another man, he would dispose of the feeling, and like that plate of macaroni cheese, stubbornly refused to submit to it.

It was a short step from the print shop to want to make his own pictures, and with a second-hand camera he commenced to learn the art of photography, firstly from library books and secondly from incessant practise. Once he felt his portfolio was proficient enough, he answered an advertisement for chief photographer with *Millennium*, a newly revamped magazine.

Jo had seen something extraordinary in the tall, tousled-haired boy who stood before her, nervously picking at his fingers. His angular face was spotted with pubescent pimples, and his suit was roughly ironed, with trousers showing a lopsided crease. She warmed to him immediately, and remembered the days when she had walked around in her favourite jeans and sloppy jumper. His portfolio, though, was nothing like the boy. It was adult, masterful and courageous. She liked it, and much to his eager surprise, gave him the job.

Although their relationship wore nothing but a professional exterior, there was always a hidden empathy between them, non-intrusive. Each kept their own secret. But was it the one that dare not speak its name?

Chapter Twelve

1976

Joan was busy typing into her word processor as Jo reached her desk. Joan, a rotund figure with a face to match, looked up and wondered whether Brian had expressed his feelings to Jo. Her usual infectious laugh was stifled into an enigmatic smile.

However, she need not have worried, Jo was not about to force the issue. 'I think Joan that both you and Brian should interview Miss Standford. I don't really see the point of my coming with you. Never mind safety in numbers and all that, we don't want to go en mass and frighten the poor woman off, don't you think?'

There! It was settled, no histrionics. She would leave the matter well alone. Anyway, this was what Jo said to herself as she walked back into her office, but secretly she wanted to go, wanted to see Jenny again. But the unknown was more frightening than the reality …

Joan and Brian were to meet Jenny at the gallery, on the morning of the 17th September, before the opening to the public that afternoon. Their early morning process meeting had gone well, and although Joan giggled with excitement and Brian agonized over the sufficiency of film and accuracy of camera angles, their professionalism won through and off they went to the gallery.

Jenny and George arrived at their hotel late on the 16th. They were shown up to their rooms, George's on the third floor and Jenny's suite on the fifth. Although night had fallen, the air was warm and humid.

Air conditioning cooled Jenny as she unpacked, and ordered a sandwich from room service. As she showered and pulled a comforting terry towel bathrobe around her she wondered if Jo would deliberately absent herself from the meeting.

Does she even know I am here? she asked herself, and then, as if presenting an argument to a third person, *of course she does, but she may not want to see me* – and then, *why should she?* The third person remained silent.

She ate her sandwich with unexpected hunger, and sipped the complementary champagne.

> *'What have I? Shall I dare to tell?*
> *A comfortless and hidden well*
> *A well of love – it may be deep-,*
> *I trust it is, – and never dry:*
> *What matter? If the waters sleep*
> *In silence and obscurity.*
> *-Such change, and at the very door*
> *Of my fond heart hath made me poor'*
> (Wordsworth, 'A Complaint')

She got into bed and allowed the champagne to carry her into a dreamless sleep.

How shrill the telephone ring can be when it is not expected. It was her early morning call. She looked at her watch, and was amazed that she had asked to be called so early. It was six-thirty. The paintings would be hung, with George's expert management, by eight-thirty, and her interview with *Millennium* would be at ten 'o' clock.

She washed and dressed and went down to breakfast at about quarter past seven. She had chosen, and put out what to wear, the night before, so there was no last-minute panic. She had chosen something that she thought Jo might like, assuming that Jo would be there.

In her nervousness she managed a cup of espresso and a slice of toast, but nothing more. Her mind full of conversations she would have with Jo, and then full of sadness should such conversations not take place.

At ten o'clock Joan and Brian arrived at the gallery, and found Jenny magnanimous in her welcome. The interview was fluid and comfortable, partly due to Jenny's personality and Joan's professionalism, and partly due to the two glasses of champagne they each quaffed.

Brian clicked constantly with his camera, carefully focusing and then refocusing in order to obtain the best perspective and capture the wealth of colour in Jenny's canvases. Finally at twenty past twelve with the interview completed, Jenny broached the subject of Jo.

She asked Joan, 'Jo Dawson, she's your editor, isn't she?'

'Why yes,' Joan replied.

'Well I think I may know her. I'm sure there was a Jo Dawson at the same college as me, in the sixties. If it was, it would be fun to catch up with her after all these years. Perhaps ... er, perhaps you could ask if she would like to meet for lunch or something.'

'Well, yes,' replied Joan. 'I'll ask her. Shall I have her ring you?'

On the back of a gallery circular, Jenny wrote the telephone number of the hotel, and handed it to Joan. She felt pleased that she had had the temerity to broach the subject.

It was half past eleven and Jo busied herself proofreading her political editor's article on 'The Changing British Society'. She was always pleased to read Angela's articles, which were succinct and challenging. Her grasp of the idiocy of political rancour amused Jo, and she knew that this current submission would delight her readers.

Jo had chosen Angela's article specifically, as she wanted to fully engage her thoughts with editorial business. She had left the past completely behind her, and could not allow thoughts of Jenny to break down the wall she had put up. No, this was just another profile to be filed in the archives of the magazine, and she would treat it as such.

It was these thoughts that she had firmly fixed in her mind, when Joan entered her office at one o'clock, and regaled Jo with the morning's events: the success of the interview and the splendour of the exhibits. Brian had, apparently, overheated his camera, with his constant clicking, and Joan was completely enamoured with Jenny.

'Where is Brian?' Jo asked, when she could finally get a word in.

'Oh, he's developing the photos. We thought that we would format the paintings within a framework, and place a photo of Miss Standford in the middle. Should make quite a good front page, don't you think?'

Jo nodded, her heart beginning to thump, despite her previous resolution. Joan smiled gleefully, and as she turned towards the door, added, 'Oh, incidentally, Miss Standford thought that she might have met you in college in the sixties.'

Jo didn't answer, her heartbeats were suddenly becoming thunderously incessant.

'Well, anyway,' Joan continued, 'she gave me her number to give you, in case you might remember her and would like to join her for lunch or something.' With the gallery circular placed on the desk in front of Jo, Joan walked out of the door.

Well! Now a decision had been forced upon her. Should she ignore the blatant request, or give into curiosity and accept the invitation. Curiosity? How inane could she be? She wasn't curious, she was fearful. How firm was her closeted life, how secure was she within her emotions. Was this a test? Could she just ring, have lunch and walk away back to her self-made hibernation? She placed a hand on her chest, trying to dampen the sound of her ever-increasing heartbeat.

Swallowing, she placated the dryness of her throat. No, she wouldn't ring, she would call in at the gallery. There she could become hidden amongst the guests, anonymous, with an opening for retreat if one was needed. Yes, that was what she would do!

She rang for Sally. 'Sal, I think I will take a long lunch, probably pop into the Whitechapel afterwards, to see what all the fuss is about.'

'OK Jo. Oh, and Angela was asking about her article.'

Jo got up from her desk, handed Sally a blue folder, and picked up her briefcase. 'Yes, here it is, can you thank Angela for another good job.'

It was around half past three when Jo stood outside the gallery entrance. She had paid off the taxi and watched it slowly disappear amongst the traffic. She was pleased to see the gallery full; no chance of being seen, then.

Best laid plans … She was met at the door by George, who handed her a glass of champagne and welcomed her to the exhibit.

'And you are?' he asked.

'Jo Dawson, editor of *Millennium*.

'Oh, Jo Dawson, aren't you that friend of Jennifer's? I'm certain I've heard her speak of you.'

Jo gulped her drink. 'Don't think so, perhaps it's another Jo Dawson.'

She needed to escape, but George had hold of her arm.

'No, I'm sure you're the one. Come on, Jennifer's over there, let's surprise her.' Protestations were of no avail, as George marched Jo over to the back of the gallery. 'Look, Jennifer! Look who I have here!'

Jenny turned round from the person to whom she had been talking, her face paling with recognition. She opened her mouth but no words came out.

'Jennifer, it's that friend you talked about, you know, Jo, Jo Dawson.' George spoke again in a louder voice.

For that moment the room appeared to be shrouded in a mist, as the two women faced each other. George, his attention drawn to another guest, left them. Who would speak first, who would break the silence?

'Hello Jo. Er, you got my message then?'

'Er, yes.'

'Would you like another glass of –'

'Er, no. Er, yes. Well, alright then.'

Jennifer walked to Jo's side and gently took her arm. 'We can't talk here, Jo. Wait, let me make my excuses and we can go back to my hotel.'

Jo felt perturbed, this was not supposed to have happened, and this was not a good idea at all.

'Not sure I can Jen.' There! The name had passed her lips. 'I have to be back at work, I … I only popped in for –'

Jenny's hand remained firm on Jo's arm. 'You can phone from the hotel and let them know you'll be delayed.'

Jenny was adamant, and so Jo finally gave in. They sat in the back of the taxi, their bodies close, yet not touching. Jo breathed in Jenny's perfume. It filled the air and challenged her senses. Perspiration threatened to run down her arms. She glanced surreptitiously at Jenny and silently gasped when she saw that she still wore the blue pendant around her neck. She wondered what Jenny would think if she told her that she still had the book of Wordsworth poems, dog-eared and extremely well loved.

On arrival at the hotel, Jenny handed Jo the telephone. She was to have no excuses; Jo had never seen her more adamant. Her insistence surprised her a little.

Sally was happy to hold the fort. 'Don't worry Jo, everything's tickety boo. Brian and Joan are in full conference, doing their usual one-upmanship, so they're happy. Angela's pleased with your comments and the paper's arrived for the print run at the end of next week. So, Jo, nothing for you to worry about. See you tomorrow.'

Jo replaced the telephone on its receiver, and plunged her trembling hands into the pockets of her tailored slacks. Jenny smiled, remembering the first day she saw Jo.

Jo's reputation as a wordsmith came under suspicion as her vocabulary failed her. Ten years of separation had dulled all sensory perception. She felt vulnerable.

'Jo, please sit down. You look like a spare part standing there!'

Jenny laughed and suddenly Jo remembered that laugh. The way the corners of Jenny's eyes crinkled and her cheeks dimpled.

'Gosh, Jen!'

'What, Jo?'

'I never thought I'd hear that laugh again.'

The laugh changed into soft concern. 'I know, Jo. Can you ever forgive me?'

'Nothing to forgive. It was another life, another time. Life moved on, things change, don't they?'

'Yes,' Jenny replied, 'but not my love for you.' There, it was out! And then, 'There hasn't been a day that I haven't thought about you, haven't … oh, but I'm being presumptuous. Perhaps you have someone else?'

Jo didn't mean to scoff, didn't mean to sound bitter, but vocalized feelings have a way of misinterpretation. 'No Jen, once bitten and all that …' And then, 'Why didn't you write?'

'Oh Jo, I did. I wrote lots of letters.'

'Well, I never got them.'

'No, I never sent them, didn't think you would ever want to hear from me again. Oh Jo, I've missed you so.'

Tears welled up in her eyes, and Jo realized she wanted so much to reach out to her. Should she? Yes, and with all her resolve lost she took Jenny in her arms, and as she did a line from a Wordsworth poem came to mind.

> 'One moment now may give us more
> Than years of toiling reason:
> Our minds shall drink at every pore
> The spirit of the season.'
> (Wordsworth 'To my Sister')

58

Was this that "one moment" that could define their duplicity? That moment when a stone thrown into a pool could create an ever-widening ripple? Round and round, swirling continuously, a never-ending dream held in perpetuity. That single step, hesitantly taken, culminating in a kiss as soft as a butterfly's wings?

Yes, Jo thought, *this was that moment which had lived within her for ten long years.* A moment buried, then resurrected. A dreamscape that had floated on the ether and finally had come to rest upon the body she now held in her arms. Silently she lifted Jenny's face and tenderly brushed the tears from her eyes with her finger.

Jenny shivered and moved deeper into Jo's arms. It was not a time for words, but a time for their hearts to steal this moment for feeling. But moments end, dreams vanish upon waking, and are forgotten in the cold light of reality. No, nothing had changed. Jenny was still afraid that this love she felt so profoundly could not shield her from the opinions of others, from the moments of regret she had taken from the past, and which now slowly pulled her into the present. Could she ignore that ghostly voice within her and give into her deep need for Jo? No she couldn't, she couldn't hurt Jo again. The truth had to be told. The very thought of denial renewed her tears.

Jo held her tightly. 'Jen, Jen, what's the matter? Please don't cry, I'm here now!'

'Yes, yes you are, and I … I don't deserve you, don't deserve your love.'

Jo looked down into Jenny's face, frowning as she saw the fear in Jenny's eyes. 'For goodness' sake, Jen, what is the matter?'

'I have a daughter!' There, it was out, and she spilled into the air the story of her life when she left Jo, Henri St Clair, the death of her father, the birth of Josey, and finally her trip to London.

It was all too much for Jo, too much for her to take in. She got up from the settee and paced the floor. She couldn't understand it. Her Jen, a man, a baby! How could she? How could she have betrayed her so? All this time, Jo had kept Jenny close to her heart. Never loving, never even thinking about loving anyone else. What a fool she had been. Anger rose up from the very depths of her being. 'I need a drink!'

Jenny knew this was not a request, and walked to the mini

bar to fetch a bottle of wine. In silence she handed Jo a glass, and poured one for herself. Jo drank it swiftly and sat down on the settee. She sat back and lit a cigarette. Still no words passed between them. Jenny, still standing wondered whether she should sit beside Jo. She chose not to, and seated herself in a chair opposite.

Jo sipped her wine and drew deeply on her cigarette. She didn't understand any of it. This was her worst nightmare. She'd wake up in a minute and be back to yesterday. So this was what love meant: betrayal, insincerity, a hobby to be discarded when one got bored. Well, she'd have no part in it. Her anger had turned to bitterness, and she silently scolded herself for her infallibility.

'Jo, Jo, please say something!'

'What is there to say Jen? You went off, did your own thing, while I, stupidly …'

'Stupidly what, Jo?'

Jo stubbed out her cigarette and looked straight at Jenny. 'Stupidly fell in love with you and stayed in love with you, despite everything, despite your going off to Paris without a word, a phone call. You have no idea how lonely and desolate I have felt all these years. How every day I've wished you by my side. Hated myself for being so weak, for being so unable to stop loving you. And now, what was it all for Jen? What was it all for?'

Jenny could bear it no longer. She rose from her chair and knelt beside Jo. 'What was it all for, Jo? It was for the love we had, the love we still have. Yes, I've made huge mistakes – leaving you, Henri St Clair – but it showed me that I could only love a woman, only be with a woman, and that woman was you! Is you! I named my daughter Josey, so that I could keep you near me. I agreed to your magazine's interview in the hope that I would see you again. What was it all for Jo? It was for the fact that I love you dearly, and always will. That's what it's all for!'

She got up, and accepted no refusal as she cupped Jo's face in her hands. 'I love you, Jo, you must believe that!'

How could Jo not believe the pleading in Jenny's eyes? How could she not believe the love she saw? She gave in. Yes, that moment was now.

If the past could be recalled for prosperity, then the present could be confined to that one moment when their kisses etched an eternal epitaph. Love was new again, full of youthful innocence.

Each kiss was the awakening of a spring flower. Each touch was a remembrance, each desire a fulfilment.

As if love had been locked in youthful discovery, it became uninhibited passion unadulterated by the passing of time. Prejudice was discounted, as a quixotic arbiter of reason. They confronted their adversaries and laughed with the magic of it all. They were united in victory, undivided in adversity. They were back again, innocently in love. With all passion spent, they lay together naked and unashamed.

Jo kissed Jenny's neck and whispered, 'And the lover is beloved.'

'Oh, so you still have it then?'

'Have what?'

'The Wordsworth.'

Jo smiled. 'Oh yes, I still have it, a little worse for wear. And you,' she added, touching the blue pendant, 'you still have the necklace.'

Jenny rose upon one arm, and kissed Jo. 'Didn't I say that I would wear it forever?'

The telephone rang interrupting their reverie.

'I'd suppose I'd better answer that.'

Jo sighed, 'Yes, I suppose you'd better.'

George Slingsbury was annoyed. No, he was more than annoyed, he was furious. He had spent all the afternoon placating disappointed guests. His excuses were lamentable in their fabrication. Where the hell was she? Three hours for lunch? Surely even catching up with an old friend couldn't take that long?

It was five o'clock and guests were starting to drift out of the gallery. Reserves had been placed on a number of paintings, but George thought more would have been sold if Jenny had been there in support. Yes, it was an angry man who rang the hotel.

'Oh you are there! Are you coming back? ... You're not? ... Well, yes, I suppose I could. It's obvious you have something more important to do, more important than staying and talking to your guests. ... Well, yes, I'll see you tomorrow. I suppose you will be coming to the gallery?' He banged the receiver down, his irritation smothering his fondness for Jenny.

Although Jenny had briefly spoken of Jo Dawson, George had always believed she was one of Jenny's college memories, and therefore couldn't quite understand how their meeting today could prompt Jenny to disengage herself so abruptly from the business at hand.

Oh well, he thought, as he tidied up the gallery, *women will be women. Don't understand them, never will!*

Although George had had many relationships, he had never had the desire to marry. He had started his long career in a variety of auction rooms, travelling around Europe until finally settling in France. His knowledge of contemporary culture fashioned his reputation and soon he became the father figure to young, up-and-coming artists.

When the rumour factory celebrated the talent of Jennifer Standford, he knew he must add her to his list of protégés. As he took this young woman under his wing, he soon began to realize his feelings were paternal. And so all through the Henri St Clair debacle he supported her. He didn't understand her, but he supported her. As he did when Frederick Standford died, and all through the custody proceedings regarding Josey.

What he couldn't understand was Jenny's sudden indifference. No matter what befell in her personal life, she would always become enthused by a new exhibition, hungry for acceptance and passionate about her painting. To disappear on the first day's showing was completely out of character. This Jo must have some kind of hold on her. *Oh well,* he consoled himself, *I expect she'll be full of apologies and explanations tomorrow.* With his work at the gallery completed, he went back to his hotel, resisting the urge to call upon her.

'Well, Sally, Jo's out for the rest of the day, then?'

'Yes Brian, she's met up with an old friend and will be in tomorrow.' Sally knew the old friend was Jennifer Standford, but discretion was forever her watchword.

'Oh, right. Can you pencil in a morning meeting for Joan and I?'

'Ok Brian.'

Satisfied, Brian left for the evening, his prints tucked securely in his briefcase. On the way home, he stopped at a Chinese and bought a takeaway. He was used to eating alone. At home, he poured a glass of whisky and ate the fried rice and chow mein from their foil containers. Fully sated, he poured some more whisky and placed a record on his record player.

It had been a good day, even Joan had been less contrite and open to suggestion. The front page would be magnificent, the best yet. He refilled his glass, lit his pipe, sat back in his chair, and listened to the strains of a Shirley Bassey record.

He wondered if the old friend was Jennifer Standford. Had they really met at college? He didn't know, apart from the fact that Jo had been acting rather strangely since the artist's profile was suggested. He didn't know, Jo had never said, had never spoken about personal things, apart from her fond visits to her aunt and uncle in Wales.

He took out his prints and arranged them on the coffee table. As he studied the photographs he began to understand why the exhibition had been entitled, 'A Welsh Metaphor'. There were landscaped, hills, valleys, pine forests and waterfalls. The colours, although brilliant, were overwashed in a misty hue, as if the artist had been looking through rain-covered windows, or tear-filled eyes.

Well Jo, he mused, I think you will like … and then he realized, this was Jo's Wales, this was her home, where she had spent her childhood and all the Christmases after that. He leant back in his chair. 'Oh. Jo, now I realize.'

He gathered the prints together, holding the portrait he had taken of Jenny, and stared at it. Yes, now he understood. Carefully he replaced them into his briefcase, poured yet another drink and turned over the LP on the record player.

He relit his pipe and thought of Douglas. Dear Douglas, whose life had been so brief. They had shared furtive, indiscreet moments together, when young apprentices in the same print shop. They had no realization of their growing feelings, and when they shared concerts, walks, and literature together their uncommon closeness was all he could admit to.

When Douglas had died suddenly, Brian was left bereft. All he had were their shared moments, and the inability to take that one step further. He thought of the loss of Douglas as his punishment. After which he never contemplated letting the "devil out of its cage". As he drew on his pipe, he now knew why there was that unspoken empathy between Jo and himself. He put on another record, poured another whisky, and continued with his thoughts of Douglas.

Chapter Thirteen

'George not a happy bunny then?'

Jenny laughed. 'No, but he'll get over it. I'll be duly reticent tomorrow, he'll sulk for a bit, but life will go on. Now, darling, are you hungry? Do you want to go out to eat?'

'Yes I am.' And then, remembering the last time they went out to eat, 'I'd rather stay here.'

They showered and dressed and ordered room service. They ate their tuna salad and drank their coffees in friendly silence. It was nearly eight 'o' clock when Jo looked at her watch.

'Oh, do you have to go, could you not stay the night?'

'Yes, of course I can Jen. But I must leave early in the morning to get to work. Joan and Brian will be champing at the bit to show me their finished work. For how long are you staying in London?'

'I have to be back in France by the thirtieth, as it's Josey's birthday on the third of December, and it's my time to have her. What about you, Jo, could we not spend at least a week together?'

'Not next week I'm afraid, as we have to get the quarterly issue out, and it's my busiest time at the magazine. However, I usually go up to Pen Marig for a long weekend once the issue is out. Would you like to come with me? We could be back well before the thirtieth.' Jo noticed Jenny's hesitancy. 'Well, think about it Jen, and let me know.'

They spent the rest of the evening quietly, drinking wine and making love. It was as if all the years had disappeared. They slept finally, and in the awakening dawn kissed and bade farewell until the evening.

It was a happy Jo who walked into her office that morning. Although she did feel conscious of the fact that she had not gone home to change, but did she care? She had arrived in before Sally, and proceeded to fill up the coffee pot. She poured the hot liquid into her cup and went back to her office and began to open her mail.

'Hello you, you're early!'

Jo smiled. 'Yes Sal, didn't want to prolong Joan and Brian's agony. I see you've pencilled them in for a ten o'clock meeting'

'Well, yes, I've never seen them so enthused. I'd better make sure the coffee doesn't run out,' Sally laughed as she left Jo's office. There seemed to be an unexplained optimism in the air that morning!

Yes, Brian was right, the front cover was magnificent. Jenny's portrait was to be edged by a framework of miniaturized photographs of her paintings. The difficulty was in deciding which of the portraits would be selected.

'What do you think, Jo?' Brian asked.

Jo didn't think, she couldn't, and she daren't reveal the fact that she loved them all, that she wanted to gather them up and squirrel them away.

'Oh, I don't know Brian, you choose.'

He looked straight at her. 'Are you sure?'

She felt her face redden, and averted her eyes. 'Yes I'm quite sure. Now, sweets, I must get on, and we have an issue to get out by the end of the week. Oh, and excellent work.'

Joan half-turned as she walked out the door. 'Oh, Jo, did you find out if Miss Standford was the same person you knew at college?'

Jo looked up from her desk. 'Er, yes,' she said.

But before Joan could enquire further, Brian took her arm. 'Come on Joan, work to do.'

It was a relieved Jo who watched the door close behind them.

The rest of the week was full of frenetic industry as the quarterly issue was compiled, typeset, and completed for its print run. Jo's days soon melted into long exhaustive nights, and intermittent times spent with Jenny.

With the closure of the exhibition and the completion of the magazine run, it was time for Jo to make her trip to Wales. Both her aunt and uncle were now very frail, and these visits came at a premium. For how long they could remain at Pen Marig, heaven only knew.

Jenny had still made no decision, and time was of the essence if they were to be back for Jenny's departure on the thirtieth. She would ask her to make up her mind when she met her that evening.

But first things first, there was the "end run" celebration to have with her team. They were full of high spirits, in more ways than one, when she finally arrived at the Pressman's wine bar. It was always their tradition that the team would head off early and she would follow them on later, once she had tied up all the loose ends of the day's business. Normally she would stay for one drink, and then leave a tab behind the bar before departing for home, but today she had more than usual to celebrate. Jenny had come back into her life, and all seemed to be well in her world.

'Well, team, how are we going to surpass this issue? You'll have to come up with something spectacular for Christmas.'

Brian put his arm around Jo. Since his secret revelation, he felt a fraternal need to keep her safe. 'Off to Wales then, Jo?'

'Yes, can't wait to get away from you lot,' she laughed. 'Just behave while I'm gone.'

They all joined in and laughed mischievously. 'Would we do anything else?' they replied in unison.

'Tab behind the bar, folks, see you in five days' time.'

Brian walked with Jo to the exit, and handed her a brown envelope as he opened the door. 'Here,' he said, 'thought you might like these.' Leaving no time for explanation, he turned and walked back to his colleagues.

Jo, bemused, but with no time to question, placed the envelope in her briefcase and walked towards the taxi rank.

'Jo seems happier,' Angela commented to Joan. 'Could be meeting up with Miss Standford. It seems they were at college together in the sixties. I would imagine it was quite a fun time, remembering the old days.'

'Well there you go, Joan, might be an article in it somewhere.'

'Um,' Joan mused. 'Might be fun.'

'Well, enough about work, where are we going after this? Chinese, Indian?'

They couldn't agree. A coin was tossed and the Indian won. Time for another drink, so Little Jimmy, now elevated from runner to the magazine's typesetter, and Brian were sent to the bar.

'Hey, look who's just come in!' exclaimed Joan, nudging Angela's arm.

'Who?'

'Anne Richards. You know, works freelance, sells gossip to scandal sheets. Was after the editor's job when Susan Brown stepped down.'

'Oh yes, the female pariah. Who's she got with her this time?'

'Some wealthy old man I expect,' poohed Joan.

'Oh God, don't look, she's coming over.'

Although they turned away to ignore her presence, there was no escaping that shrill harridan voice.

'Hello darlinks, hard at it I see.' And then, without drawing breath. 'So someone finally got to Jennifer Standford, what a coup!'

They ignored her sarcasm, rose to their feet and headed quickly to the bar with a unified, 'Can't stop, must join the boys.'

If Anne had felt their animosity, she was impervious to it, and returned to her male escort without a second glance.

Chapter Fourteen

Anne Richards knew right from an early age how cruel life was. Many years of paternal abuse closed her heart to emotion, and set her firmly on a course of self-preservation. She moved in and out of characters with schizophrenic regularity, evading any discovery of her true thoughts.

She gained knowledge through voracious reading and learnt to match her personality with pseudo empathy to anyone in whose company she found herself. She drifted from one job to another, never allowing herself to become attached to anything or anyone. She had set her sights towards a higher goal where power and ambition outshone any personal commitment.

Her reputation grew larger than her likeability, until she realized that there was power in the chosen (if not reliable) word. Scandal begat inquisitiveness, and inquisitiveness begat altruism. Soon she was able to sell her revelations to the highest bidder.

Her sexuality, although ambiguous, was confined to the wealthy. The older the better, for then she could prey upon their gratitude, but unlike the mantis chose not to decapitate them until their fear of it reduced them to substitute any communion with monetary recompense.

Her annoyance at *Millennium*'s interview coup with Jennifer Standford would not go away. And she still bore a grudge over the rejection of her application for the editor's post. She would not allow a small-time magazine to outwit her, and as she walked back to her latest conquest, she plotted her revenge.

In the taxi Jo took out the envelope from her briefcase, and was confronted with copies of the photographs Brian had taken of Jenny. She need not have wondered why, for she knew that Brian shared the same sexual proclivities. Unspoken, and yet apparent to those made of the same cloth. She felt no embarrassment, no shame. If Brian knew, then her secret would be safe. She would not mention it on her return, but just thank him for his thoughtfulness.

Jenny had spent an anxious day. She remembered too well her last encounter with Jo's aunt and uncle. How much had Jo told them? How many excuses had Jo made for their long absence? Would light be made of their renewed "friendship". Yes, it was a very anxious Jenny who opened the door to Jo that evening.

Jo, still feeling heady from the wine, held Jenny in her arms and kissed her passionately. She had never felt so much love, so much happiness. All was right with her world.

'Come my darling, sit down, and let me show you these.'

They sat together on the settee and Jo showed the photographs that Brian had taken. As she spread them out on the coffee table she touched them lightly with her fingers, tracing Jenny's face on each one.

'What do you think, darling? Aren't they wonderful?'

Jenny was thrilled. 'Oh gosh, yes Jo, they are really very splendid. Can I take a couple for Josey?'

'Of course you can. Now, what have you decided about Wales?'

'I don't know Jo. You say that they are very frail, are you certain that they won't mind my coming with you? After all, they weren't very happy about us the last time we visited.'

Jo laughed, and placed her arm around Jenny. 'Don't be silly, they'll be fine. They've always wanted what's best for me, and if you are what's best, then I know they will be happy.'

'Resigned, you mean.'

'OK, resigned. But does it matter? You'll be back in France in five days' time, and who knows when we will meet again. Come on Jenny, we have this moment, let's not waste it.'

It seemed that evening, as they lay together, that they had suddenly discovered their secret garden. They could walk through it with impunity, and touch the flowers with tenderness, feel the grass between their feet, and the rush of doves above their heads. They were a couple, two people oblivious to anything but the love they felt for each other. Holding, kissing, loving, became a renewal. An awakening. A dawn chorus, an unexplainable relationship between woman and woman. No harm would befall them. They were immune, and within their immunity their love blossomed into an extravaganza of colour.

Jo kissed Jenny on her lips, tracing their outline with her tongue, and moving her body closer to hold fast the trembling between them. Jenny rose up to meet Jo as she held her arms around her body. They met, and perspiration glued them together. Lips, tongues, hands explored every nerve tantalizing each neuron into involuntary submission, until they both lay quivering like saplings in the autumn breeze.

Their love was never stronger, never more complete, never more absolute than that day, and in the early hours of the morning promises were made.

Tom and Doll looked forward to Jo's visit. Although now very frail, with the future of the farm in question, they were happy to know that their Jo would arrive soon. Having no children of their own they had always found solace in the company of Jo. She had grown, as Tom had remarked, into a woman of stature. A woman who knew her own mind, stubborn (like Tom) and secretive. One never knew what she was thinking, what she was feeling. She was an enigma, but he loved her so much.

Whatever she wanted – and in his heart he knew – he would never judge her, never condemn her for what happiness she could find. For hadn't he found happiness when his young Jo came to live with them? No, despite his wife's misgivings, he would never judge Jo. So when she phoned and told him she would be bringing her friend along, he stood firm in his resolve.

Doll on the other hand was more alienated. The Earth Mother, the barometer of normality, husband and wife, and nurture, was all she knew, and was all she wanted to know. However, her love for Jo and her fondness of Tom tempered her feelings, and she too would submit to the realities of Jo's life.

Dilys from the post office had been that morning to help Doll clean and bake, and Dai from the village had been in to cut the logs for the fire. At four thirty, Doll tripped around with a duster, making certain all was in order, and Tom sat out in the yard awaiting the arrival of Jo and her friend.

He filled his pipe with ready-rubbed tobacco and sat back on the seat watching the evening sun dip slowly beneath the hills, until Marling Rock became a shadow to haunt the autumn sky. What joy he had in his memories: collies barking, Jo running up behind him, hair all tousled in the wind. Cows coming home for milking, and sheep lazily grazing the deep greenness of the valley. Happy days, not to be duplicated. The farm was to be sold, and he and Doll were to reside in a tithed cottage in the village. If only ... well, "if onlys" don't happen. He never had a son and Jo chose a different path to follow. No point in thinking about "if only".

Just then a car rolled up, stopped, and out leapt Jo. If his legs could have carried him he would have run to meet her, but arthritis only allowed a slow gait.

'Hello *cariad*, it's good to see you.'

'Hello Uncle, how are you? How's Aunty?'

'We're very well. Now did your friend come with you?'

Jo turned back to the car. 'Yes she did.' And then turning towards Jenny, who had opened the passenger door, 'Come on Jen.'

Jo held Jenny's arm as they walked towards Tom, who after a brief hesitation, bent down and kissed Jenny. 'Hello *bach*, nice to see you, it's been such a long time.'

Reassured, Jo kept hold of Jenny's arm and walked into the house. Aunt Doll was busy cutting a cake and filling up the kettle for tea.

'Hello Aunty, how are you?'

Doll turned, looked at Jo and Jenny, wiped her hands on her apron and held her arms open in greeting. Jo remembered the comfort she felt the first time she was held in her aunty's arms. Memories flooded into her mind. She was at home. Never would she feel so secure as she did standing in the kitchen with Aunt Doll's arms around her.

Finally she drew back. 'Aunty, you remember Jennifer?'

'Yes, it's very nice to meet you again. I hear from Jo that you have become quite famous with your painting.' And then, in a half-whisper, 'It's nice that you've kept in touch with our Jo'.

To avoid any embarrassment Jo moved towards the stairs. 'Same rooms then, Aunty?'

'Yes, the same rooms.'

Jo helped Tom carry the cases up the stairs, and was amazed to see how breathless he was. Age and toil had wearied him.

The rooms were tidy and clean, with lavender, and sweet-smelling laundry, and blossom-coloured eiderdowns. Jo's past neatly held in a time warp. They unpacked and decided to go for a walk before supper. Doll would have wanted more conversation, but Tom was glad just to have his Jo here with him.

'Marling Rock then?'

'Yes, Marling Rock.'

As they walked up the path to the tree on the hill, Jo slid her hand into Jenny's. 'I loved your paintings.'

'Not as much as I loved painting them.'

It didn't seem a time for more words as they sat beneath the tree and looked across the fields and down into the valley. Jenny, feeling Jo's mood, put her arm around her and pulled her head onto her shoulder.

Eventually Jenny spoke. 'What will happen to Pen Marig and Marling Rock after ...?'

'You mean when Doll and Tom leave?'

'Well, er, yes.'

'I don't really know. They were tenant farmers, so I suppose the farm will revert back to the owner.'

'Who's he?'

'Oh, do you remember Guy, the lad in the garage? Well, his father owned Pen Marig, and when he died he left the farm to Guy, so I don't really know what will happen to it. I hate the fact that this may be the last time I will be able to sit here.'

'Well, let's make it special Jo.'

'It is special Jen, you're here.'

Their conversation dwindled into the shadows of the sky. Darkened by the night, but highlighted with the spasmodic twinklings of the stars. Jo was reminded of Wordsworth.

> *'Earth has not anything to show more fair:*
> *Dull would he be of soul who could pass by*
> *A sight so touching in it's majesty'*
> (Wordsworth, 'Westminster Bridge')

She clung to Jenny, her only reality. She was not going to be hampered by thoughts that could depress her. She kissed her neck. 'As long as I have you my darling, I will never be lonely.'

Jenny sighed. 'You will always have me, but ....'

'No buts Jen. We have now, let's not think about tomorrow.'

And so they didn't. They spent the rest of the five days in complete happiness. Even Doll, now resigned, was happy for them. She didn't understand it, but if it made her Jo happy ...!

The day before they were due to return, Jenny asked Doll and Tom if she could make a sketch of them. Flattered, they agreed, and so Jenny sent Jo off to walk the valley, and set to work sketching.

She was pleased, even though she would not let them see, with the finished work, which she placed safely away from prying eyes. *This*, she thought, *would be her legacy to the two people who loved her Jo.*

On her last day at Pen Marig, Jo had arranged to take Aunt Doll on a shopping trip to Aber. Jenny was happy to stay behind and wander through the valley with her sketch pad.

'Make sure Jennifer has lunch,' Doll demanded of Tom.

Jennifer winked at him, pleased to know that on her second visit to Pen Marig the pair had discovered a mutual friendship. 'I'll be back by one,' she whispered, and was greeted by a smile of gratitude from Tom.

Lately life with Doll had been one long irritant. His inability, through degrading bones, to escape to the hills had caused a constant strain on their relationship.

Jenny and Tom sat patiently in the yard, waiting on Doll to finish her primping. The visit to Aber was a real occasion for her, and she was not going to shop without the appropriate apparel. Finally she arrived at the door, and walked to the passenger seat of Jo's car.

As they watched Jo's car drive slowly down the hill towards the bottom gate, Tom mused, 'Women and cars, eh? Never thought I'd see the day!'

'Life moves on Tom,' answered Jenny.

Tom sighed. 'Yes it does.'

Jenny looked at him as he puffed steadily on his pipe, his eyes gazing down the hill, glazed in vacant stillness. They sat a while in silence, where a mutual empathy seemed to enfold arms around their thoughts.

Tom refilled his pipe, brushed the flakes from his jacket and reached into his pocket for his matches. 'What will you do now, then?'

The question took Jenny by surprise. 'What, now?'

'No, not now! When you leave here.'

'Well I … I have to go back to France.'

'And Jo? What about Jo?'

Jenny, stunned by the suddenness of Tom's question, lit a cigarette, inhaled deeply, and turned towards her inquisitor. 'Truthfully Tom, I don't know. I have commitments in France, and Jo has her own commitments in London. We haven't really spoken about it.'

'Then you'd better,' insisted Tom. 'Jo is too precious to me to be let down once again.'

From his conversation it was apparent that Tom was more aware of life's differences than one first realized. Jo was his lost lamb. His *raison d'être*. His paternity had generated hope, but hope did not spring eternal. He had no legacy to leave, no material wealth, no deeds laid down for history. No nothing to leave but his love, and protection. He had to know, had to be sure that his Jo would be safe in the world she had chosen for herself. Doll would never understand, but he did. Love could only be love. Whether hidden by a coat of many colours, or held transparent in an opaque vapour, it was still love. He reached out and touched Jenny's arm.

'You'll take care of my Jo, won't you?'

'Yes, Tom, I will try.'

Tom got up and walked towards the house, and Jenny knew there would be no further conversation.

Doll felt a youthful delight as she gazed into the shop windows. Short skirts that hardly covered the knees. Long trailing dresses that scraped the ground. Hats that flounced and flaunted decadency. Mannequins, red-lipped and black-eyed. Fashion had left her in its wake, in yesterday. She would content herself with a pair of serviceable court shoes and a leather handbag.

Unpersuaded to try something different, they sat down in Sharon's Tea House to drink tea and eat buttered scones.

'Have you enjoyed yourself, Aunty?'

'Oh yes *cariad*, it's been a nice trip. But …'

'But what, Aunty?'

'I'm worried about Tom. He's so irritable and short-tempered lately. I know it's because of Pen Marig. I know he'll be lost without his precious farm, but what can we do?'

'He'll get used to it Aunty,' Jo consoled, although in her heart she knew that Tom would never get used to it.

'Will he Jo? Farming is his life. if only –'

'If only what?'

'Oh never mind Jo, I'm just being stupid. Yes, I'm sure you're right, he will get used to it.'

She spoke no more about it, and they departed for home.

Jo took Doll's packages to her bedroom and returned to the kitchen. 'Where's Jen?'

'Oh,' replied Tom, 'gone into the village to buy some gifts to take back with her.'

'Oh right, I'll go down to meet her then,' replied Jo, glad of an excuse to leave. She felt suffocated by her aunt and uncle's sadness, which seemed to drain all life from the house. Yes, she would walk down to meet Jen, and try to shake off the anxiety she felt.

What would she do without her adoptive parents, without Pen Marig? The thought of it was too much to bear. This had always been her home, her sanctuary. The light in the window that had guided her home when her world had become so desolate after Jenny left for Paris, all those years ago. She had drawn strength from her uncle, who taught her about the wonder of nature, the joy that a newly born lamb could bring. The spring flowers in the valley that danced happily in the April breeze. Yes, he had taught her that life was beautiful, if one only looked beneath the surface.

Unwanted tears burnt her throat as she forced them back. Crying had never been easy for her. A sign of weakness to which she would not concede.

Just then, Jenny appeared on the road.

'Hello you! Hey, what's the matter?'

'Just thinking, Jenny, that's all.'

'I know Jo, I know. It must be really awful for you.'

'Yes it is.' Jo linked her arm in Jenny's. 'Let's not talk about it any more Jen, otherwise I may not be able to hold it all together.'

'Do we have to be back straight away? Can we not go up to Marling Rock? We really have to talk, Jo. I know it may not be the right time, but really we should.'

Jo leaned towards Jenny and kissed her on the cheek. 'Yes, let's. Marling Rock then, one last time.'

Tom had left Doll preparing supper, and sat in his usual seat in the yard. He sighed as he watched the two shadowy figures open and then close the bottom gate, and walk arm in arm up the hill towards Marling Rock. He knew that this would be Jo's last time at Pen Marig, and was glad that Jenny had been here with her. She seemed happy with her friend, and that was consolation enough for him. No recriminations, no judgement, just consolation.

As they sat down under Jo's tree, they held hands and bent their heads together, involved with their own thoughts.

After a while Jenny spoke. 'You know I have to go back to France on the thirtieth, and you know that I have to keep access to Josey, and you know ...'

'Yes, darling. Yes I know this may be the last time we will be together for a long time. But we can write, telephone, can't we?'

'You know we can't, Jo. Any hint of impropriety will mean loss of access, and I've fought so hard to get it. Henri's family would only need a sniff of scandal, and I would lose Josey, and I couldn't bear it.'

'But how would they know, Jen?'

'Oh they would know, they have spies everywhere. I don't think you realize how influential the St Clair family are. But darling, it will only be until Josey reaches sixteen.'

'But that's five years, Jen!'

'I know, and if you feel you can't wait, Jo, I'll understand. I will hate the very thought of it, but yes, I'll understand.'

'Oh for God's sake Jen, how could I love anyone else?'

They held each other tightly as if to transfer life from one to the other, and spoke no more of it.

Lunch and supper came and went, and after packing for an early morning start, they returned to the sitting room to spend the evening with Doll and Tom.

Tom felt in an ambivalent mood. 'Come, Doll, fetch that bottle of malt from the cupboard, I think this is that special occasion.'

Doll dutifully walked to the sideboard and retrieved an unopened bottle of malt whisky, and four lead crystal glasses. She had lit the coal fire earlier, and the warmth of the flames created a cosy ambience.

'Well girls, you're off tomorrow, and we'll be off in a couple of weeks. Doll and I hope that you have enjoyed yourselves. But you mustn't be strangers. It may be different, but we'll make our new home as welcome as we can for you …' His voice trailed off.

'Don't worry Uncle, wherever both you and Aunty are, I'll always feel at home.'

He smiled and poured the whisky into the glasses, and handed a glass in turn to Doll, Jo and Jenny, as they sat around the fire.

'To Pen Marig,' he said, as he raised his glass.

'To Pen Marig,' they all said together.

The rest of the evening was spent in merry banter and reminiscences. Laughter filled the room, brought on by Tom's revelations of Jo's childhood, and the frequently drunk whisky. It was a happy time, and one to be written down for posterity.

Next morning, a hearty breakfast and cups of strong coffee ensured that Jo's hangover would be well abated before she drove back to London. With cases packed and stowed in the boot of Jo's Ford Escort, they said their farewells.

'I'll be back for Christmas,' Jo consoled a tearful Doll. 'It may not be Pen Marig, but anywhere you and Uncle are will be home for me.'

Doll sobbed, unable to reply.

They journeyed home in silence, Jo unable to articulate the sadness she felt. Jenny, acknowledging her feelings, rested her hand on Jo's leg in loving commiseration. Jo dropped Jenny off at her hotel, and drove home to unpack and shower, arranging to meet Jenny again that evening.

She felt slightly claustrophobic as the walls of her two-bedroomed flat closed in around her. She missed the open space of the Welsh valleys and hills, and as thoughts flooded over her she sat down on her bed and cried.

At eight o'clock, she had finally gained control of her emotions and rang Jenny. 'I'll be over in about thirty minutes.'

'OK darling.'

After Jo had left, Jenny busied herself repacking for her trip home to France. She had bought a Welsh doll for Josey and carefully wrapped it in tissue paper, placing it deep inside her case to keep it safe from breakage. She also placed a brown envelope on the coffee table. This was her surprise for Jo. Excitement presented as impatience as she waited for Jo's phone call.

'Come on Jo,' she said to herself, 'we don't have much time.'

Champagne, smoked salmon and marshmallows had been ordered from room service. They were to arrive at around eight.

Placing down the telephone receiver, Jenny suddenly felt like she had all those years ago, when she stood anxiously by the porter's window. A youthful trepidation, a need to turn and run away. She felt exposed and insecure. A child nervously hiding from her mother, a plate accidentally broken.

The door bell made her jump. A moment was needed before she could open the door. She did, and there stood Jo.

She could have cried, if she hadn't felt so uncommonly nervous. There Jo stood, large sloppy jumper, blue denims and white plimsolls. Whatever they had together, seemed to be encapsulated in this frozen sculpture of the past.

'Well, aren't you going to let me in?'

Jenny stood back. 'Er, er … yes, of course.'

Jo was reminded of the sarong in *A Town like Alice*, and hoped that for one night they could relive the first time they had discovered their love.

'Oh Jo, Jo!' No more standing back, as Jenny rushed into Jo's arms. 'I don't think I can ever love you as much as I do now.'

'Ssh, my darling.'

'I can't ssh Jo, I need to tell you, show you, I can't be silent.'

However, she had to, for room service arrived, and the spell was broken.

'Umm, champagne, smoked salmon, strawberries … and what else?'

Jenny laughed outrageously. 'Marshmallows!' Then grimaced, 'But no fire to toast them.'

'Don't worry, we'll drink the champagne and pretend.'

Their world was never more complete than that night. They were childishly, stupidly in love. They dipped strawberries in the champagne and chewed the cold marshmallows. Giggles were transformed into kisses and kisses into unashamed intercourse. Quietly they lay together, astonished by the explosiveness of their familiarity. Like volcanic eruptions, they fell into the black hole of the universe. If they flew too near the sun they would never have known, for their love on that evening insulated them from any solar intrusion.

Reluctantly they arose, showered and sat, dressing-gowned, on the settee.

'I'm famished,' stated Jenny.

'Yes, now I come to think of it, so am I.'

'I'll order something. What do you want?'

Jo, still needing to keep the evening alive laughed, 'Beans on toast.'

Jenny laughed. 'Yes of course, what else would it be, beans on toast it is.'

Room service was called, and a very astonished waiter shouted to his colleagues, 'Room 508 wants beans on toast. Can we do it?' It was obvious that they could when the trolley arrived with covered plates, under which beans on toast were carefully placed.

They ate enthusiastically, and poured some more champagne from the second bottle they had also requested from room service.

'I bet they think we are really mad. I expect this will be a story to tell their grandchildren. Do you know, there were two ladies who ordered beans on toast, and … champagne!'

Jenny and Jo chuckled at the thought of it.

With the food eaten and another glass of champagne poured, Jenny sat down beside Jo and handed her the brown envelope she had previously placed on the coffee table.

'This is for you.'

'What is it?' Jo quizzed.

'Open it and see.'

Jo opened the envelope and took out two sheets of paper. 'Pro-forma contract for sale.' She could read no further. 'What does it mean?'

'It's yours, my darling.'

'What is?'

'Pen Marig.'

'But I don't understand. How? When? Where?'

Jenny took Jo's shaking hands into hers and told her that once she knew Pen Marig was to be sold, she'd explored the possibility of buying it. During the time Jo and Doll were in Aber, she had walked to the village and spoken to Guy. His father had left him Pen Marig and all the land, but he really didn't want to farm the land himself. He viewed his inheritance as his way out of Wales. He had always wanted to travel, and with money from the sale of Pen Marig could fulfil his dream.

When Jenny offered him a lifeline he took it with both hands. Jo would keep the farmhouse and Marling Rock, and lease the rest of the land to Ewan Thomas who wanted to increase his dairy herd. The deal had been struck that Thursday afternoon, and it would be left to solicitors to complete the conveyance and transfer the deeds to Jo.

The morning came with no appetite for breakfast. Jo, still reeling from Jenny's news, pushed a glutinous mound of cold scrambled egg around her plate. Time was short, and she had to leave soon, but how could she leave with the matter unresolved? Somehow she had to persuade Jenny to take part ownership of Pen Marig. She could not accept the gift unconditionally.

Jenny glanced at Jo. 'Whatever is the matter with you?'

'I just can't allow you to do this.'

'Do what?'

'Buy Pen Marig.'

'But I need to do this Jo. Need to know that there is somewhere you can go, somewhere that you can call home, and Pen Marig is that somewhere.'

'I understand all that Jen, but this has to be something we can both share, this has to be our special place. Tom and Doll will not be with us for much longer, and after them, all I have is you. If anything happened to me, I would leave Pen Marig to you, so I can't see the problem in putting the deeds into both our names.' Jo half-laughed. 'At least it would save all the hassle with probate.'

However Jenny could not agree. She told Jo that there would be speculation if it was to be known that they were so materially connected. Jo had to finally agree.

'All you have to do, Jo, is to retain your own solicitor, liaise with Guy's, and complete the sale and transfer. You will find that there is also an open cheque in the envelope.'

Jo began to argue, but it was of no avail. 'But the money Jen, the money! Won't someone know that you have withdrawn so much from your account?'

'No my darling, this is my own private account here in

London. It is the inheritance that my father left me when he passed. I haven't touched it, was saving it for when I returned to England for good.'

Jo lifted up her hands. 'Well then, when you come back to me, you must promise me that you will add your name to the deed.'

'I promise Jo, with all my heart I promise.'

The matter was settled.

Their final goodbye could have been a remake of *Brief Encounter*. But it was Jenny, not Celia Johnson, who stood in the hotel passage and watched as the lift doors closed behind Jo, slowly carrying her away. No Trevor Howard to wipe the grit from her eye, just an empty hotel room and a box of tissues.

Chapter Fifteen

Anne Richards' mind was encyclopaedic, a network of catalogued trivia. She would not forget the indifference shown by the team from *Millennium*, and as she walked back to her escort in the Pressman's wine bar, plans of revenge were already formulating.

How was it, why was it, that *Millennium* had succeeded in obtaining an interview with the reclusive Jennifer Standford? Nobody else had managed to do so, not even her, and she invariably found ways of extracting an interview from even the most reluctant of celebrities.

Yes, she would do whatever it took. She feared no retribution. Hadn't she, a long time ago, sold her soul to that highest of bidders: power? Malevolent and uncompromising power. It fed her greed and reduced its subjects to malleable puppets. She was the pin that winkled out the soft tissue of embedded secrets. The scalpel that dissected skeletons in her adversaries' cupboards.

One could have no pity for Anne! Her reckless abandonment of childhood dreams had dictated her chosen path. The hunted became the hunter, the abused the abuser. If retribution was to be had, it would be hers. Once she had created the illusion of friendship, she would pounce like the insatiable mantis, with the resultant decapitation. She would devour her prey, then move on. The hungry rattler, but with muted warning before the strike.

Yes, those upstarts from *Millennium* had something to fear. She thought Joan intelligent but of no substance. Angela rigid in conformity. But Jo Dawson ...? Yes, what of Jo Dawson? The elusive butterfly, calmly going about her business. Solitary, industrious, mysteriously obscure. Yes, there had to be another side to Jo Dawson. The thought tantalized her. She would explore further. Happy with her resolution, she drank champagne cocktails, and beguiled her escort with feminine witticisms.

Anne had learnt her craft at a small, mediocre North London

newspaper, with an equally mediocre circulation. After tiring of reporting the mundane, interspersed with the occasional suburban rhetoric, she decided the paper should raise its game and compete with its contemporaries. Subtly she worked on the gullibility of the editor, and as chief reporter, fashioned the tabloid to engage its readers' curiosity for salacious gossip. As circulation increased, Anne's thirst decreased. She had drunk the well dry. It was time to move on.

Reputation creates a habitual following, and soon Anne's talents were highly sought after. Gossip became her opiate, scandal her addiction. Truly the hunted had become the hunter. But words, however bought, were of no monetary value. This she had to find elsewhere.

As she had no penchant for youth, she set her sights on the elderly but wealthy suitors, who were happy to pay for the flattering crumbs she offered. She took her sledgehammer, cracked the nut and devoured its soft kernel. There was, however, one last nut to crack: *Millennium*. They would pay for their indifference.

The next day she set to work. This would be a private mission, without the aid of her researchers. If she was to bring down *Millennium*, it had to be done covertly. Jo Dawson was renowned for her fairness, her sense of propriety, and for her privacy. *Surely,* she thought, *no one could be that virginal?* She would go back, as she always did with her subjects, to the beginning.

After hours spent at Somerset House, she obtained Jo's birth certificate. Now she could start. Annoyance inflamed her, after her research offered no information after 1950. It seemed that Jo had disappeared. Finally, Anne conceded that Jo must have lived somewhere, but if not in London, where?'

Suddenly an idea formed. Hesitant at first, but gathering momentum as logic prevailed. Perhaps she was looking at it from the wrong angle. Since her encounter with the people from *Millennium*, the question of 'Why?' had embedded itself in her mind. Why had they succeeded, why did Jennifer Standford agree to talk to them where all others had failed? Yes, perhaps Jennifer Standford was the way into the mystery that was Jo Dawson.

Now, she was on a roll. She went back to Somerset House, and trawled the archives. Jennifer, born of Kate and Frederick Standford. No record after 1944, but then a reappearance in 1945, but only of F. Standford and Jennifer. Once again, no further record until 1963. Then she found a J. Standford residing in Flaxman Square, South West London. Back now, to the Land Registry. In 1941, Flaxman Square was owned by an A. Leggat. From a trawl of the London telephone directories, found a number of A. Leggats. This would take more time, but she had expected that. She would now enlist the help of her very private detective, whose discretion, she knew, could be relied upon. He was the old-style gumshoe who took on any case if the payment was right. She had used him on several occasions to hunt out certain indiscretions for her exposés, so this should be a doddle for him.

She telephoned him the following day, and advised him of the job he was to carry out. Yes, it would take time, but yes, as in the past, she would make it worth his while. With part of her exercise completed, she went back to work on her next exposé.

Chapter Sixteen

During the next three months, Jo busied herself with the task of collating articles for the Christmas issue. She felt flat and stale, like champagne left over from the night before.

Her team, oblivious of her reduced enthusiasm, beavered away. Joan fetched articles on her latest celebrity. Angela produced an unequalled resume on 'The Value of Christmas', and Brian, full of mastery, photographed the changing seasons for the magazine's Christmas calendar. The agony aunt's column was full of compassion tempered with pragmatic solutions, and Betty had excelled herself with the influx of advertisers. Once again, her team had triumphed. The Christmas issue was completed, printed and distributed with their usual efficiency.

It had been three months since Jo had seen Jenny. Although she immersed herself in work, it didn't seem to fill the hole left by her departure. Wearily, after a long day at the office, she would drive back to her apartment. Sometimes, when her thoughts were elsewhere, she couldn't remember how she got there, but once in, depression took over, only abated by more than a few glasses of wine. She was trapped by her feelings, disgusted at the selfish thoughts she had. Why should she live such a lonely and unfulfilled life? Had she, like Adam, bitten into the forbidden fruit, only to find sourness in its tasting? Had she condemned herself to the Apocalypse, as horses trampled over her very existence? She had no answer except her love for Jenny, but for how long could she sustain it?

It was the 20th December, and the team sat in the wine bar, as usual. They had ordered drinks and were happily ensconced at their table when Jo arrived.

'Hello Boss,' Brian said, as he pointed to the chair they had left for her. 'Not a bad one, eh?'

'No, not a bad one, should be happily received. Oh, by the way

Brian, the calendar is really good, I'm sure that it will sell well.' She sat down, lit a cigarette and lifted the wine glass to her lips. 'Thanks all of you, yet again another good job, I'm really proud of you.' Suddenly, a tear threatened to form. *What an idiot,* she thought, and quickly bowed her head, and fidgeted with a beer mat.

'Well Boss,' said Brian, taking up the baton, 'we couldn't do it without you. So, and I hope you won't be embarrassed, me and the team have bought you something. Yes I know we don't normally do presents, but we thought, just for once, we would let you know how we all think about you.' As he finished his sentence, he deposited a neatly wrapped parcel on the table in front of Jo.

As they all giggled to diffuse any tension, Jo slowly untied the gold ribbon, and carefully unpicked the cellotape which adhered to the wrapping paper. A box was revealed. A box which held a white crystal paperweight, inside of which was a miniature red rose glistening with drops of silver dew. The card was simply printed with 'Our love to you, Boss'.

She could say nothing, as that previous tear threatened to fall.

'Time for another drink I think,' said Brian, as he leapt up from the table. 'Don't want to embarrass the boss too much!'

Thankful for his interruption, Jo sighed, and then smiled at the people around the table. 'I really don't know what to say. It's … it's.'

'Don't have to say nofing,' replied little cockney Jimmy. 'We all know where we would be without your support.'

Brian returned with a tray full of drinks, and the party was soon in full swing. For the first time, Jo felt happy and comfortable. Yes, these were her family, and she loved them all.

Around ten, Jo stood up to leave. 'Well folks, must be off.'

'Up to Wales?' Brian asked.

'Yes, up to Wales,' Jo replied.

'I'll walk out with you.'

'There's no need Brian, you go back to the team.'

But Brian insisted. 'No, I'll walk out with you.'

As they walked out to the front of the wine bar, his joyful countenance became serious.

'What's the matter Brian?'

'Don't know if it means very much, but Anne Richards is scouting around for information.'

'Information? I don't understand, Brian. What is that to do with me?'

'She's had her associates asking questions about Jennifer Standford.'

'So? Brian, I still don't understand why you are so concerned?'

'Well, don't forget that revenge is a dish best served cold, and that woman could freeze an iceberg when she is really put out.'

'Put out about what, Brian? I still don't understand'

'Put out about our last issue, with Jennifer Standford as our headliner.'

As history had exacted silence about her proclivities, Jo feigned ignorance. 'Oh, I'm sure, Brian, Miss Standford wouldn't worry about what Richards has to say!'

'But would you, Jo? I'm sorry, but you know that I'm very fond of you, and I know that I may be presumptuous, but I know, Jo … I know.'

'Know what Brian? What do you know?'

'I know that you and Jennifer Standford are more than just college acquaintances.' As Jo's face whitened Brian carried on, 'Oh don't worry Jo, your secret's safe with me. I know, because I once felt like you do, but my feelings were lost when he died, and I never had the inclination to find someone else. It was imperative that you should be aware of Anne Richards and her vicious ways. Well, I won't say any more, but just be careful.' With a hug, Brian turned and walked back into the wine bar.

Should Jo be worried about Brian's information? She wasn't sure. She knew Anne Richards was ruthless and uncompromising. However, what more could she glean that hadn't already been told in the *Millennium* article? As the taxi brought her home, she put Brian's warnings to the back of her mind. She had better things to do than worry about the intrigues of a malicious harridan.

She had kept the news of her ownership of Pen Marig from Tom and Doll. This would be her Christmas surprise. Collusion with Guy had created a delay in their move to the village, so they would spend Christmas at Pen Marig, and move – as they both thought – into the cottage next door to the post office in the New Year.

Inebriation and high spirits hastened Jo's packing. No presents to be wrapped this year: Pen Marig would be the present they could keep until life finally left them.

Yes, she was full of joy and anticipation as she went to sleep that night. She would leave early the following morning.

The drive up was slow. Rain and wind pounded the car, impeding progress. Finally she arrived at Pen Marig.

Doll, with the aid of an umbrella, helped Jo carry her bags to the house. Jo was bewildered. Was Tom ill? Why had he left Doll to tote the luggage? Shaking the rain from her jacket she asked, 'Where's Uncle?'

Doll placed the opened umbrella in the boot room, and muttered, 'Where do you think he is? Out on the hills.'

'But ...'

'Yes I know but stubborn as a mule he is. Out with Tess.'

'Oh,' replied Jo, not wanting to add anything conciliatory to the conversation.

'Yes, oh is right! Won't have a walking stick!'

'But how ...?'

'How indeed? That damned old shepherd's crook!'

Jo was aghast, she had never ever heard Doll use any kind of expletive, no matter how angry she had been. 'Look Aunty, I'll go and find him.'

'But *cariad* you'll get soaked!'

'I'll be OK. Won't be long.'

Stubborn as Tom, Doll thought as she watched Jo walk up the hill.

Jo fastened her jacket collar firmly around her neck. She could hardly see, as the rain lashed her face, with the wind whistling around her.

Suddenly as she reached the brow of the hill and she saw Tom, his upper body bent over, head resting on his hands, as they held the shepherd's crook. His silhouetted figure both amazed and frightened her, and she understood Doll's momentary lapse into subdued blasphemy.

She ran the last couple of yards, calling to him, but her words were carried away on the wind around her. When she thought she was near enough to approach without startling him, she called his name again.

He half-turned and with squinted eyes peered through the mist. 'Is that you, Jo?'

'Yes it is, and why for goodness' sake are you out in this

weather?' She didn't wait for an answer. 'You know Aunt Doll isn't happy with you, and come to that neither am I. Do you want to catch pneumonia?' She tucked her arm in his. 'Come on, its time to go home.'

Just then a young collie raced up the hill and sat obediently beside Tom. As he bent down and patted her, his words, almost lost to the wind, were, 'This is my home, Jo.'

The kettle boiled on the stove, as Doll peered through the kitchen window, impatiently wiping at the condensation with her tea towel. How difficult life had become for her. *Almost fifty years of marriage to Tom would,* she thought, *have prepared her for the ravages of time and the physical deterioration of old age.* But Tom's incapacity to let go drove her to distraction. The farm had been his life, and she just an interloper, standing stoically in the background to smooth his fevered brow, and keep safe his hearth and home.

But soon there would be no hearth and home. She had watched helpless as his strength slowly sapped away, as his mistress, his life's blood that was Pen Marig, was taken from him. How long he would last in the village, heaven only knew. Again she wiped the mist from the window, as the whistling kettle interrupted her thoughts. Irritated she glanced once more out of the window. *Where are they?*

She was pouring hot water into the teapot, when Tom and Jo walked into the boot room, followed by Tess the collie. Jo grimaced. Doll had never allowed dogs in her home. *We'll wait and see,* she thought. So she did, and no mention was made of Tess.

Tom washed at the kitchen sink in silence, while Jo went upstairs to bathe and change. She didn't realize how cold she was until the hot bath water breathed her circulation back to life.

Tom was already sitting at the table when Jo entered the kitchen. Tea was poured and Welsh cakes buttered. They ate in companiable silence, as Jo felt unable to loosen the tension between them.

'You found him, then?' Doll said, stating the obvious.

Tom grumbled an undertone. Jo remained silent.

Finally she could bear their anguish no longer. She placed her cup in its saucer, sat back in her chair and told them her news.

Tess moved and scratched, as if telepathically she knew the ensuing silence had to be broken. Tom bent down and gently stroked her. As he straightened up in his chair, a tear fell from his eye. Doll stared, and then reached out her hand to touch his.

After what seemed an eternity, Tom rose from his chair and walked over to Jo. His weathered hands gripping her shoulders as he lifted her bodily from her chair. He held her as a father would hold a child, tenderly at first, but then as the love flowed from him unrelentingly.

'That's enough Tom, don't want to smother the poor child.'

Tom released his grip, but still gently held Jo to him. 'I don't know what to say *cariad*, I just don't know what to say.'

'Nothing to say,' replied Jo. 'It was all Jenny's doing, she arranged it with Guy on her last visit.'

Doll dismissed Tom and Jo to the front room, and set about tidying the kitchen. Emotion swelled her heart, but it was an emotion best kept to herself.

For the rest of the holiday, Doll cooked, and Tom and Jo spent the daylight hours roaming the hills of Pen Marig. Tess was learning well, but then, that was always down to Tom's innate expertise. Life was good for all of them. Doll smiled, as she unpacked her treasured ornaments and placed them back in their stained glass cabinets. The best china was again situated on the Welsh dresser her father had made. The fire dogs were polished and rehomed back in the open grate. Yes life was good for all of them.

Alas, time wasn't a vacuum of space, suspended in animation, it marched on perilously, changing days into night and night into days. Soon it was time for Jo to leave, but this time she could leave without sadness.

'One last day on the hills, Jo?' Tom had asked, as he glanced at Doll, who nodded.

'Yes Jo, you go off with Tom. I've packed some lunch, and we will have dinner when you return.'

Tess walked quietly at Tom's side, as the three of them set off up the hill. Tom stopped at Marling Rock and laid an old mac on the ground. 'We'll sit here for a while, Jo,' he stated as he seated himself against Jo's tree.

'OK.'

Tess sat beside him and looked up with a loving gaze. Tom

took out his pipe and began to fill it with tobacco. Jo lit a cigarette and they both puffed away in silence. After a while Tom spoke.

'Jo,' he started, then stopped.

'Yes, Uncle.'

'Jo, Doll and I' – he always put Doll first as if she was the instigator of the tale – 'Doll and I are very worried about you.'

'Why, Uncle?'

'You have given us so much, but you have so little.' Tom, being of limited words, conveyed his feelings in the one sentence. 'All I can do, all we can do, is to thank both you and your friend.'

Jo, knowing she should not embellish the simplicity of his gratitude, replied, 'That's alright, Uncle.'

They sat quietly together, each with their own thoughts, then Tom spoke again. 'How is Jennifer?'

Jo, shocked at his forthrightness, took a moment to reply. 'She's in France.'

'Really!'

'Yes, she has commitments there.' Should she tell Tom about Josey? Would that confuse him even more? She decided not to.

'And you, Jo,' he continued, 'where are your commitments?'

She had no hesitation with her answer. 'Why here, Uncle, here with you and Aunty, and with …' – she sighed – 'with my work in London.'

'But aren't you lonely Jo, down there with no … companion. Can't you find someone else to share your life with?'

Jo shivered, the cold December air chilling her bones. Tom placed his arm around her and pulled her to him. After a while she spoke. 'I know you won't understand Uncle, but as Pen Marig is your obsession, so Jenny is mine. I can't help it. It's just a need I have that won't go away.'

Tom was silent for a moment, choosing his words carefully. 'You're right, Jo, I don't understand. I don't understand how you can spend your life waiting for someone who's never there. Why can't you be in France with her, or she in London with you? I just don't understand it.'

'It's complicated Uncle. You and Aunt Doll have accepted the situation because you love me. You probably don't understand it, but you accept it. Unfortunately other people are far more judgemental, and Jenny isn't brave enough to suffer the slings and arrows. It's …'

'So you're willing to spend the rest of your life alone!'

'If that's what it takes, then yes, but I'm not alone, I have you and Aunty, and Pen Marig, and perhaps one day Jenny and I will be here together.'

The subject was dropped.

'Come Jo, it's cold, let's go home.'

Chapter Seventeen

Robbie Dewhurst was a gumshoe, plain and simple. Not as infamous as the fictional Philip Marlow, or charismatic as Poirot. He was dogged in his pursuit and comfortable even if the outcome was none too reputable.

He sat in his two-roomed flat above Baker's fish and chip shop, and sifted through his notebook. He had found the A. Leggatt who used to own Flaxman Square in the late 1960s to 1970s, who although his memory was spasmodic, did seem to remember a young woman who rented No. 45. He thought she might have attended a college nearby but wasn't certain.

When given the instruction from Anne Richards, he had prudently purchased a copy of *Millennium*, as he knew she would not pay for any duplicated information. He knew he had to come up with something new. He sat back in an overly sprung armchair, lit a cigar and scratched his slightly balding head.

His ability for ferreting out the iniquitous had let him down. Ultimately he realized that apart from becoming famous as an artist, Jennifer Standford's life was quite un-eventful, and certainly free from any hidden scandal.

He closed his notebook and threw it onto the table. He was becoming increasingly tired of his life. Tired of the hours spent dogging his victims' footsteps. Tired of being cold, wet and hungry when his pursuits dictated long nightly vigils in all weathers. He had made a comfortable living from his assignments, by being frugal and prudently squirrelling his cash away. Not wanting to submit to a pun, he now felt that perhaps his rainy day had come.

He poured a vodka into a glass, walked over to the telephone and thought, *time to bite the bullet.* He downed the drink in one gulp and dialled Anne Richards' number.

'Hello.'

'Miss Richards, it's Dewhurst here.'

'Yes.'

'Bad news I'm afraid.' He waited for the explosion.

'What is?' Anne demanded.

'Can't find anything more than what was reported in that magazine.'

He heard the splutter. 'Then you'll have to go back and search some more.'

Now was his moment. 'Sorry, no can do!'

'What?' Another splutter followed by an expletive.

'I ain't doin' no more, I've 'ad enough.'

It seemed minutes before she replied. 'Well, don't think you'll get paid!' she shouted, slamming down the receiver.

He laughed as he poured another vodka, and raised it towards the telephone. 'And good riddance to you too!'

Anne Richards was at a loss. She had counted on Dewhurst to provide the ammunition she needed to exact her revenge. Now what did she do? Grudgingly she accepted she would have to wait. Her current businesses dictated her time. Too many irons, too many fires.

Chapter Eighteen

Jo was spending Easter in Wales when the news came. During the past three years, as Tom and Doll's health had deteriorated, she had made her visits more and more frequent, wanting to be with them as much as she could.

She answered the phone to an excited Angela. 'Jo, Jo!'

'What, sweetie? What's happened?'

'We've been nominated.'

'Nominated for what?'

'Magazine of the Year.'

'Oh gosh, really?'

'Yes really, Jo.'

'OK Angela, I'll be back on Wednesday, we'll talk then.'

She thought the grin would never leave her face. Finally recognition for all the hard work done by her and her team.

'Well?' asked Joan. 'What did she say?'

'Too stunned to say much, I think. Anyway she'll be back on Wednesday.'

'Well,' said Joan, as they all sat having lunch in the canteen, 'it doesn't mean we've won.'

'Oh shut up Joan,' they all shouted.

Tom thought the accolade well deserved. Doll, who didn't quite understand such things, didn't think anything except regret. Regret at being so insistent on education, without which her Jo might never have left Pen Marig. Never have had her head turned (as she put it) by the ways of that other place – meaning London. Life would have been so simple. *She would have been courted, married, and had a couple of babies beside her, instead.* Doll shook the thought out of her head.

May came with the night of the media awards. Jo dressed carefully

95

in silver-grey culottes, burgundy blouse, set off by the gold necklace Doll had given her many Christmases ago.

She was picked up by Brian, who arrived promptly at seven-thirty. He looked so distinguished in his dinner suit and velvet bow tie. She told him so, and ignored the blush that rushed to his cheeks.

He handed her a corsage of orchids and bowed. 'Are you ready, boss?'

'Yes my dear, I'm ready.'

In the meantime the village of Cymgurig was in uproar. Guy's colour television had been borrowed and exchanged for the black and white one housed in the Three Bells public house. Both villagers and farmers were invited (if not shanghaied by Tom) to watch his Jo.

'She's going to win something,' Doll had proudly regaled her friends. 'Didn't I say she'd be someone someday?' she had said, repeatedly, to ears that had closed after the sixth time of telling.

Chairs and tables were arranged in a semi-circle in front of the television. Doors and windows opened to the warm night. Barry, the landlord, had got in two extra barrels of beer, whilst Gwyneth did sandwiches.

'What's the prize she's winning?' asked Dai.

'Might not win,' replied Tom.

'Well let's hope she does after all this fuss,' grumbled Dai.

Gladys the postmistress spoke about the benefit of a good education, whilst Doll sipped her port and lemon in quiet appreciation.

Chapter Nineteen

As Jenny sat by the window, the aeroplane drifting towards France, she mused how relative time and space were. In almost an hour she would reach her destination, and yet her plane seemed to be held in suspension. If only life was this uncomplicated. If time and space could hold one's heart in the palm of their hands and life could be calmed within their infinite stillness. Yet things were to change.

Two years later, when her quarterly *Millennium* was posted through the door of her cottage, the nomination headline leapt off the page. She returned to her kitchen, poured coffee and sat down at the table.

Page two revealed a picture of Jo and her staff, under which read the caption, 'Nominated as Best Magazine', with a short resumé of the magazine's history.

Jenny stared at the photograph, and her eyes watered. 'Hello darling,' she whispered.

As she touched the picture with her finger, she knew she needed to be there. How would she persuade George that it was something she must do? George was due the next evening. He would stay overnight.

She cooked dinner, and chilled two bottles of his favourite Chablis. Although anxious, she felt excited at the prospect of returning to England. Once she had placated George with chicken and Chablis, she jumped in with both feet. No time for hesitation, seize the moment, that was best.

'George, I'm going to England next weekend.'

'Why?' George asked.

She took another sip of wine and placed the magazine in front of him. 'Because ... because I need to be there.'

As he read the article his response amazed her. 'I see, this is your friend's magazine. Do you want me to book the flight?'

'Um … Well. Yes?' Jenny was confused. Why had George not tried to dissuade her? Had he guessed?

No more was said, the subject was closed for that evening. The arrangements were made. George was left to organize the next exhibition, and Jenny packed for the flight to England.

Chapter Twenty

Brian was a proud escort as he held Jo's arm and led her towards the limousine. All was chatter and gaiety among the *Millenium* team. She felt happy and comfortable. Yes, these were her family.

As they left the car and stepped onto the red carpet the crowd clapped and whistled. The obligatory reporters shouted questions and the photographers snapped their pictures. Everyone was happy and excited.

Awards are a long affair. Accolades are protracted. People from the nether regions thanked others in one boring soliloquy after another. Champagne and nibbles became everyone's salvation. The wait was interminable. Best this, best that ... it quite amazed Jo. An interlude came, the inevitable comfort break. Jo's team were becoming fidgety. 'Why do these things take so long?'

Finally, 'Best Magazine Category.' They all held their breath. 'And the winner is – *Millennium!*'

The team shrieked, Cymgurig shrieked, and Jenny cried.

Jo was succinct in her speech. 'This award does not belong to me, but to my team, without whom I would not be standing here this evening. Their dedication and support has made *Millennium* what it is. So I would like to thank my colleagues, my Aunty Doll and my Uncle Tom whom I love very much, and ... ' – she hesitated – 'and Wordsworth, who inspired me and gave meaning to the written word. Surely, a poet one can never be without.'

As they walked down from the stage, Brian took Jo's arm. 'I've a feeling she's here.'

'Who's here?'

'Your Wordsworth.'

Jo shivered, Brian's arm supported her.

'I'm sure she is Jo. I have that feeling. '

But before Brian could elaborate, Angela bounced towards

them. 'Well Boss? What a night! We're all off now to the party. Coming?'

Brian's words had disconcerted Jo. Surely the excitement of the evening had beguiled him with romantic fantasy. 'Yes, yes, of course.' Feeling steadier, she let go of Brian's arm and followed Angela.

As they walked towards the stairs leading to the banqueting hall Angela let out a yell.

'Good Lord, isn't that Jennifer Standford talking to Joan? Gosh I didn't know she would be here.'

Jo slowed her steps, and with a feigned smile walked towards Joan.

'Isn't this a surprise?' Joan beamed.

'Well yes, it is,' replied Jo, as she moved towards Jenny and gave the theatrical two-cheek kiss. 'How are you?' And then, 'it's very good of you to find the time to come, you must be very busy.'

'Well yes, but I felt I must support you all, especially after the wonderful article you did for me.' She turned to Brian. 'Your photographs were wonderful.'

Brian beamed.

Little Jimmy shuffled, and then said, 'Well people, I'm ready for some real food. I'm starving.'

They all laughed.

'Would you like to join us Miss Standford?' Angela asked.

'Well yes, if that's alright with everybody. But please call me Jennifer.'

The *Millennium* entourage strolled into the hall, to placate their hunger and quench their thirst. The noise of chatter, laughter and the inevitable back-slapping pounded Jo's ears. She wanted to talk to Jenny, but the setting hampered the prospect.

As she stood sipping champagne, waiting for the buffet queue to diminish, she felt a light touch on her arm. She turned to the side and saw Jenny. As always her heart threatened to jump out of her body.

'Hello, darling.'

'Ssh! People will hear you!' Jo hushed her, shocked at Jenny's openness.

Jenny's response was to smile. 'I don't have long Jo, I have to catch the six-thirty plane tomorrow morning.'

Jo said nothing. By now her heart had completely stopped.

Jenny whispered, 'Can you get away?'

'Yes, but later.'

'Can you leave about eleven?'

'Yes,' replied Jo.

The party got under way and was soon in full swing, winners congratulating winners, losers consoling themselves with numerous glasses of alcohol.

Once again Jo felt Jenny's hand on her arm. 'Shall we go?'

Suddenly Brian walked over to them.

'Brian?'

'Yes Boss, I know, you have to go now.'

'Yes.'

'Don't worry, I'll let everybody know. What was it, some sort of headache?'

He pirouetted and flounced back to join the mêlée.

'Does he …?' Jenny asked.

'Yes,' was all Jo could answer.

They collected their coats and as they walked towards the door, Jenny nudged Jo's arm. 'Hello you.'

Jo turned and smiled. 'Hello yourself.'

As they walked out of the door, Anne Richards smiled, her red lips tightening into a thin line. 'Well, well, well,' she muttered to herself.

Jo hailed a cab.

'Where to?'

'Forty-five Flaxman Square.'

'But …'

'Yes. I bought it two years ago. Thought it would be a nice home for Josey and I when we come to England. George often stays there when he's in London.' And then, 'Well, it saves on hotel bills.'

'Flaxman Square!' Yes, Jo remembered Flaxman Square.

But if visions were held in memory, disappointment grew in reality.

'Moving about in worlds not realised,
High instincts before which our mortal nature
Did tremble like a guilty thing surprised.

But for those first affections,
which be they what they may,,
Those shadowy recollections
Are yet the fountain-light of all our day.'
(Wordsworth, 'Imitations of Immortality')

This was not the fantasy with which Jo had comforted herself. The house was flat, cold in decor and monastic in ornamentation. Jo shivered. In her dreams she had expected more.

She sat down on the black leather settee, empty and devoid of emotion. As she looked at the grey-flecked carpet it seemed all her remembrances had floated away, like dandelion seeds in the autumn breeze.

As Jenny walked towards her holding two glasses of wine, she had to ask the question. 'How did you manage it? I can't believe it. You said five years, yet it has only been two. Surely you –'

'Yes, yes I know,' Jenny interrupted Jo. 'I know, but I had to be here for you.' And then, 'George arranged it. I think he knows.'

'What! Everything?' quizzed Jo.

'Yes, I think so.'

Jo again, stated, 'But you said five years Jen, and I was prepared to wait, but now, well now, I don't think ...'

'Oh I'm so sorry Jo, this is just a flying visit, I have to be back tomorrow. Would it be unfair of me to ask you to wait for another three years?'

'Well if it has to be, then yes, I'll wait. But no longer Jen, I don't think my heart could bear the strain.'

'Oh silly you, I promise just another three years, and then I can come to stay, and all will be as it should be!'

Jo was not that sure. Jenny's love for Josey could determine their future together. But she did not vocalize her doubts. At this point in time she was just happy to have Jenny here. Pushing the thought to one side, she took Jenny in her arms.

Their kisses were like none before. Burning adherence to a painful passion. Focused, yet chaotic. Desperately clinging on to each other, as the last leaf of autumn clings to its solitary branch, down they sank into the dark abyss where the future has no relevance.

Afterwards they lay together, fearful of separation, and surrendered their love to the night.

The next day, as Jo watched Jenny's plane glide up from the runway, she wondered whether she would ever see her again.

Anne Richards relied on her instinct. She had a nose for it, inquisitive and uncompromising. She had waited a long time with the thought of revenge festering deep within her. She had contained her anger at Dewhurst's failure and betrayal into implosive resentment. A resentment heightened by the success of *Millennium* and, with it, Jo Dawson.

She had attended the awards night, and although not among the nominees, used the opportunity to network with potential clients. Never did she expect the added bonus of seeing Jo Dawson prematurely leave the celebrations with Jennifer Standford.

Well, well, well, she thought, as she returned to her companions, silently salivating at the prospect of a hidden agenda. Could she exploit the incident, convert it into financial gain?

As she sipped her champagne and charmed her attentive clients, she started to formulate plans. *If a job's worth doing ... um – do it yourself!*

Chapter Twenty-One

'By grief enfeebled was I turned adrift,
Helpless as sailor cast on desert rock;.'
(Wordsworth, 'The female vagrant')

It was a warm summer evening. Jo had showered and dressed in T-shirt and shorts, and was sipping an iced tea, when the phone call came.

'Hallo.'

'Hallo Jo. It's Doll, she's quite poorly!' Tom's voice was bleak, and unusually hushed.

'How poorly, Uncle?'

'Quite poorly!' Tom was not given to overstatement.

'Right, I'll come up.'

Her hands shook as she leafed through her address book and found Sally's home number. Still shaking, she dialled.

'Yes?'

'Sal, it's me, Jo. I have to go to Wales, my Aunt Doll is ill.'

Sally's reply was brief. 'You go, Jo, don't worry about a thing. And I hope she'll be alright.'

Jo changed into jeans and sweater, threw an overnight bag into the car, and drove off towards the motorway.

As Tom and Doll had slowly succumbed to old age, Jo had been dreading the day when the phone would ring.

What would she do without her aunty? Without those big plump arms around her. That sharp tongue that scolded her when she did wrong, and then those steel blue eyes that softened with the wrinkled smile that encouraged her. She shook the thoughts out of her head; she must concentrate on arriving safely.

It was still fairly light when she drove through Cymgurig. *Thank God,* she thought, *for the summer evenings.*

Tom was waiting at the bottom gate, puffing absent-mindedly

on his pipe. As she approached, he opened the gate and she drove in. She jumped out and opened the passenger door as Tom closed the gate and walked slowly towards her. They drove up to Pen Marig in silence, neither of them wanting to talk.

As Doll lay in her bed, she thought about her life. She was twenty-five when she finally agreed to marry Tom. He had farmed Pen Marig with his father, and when his father died, took over the tenancy. When his mother died a year later he decided it was time to take a wife.

Doll had known Tom from school. At the age of seven she had come to Wales to live with her foster parents when her parents died. Her brother, Jo's father, stayed on in London with another family, and in later years worked as a hospital stoker. There was no affection between them, and she stayed with the people who had taken her in, who eventually adopted her. She first met Tom at school, and although she never thought of him as handsome, his ruddy face and deep brown eyes held a certain charm. Very soon they drifted into the courting phase, and finally she accepted his hand in marriage.

They had a comfortable marriage, and very quickly Doll fitted into the role as the home-maker and farmer's wife. Doll's only sadness was her inability to bear children. She had so much wanted to give Tom a son, someone to carry on the inheritance that was the Pen Marig dynasty. Therefore, when she had the opportunity of taking in Jo, she did not hesitate.

She had known from an early age that Jo was different, and despite her persuasion, could not imprint feminine ways into the tomboy. She'd say, and repeatedly, 'Tom, if that girl hasn't got her head in a book, she's up to her elbows in farmyard muck.'

'Leave her alone,' Tom had rebuked. 'Plenty of time for frills and fancies.'

But after a while she realized there would never be such a time, and her fears were further enhanced by the weekly struggle to separate Jo from her favourite dungarees in order to insist she wore a dress for Sunday chapel.

As for Jo's poetry, she didn't confess to understand it, and although prose was quite beyond her, she thought some of it rhymed beautifully.

'Yes,' she sighed, she had had a good life. She loved her Tom, but even more so her Jo. If she was to have one regret, it would be the relationship between Jo and her friend. It was a regret that there were no adopted grandchildren to spoil. However, she felt glad that she had shown acceptance, even though it had dismayed her sensibilities.

Jo walked into the kitchen. Gwyneth from the pub was making tea.

'How is she?' asked Jo.

Gwyneth shook her head and sniffed back a tear. She lifted the teapot. 'Would you like some tea Jo?'

'No thank you Gwyneth, I'll go straight up.'

Tom stood by the kitchen sink and stared out of the window. Gwyneth tenderly placed an arm around his waist.

Tom and Doll's bedroom was bright and cheery, with the sun dancing shadows on the walls. A faint smell of lavender hung in the air. Jo drew in a sharp intake of breath as she glanced at the wizened frame that now replaced that once buxom body.

As she drew nearer to the bed she heard an almost inaudible sound. 'Is that you Jo?'

Jo sat down on a chair beside the bed, and took hold of Doll's hand. 'Yes Aunty, it is.'

Doll sighed, and attempted a half-smile.

'How are you, Aunty?' The question was superfluous, but what could she say in these circumstances?

'Not so good Jo, not so good. I'm glad you're here. Have you had something to eat?'

Jo thought, *always the Earth Mother, always the worrier.* 'Yes Aunty,' Jo lied.

'Good.'

'I'm sorry Jo, but I'm feeling quite tired.'

'That's alright Aunty, you just rest. I'll stay here for a while.'

And so she did for over an hour. Holding Doll's hand and listening to the rasp of breath as she tried to sleep. Finally, when cramp threatened to afflict her legs, she stood up, bent over and kissed Doll on the cheek, and quietly left the room.

Once back in the kitchen, she sat down at the wooden table and took the mug of tea Gwyneth offered. Tom ceased his vigil out of the kitchen window, and sat down on the seat next to Jo. They sat in silent grief, not knowing what to say to each other.

After two more mugs of tea, Tom spoke. 'Doctor's coming later.'

'Right,' replied Jo.

The kitchen was eerily silent. No usual conversations, no whistling of kettles, or whisking of scone batter. Even the range that once crackled with Doll's baking looked bleak and cold.

Jo couldn't stand it any longer. 'I think I'll go up and sit with Aunty.'

'Right,' Tom and Gwyneth both said together.

Doll was still sleeping, but her breath was even more laboured. Jo became frightened, and ran back down the stairs.

'Tom,' – no time for the usual 'Uncle' – 'I think we should get the doctor now.'

Tom strode over to the phone, dialled a number and spoke abruptly. 'Doc, can you come now.' He had obviously said yes, as Tom turned back and stated, 'The doc's coming now.'

It seemed to take hours, although in truth it was only twenty minutes, before the doc arrived. He nodded to Tom and went upstairs.

Tom paced the kitchen floor. Gwyneth made a poor attempt at washing up, and Jo dragged deeply on her cigarette.

Finally the Doc returned. 'Jo.'

'Yes.'

'She wants to see you, and then Tom. It won't be long now.'

No time for sugar-coating the pill. As Jo raced up the stairs, Gwyneth made yet another pot of tea.

The room had darkened with the fading sun. A bedside table lamp offered the only light.

A small voice spoke. 'Jo, Jo?'

'Yes Aunty, I'm here.'

Jo sat on the bed beside Doll and forced back the tears. Doll would never have wanted any show of outward emotion.

As she took Doll's hand and raised it to her lips, Doll spoke again. 'Jo, you have always been a joy to me, and I know I have never told you how proud I am of you.'

'Ssh, Aunty, save your strength.'

'No Jo, I have to say this, have to tell you, how happy you have made me and Tom. But ...'

'But what, Aunty?' Jo leaned closer as Doll's voice became weaker.

'But you must follow your own path. I was wrong, Jo, but all I need is for you to be happy. You are happy aren't you?'

'Yes Aunty I am. Now don't say any more, I'll fetch Tom.'

She raised Doll's hand to her lips and kissed it.

She went down to the kitchen, and Tom strode up the stairs.

Finally, with him gone, she was able to let go. Tears flooded her eyes, and fell down her cheeks, unheeded and unashamed.

Gwyneth walked over and patted her shoulder. 'There, there, don't cry, it's for the best.'

But Jo did cry, she couldn't stop, and Gwyneth decided to say no more.

Tom came down from the stairs, called for Tess and walked out of the house. The doctor went up, and after a short time returned.

'She's gone.'

Jo looked up at him, and as if reading her thoughts he said, 'She went peacefully, without pain. Don't worry, I'll make all the arrangements.'

'I'll go and find Tom,' was all she could reply.

She knew where Tom would be, and walked slowly up the hill towards Marling Rock. Her head was full of thoughts, memories of the years spent with her aunty. How she would miss those big cuddly arms, the flour-coated aprons, the shrill voice as she greeted Jo on her visits. She turned back and looked at the empty doorway far below the hill, and thought she could see Doll standing there, arms folded, head to one side. Her heart leapt and tears began to fall again. Quickly she wiped her eyes, and lit a cigarette. She couldn't let Tom see her this way. She had to be strong for him.

She came across him sitting under the tree, smoking his pipe. Tess lay beside him with her head on his lap. It was a warm evening, with the sun slowly drifting away, leaving a faint glow horizontally along the hills. If there was no sadness in that moment, she would have marvelled at its splendour.

She sat down beside Tom and took his hand in hers. No words were spoken, as they sat immersed within their own personal thoughts.

The day of the funeral came, with the Cymgurig chapel packed to its rafters. All who knew and loved Doll were there to pay their respects. There were no flowers, at Doll's request, save two red roses – one from Tom and one from Jo. The service concluded with the singing of 'Bread of Heaven', Doll's favourite hymn, which with full choral enthusiasm resounded all over the hills.

Doll would have smiled down when she saw that Jo had worn a skirt. 'Just for you Aunty,' she had said as she dressed that morning.

After two more days, Jo would leave Pen Marig and return to London, so she and Tom spent the time sorting Doll's things. Gwyneth had been marshalled to ensure that Tom ate properly, and Dai was to keep an eye on him.

With things sorted and Tom organized, Jo felt she was able to leave him without worrying too greatly. They kissed goodbye and she promised to ring him a couple of times a week.

'Don't have to do that Jo, I'll be alright.'

'Well I will, Uncle, and that's that.'

She returned home to a forest of post and junk mail. *Need a drink to sort through all that,* she thought. The flat was warm with its unopened windows, and she quickly changed into a summer shirt and shorts. *There, that's better.*

She poured a Scotch and Coke, and sat back in her chair. The alcohol brought a kind of relief, and gradually the tension of the past two weeks began to loosen. It was too late to ring the office. She would go in tomorrow.

Right, now the post. She sifted through, placing the junk mail to one side, and putting the rest on her lap, began to open them. She was beginning to grow weary of bills, and circulars, when she came across a blue-edged envelope.

She frowned, and then gasped when she recognized the handwriting. She looked at the postmark: it had been sent from London a week ago. With trembling fingers she opened the envelope.

My dearest Jo,

George was in London a week ago, and read in the newspaper the obituary of your Aunt Doll. It seemed that your colleagues at the magazine wanted to do something for you, while you were away in Wales.

I really don't know what to say to you Jo, how to mitigate your loss. I know how much you loved her, and how much you will miss her.

Oh Jo, Jo! I wanted so much to be there with you, but I couldn't. Josey had started at Julliard, and it was on the same day as your aunty's funeral. It would have been too difficult to explain why I couldn't be there with her on her special day.

If it's any consolation, I was there with you in spirit, and cried with you in your sadness.

I know that this is not what you want to hear, but I still do love you so very much.

Please take care my darling, my thoughts are always with you.

Yours forever,
Jen
P.S. I have asked George to post this to you.

She glanced at the top of the letter hoping to see an address, but there was none. Jo didn't know whether to laugh or cry. She was lost in the irony of it. *Yes,* she thought she could send this one, *but none of the others!* So now yet another reason why they couldn't be together. She sighed and poured another Scotch, this time with less Coke.

She read the letter again, with cynicism. Well I suppose if she still loves me, that's better than nothing. She gulped down the drink and inwardly scolded herself for being so bitter. Had she not known what it would be like? Had she not given into her addiction the last time they met? She remembered her aunty's words: 'You must follow your own path.'

She poured another drink, lit a cigarette, and pondered on exactly what her path was, and where it would lead her. She became more and more inebriated, and then her ponderings were over. She knew exactly where her path lay, and hated herself for her weakness.

Her mind flew in a fantastic wonderland. She would find someone else. She would visit "those clubs" and she would have one-night stands. She would, she would ... But she knew she wouldn't, she knew she was shackled by her love for Jenny. There was no escaping the fact, she was a prisoner of her own ill-fated desires.

Chapter Twenty-Two

It's funny how life has a way of turning in on itself. How something as innocuous as an obituary could have such a devastating affect. Anne Richards scoured the columns of the dailies, a habitual process, to ensure no possible source of information could escape her curiosity. Society pages and personal columns were her first port of call. Any snippet of submerged scandal was voraciously seized upon and committed to her notebook, to be resurrected at a later date. She drank her black coffee and puffed on a Tom Thumb, carefully jotting down bits of news.

As she turned the pages of a broadsheet the word *Millennium* caught her eye:

It is with sadness that the friends and colleagues at Millennium send their heartfelt condolences to their editor Jo Dawson on the passing of her Aunty Doll. All our thoughts are with her and her family in the Welsh village of Cymgurig.

Anne Richards could have lit up the whole of London with the beam that widened as each word was read, and then reread.

Cymgurig? Where on earth was Cymgurig? A road atlas was fetched and the glossary perused. Llanidros, ah, Cymgurig! She turned to the page, drew her finger down and then across. The name was hardly visible to the naked eye, but once a magnifying glass enlarged the words, she found the nearest town was Llanidros. *Ah,* she thought, *so now I know a little more about you, eh, Jo Dawson.*

She looked at her date planner and found she had a couple of days free at the end of September. She drove to the office in good spirits and even managed to smile at the receptionist. She called her PA.

'Phillip.'

'Yes, Miss Richards?'

'I want you to find a good hotel in Llanidros and book me two nights for the 28th and 29th September.

'Yes Miss Richards. Um, where's Llanidros?'

'North Wales, you idiot.'

'Oh, right.'

'Something's up,' Phillip said to Gwen the receptionist. 'She's even humming!'

'Yes,' answered Gwen, 'she smiled at me this morning. Well, someone's for the high jump!'

They both giggled, but as they knew better than to annoy Anne Richards, went back to their respective low profiles. After all, a job was a job and they were well paid for their complicity.

Jo phoned Sally early the following morning. 'Hi Sal, I'll be in about ten-ish.'

Sally busied herself sorting Jo's post and ensured the coffee was hot. She was pleased to have Jo back. The office had seemed quiet without her. They had all discussed what to say about her loss and decided that a copy of their obituary left on Jo's desk would express their feelings, without any additional need for words. It was mid-August and the room was beginning to warm. Sally turned on the fan and allowed the soft breeze to cool the atmosphere. She stood back in the doorway and surveyed the desk. *Yes,* she thought. *Everything in order, just as Jo likes it.*

'Morning folks,' a loud voice called out behind her. She turned round and saw Jo marching in that old familiar way down the aisle between the desks.

She stopped at Jimmy's. 'Well James,' she smiled. 'Been behaving yourself?'

'Yes, Boss,' Jimmy grinned, saluting in his comedic manner. She was reminded of Benny Hill, and smiled.

As she walked on further towards her office she winked at both Joan and Angela. 'Alright girls?'

'Yes Jo, we'll catch up later shall we?'

'Okey dokey.'

Sally was already pouring coffee when Jo approached her.

'Hello Sal, efficient as ever.'

Sally smiled and placed the cup on Jo's desk. 'Post's been

sorted, and I've put the fan on. Hope it's not too cold for you, I've put it on the lowest setting.'

'No my dear, I'm sure it will be fine.'

'Well, buzz me if you want anything.'

Jo smiled and sat down at her desk, and set to work on the post. After about an hour, she buzzed for Sally.

'Yes Jo?'

'Can you deal with the non-urgent stuff? I've finished dictating for today.' She handed Sally a spool of tape. 'And now I think I ought to catch up with the team. Perhaps a working lunch. Can you ring the canteen and arrange for sandwiches and coffee? We'll meet in the boardroom, say about an hour. Is that OK?'

'Yes Jo. I'll organize the food and let the others know.'

Jo sat at her desk, lit a cigarette and watched the breeze from the oscillating fan turn the smoke into circles. She was glad of the quietness as she reread the obituary placed by her staff. How kind their thought had been, and how prudent of them to let the words speak for themselves. She wondered how Tom was, and decided to phone him when she got home.

As she took the last couple of drags on her cigarette she allowed her mind to wander back to the blue-edged letter, and suddenly felt both angry and alone. Irritated at her lack of composure, she stubbed the butt into the ashtray, and walked out of her office towards the boardroom.

Working lunches had always been the arena for productivity, mixed with laughter. Jo enjoyed the camaraderie and fresh ideas that poured from her staff, and today was no exception. They were all glad to have her back. She was their captain and although the ship never veered from its course, without her at the tiller there were occasions when it became lost in the doldrums. After the usual niceties, they all got down to the business of the day.

Helen was getting bogged down with work on the agony column. 'Post just seems to increase daily Jo.'

'Well Helen, that's down to your popularity. Take someone from the typing pool to help you. Call them a junior assistant or something.'

Helen beamed.

'Now, Joan, who have we got as a headliner this quarter?'

'Well Jo, its Harriet Cole. Will make a good story I think?'

Harriet Cole was a missionary type and foster mother, who spent a lot of time in Africa, and Joan felt that perhaps more attention should be drawn to such selfless individuals.

'Sounds great, Joan. Hope I'm not going to be faced with exorbitant expenses for travels to Africa.' Jo grinned mischievously, and they all roared.

'No. No, she's back in England for a while, trying to raise more money for a school out there. Petrol account may be a bit steep though!'

'No worries, Joan, perhaps we could use some of the money from the sale of the Christmas calendar, to boost her coffers.'

Paula, who looked after fashion, regaled her audience with the latest Paris, Milan and London designs.

'Jeans are out then,' Jo groaned, feigning a tearful grimace. Again more laughter. It was so good to be home, Jo mused.

Angela's piece on 'A Woman of Our Time' was as usual magnificent, and Brian's photography entitled 'A History of Britain' delighted them all.

'I don't know why you don't have your own exhibition. I'm sure it would be received well.' Brian blushed and stammered an incoherent reply. Jo jotted a note in her diary. 'I'll see what I can do.' Again Brian blushed.

'Now, Jimmy, what are we going to do with you? I think you've finally run the gauntlet of the office postal service, and the typesetting room. Perhaps it's time for you to do something different.'

Jimmy opened and closed his mouth, excitement strangling his vocal cords.

'Right then, I'll leave it up to you Jimmy. Brainstorm some ideas, and when you've done that come and see me, and we'll do something for the Christmas issue.'

Angela, the earth mother, ruffled Jimmy's hair. Brian slapped his back. 'There you are, mate.'

The meeting drew to a close, with its usual joke-telling and anecdotal stories.

'Go on you lot, you're like a load of monkeys. Off with you and do some work.'

Jo could still hear the ring of laughter as she sat back and drew quietly on a cigarette. Yes, she was glad to be back. Thinking they all had gone, she was surprised to see Brian hovering in the doorway.

'Yes Brian, what is it?'

'Can I have a word, Boss?'

'Of course, sit down.'

'Well, well I was speaking to Phillip in the Pressman's ...'

'Phillip? Phillip who?'

'Oh sorry, he's that Richards woman's PA. Well he was saying that she asked him to book a hotel in Llanidros, and I remembered that was near where your uncle lives. Might not be anything in it, but it seems a bit of a coincidence, don't you think? I mean, she never does anything without an ulterior motive.'

Should Jo be worried about this? She knew Anne Richards was the proverbial dog in the manger, but what was there for her in Llanidros? Suddenly a thought rushed into her head. Oh God. Pen Marig. The obituary.

She shuddered as if a ghost had walked over her grave. 'OK Brian I'll look into it. And thanks for letting me know.'

He stood up and frowned. 'Just be careful Boss.'

'Yes, yes I will.'

Left alone to ponder the conversation, Jo decided to search further into the background of Anne Richards. Perhaps on this occasion she could beat her at her own game. That afternoon she called Sally into her office.

'Sal, what do you know about Anne Richards?'

'Not much really, apart from the fact that she's an inveterate scandal-monger who enjoys destroying people's reputations. Oh, and did you know, all those years ago, she was put forward by your predecessor Susan Brown for the editor's position here?'

'No. No, I didn't know.' So there Jo had it, that was the reason why Anne Richards was so hell bent on revenge. Jealousy, plain and simple jealousy.

'Well Sal, I want you to find out all that you can about her. And this will be strictly between us.'

Sally frowned. 'Why yes of course Jo.' She left the question of 'Why?' unspoken. She had known Jo long enough to know there was a good reason for her request.

Still frowning, Sally left Jo, and set off for the magazine archives.

Brian was not a happy man. Phillip's announcement had perturbed him. He decided to telephone him and ask him out for a drink. Perhaps he could pump him for more information.

Phillip Green hated both his job and his employer. Its only redeeming feature was that it paid well. As a compulsive spendthrift the necessity to keep his salary outweighed any crisis of conscience. No "road to Damascus" moment for him, even though Anne Richards's demonic light shone all too clearly.

He liked Brian. He had an air of naivety about him that made Phillip feel slightly tarnished, and self-analytical. *Perhaps,* he thought, *they may become good pals.*

"Good pals" was not, however, on Brian's mind. He could not understand how someone so outwardly nice could work for and be paid by such a hateful person. Why was he like Judas, selling his soul for thirty pieces of silver?

No, his sole intention was to meet him and pump him for information.

Phillip had already ordered the drinks when Brian arrived, slightly late, at the Pressman's wine bar.

'Hi,' Phillip beamed. 'Vodka OK?'

'Yes, thank you.'

'Shall we sit down?'

'Yes, OK.'

They walked towards an empty table in the corner of the room, moved aside a couple of empty wine glasses, and sat down.

'Nice of you to call, Bri.'

'Well I thought I'd return the favour.'

'Well Bri, how's tricks?'

'Oh you know, pretty hectic this time of the month, quarterly issue and all that. What about you?'

'Well, good. Well, that's when I'm not running myself ragged after Richards.'

'Why do you stay with her?'

'Money, old thing, need to maintain my lifestyle.'

'Yes, well I suppose so. What's she got you doing now?'

Was this the right time to pursue the matter? Perhaps a little inebriation might prompt a loose tongue from Phillip. He downed his drink then rose from the table.

'Another one, then?'

'Oh yes, why not?'

Brian walked to the bar, glancing briefly at Phillip. There was something quite strange about the man. It niggled him.

He returned with the drinks – a double for Phillip – as Phillip was lighting a cigarette.

'Well Phil, where were we?'

Phillip sipped his vodka, and peered at Brian over the top of his glass. 'Can't tell you Bri. You know what the old dragon's like, more than my job's worth to gossip.'

They both laughed at the irony of it.

'Well I suppose another poor celeb's going to be sent to the gallows? Don't know how you can work for that woman.'

'Well let's say, Bri, it has it perks, trips out and all that. We're off to Wales at the end of September, and after that who knows. Must go where the story is, and she can't do without her gopher.'

They both laughed.

'Suppose I'd better buy a phrase book,' Phillip continued. 'Do they speak English in Wales?'

Brian felt humourless, but joined in with Phillip's mirth. Anxious not to overplay his hand, he decided they'd have one more drink and then he would bid his farewells. Had he got what he came for? He wasn't sure.

Chapter Twenty-Three

Jenny had fought with herself over whether to send the letter to Jo. She knew George would post it for her when he visited his London gallery. She had longed to say that she was coming over, coming to be with her, to stand beside her as she said goodbye to her aunty. She had longed for it, hoped for it, but dared not.

Josey had been accepted at Julliard School of Music, and at fourteen was one of the youngest pianists ever to have been accepted. Henri had paid for Josey's tutelage by one of France's most renowned professors, who had been instrumental in obtaining a place for her at this prestigious music college. 'We've gone as far as we can Henri, now it is time for her to be taught by the masters.'

Why oh why, Jenny had agonized, did Josey's inauguration have to be on the same day as Doll's funeral? Fate once more had conspired against her. Was this her punishment?

How would Jo receive her letter? Should she add her address, telephone number? Go with her instinct and against her fears? Why was it so difficult to write this one letter, when all the others were prolifically written, and yet entombed in a bureau drawer?

As she read it through, the selfishness of her choice stood blatant and undeniable. Would she ever be free from this constant emotional tug of war? Without further delay, she placed the folded page in the envelope and sealed the flap. There it is done, no more procrastination. And then, as she placed the letter down on her desk and sighed, perhaps no more Jo!

Tom was glad to receive Jo's phone call, although his pride would never let him admit it.

'Yes Jo, all's fine. Evans moved his cows into the bottom field yesterday. I'm taking Tess to the trials next week, up against Gareth's Ben, but Tess will do well. How about you. Are you OK?'

'Yes Uncle, I'll be up at the end of September, but will ring on the weekend to confirm date. are you eating OK? You know aunty will be looking down at you, don't want her rattling the rafters, do we?'

'No *cariad*, no we don't.' He laughed an affectionate laugh at the vision of his Doll giving him "the look" from above.

They chatted a little while longer and then said their goodbyes.

Jo put some sausages in the oven and peeled some potatoes for boiling. Pondering at what to have with them she chose a tin of marrowfat peas. Baked beans were never a part of her larder. Glass of red tonight? Yes.

She sat down and pondered Brian's conversation. She would make sure she was at Pen Marig on the dates Anne Richards was supposed to be in Llanidros. No way would she allow her to have contact with her uncle. Whatever it was she was looking for, she wasn't going to find it at Pen Marig.

Chapter Twenty-Four

Henri St Clair was not given to pride, unless it involved his daughter. Even at the age of six he knew she was someone very special. Whenever he walked by the Great Hall in the Chateau, he would see her kneeling on the piano stool, giving her enough height to enable her to run her fingers along the black and white keys of the baby grand. Often he would stop and listen, and soon began to realize the random notes were in fact little tuneful melodies.

'Ah,' he thought, *'she's her mother's daughter, full of untapped talent.'*

Despite his mother's disapproval, he took Josey to every opera and concert in Paris, and watched admiringly as she soaked up the genius of the composers. Josey loved these outings and became besotted by the heroism of Tchaikovsky and the magic of Brahms. Her dreams at night were full of dancing crochets and quavers, with fingers that moved across the scales as she slept.

Professor Neimann was sent for and Josey's tuition began.

Josey loved her father, adored her mother, but feared her grandmother. Now she could finally disengage herself from the "old guard" disciplinarian.

'If you don't rein that child in, Henri, she will end up just like her mother!'

'Well,' Henri answered his mother belligerently, 'that wouldn't be a bad thing, Mama. You only have to visit our friends, and see her paintings hanging from their walls. No, Mama, I am not going to stifle Josey's talent. Only time will tell if I am right or wrong.'

'Well if you're wrong, then you will have to pick up the pieces.'

Alas for Madam St Clair, Henri was right, and at the age of 14 Josey was selected for Julliard.

It was a weekend in June, on one of her access visits with Jenny, that Josey told her about Julliard.

'Oh my darling, that's wonderful.'

'Will you come Mama?'

'Yes, of course I will. what's the date? ... Right, I'll put that in my diary right now!' she opened the drawer in her desk, and pushing her letters to Jo to one side, removed her diary and made the appropriate entry. 'There, that's done. Now what shall we do for a special treat?'

'Oh let's not go out, let's have lunch in the garden and sunbathe. I'll play you something while you chop tomatoes.'

Jenny laughed and began to prepare lunch.

She had bought Josey an old piano on which to practise during her visits and felt her heart swell with pride as she listened to a Mozart intermezzo. 'Ah, Mozart?'

'Yes Mama, we'll make an expert out of you yet.'

They both giggled and returned to their respective tasks.

After lunch they sipped iced lemonade and lazed in the sunshine.

'No sketching today Mama?'

'No, too hot, anyway I want to hear all about the things you've been doing.'

'Keeping out of Grandmama's way mostly. Oh why can't I come and live here with you?'

'Oh Josey, I wish you could, but you know that is not possible, you know you have to stay with your father until you are sixteen. Anyway you're off to Julliard, and I have to go to Cologne in September to promote my new exhibition.' She patted Josey's arm. 'Don't worry sweetheart, time will soon go, and then we'll take a trip to England. Perhaps, if you like it there, we could stay awhile.'

'Ooh Mama that would be wonderful.'

The rest of the afternoon was spent lazing in the warm sunshine, interspersed with happy conversation.

Once Josey had retired to bed, Jenny settled down on the veranda to relax with a chilled Moselle, and watched the dusky evening sky change into star-studded black velvet. She loved this time of the day, when she could commune with the heavens and commit all her secrets to their twinkling delights. Normally this would be the time she would sit and write a letter to Jo, but these times were always postponed whenever Josey visited.

Tomorrow would be Sunday, and Henri would come and take

Josey back to the chateau. She consoled herself with their earlier conversations. Only two more years to go, and then she could return to England.

She sat for a while, holding the pendant between her fingers, and thought of Jo. Would two more years widen the gulf that had already been carved between them? Could she dare to hope that they had not reached the point of no return?

She poured another glass of wine and lit a cigarette. As she watched the moon disappear behind a grey cloud her mind wandered back to the time she had spent in England and at Pen Marig. She shivered rather from her memories than from the chill of the night.

The next morning, Josey was already up when Jenny walked into the kitchen. She had laid the table, buttered the croissants and heated the coffee pot.

'My, my, you're an early bird.'

'Yes Mama. Papa will be here at two, so we don't have a lot of time.'

'Time for what, Josey?'

'I want to play you some music I've written, and then we can go and look at all your lovely paintings.'

'But they're at the studio, will we have time?'

'Of course Mama, so hurry up and eat your breakfast.'

'Yes mademoiselle,' Jenny laughed. 'Look, I'm eating, I'm eating.'

Josey laughed her infectious laugh and soon they were both consumed in childish gaiety. Soon the breakfast plates were stacked in the sink, and when they had finished washing up, Josey marshalled Jenny into the sitting room.

'Now Mama, this is for you.'

As Josey's fingers caressed the piano keys, Jenny wondered how she could have borne such a gifted daughter.

'Well Mama, what do you think?' Josey pirouetted on the piano stool, eyes bright with excitement.

'Darling, it's beautiful, what's it called?'

'Well, I've called it "A Jamais Mama", "Forever Mother".'

A tear threatened to escape from Jenny's eye. 'Oh darling, how lovely. Play it again.'

The morning was racing by, and as they drove to Jenny's

studio, she thought how one day she and Josey would look back and realize how precious these days were.

Jenny's studio, a refitted cowshed, lay in a lane surrounded by green fields and hedgerows. She had chosen this place for its solitude. *Did it subconsciously remind her of Pen Marig?* She kept that thought to herself.

Jenny had changed her style for the Cologne exhibition, concentrating more on portraits and architectural pieces, which she thought the German collector would prefer.

Josey, a typical teenager, gave honest and succinct observations, and was, Jenny thought, her best critic.

'They're very good Mama. Different, but very good. I'm sure they will sell very well.' Then suddenly, pointing to some canvasses in the far corner of the studio 'What are these, Mama? You haven't shown me these.'

Jenny blushed. 'Oh they're just old ones, not my best works...'

'Let me see, oh please let me see!' She ran to where they stood, not waiting for a reply. 'Why, Mama, these are wonderful. Who are they?'

Josey, in her adolescent enthusiasm had unwittingly unwrapped Jenny's past. What could she say, what excuses could she make, as Josey looked at the portraits of Doll, Tom and Jo.

She drew a deep breath. 'Well darling, do you remember me telling you about my early days at college? Well these are my friend's aunt and uncle. I drew them whilst on holiday one Easter. They have a farm in Wales.'

Could she get away with it?

Josey took out the portrait of Jo. 'And this one?'

'Oh that's Jo, a friend from college.'

'She has a nice face. A little sad perhaps, but nice. Do you see her any more?'

'No, we lost touch. She's a magazine editor now.' Further explanation, she thought, would satisfy Josey's curiosity. 'I met her briefly when I did that article.'

'Oh yes Mama, that was a lovely piece. What a pity you didn't keep in touch.'

'Never mind dear, I expect she has lots of other friends. It was such a long time ago. Now come on we must get back, your father will arrive soon to take you home.'

There, thankfully, the matter was dropped.

'Do I have to go home Mama?' Josey grumbled as they drove back to the cottage.

'You know you do, but we'll have Christmas together, and time will pass quickly once you start at Julliard.'

Josey pouted, as she always did on these occasions. 'You will come, won't you Mama?'

'Of course I will darling.'

Thus, as Jenny wrote her letter to Jo, she pondered upon the price she had to pay for a mother's promise.

Work on the magazine's quarterly issue was almost complete. Jo had rung Tom and made arrangements to drive up on the 27th September. A germ of an idea had formed. She would ask Brian if he would like to join her. *This*, she thought, *might divert Anne Richards' attention away from any sinister agenda.*

She packaged the request as an opportunity for Brian to photograph some autumn scenes for the Christmas calendar.

'Gosh Jo, I'd love to. Are you sure I won't be in the way? After all this is your special time with your uncle.'

'Certainly not, he'll welcome some male company.'

The trip was organized, and as they drove through the Welsh countryside, Brian's enthusiasm pleased her.

Gwyneth had baked the previous day, and Barry had ensured plenty of cut logs for the kitchen range. Dilys the postmistress's daughter had cleaned and made up the beds with freshly laundered linen. Tom, satisfied that all was in order, walked down with Tess to the bottom gate to await Jo's arrival.

Although he had wondered why Jo was bringing a man with her, he would not labour the point. She'll tell me, he mused, if she wants to! 'No Doll,' he looked up to the heavens, 'I won't ask!' He smiled and puffed contentedly on his pipe.

As Jo's car appeared over the brow of the bridge, Tom opened the gate.

'Who's that?' Brian asked.

'That, Brian, is my Uncle Tom.'

'I must take some photos. Can you stop, Jo?'

Jo laughed as she thought that this was going to be a fun couple of days. No need to worry about keeping Brian occupied.

She had hardly drawn the car to a halt when Brian leapt out.

'Brian, you snap and I'll drive through.'

Tom, although not a patient man, stood still while Brian focused his lens and clicked his camera. He didn't quite understand why this man should use the words 'magical', 'stunning' and 'exquisite' which accompanied every whirl of the shutter. To his relief Jo stopped the car inside the gate and beckoned Brian in.

'I'll walk up, Jo. Tess needs the exercise,' said Tom, glad to be away from the imposition of the camera lens.

Jo parked up, and Brian fetched the cases from the boot.

'Yes I know, Brian, I'm very lucky. Come, I'll show you to your room.'

She walked up the smooth wooden stairs with Brian following, and as he placed the cases into their respective rooms Jo wished that it was Jenny and not Brian standing in front of her.

As they walked back down to the kitchen, Tom was already filling up the kettle.

'Everything alright Jo?'

'Yes Uncle, and this is Brian, he's –'

'Takes photographs.' Tom finished her sentence.

They all laughed, and Tom remembered the days when he, Doll and Jo shared moments of laughter together.

The rest of the day was spent without Brian and his beloved camera.

'Will he be OK? I mean, he doesn't know his way around here,' Tom had questioned.

'Uncle, as long as he has his camera he'll be OK. Anyway, Uncle, how are you, how have you been?'

'Not bad Jo, not bad at all. Tess keeps me busy and' – he looked towards the heavens – 'Gwyneth makes sure I eat. And you, Jo, how are you?

'Busy.'

'That was not what I asked. Heard from Jennifer?'

'No Uncle, not for a long time'

'Oh well Jo, Brian seems a nice chap.'

'Yes, he is Uncle. He's just my photographer, and a good friend, but that's all, so don't you be getting any ideas. I brought him here to take some photos for the Christmas calendar and –'

Tom walked over to her and cradled her in his arms.

'Oh well, one day perhaps, Jo, eh?'

'Perhaps, Uncle. Now what are we going to have for supper?'

The subject was dropped and Jo busied herself with preparing vegetables to go with the steak pie Gwyneth had made.

The weather was uncommonly warm for September. Brian disappeared every day with sandwiches and his beloved camera, and as was their way, Tom and Jo roamed the hills and valleys around Pen Marig. Jo was careful to walk slowly, so as not to embarrass Tom, who now found it more and more difficult to climb the slope up to Marling Rock, which stood beside the river that ran through the valley on the other side. Mindful of his increasing arthritis, she ensured that they would make frequent stops to sit and admire the landscape.

On her visits to the village, she was surprised not to hear her neighbours talk about any strangers passing through. Normally this would be grist to the mill for the pub inhabitants, but there was nothing. So had Anne Richards not come? Had Jo got the dates wrong? No, the fates had conspired to help her: Anne Richards had found something more substantial in which to plant her teeth.

The society columns had printed Jennifer Standford's daughter's entrance into Julliard. Anne would take herself to France and infiltrate the St Clair dynasty. Her hands, raw from rubbing gleefully, itched with anticipation. Why bother with the peripheral when she could go straight to the centre?

Phillip had been commanded to cancel the Llanidros bookings, and arrange flights for Paris. Gwen was instructed to search the archives for anything on the St Clair ancestry, and in particular on Henri St Clair.

The next thing to do was to find a way in. She rang her French counterpart. 'Hello darling. I'm coming over, can you put me up for a few days?'

Suzanne Martine squealed with delight. She liked Anne tremendously. They were both cut from the same cloth. It would be exciting to share gossip with her.

'Of course, *chérie*. When?'

'Next week. I'll have Phillip ring when I know the dates and arrival time.'

'Lovely. Michelle can meet you from the airport.'

There, that was done. Anne sat back in her chair and lit a Tom Thumb. She felt very pleased with herself.

Suzanne and Anne's friendship had blossomed over the years. They were governed by the same predatory instincts, with a common insatiability for deposing their subjects. Their infamy was an umbilical cord that stretched easily across the Channel.

Although Suzanne had stayed with Anne in London, this would be the first time Anne had made a reciprocal visit.

Chapter Twenty-Five

Suzanne's apartment was opulent to the extent of overindulgent extravagance. Plush gold and scarlet drapes hung from ornamental rails. Moulded architraves separated walls from ceilings which were festooned with crystal-studded chandeliers.

Suzanne was born in and married to wealth. It bored her, but gave her the means to open doors, and creep into the lives of others. Scandal-mongering was not a dalliance, but a necessary alleviation from the mediocre. As with all opiates, it consumed her until no one was safe from her malignancy. Yes, Suzanne couldn't wait for the arrival of her fellow conspirator.

After a couple of days of catching up and shopping, it was time for Anne to approach the subject of Henri St Clair.

'Henri? Oh yes *chérie* – we've dined at the chateau many times. A nice man but ruled by that harridan of a mother. Has a daughter you know ... Married? No, had an affair with that Standford woman. ... Where does she live? Oh somewhere near Rheims. Has a studio there, sees her daughter on weekends I think ... Reclusive? yes, I suppose you could say that.'

Anne listened intently to her friend, savouring every snippet. 'I understand the daughter is at Julliard.'

'Oh yes, a shining star. In fact she has a concert next week. We could go, and I'll introduce you to Henri.'

'That would be lovely Suzanne.'

Could things have gone better for Anne?'

The evening of the concert came. They dressed carefully in their newly bought Paris gowns. Their expertly coiffured hair was studded with diamante clips, which matched their equally studded stiletto opened-toed sandals. Satisfied with their appearance they sat in the chauffeur-driven limousine drinking pink champagne.

The music was a delight. Josey was truly gifted. After two standing ovations the audience began to disperse.

Suzanne linked arms with Anne. 'Come, I'll introduce you to Henri.'

They walked through the auditorium and around to the back of the stage, where a small group were huddled in conversation. Josey and Jenny were cuddling, while Henri looked on, beaming from ear to ear.

Madame St Clair stood clutching her sequined bag, nodding in refined appreciation.

'Darling, it was wonderful,' Jenny cried.

'It was, wasn't it Mama!'

Henri joined in. 'I loved the Brahms.'

Josey laughed. 'It was Chopin. Oh what a philistine you are Papa!'

Henri grimaced, red-faced. 'Well poppet, whatever it was, it was charming.'

'Hello Henri.' Their gaiety was interrupted by Suzanne.

Henri turned. 'Oh Suzanne, how lovely to see you. Did you like the concert?'

'I adored it,' she simpered. 'Josey, you must be delighted. You're so, so gifted.'

Josey beamed. Suzanne turned to Henri. 'Oh Henri, can I introduce you to Anne Richards? She's a very dear friend of mine from England. I couldn't let her go home without giving her a treat.'

'Why yes, hello.' Henri bowed, and took Anne's hand in welcome. 'Let me introduce you to my family. Josey, my very talented daughter.' Josey smiled. 'My mother, Madame St Clair, and Josey's mother Jennifer Standford.'

Anne ignored Madame St Clair. 'Oh yes, Jennifer Standford, I've heard so much about you. I believe you paint very well!'

The sarcasm was not lost on Madam St Clair. She may not have approved of Jenny, but she was her granddaughter's mother. The honour of the St Clair family had to be upheld. She took a step forward. 'Oh yes, and what is it you do, my dear?'

Anne squirmed under the steel gaze. Had she met her adversary? Years of calculation came to her aid. 'Oh nothing as talented, I'm just a mere columnist.'

She turned to Jenny. Flattery might diffuse the situation. 'Perhaps I could visit your studio while I'm here?'

Josey enthused. 'Oh yes Mama, please let her, then she can see how wonderfully you paint.'

Jenny nodded, both to placate her daughter and to disguise the dislike she had for this woman.

Henri, however, ignorant of this, invited them all back to the chateau for a celebratory party. The invitation was accepted with enthusiasm by Suzanne and Anne. Wine and food were consumed with relish, and when it was time to depart to the drawing room, they were treated to an impromptu recital by Josey.

Anne, needing to diffuse her recent faux pas, beguiled Henri with humorous anecdotes. He, like a rabbit caught in a car's headlights, fell prey to her charms. It had been a long time since his masculinity had been massaged so adeptly. Perhaps, he thought, romance hadn't been quite lost to him?

Madam St Clair, however, was not to be moved. Her shrewd and undeniable objectivity bore credence to her apprehension. 'That woman's not right for you, Henri. She's not quite what you think she is!'

'Mother, I'm 45 years old, don't you think it's time you stopped interfering in my life. First Jennifer –'

'Oh yes, Henri, I was right about that, wasn't I? And look how that turned out!'

'Yes, but we do have Josey to show for it, so please don't continue Mother. If I want to see Anne, then I will.'

Henri stood adamant, but Madame St Clair had the bit between her teeth. 'Oh yes, Josey, and she can't wait to scurry off to live with her mother!'

Henri was amused by the irony of it all. 'Well Mama, no different than my still living with you!'

He stomped out of the room, his repartee resounding heavily on Madame St Clair's ears.

Chapter Twenty-Six

Josey loved living with her mother. She would practise in the morning and then join Jenny at the studio for lunch. She was only nineteen, and yet her life was full. Could she be happier?

Even though the love of her daughter was all-consuming, there were moments when Jenny felt numb with loneliness. She had promised herself to return to England once Josey had reached sixteen, but events had overtaken themselves. Three years on, and Jenny was no nearer to her dream. Her letters to Jo had become more infrequent, more desolate. When would there be a time? Perhaps now with Josey settled on her career path?

Yes! She would write to Jo, and this time she would send the letter. She would give the letter to George, who would post it. With Josey sound asleep, she sat down on the veranda and began to write.

> *My dearest Jo,*
>
> *I'm coming home!*
>
> *Can I dare hope that you would still wish to see me? I have been such a fool Jo. I should never have left you. Never have wasted my life, your life, our life!*
>
> *If there is to be one solitary constant it is that I have kept my promise to always love you.*
>
> *If your love has been lost within all these years of separation and my own selfishness, then I will understand.*
>
> *I will move into Flaxman Square permanently by the end of next month, if you can find it in your heart to visit me.*
>
> *How do I love thee? Unlike Elizabeth Browning, alas I cannot count the ways.*
>
> *Yours always, Jen*

When she had finished, she folded the page and placed it in her drawer. She would address it and give it to George tomorrow. Satisfied with her decision, she poured a glass of wine and sat back in her chair.

As she gazed out into the night, she dreamt of other moonlit skies, when she and Jo had sat and gazed over the Welsh valley. Her heart leapt at the thought. She drew the pendant to her lips, Oh Jo, Jo, shall we ever have those times again?

The events of the next two days overtook all the resolutions Jenny had made.

Chapter Twenty-Seven

It was early the next morning when Henri telephoned the cottage. Jenny was fixing breakfast when Josey burst into the kitchen.

'That was Papa. He's coming down with Anne. She wants to see some of your paintings!'

Jenny raised her eyebrows in dismay. She had wanted to see George. It was Wednesday, and he was going to London on Friday. She needed her letter to be delivered.

'Does he have to?' she was irritated.

'Well yes, Mama. I want Anne to see how clever you are.'

Still irritated she poured coffee. She would have to see George tomorrow. She would telephone when the visitors had gone. 'Well, I have to go to the studio this morning. You'll have to wait for them and bring them down later.'

Josey felt deflated. 'Well, I suppose so, if that's what you want!'

'Yes it is! Well I must get going.'

'But what about breakfast, Mama?'

'Oh, I'll have something at the studio.'

Josey could not leave it there. 'What's the matter Mama? Is it because Papa is bringing Anne?'

'Certainly not. I … I just wanted us to have some time together. After all, you are off on your tour next week.'

Josey kissed her mother on the cheek. 'Never mind, they'll only be here for today, we'll have lots of time for ourselves. You go, Mama. I'll tidy up. Do we have any cake?'

'Yes, it's in the pantry.'

'Right, I'll give them coffee and cake, and then bring them down to the studio. Is that OK?'

Jenny half-smiled. 'Of course darling.'

With that, Jenny left Josey to busy herself. Josey hummed as she tidied. To Josey everything was wonderful: her life, her mother, even her father. Although she wasn't fully enamoured with

Anne, she had seen a sudden lightness of step in her father's gait. It was obvious that Anne maybe could make him happy. She would make this day pleasant for him, and Anne, if needs be.

The morning had grown warm. Sunlight beamed through the opened lattice windows. Shadows danced on the pink distempered walls, and gnarled oak beams stoically carried the weight of the plaster ceilings on their shoulders.

Josey raced to the kitchen when her father arrived. 'Come, Papa, I've made tea. Can you cut the cake?'

He smiled at his daughter. 'Anne darling,' he called as he walked towards the kitchen door. 'Make yourself at home'

Anne surveyed the lounge. French chic. Chintz-covered chairs with matching curtains. *Ugh,* she thought – *not for her!* Was this the time to rummage? She would never get a better opportunity. She listened: Josey and Henri were gaily chatting in the kitchen. Could she? Yes of course she could. She glanced around the room. Cabinet, oak table, upright chairs, writing bureau. Ah! Writing bureau!

She acted swiftly. Time was of the essence. She pulled open a drawer. Nothing much, scraps of drawing paper and pencils. She listened: laughter could still be heard from the kitchen. She pulled open another drawer. A piece of paper lay over the top of some blue-edged envelopes by the side of which a diary was laid. She felt she had drawn the winning ticket as she turned over the page and read:

'*My dearest Jo, I'm coming home ...*'

She read on, her juices flowing. At last she had the key to Pandora's box. Her hands shook as she rifled through the envelopes. Each one marked 'Jo Dawson', with a London address.

The voices in the kitchen became louder. She had to be quick. She took a few envelopes from the drawer, and deposited them in her handbag. She would savour this delicious fruit later.

After the coffee had been drunk, and cake eaten, Anne feigned a migraine. 'Do you mind, Henri, if we visit the studio another time? These wretched heads are really debilitating.'

'Of course not *chéri*, I'll take you straight back to Suzanne's.'

Josey watched their car drive off down the lane. She felt

bitterly disappointed, and wondered how a migraine could take hold so quickly.

'Oh gosh, Mama!' She picked up the receiver and phoned the studio.

Jenny was less disappointed; actually, was not at all disappointed. Now she had time to talk to Josey about her leaving. She would see George the following morning.

Josey was playing her piano when Jenny arrived back at the cottage.

'I'll prepare lunch,' she called out as she passed the sitting room.

She opened a bottle of Moselle to accompany a cheese omelette and salad. As she laid the table she called out to Josey. 'Almost ready, darling.'

'OK Mama, won't be a minute.'

From experience Jenny knew Josey's minute could turn into ten or more, so she poured a glass of wine and sat down at the kitchen table. She would cook the omelette when Josey had finished, thus avoiding any burnt offering. She would talk to Josey after lunch.

Anne sat comfortably in one of Suzanne's burgundy leather armchairs, drinking the cognac she had previously poured. Suzanne had left a note for Anne: *"Don't wait up Cheri, might not be back until tomorrow."*

'Oh good,' Anne thought. Now she had time to read her contraband. Her handbag, which she had so jealously guarded, lay on the marble coffee table. 'Now, let's see what secrets you've been hiding!'

She took another sip of cognac. She wanted to savour the moment. Carefully she slid her index finger beneath the flap of each envelope. She had wished she'd taken the folded letter, but its loss may have been discovered and she would lose the element of surprise. No, she had to be content with the few she had stolen.

As she read them, it didn't take a genius to realize they were love letters, full of passion, yet tinged with sadness. As she read and then reread them she found no adjective to describe the elation she felt. She could almost taste victory.

She drank more cognac. A plan had to be formed. She must calculate her moment to strike. Revenge, after all, is a dish best served cold. Could this be the exposé of the century? No! There was no longevity in it. Her spoils had to be substantial. At last she could fulfil her dream of revenge. Her Goliath was about to be slain.

She cared not for Jennifer Standford, she was insignificant. Whereas Jo Dawson ... Yes, Jo Dawson! She would have her crown, *Millennium*. It should have been hers. 'Yes my dear,' she hissed, 'it's mine for the taking.'

A momentary thought rested upon Henri, but was quickly dispensed with. He was expendable, a means to an end.

She gently placed the letters in their envelopes. A delicious treasure not to be tarnished by heavy-handedness. She poured another cognac and walked to the telephone.

'Henri, hello ... Yes I'm a little better. Do you have Jennifer's number? I really must phone to apologize. ... You have? Right, I'll get a pen.'

Jenny was tidying up after lunch when the telephone rang. 'Oh Josey, can you get that?' she called from the kitchen.

'Yes Mama.' Then, 'Mama it's Anne, she wants to speak to you.'

Jenny stood in the doorway shaking her head. 'No,' she whispered, but Josey was adamant.

'She says it's quite urgent.'

Jenny shrugged and took the receiver from Josey. 'Well Anne, what is it?'

'Oh darling, I just wanted to apologize for my quick exit.'

'No need!'

'Oh, but there is. I think I must apologize properly!'

Again, a rather irritated Jenny advised there was no need.

'I'm sure you really would want to meet me. Especially if – now how can I say this – especially if you value your friendship with Jo Dawson!'

Fear gripped Jenny's heart. 'I don't know what you are talking about ...'

'Oh I think you do. Now I'll expect you at ...' – she gave Suzanne's address – 'Shall we say at seven this evening?'

Anne replaced the receiver and walked back to her armchair. She had a few hours to wait. Could she contain her excitement till then? Yes of course she could! She would cook a light meal, shower and change, then she would stalk her prey, like a fox around a chicken coop.

Jenny still held the receiver long after Anne had replaced hers. What had just happened? What was that conversation all about? She felt very frightened. She knew a little of Anne's reputation. There was no avoiding the issue, she had to accept the unwelcome invitation.

She replaced the receiver and walked back into the kitchen. Josey was pouring coffee.

'That was Anne Richards.' But Josey already knew that.

'She wants to discuss a commission. She's staying at Suzanne's, so I'll meet her there. Will you be alright for a couple of hours? I'll leave about six-ish, should be back by nine.'

'Of course Mama, I've a lot of rehearsing for the tour next week.'

There, it was settled. A little white lie, but no harm done.

Jenny drove slowly, she was too nervous to drive fast. She played a tape. Normally the music would calm her, but this evening it seemed to heighten her tension. She switched it off, leaving silence the only background to her thoughts.

On her arrival, Anne preened. 'Would you like a drink?'

'No thank you. Just say what you have to say, and I'll be off.'

'Oh come, come Jennifer. Don't be so eager, please do sit down.'

Jenny sat down on the edge of the settee.

'Well my dear, where were we?' Anne carried on the conversation as if there had been no break in time from the afternoon's phone call. 'Oh yes, Jo Dawson! Not just a friendship then?' she reached into her handbag and placed the envelopes one by one onto the coffee table as if one was dealing a deck of cards.

Jenny stared, she felt sick, but still she said nothing.

'Why, my dear! Not even a protestation. Come now aren't you even curious?'

No she wasn't curious, she was angry. How dare this woman steal from her, invade her privacy. She wanted to hit her, wipe that smug look from her face, but she knew such action would only inflame the situation. 'I'll have my letters back please.'

'Of course my dear.' Acid dripped from Anne's words. 'But I want –'

'Well, yes, of course there's a price. How much do you want?'

'Oh Jennifer, Jennifer, tut tut. Pieces of silver? I think not.'

'Then what is it?'

'I want *Millennium*, I'm sure you can persuade your friend to hand it over.'

'I don't see how, she's only the editor.'

'Oh dear, didn't she tell you? She bought the magazine five years ago. My, my, my, what secrets we have!'

Jenny got up from the settee. 'Oh do your worst. I really don't care.'

'Really! Well I'm sure Josey would!'

'You leave Josey out of this.'

'Then do as I ask. I want *Millennium*.'

'And if not?'

'Then I'll bring you all down. You have four weeks, and then I'll see you in London.' She handed Jenny a business card. 'There, I think that's our business finished.'

Jenny sat in her car, gripped with fear. Murderous thoughts bombarded her mind. In that moment she found herself drifting into that dark place where one could be led to kill another. She lit a cigarette, the smoke filled the car. She wanted to disappear into the darkness. She drove home to the cottage, bereft of all reason.

Josey was still playing as Jenny walked into the sitting room.

'Is that you Mama?'

'Yes darling, you carry on, I just have to phone George.'

Josey swivelled on the piano stool. 'Meeting go well? Did you get a nice commission?'

'Er, yes. I'll tell you about it later. You carry on practising, and I'll call you when supper is ready.'

Josey returned to her piano, and Jenny to the dining room.

'George.'

'Oh hello Jennifer.'

'George, I want to go to London on Friday. Can you book me a seat on the plane?'

George frowned. They had never discussed her going earlier. 'Well of course. What about Josey?'

'She starts her tour in one week. She can stay with her father until then.'

'Oh, OK. I'll ring back to confirm.'

'Yes, and thank you.'

George put down the phone, a little bemused by the request, but he did as he was asked and booked a seat out from Paris at ten o'clock that Friday morning. He called Jenny back with the details and arranged to take her to the airport at eight o'clock.

All that was left was for Jenny to tell Josey!

She picked at her supper.

'Not hungry Mama?'

'No, not really.'

'Is something the matter?'

'Not especially, but I have to go to London on Friday.'

'Oh!'

'Yes.' Another lie was to be told. 'George has booked the Whitechapel again so I need just to check that all is in order, enough hanging space etcetera. Yes it is a bit of a bore, I know, but its necessary.'

'Well of course Mama. I'm disappointed, but I can stay with Papa until I leave for New York.'

'Are you sure?'

'Yes, of course Mama. Please don't worry so.'

Was now the time to broach her move back to England? Perhaps not. Now she was coming to Jo not with promises but with "the Sword of Damocles". No, the time was not now. She felt a tear form, she rubbed her eyes.

'Are you alright Mama?'

'Yes darling, just a little grit in my eye!'

George rang to confirm final details. He would meet her at the cottage and they would drive up together. She packed a case. She would exchange her money at the airport.

She had one last day with Josey. She would make it special. And it was; they laughed as they picnicked in the meadow and reminisced about Josey's childhood.

'It may have been a bit grim Mama, but I always had you to come back to.'

They cuddled and then dipped strawberries in cream.

'Come Josey, sit still, I want to draw you.'

'Oh no, not again Mama!'

'Yes, again. I want to catch you at the time before you became really famous.'

They both laughed, and dutifully Josey sat still.

They returned early that evening. Henri was to pick up Josey, and George would collect Jenny.

For Josey, a fitful sleep. For Jenny, none. She arose at four 'o' clock made coffee and sat out on the veranda. The birds were waking from their sleep, and the sun was attempting to appear above the blue-tinged clouds.

Even the nicotine from her cigarette could not dispel the nervous murmurings which circled her stomach. What was she to say to Jo? If indeed Jo would still want to see her. She had wanted to come with love, and not with an asp to strike at her heart. What price a memory?

The airport lounge was hot and sticky. She had an hour and a half to wait for her flight. George ordered an absinth and Jenny a cognac.

'Jenny?'

'Yes George.'

'I assume you're eventually going to tell me what's up. It's unlike you to be so impulsive. can I assume – and I apologize if I'm wrong – it has something to do with your old friend Jo.'

Jenny looked up at him, tears streaming down her face. 'Oh George, I don't know how to begin.' But begin she did, and once started she couldn't stop. Words tumbled out from her.

Anger filled his heart. 'For goodness' sake woman, couldn't you have kept the drawer locked, or at least hidden your letters away?'

'Yes, yes,' she cried pitifully, 'I know. But there's only ever been Josey and you at the cottage. I just didn't think.'

'Didn't think! Good God, Jennifer, every one knows that woman's the devil incarnate.' He stopped as he saw the fear in Jenny's eyes. 'Oh well it's done now.'

But it wasn't done. She still had to confront Jo.

'Old sins cast long shadows'

Part Two

Part Two

Chapter One

'Long time have human ignorance and guilt
Detained us, on what spectacles of woe
Compelled to look, and inwardly oppressed
With sorrow, disappointment, vexing thoughts,
Confusion of judgement, zeal decayed,
And, lastly, utter loss of hope itself
And things to hope for!'
(Wordsworth, 'Imagination & taste how impaired and restored')

Jenny stood in reception. Lucy smiled in recognition. 'Ah yes, Miss Standford. I'll tell Sally you're here.' Jenny listened while Lucy announced her arrival. 'Sally? Jennifer Standford's here to see Jo. Won't be long, Miss Standford, please sit down.'

Jenny pondered on the statement, 'She won't be long'! But how long had it been since she had seen Jo? Did absence make the heart grow fonder, or was it a case of out of sight, out of mind? From her seat she watched the door. Would it open? And if it did, would it present an invitation or a dismissal? Her nerves, almost shattered, denied the prospect. Jo would see her. She had to!

The door opened and Sally walked towards her, arms outstretched. 'Hello Miss Standford, how lovely to see you again. I'll take you up.'

Jenny rose up and followed Sally to Jo's office.

Jo looked up from her desk, and not forgetting her manners, said, 'Oh hello Miss Standford, what a nice surprise, are you well?'

'Yes, thank you.'

Once the niceties were over Sally left the room.

Jenny marvelled how the years had not changed Jo. She still had that earthy blush to her face. Still those dark brown eyes that could penetrate all thought. Still had those lips ... But they had become estranged. She saw no look of welcome, no acknowledgement of secret affection.

'I wrote you a letter ..."

'Oh yes?'

'To say I was coming back to England.'

'So!' Jo remained unmoved. 'Well, you're here now. What do you want?'

Jenny lowered her eyes, and half-whispered, 'I wanted to see you!'

Jo dismissed the words. Again she said, 'Well, you're here now. What do you want?'

'I wanted to see you, I must speak to you!'

'Well you have, now you can go.'

Jenny fumbled with her handbag. She had expected animosity, but when it came, it gripped her heart with icy fingers. *Nothing much to do now*, she thought, as she opened her handbag and pulled out a package.

'I'll go then?' she waited for a reply, but there was none. 'Then I'll leave these with you. I'm staying at the Adelphi. I'll ... I'll leave the room and phone number, in case...'

Jenny did not want to meet at Flaxman Square. She had done enough damage to Jo. No way would she heap past memories upon her.

Jo didn't look up until the door had closed. What had just happened? How dare she! How dare she walk back into her life, as if the years that had passed had been dismissed. Anger consumed her. She threw the package into her briefcase, and slammed the lid shut.

'God damn her! God damn that bloody woman.'

She went back to her work, but concentration failed her. She needed to think. Needed to go home. She picked up her briefcase and jacket, and left her office. She feigned a headache, and felt guilty when Sally offered her commiserations.

'You'll be alright for tomorrow?'

'Yes, should be,' Jo mumbled.

She drove home, and once inside her flat, threw the briefcase and jacket onto the sofa, and marched into the kitchen. She poured a glass of wine, and walked back into the sitting room. Anger stormed the ramparts as she gulped down the wine and lit a cigarette.

She couldn't believe the audacity of the woman. What did she expect? They would be as they were? She would nibble at the crumbs she offered and be thankful for them? No! After 12 years of silence, Jo had had enough. She had to sever the connection. No ties, no obligations!

She took another gulp of wine, opened her briefcase, and took out the package. Once opened, it revealed several bundles of envelopes, which on close inspection were addressed to Jo. 'What on earth!' She slit one envelope and took out two sheets of paper.

My darling Jo…

As she opened each envelope and read each letter, she realized that these where the love letters Jenny had written to her.

So many questions, so few answers! Jo got up from the armchair and walked back into the kitchen. As she poured another glass of wine she knew that she could make no sense of it. Why now? Why hadn't she sent them? Did she think that these would compensate for all the heartache and loneliness that Jo had suffered over the years? But no, they didn't, in fact they had the opposite effect.

God damn you Jenny! I'll not fall into this trap again. I'll not be resurrected only to be thrown to the lions. *Sever all ties,* she thought. *What was left? Pen Marig!*

There, she said to herself, as she wrote the cheque. No more handouts. She can have her money back, and that will be an end to it! Bitterness had suffocated her feelings for Jenny, until there was nothing left.

She took the paper on which Jenny had written the details of the hotel, and called for a taxi.

Jenny had wished for the phone call from reception, announcing Jo's arrival, but none came. Then there was a knock on the door. She hadn't ordered room service. Perhaps they had made a mistake. The mistake was thinking that Jo would ring first.

'Oh Jo, you've come! I'm so glad.'

'Don't be, I won't be long!' Jo replied as she pushed Jenny aside and walked into the room.

'I've read your letters, but aren't they a little too late, don't you think?' Sarcasm flowed unrestrained from Jo's lips.

Jenny's eyes burned, and her heart raced. 'But Jo, I –'

'You what, Jen? Thought I'd come running like I always did? Hoping my cup would be half-full and not half-empty. Well you're wrong Jen, I'm tired of it all. I have a good life now, I don't need any complications. And let's face it Jen, you certainly don't, otherwise we would have been together all these years.' Jo was on a roll now, with her previous glasses of wine, she felt that she may have finally won the war, even if it were to prove to be a pyrrhic victory.

Jenny tried to interrupt. 'But Jo I really do need to talk to you!'

'I just don't believe you Jen. You want to talk to me now? Did you lose your voice over the last twelve years? Well you may have found it now, but it's way too late. I don't want to hear it! From today I want to cut all ties with you. No obligations.' She handed the envelope to Jenny. 'Here you are, the money you paid for Pen Marig.' And as an afterthought, full of sarcasm. 'It's the full market value, so you won't lose out.'

She carried on, with Jenny only able to stare in disbelief. 'You can keep the letters. They may in retrospect remind you of what might have been. So go back to where you came from. It's over Jenny!'

Jo turned on her heels and walked out of the room. She walked down the steps of the hotel.

'Taxi, madam?' asked the concierge as he lifted his hat.

'Yes please.'

The taxi was hailed and Jo returned to her flat.

As Jenny stared at the door it appeared as a bottomless pit into which Jo had disappeared. She looked at the letters Jo had left on the table and shook her head in hopelessness. She had wished that these would in some way heal the rift between them but now realized she had handed Jo a poisoned chalice from which to sip.

What was she to do? What could be done? Who could she turn to?

The threat of Anne Richards would not go away. Her own reticence to acknowledge her true self had led to this disaster. But what was even worse was that she had unwittingly involved her beloved Jo into this unimaginable nightmare. She must speak to Jo again. She must bring closure to this whole sorry mess.

She would try to sleep on it, and formulate a plan tomorrow.

Chapter Two

Jo paced up and down her flat, her footsteps pounding the floor in anger. But at whom was she angry? Herself, for hating Jenny, or for still harbouring the feelings she had? Love and hate! A very fine line to tread, especially when emotions kept an unsteady gait.

She knew she had to get away. She had some holiday coming. She would take it. She would go to Pen Marig. She would be safe there.

She took the next day to rearrange her work schedule, and left for Pen Marig the following morning. She would take the train. The journey would aid contemplation.

Two days had passed since Jo had gone. As Jenny didn't know where Jo lived, she decided not to phone the magazine and be rebuffed by Jo, but to visit instead.

Joan was surprised to see her. 'Oh I'm sorry, Miss Standford, but Jo is on holiday. Did she not tell you?'

'Oh dear, she must have forgotten. Never mind I'll catch her when she returns. Where did she go, did she say?'

'Well, er, no she didn't. but I expect it's Wales, it usually is.'

'Thank you, and if she should call, perhaps you could let her know I popped by.'

'Well yes I will. Er, was it important?'

'No. No, I might be exhibiting again, and thought perhaps ... No. Never mind, I'll ring her later on in the month.'

She left the building, wondering what to do next. She would go to Pen Marig. If Jo wasn't there she would write her a letter, explaining everything, then go back to France and think of another way to diffuse the Anne Richards situation.

She settled her bill at the hotel, and hailed a taxi to the train station. It was a long journey, and with each mile her heart grew heavier. She felt like crying, but the crowded compartment leant no possibility for tears.

She arrived at Aberystwyth just before five 'o' clock and found a taxi to take her to Pen Marig. As if in slow motion, she recalled every hedge, hill and lane, and remembered how carefully she had set each scene onto canvas, all those many years ago.

Oh Jo, Jo, what have I done?

She could think no more, as the taxi driver announced her arrival at Pen Marig. As she saw lights shining from the farmhouse windows, her heart beat so fast, she felt the breath leave her body. She lifted her hand to knock on the door. She then thought, *this was a very bad idea,* and turned to go.

A voice called, 'Who's there?'

Jenny, feeling her legs shake uncontrollably, replied, 'It's me Jo, Jennifer!'

If Jo had thought her addiction to Jenny was over, she was wrong! As they stood face to face, the rawness of it burnt her throat. She gulped, 'What are you doing here?'

Jenny clenched her hands. The act seemed to stabilize her. 'I had to see you Jo! Joan told me you'd taken time off. I just … just hoped you were at Pen Marig.'

'Well you were right.' Jo hesitated. 'Er, I suppose you'd better come in. Er … now you're here!'

It seemed to Jenny that she walked into yesterday as she was shown into the kitchen. It was still the same. Nothing had changed. Still the shiny black-leaded stove. Still the butcher's table, with its uneven top from years of scrubbing. And yes! Still the old butler's sink in which Tom would wash before every meal. As she did not know what to say, she remained silent.

As if Jo had read her mind, she uttered, 'Haven't had the heart to change anything, since Tom passed away.'

'I'm so sorry Jo …'

'Why be sorry?' came the retort. 'I'd lost the only one unconditional love in my life' - Jenny flinched at the word "unconditional" - 'and where were you? Well, it's over and done now.' Jo stopped, and trying not to look at Jenny, turned towards the stove.

'I expect you'll be wanting a cup of tea or something?'

'Er, yes, if it's not too much trouble.'

They had become strangers, with no hint of familiarity between them.

'Of course not. Are you hungry?'

'No, not really,' Jenny replied and smiled a faint humourless smile.

They drank their tea in silence. There was no remembering in conversation. Could they go back to how it was? No! Not when one tries to clutch at straws with a closed hand.

> *'For love, that comes wherever life & sense*
> *Are given by God, in thee was most intense;*
> *A chain of heart, a feeling of the mind,*
> *A tender sympathy, which did thee bind.*
> (Wordsworth, 'Incident')'

Jo finished her tea, looked up at Jenny, and found herself in danger of losing all her previous resolve. She jumped up from the table and said, 'I expect you'll want to bathe and change. Too late for you to leave tonight. The room opposite mine is made up. I keep it tidy for Brian when he visits.'

'Are you sure?'

'Yes. You won't be disturbed, it's time for my evening walk with Tess.'

Jo whistled, and out bounded a black and white collie from the parlour. With her jacket on, Jo went outside, quickly followed by Tess. Tess had been the name of Tom's favourite collie, and so she had used it for her own dog, hoping it would hold Tom's spirit close.

They walked up the hill towards Marling Rock. No sheep to herd now. Tess ran off, stopping only to glance back at Jo.

At least, Jo thought, *she always wanted to know where I was. God damn that woman, why is she here?*

Chapter Three

During the past 12 years, Jo had pragmatically resigned herself to the life she now had. There had been occasions when she might have been tempted to find another companion, but she knew no one could compete with that all-consuming first love. No, there could be no one else.

Finally she reached Marling Rock, and sat down under her tree, lit a cigarette and again thought, *God damn that woman!*

Tess sat down beside her and rested her head on Jo's knee. 'What are we going to do Tess?' The collie looked up and licked her hand. 'Oh Tess, if life was only that simple, a lick to kiss it better!'

Jenny carried her case up the scrubbed wooden stairs and consoled herself with, *well at least she didn't tell me to go.* She bathed and changed into a jumpsuit, and went to go downstairs. On the landing she stopped, and looked at the door opposite the one she had left. On it were still the etched letters on the wooden plaque. 'Jo's room'.

Should she enter? Dare she enter? Yes she would! She carefully turned the knob, and feeling like an intruder, opened the door and took a hesitant step inside.

As with the rest of the house, time had stood still. She smiled, as she looked at the collie pictures on the wall, and the train set sitting obliquely on the shelf by the window. Two photographs of Tom and Doll sat on the mantelpiece above the redundant fireplace.

The bedside table held a clock, a book and a photograph frame. She took up the book and realized it was the Wordsworth she had bought Jo all those years ago. *Oh well,* she thought. But a bigger surprise was to befall her, when she lifted the photo frame and saw the photo of herself which she had given to Jo so many years ago.

Feeling bereft, she backed out of the room, closed the door behind her and went downstairs into the kitchen. As she sat down at the table quietly smoking a cigarette, she decided then that she would not talk to Jo about Anne Richards, but go back to France and find some other way out of this unholy mess.

She had been stupid to think that she could involve Jo in this debacle after she had taken herself out of Jo's life for these past few years. She had reaped what she had sown when she consigned her feelings to the fear of discovery. Yes, she was adamant, she would leave tomorrow, and she would not tell Jo.

'Well Tess, another cigarette I think? Then we'll go back home.'

Tess nestled her head in Jo's lap, and heaved a deep sigh of contentment. Jo felt comfortable and thought how wonderful it would be if her own life was that easy. The sun was lowering itself beneath the hills, its warmth ebbing from Jo's bones. 'Time to go home, I think.' She looked down the hill to Pen Marig, and wondered what was waiting for her in that grey brick house with its lighted windows.

She inhaled deeply on the last dregs of her cigarette, stubbed it out with her foot, and realized she could not quell the anxiety that rose up from deep within her stomach. She knew that she had felt this way before, but that was a happier time. What was it someone had said: "Obsession is only the unfullflment of dreams"?

When she reached the house, and turned the knob on the door, she knew that she was in deep danger of falling apart. She took her shoes off in the boot room and went into the kitchen.

Jenny was sitting at the kitchen table twirling her lighter in between her fingers. She looked up and smiled when she saw Jo. How wonderful Jo looked, with her brown tousled hair, red weather-beaten face and those brown eyes.

'Oh Jo!' she whispered.

Jo pretended not to hear and strolled over to the stove. 'You must be hungry.' But not waiting for a reply, 'I know I am.'

'Blethyn, Dilys's daughter, brought up some lamb stew yesterday. Didn't want me to go without food. A good thought, knowing how I don't cook. If I warm it up would you like some?'

'Well yes Jo, that would be nice. And yes, I think I am hungry now!'

'We'll have some wine while it's heating,' said Jo taking a bottle of white from the fridge, and collecting two glasses from the Welsh dresser. She sat down at the table opposite Jenny and poured the wine into the two glasses. 'There you are, hope it's not too cold!'

Jenny took one sip, coughed lightly as the cold liquid caught in her throat. 'How's the magazine doing? I'm afraid I forgot to keep up my subscription, and ...'

'It's doing very well. I had quite a few offers to sell after we won the media prize, but there was no way I would do that. Instead we formed a limited company. Sally, Brian and Little Jimmy each have a fifteen per cent shareholding, and I have the remaining fifty-five per cent. It's more a family-run magazine now. Everything I could wish for, really.' The last sentence was spoken with more of a sigh than a statement. 'And you? Any new exhibitions in the offing?'

'Well yes, George has arranged for me to show at the Whitechapel again, but I'm not too sure what to do at the moment.'

The small talk continued until most of the wine had been drunk and the stew was fully warmed through. Jo put it onto plates and placed them on the table beside the cutlery she had laid earlier.

'I'm so glad that everything has worked out well for you Jo.'

Jo looked at her plate. She couldn't eat. All she could do was look up and scoff, 'So glad? You disappeared from my life and you're so glad? You didn't forget to renew your subscription, you cancelled it! Then disappeared without a trace. What was it, Jen? You wanted to erase me from your life! When Josey passed sixteen, I waited for you. What happened, Jen? You decided that I wasn't worth the trouble?'

'No, no, Jo it wasn't like that!'

'Well, what was it like? You made a promise?'

'Yes I know, but it's so hard, so hard to explain. Josey had won a scholarship at Julliard, and ... and ...!'

'And what, Jen?'

I couldn't ... I couldn't let anything stand in her way. Scandal would have ruined her chances. She was going to become a brilliant concert pianist. I had to make a choice, Jo.'

'Oh well, you did! But what I don't understand is why you are here now?'

'I just wanted to see you.'

'It must be more than that Jen? What is it? Is Josey so famous that it doesn't matter any more?'

'No! No!' the emphasis was pronounced. 'I began to realize that I had to finally live my own life, and I hoped beyond hope that it was with you.'

By now the lamb stew was beginning to coagulate on the plates. Hunger seemed to vanish, as each sentence was spoken. Jo still did not believe what Jenny was telling her. All these years she had suffered the heartache of her love of Jenny, and now, the insolvency of her emotions had left her bankrupt.

Jo couldn't comprehend Jenny's statement. There had to be something more to it. 'Where is Josey now?' She wanted to add, 'Out of harm's way?' but decided the sarcasm wasn't warranted. Instead, she offered the question and awaited the answer.

'She's in New York.'

'Oh,' Jo replied. And thought, *well, far enough away, then!*

Jenny rushed to continue, not wanting Jo to discover the real reason for her visit. 'I have been so lonely without you Jo, and there hasn't been a moment when I haven't thought about you, and I just needed to see you. Needed to confirm that absence does make the heart grow fonder. But there again, I don't expect you to welcome me with open arms. I have betrayed the love that we had together, and damaged it beyond all possible repair. I came because I needed you to know, that despite all these years, you will always be my first and only love. Even though I never had the courage to admit it.'

Jo looked up at Jenny, and felt a tenderness, a feeling that she hadn't felt in such a long time. She got up from the table and walked towards her. She gently lifted Jenny from her chair, and folded her arms around her. Finally, Jo's fast was over.

They held each other, suffocating and all-consuming. There was no need for doubt, it was for them a wasted emotion. They stood there, moulded together, as if cryogenically frozen. A singularity in time and space. There was no need for pragmatism, for they had created their own unfathomable fairy story. Together they were invincible. Apart they were soulless beings floating through an ethereal wasteland. Words failed them. Time eluded them. Magic consumed them, and when they finally lay together, the night secured them.

In the morning, the dawn birds sang away the darkness, and Jo stirred with their joyous call. She sat up on one elbow and gazed fondly at Jenny's face – could she call it an apparition? – languishing in sleep on the pillow beside her. Had that night really happened, or was it just a dream?

As if to answer her silent question, Jenny stirred, looked up at the face peering down above her, and whispered. 'Hello you!'

'Hello you. Want some breakfast?'

'No, darling, I'll just stay here for a while if I may.'

'Of course, you stay there. I'll take Tess for a walk.'

Jo walked up to Marling Rock. 'Away Tess,' she commanded and watched the collie bound up the hill.

Jo's happiness was pragmatic. She had her Jen back in her life, and even if it was for one day, she would cherish the moment forever. Love in perpetuity has no hindsight, yet there was a retrospective lineage of all things possible.

She reached Marling Rock, with Tess nowhere to be seen. She whistled. No response! But then, just as the sun was rising over the valley, she saw her black and white bundle of fur bounding up the hill, with Jenny in her wake.

At the top Jenny puffed and gasped. 'I need more exercise I think!'

Jo laughed, 'Well stay, then!'

If only I could, Jen thought, and sat down beside Jo at the foot of the tree.

'Remember, Jen?'

'Oh yes I do, I remember.'

Tess came back from her escapades and sat down beside Jo, nestling her head in Jo's lap.

'She's lovely Jo, I'm so glad you have her.'

'Yes she is lovely. Every day I imagine Tom's spirit within her. We have a second sense like that, I think.'

Jenny gently squeezed Jo's hand and said, 'Oh Jo! I'm so sorry about Tom, you must miss him dreadfully.'

'Yes I do, I knew that he would have always been there for me, always would have patiently listened to my pronouncements about love and life.'

'You mean you and me, Jo, don't you?'

'Oh well, Jen, fortune favours the brave. And anyway I had

Brian, he has been an absolute rock over the years: Not quite the same as my beloved Tom, but a really good friend.' She sighed and continued, 'He stays at Pen Marig when he needs to be on his own, or to mull over the next photo session. Yes, he has been a very dear friend.'

Jenny squeezed Jo's hand again. 'Jo ...'

'Please don't tell me Jen that you have to leave!'

'Yes, I do, but not for a couple of days. I have to go back to France. There is something that I have to do, some loose ends I have to tie up, and then, and then I'll be back for good. Remember Jo, remember *Now Voyager*, "don't let's ask for the moon, we have the stars".'

Jo wanted to believe her, but there had been so many broken promises. *Oh well*, she thought, *let's not dwell on tomorrow*. She turned and smiled at Jen, and got up. 'Home, I think!'

They walked hand in hand down the hill, towards Pen Marig, quickly followed by Tess.

Yes, tomorrow was another day.

Chapter Four

Two days later, Jenny returned to France. George had been busy. The date for the exhibition at the Whitechapel had been confirmed. All that was needed was for the paintings to be chosen, crated and air freighted to London. They busied themselves, choosing what was to be shown.

Later that day she decided that she would have to ring Anne Richards.

She had no sleep that night. Words and phrases that she would like to say to Anne Richards raced through her mind. How could she keep Josey safe from scandal? How could she betray Jo? *Millennium* was out of reach, Jo would never give it up. Could she appeal to Anne's better nature? Did Anne Richards have a better nature? By break of day, she had decided again to offer money for her silence. But would that be enough?

She rang first thing. She couldn't wait any longer. 'Anne.'

'Yes.'

'This is Jennifer Standford.'

'Oh yes, so you're back then?'

'Yes, we have to talk.'

'Right! You know Lombardi's?'

'Yes.'

'Say ten o'clock there?'

'Yes.'

Lombardi's was a well known watering hole inhabited by various media personnel, and was Anne's territory. Jenny knew that she would be treading on quicksand, she would allow no histrionics to gather a crowd, but just state her case in a matter-of-fact way.

She arrived early, ordered a cappuccino, and sat down at one of the tables outside.

Anne arrived shortly after, and ordered a glass of brandy. 'Well, did you resolve anything whilst you were out of the country?'

'Yes I did,' replied Jenny, trying to sound bullish. 'Yes, I did, and you can't have *Millennium*. It's a limited company now, with multiple shareholders, and I don't think –'

'No, you don't think,' interrupted Anne. 'I'll just have Dawson's majority holdings, as I doubt whether she would relinquish her stake to the, what can we say, the subordinates.'

It was obvious to Jenny that Anne Richards had done her homework. She leant forward, and looking at Anne straight in the eye, said, 'Look, why can't we compromise? If it's money you want, I have enough. Tell me how much and it's yours, no questions asked.'

Anne Richards took another sip from her brandy glass, tipped back her head and laughed out loud. 'Compromise, compromise, I don't think so! You have more to lose than that Miss Standford. I wonder what your daughter would say, when her career is in ruins? Who would want a concert pianist with a deviant for a mother? No, Miss Standford, you either acquiesce to my demands or I will reap such a media storm, that there will be nothing left in its wake. Go back to your precious Jo Dawson, I'll see you in London.' And then with inhuman sarcasm, 'I assume you'll leave me a complementary ticket for your exhibition, and … don't be foolish, make sure it's not your last.'

Blind fury overwhelmed Jenny as she stood up from the table. 'Oh, do your worst, I don't care any more!'

'Oh I think you do,' Anne snarled. 'Go home, Miss Standford, there's no more to be said. I'll see you in London.'

Jenny left with Anne's words ringing in her ears. Yes she did care, she cared very much, but what could she do now? She was helpless, and in desperation whispered to herself, 'Oh why can't she just disappear under the rock from which she came?'

At home, she flung her coat and bag on a chair, sat down at the kitchen table and burst into tears. Flights of fancy bombarded her brain. *I'll tell Josey. No, I can't, what would she think? She would hate me. I would lose her! No, there was nothing that could be done.* Panic gripped her heart and once again she secretly desired Anne's disappearance.

George walked in on this furore.

'My God, Jennifer, what is the matter with you?'

Jenny sighed, lit a cigarette and proceeded to relate Anne's threats to George.

'Mm,' he said, when she had finished. 'A tricky one.' Then, as he saw the blood drain from Jenny's face, 'But not unsolvable.'

'I don't understand George ...'

'Now let me see. Richards insists on having Jo Dawson's holdings in *Millennium*. Jo is hardly going to agree to that, and as you haven't told her about all this, she is more unlikely to when you do tell her. So the first thing you must do, no matter how hard it will be, is to talk to Jo. Unfortunately as her main interest is in *Millennium* she may only see Josey as your problem. Then what about Josey? Well, she's in New York, so we don't have to worry about her at the moment.' He had to be clinical, any hint of subjectivity would clearly take Jenny over the edge.

'You'll have to go back to London. You'll have to tell Jo. The exhibition opens in four weeks' time. You'll have to go back before then. You can't wait until that Richards woman arrives. You have got to stop her in her tracks.'

'But how can I do that?' Jenny was becoming more desperate with every word spoken by George.

George raised his hand and scratched his head. 'You go and talk to Jo, I'll wait for Josey to return from New York, and try to mitigate the situation.'

George had hardly got the words out of his mouth when Jenny let out a yell. 'But how, George! You can't, you can't! She'll never understand!'

'She might, Jennifer. It's the early seventies, people are more aware, more tolerant, and we just have to gamble that she is among the enlightened populous.'

'But I should be the one to tell her. I –'

'No Jennifer, you'll get too emotional, and there's no guarantee that you won't bottle out and not tell her at all.'

'I don't know, George, I don't know. How can you be sure?'

'I can't, but is there any alternative?'

Jenny shook her head and resigned herself to George's reason. She wanted to put off the inevitable. 'No there isn't, George, but can we wait until I see Jo?'

'Yes, OK, but she will have to be told eventually.'

Jenny was pleading now. 'I know, I know. But ... but we can wait, can't we?'

They left it at that.

Over the next two weeks, George and Jenny finished choosing paintings to be crated and ready for airlifting to London. Jenny would fly ahead of the transported cargo, and arrive at Flaxman Square two weeks prior to the gallery opening.

The momentum of their industry left no time for Jenny to waiver from George's planned solution. She would go to London. She would tell Jo. Whether or not she would remain resolute once ensconced in Flaxman Square, she did not know.

Chapter Five

Jo returned to work in a flamboyant mood. Her fast was over, and very soon she would be able to live her life with Jenny, in exactly the way she had dreamt. Her team, as always, had kept her ship on an even keel, so much so that she knew she would be able to relinquish some of her time spent at the magazine. Time to consult with them. Would her excuse to spend more time at Pen Marig ring true? She would make it a plausible case for reducing her hours.

Lunch was sent to the boardroom, and the troops were assembled. After the normal repartee, Jo quietened them down.

'Well, people, you know I'm afraid that I will need to spend more time at Pen Marig. After visiting the contractors last week, I realize that the renovations I have in mind will take a lot of overseeing.' This she knew was a white lie, and she hoped that she would be forgiven for it. 'I know that you are all fully capable of running the magazine in my absence, but would you be happy with the increased responsibility?'

Little Jimmy shuffled in his seat. 'Would we be able to talk to you? Er, er, you won't be cutting off the phone will you?'

Jo laughed, 'Well if I do, we can always use a carrier pigeon.'

Sally nudged Jimmy's arm. 'Don't be daft Jimmy, Jo will be in Wales, not moving abroad, so don't you be worrying about all that.' And then, 'How long will the intervals be, Jo?'

'Not too long, a couple of weeks at a time, but I'll make sure I'm back the week prior to the quarterly run. In fact, I'll make such a nuisance of myself you'll all wish that I'd stayed away!'

There was a resounding 'No!' from all of them, and once again the room filled with laughter. They finished their lunch, and set to work discussing the articles for the next quarterly edition.

'Oh by the way Jo,' Brian spoke, looking straight at Jo. 'It seems that Jennifer Standford is exhibiting again at the Whitechapel. Do you want us to cover it?'

Jo drew a silent breath. 'Well Brian, what do you think?' And before he could answer, 'It would be good for us, I suppose.' And then, with a little hesitation and feigned ignorance, 'I'll leave it to you. You know when it is?' Brian nodded, and the matter was closed.

Jo then turned to Sally. 'I think, Sally, that we ought to rationalize your workload. Perhaps we will need to find someone to take over your PA duties. What do you think?'

'Well yes, Jo, but who would we get?'

'What about Julie? She's been excellent assistant PA. Good telephone manner, and quite efficient at dealing with awkward situations. What about her? You could train her up on most of your duties. She could PA for you on normal correspondence, whilst you remained responsible for my personal stuff. What do you think?'

Sally smiled, with some relief. 'Seems like a good idea. When do you want me to tell her?'

'Why not now? We could see how she shapes up, and make it a permanent thing if it pans out well.'

Jo sipped the last of her coffee, and then discussed additional secretarial help for both Brian and Little Jimmy. The meeting was closed and Jo went back to her office, feeling satisfied with the outcome.

Sally followed her in. 'We have a few items to deal with Jo. Can you fit me in before you start?'

'Of course, let's do that and then you can speak to Julie.'

Sally sat down and proceeded to work through the in-tray. 'Had a letter from Scotts (they were the outside accountants of the magazine) and they think that we should consider floating the company.'

'That's a no, Sally.' Jo was adamant. 'Start that process and we'll have all our competitors lining up for hostile takeovers.'

'Alright, I'll write and let them know.'

'Anything else?'

'Well yes, Jo. We had a request from Anne Richards.' Jo raised her eyebrows as Sally continued. 'Yes she asked whether she could do a profile on you and the magazine.'

Again Jo's eyebrows raised. 'That's a resounding no, Sally. That woman is poison, we certainly don't want anything to do with her.

Anyway, you found nothing substantial in the archives to clip her wings?'

'No,' Sally replied, and then added, 'I thought you might say that, so I've told her in no uncertain terms that we are not interested.'

'Anything else Sally?'

'No Jo, I can't think of anything else at the moment.'

Chapter Six

Jo was reading Little Jimmy's article on 'Space Exploration' when the telephone rang.

'Hello.'

'Hello, is that Jo?'

'Yes.' Jo's heart quietly raced as she recognized the voice at the end of the phone.

'It's Jennifer Standford.' and then a pause. 'Jo? Are you there? Can you speak?'

'Er, yes. Sorry, didn't recognize your voice.' What a lie. But that was all she could think of to say. 'How are you? '

'I'm well, and back in London.'

'But I thought that you weren't coming back for another week?'

'Well yes, I was, but wanted to get here early to make sure the paintings arrived safely and that all was OK for the opening.'

Jo could hardly speak the words. 'Are you here to stay?'

'Yes.'

Oh what magnitude of relief that single word inspired!

'Where are you?'

'I'm at Flaxman Square.'

Monosyllabic now. 'Flaxman Square? What? Back for good?'

'Yes Jo. But that's a long story. Can you come? I'd love to see you'

'Well I'm a bit tied up at the moment, but I'll try and leave early.'

'Yes.'

They left it there, and Jo set to her work with renewed vigour.

The house smelled stale from lack of use. Jenny opened all the windows to let in the very much needed air. A slight wind blew the curtains, and she wondered whether she would have time to change them. She sighed. No, she wouldn't, if she was to unpack and go shopping for groceries to fill the empty larder.

With unpacking completed, she bathed and changed, and left the house for the shops. *What would Jo like?* she asked herself as she surveyed the shelves of the corner shop. She didn't know, for time had taken away those little subtleties that bind a continued relationship.

She smiled as she looked at the tins of baked beans on the shelf, and felt the temptation to pop two in her basket. Pragmatism halted the urge, as she realized that time had consigned those heady, carefree moments to the history books.

Once home, she looked at the eggs, bread and ham she had placed on the kitchen table, and grimaced. *Well, I hope Jo likes omelettes.*

It didn't matter if Jo liked omelettes, she felt euphoric at Jenny's arrival. She left the office at three 'o' clock and drove to Flaxman Square. She parked outside the house, switched off the engine and sat. She was in no hurry! As she looked up at the bedroom window, she saw a young girl, leaning on the ledge laughing and calling to her, 'Wait there Jo, I'll come down and open the door!' She smiled and pondered the youthfulness of eighteen-year-olds. Finally she reached for the carrier bag on the passenger seat, alighted from the car and walked up to the door. She had hardly rung the bell, when the door opened.

'Hello Jo.'

'Hello you.'

They stood there looking at each other, as if it were for the first time, tentative and a little embarrassed.

'Come, Jo, we'll sit in the kitchen, it's cosier there.'

Jo obeyed, and followed Jenny inside. She reached for the carrier bag. 'Look, I've bought some champagne. We ought to celebrate your ... er, homecoming?'

'Oh how lovely Jo. I'll get some glasses.'

She did, and Jo opened the bottle. 'Shall we keep the cork?'

'Oh yes, let's.'

They drank and chatted, and allowed the champagne to loosen their reticence.

'Well Jen, back to stay?'

'Yes my darling, back to stay.'

Would Jo ask? Could she ask? Yes she could! 'Jen, you know how happy I am that you're here, but why a week early?'

'I told you, Jo. I needed to ensure that all was OK at the gallery.'

'Yes I know Jen, but I have a feeling that that's not all it is.'

Jen sipped her drink. She did not want to tell Jo about Anne Richards. She had hoped to stave off the moment for as long as she could. For the first time since leaving France, she had felt comfortable with herself. She knew it would be bad timing to introduce the subject of Anne Richards now. Not when, at this sacrosanct moment, she felt that she and Jo were quietly drifting back into the space where time was immaterial, and where love was the only constant in an inconstant world. She had to change the subject.

'Come Jo, let's eat!'

They set about in the kitchen. Jenny whipped the eggs, and Jo cut up the ham. As eggs spilt over the bowl, Jo giggled.

'Good Lord, you're hopeless Jen.'

'Yes I know I am, without you!'

'Don't be daft. Look at where you are. Renowned artist, selling all over the world. No my darling, you're not hopeless.'

With scrambled omelette put on to plates, they sat down at the table.

Jenny looked at the mess on the plates. 'Are you hungry?'

'Well I was,' laughed Jo.

'Do you remember? When it was just beans on toast?'

'Oh yes,' laughed Jo. 'Oh yes, I remember. You gave me the Wordsworth.'

'Ah yes,' and they both quoted the text together: '"and the lover is beloved."'

Jo reached across the table and stroked Jenny's hand. 'I was so afraid then.'

'Afraid of what Jo?'

'Afraid to read in it what I'd hoped it meant. That you loved me too.'

'Oh Jo, I did, I do, I always will. From the moment you gave me the necklace. See,' she said as she held it between thumb and forefinger. 'See, I told you that I would wear it forever.'

'That was our first kiss.'

'I know. How young we were then Jo. Brave and without thought for anyone else.'

'Yes, my darling, but we can't go back, we must go forward. Do you have the courage to do that?'

'I think so Jo. At least, when I'm with you I think so.'

Jo had to be happy with that.

They giggled and across the table found in each other's eyes a glimpse of long-lost youth. How bittersweet it felt. The rediscovery of that first fragile love. Tender, uncertain, a forbidden stolen apple not quite ripe for the eating. The innocence of the words 'I love you' lay soft upon lips that were frightened to kiss.

Jo stood up from the table and gently took Jenny's hand, and led her upstairs towards the bedroom. Jenny marvelled at the strength of Jo as she was lifted in her arms. She felt secure and cherished. Yes, she had come home, and knew that whatever happened this was where she should be.

Next morning, Jo awoke early, and lifting herself up on her left elbow, gazed lovingly at Jenny asleep next to her. Should she wake her? She had to go back to her flat to change ready for the office. Could she leave without saying goodbye? She lifted up her right arm and softly traced the outline of Jenny's face with her finger. It was a gentle touch so as not to awaken her, and yet it did.

'Hello Jo. What time is it?'

'Five o'clock.'

'Good grief Jo, it's the middle of the night!'

Jo laughed. 'Want some tea?'

'Yes please.'

As Jo left the room and went downstairs Jenny got out of bed and went to the bathroom. As she put on her dressing gown, she wondered when she could find the courage to tell Jo about Anne Richards. *Not now,* she thought. *No, not now.*

After their tea and buttered toast, Jo washed and dressed and got ready to leave for her flat.

'What will you do today Jen?' And then she laughed. 'Don't worry about shopping for dinner, I'll take you to Raymond's my favourite restaurant. Pick you up about seven?'

Jenny gave a slight grimace, and on seeing it Jo said, 'Oh don't worry my love, you'll find no prejudice there.'

Jenny smiled, and replied, 'Yes that would be lovely. I'll see you then.'

They kissed goodbye, and Jo drove home to get ready for work.

Brian found her quietly humming at her desk as she read through the post.

'Something I should know about?'

'Not really Bri, just happy.'

Brian knew that Jo's happiness coincided with the pending Standford exhibition. 'Will you go?'

'Sorry Bri. Go where?'

'To the Whitechapel. Don't you remember' – of course she did – 'we discussed covering the exhibition?'

'Oh that!' Jo feigned innocence.

'You've seen her, haven't you?'

Jo could lie no longer. 'Yes Bri, I have. It was like she's never been away. Am I being foolish?'

Brian hesitated. 'Are you sure, Jo. Can you go through all that heartache again?'

'Yes I'm sure Bri. When I'm with her, nothing else seems to matter. But what about you? Is there a special someone in your life?'

Brian sighed. 'No, no one special.'

He couldn't tell Jo the real truth. Although nothing had happened with Douglas he felt that his death was a punishment for his sexuality. He would have one-night stands to satisfy his desires, and then be repulsed by them, spending hours soaking in the bath, until the cold water chilled him. No, there was no one special.

Yet Jo had opened up the box, and he felt that perhaps he must explore further. 'Are you not ashamed of what you feel?'

'I don't know what you mean Brian,' Jo answered, using his full name. She felt this was not the time for informalities.

'Don't you ever feel that you've wasted your life?'

'No I don't Brian. You are what you are, and if that means you divert from the path of the norm, then so be it. But there again what is classed as the norm these days? Although it has taken a long time, society is beginning to believe that alternative lifestyles are not of the Devil's making. Be honest Brian, can you say you are happy avoiding your own sexuality?'

Brian blushed and picked at his fingers. Jo thought it was so reminiscent of the first time she saw him. 'Oh Brian what am I going to do with you?'

'Just be my friend Jo.'

'You know I am, and always will be. How could I not, when you have supported me all these years. I just wish ... I just ...'

'What, Jo?'

'I just wish that you could find that someone special, then you would know how happy it is to feel comfortable in your own skin.'

'Perhaps one day Jo.'

Jo felt she needed to lighten the situation. 'Well when you do, I'll need to vet him first.'

They both laughed and Brian was about to leave the office, when he stopped. 'Oh, I forgot what I came in for. Oh yes, Anne Richards phoned again. She still wants to profile you and the magazine.'

Irritated, Jo replied, 'Oh just ignore it Brian. I've said no once, let that be an end to it.'

Jo was perturbed by Brian's confidences. She had always thought of him as her brother, her kindred spirit, and wondered how she could help him. And then as Brian closed the door to the office, she had a germ of an idea. But this could wait until their next directors' meeting.

Jenny did go shopping, but not for groceries. She wanted to buy Jo something, but could not think what. These past two days had been her happiest for a long time, and she felt the need to commemorate them. After hours of searching she had found nothing, and took a taxi to the Whitechapel. The paintings had arrived and were safely housed in the secured basement. Carter the security guard doffed his cap as she walked in.

'Yes ma'am, can I help you?'

'Yes, I would like you to open a crate for me. Can we go down to the basement?'

'Are you sure ma'am? Should we not wait for the, er the professionals?'

Jenny laughed. 'Well if we damage it I'll take full responsibility.'

'And you are?'

'I'm Jennifer Standford, you know, the one who painted these pictures.'

Carter stepped back, blushing. 'Sorry ma'am.'

Again Jenny laughed, and they proceeded to the basement. She pointed to a crate which he duly opened.

'Yes that's the one.'

'Ah very nice. What is it? A picture of a farmhouse, with a tree!'

A very patient Jenny, pained by the man's lack of appreciation for the arts, laughed and said, 'Well I suppose it does look like that.'

After taking the painting from its crate, they returned to the gallery, and the security guard went off to the office to find some brown paper, returning shortly after with it in his hands.

'Will this do?'

'Yes, that will do very well.'

They wrapped the painting with care, and Jenny went to the office to call a taxi.

At home, she unwrapped the painting and leant it against the sofa. She poured a drink and sat down to survey the scene. *Yes,* she thought, *Jo will like this.* Yes, it was a farmhouse, and it was a tree, but it was hers and Jo's farmhouse and tree.

It was one of the paintings she had consigned to her attic. Every now and then she would go there to sit in front of it and remember her times at Pen Marig. She had been loathe to sell it, and therefore squirrelled it away beyond prying eyes. *Yes,* she thought, *this will make a lovely present for Jo.*

Chapter Seven

Jo telephoned the restaurant from her office, and booked a seven-thirty table. She arrived home at five 'o' clock, washed and dressed and drove to Flaxman Square. She felt the giddiness of that long ago eighteen-year-old, and wondered whether the feeling would ever stabilize. She hoped not!

Jenny had taken care to dress. She wanted to look nice for Jo. She looked in the bathroom mirror and subjectively looked at the image before her. Had she aged? Yes she had, but did age weary her? No it didn't. She was young again. A youthful bloom enhanced her sparkling eyes. She sighed and felt pleased with the vision. Would Jo like it? She hoped so.

Jo, did like it, and held her close, trying not to crush the newly ironed beige suit. 'God Jen, you look beautiful!'

Jenny blushed. 'What time do we have to leave for the restaurant?'

'Oh about six forty-five. Why?'

'Because I have something to give you,' Jenny replied as she reached behind the sofa and brought out the brown paper package. 'I've kept this for you, hoping that one day I would be able to present it personally.'

Jo gasped with surprise as the brown paper fell away. 'Oh my God, Jenny, this is, is …'

'Yes, your Pen Marig. Don't you remember Jo, all those years ago when you went to Aberystwyth with your aunty, and left me at Marling Rock.' Jo nodded, still speechless. 'Well this was the result. I've kept it hidden in the attic at my studio all these years. This was never to be sold.'

Jo tenderly outlined the farmhouse, the bottom gate and Marling Rock with her finger, and then with another gasp, 'And those two figures leaning on the bottom gate … ?'

'Yes Jo, that's you and I. After completing the painting, I felt that it wasn't quite finished, and then I knew that this was our special place, so I had to add the figures.'

'Oh Jen, I love it. But isn't this very valuable?'

'Only to you and me Jo. As I said, this painting was never to be sold, so please accept it with all the love I felt when I painted it.'

Jo nodded, there was nothing more that needed to be said.

They reached the restaurant at seven 'o' clock and once sat at the table the wine list was presented.

'Hello Jo.'

Jo looked up. 'Hello Raymond, how are you today?' And then nodding towards Jenny, 'Raymond, I would like you to meet my friend Jennifer Standford.'

Raymond reached out and took Jenny's hand. 'I'm so pleased to meet you. You are the famous artist that Jo has told me so much about.'

Jenny blushed, and Jo interceded. 'And you Raymond? How is Steve?'

'Poof,' he grunted. 'Gone off with a younger model.'

'Oh dear, I'm so sorry.'

'Don't be.' And with a flippant shrug of the shoulders he continued, 'Good riddance is all I can say.'

As if a light had been switched on in Jo's brain, her previous germ of an idea began to gather momentum. 'Never mind Raymond. What if we wrote an article on the restaurant? That should buck you up a bit. What do you think?'

'Well I suppose so Jo. Sorry. No, that would be very nice.'

'OK, I'll send Brian and Joan around. I'm sure between you all we could create something special for the magazine.'

'Lovely, would you like to order now?'

'Yes that will be fine.'

Raymond flounced off to fetch the menu.

'Oh by the way,' Jo said, as she sipped her drink, 'Do you remember Anne Richards? You know, that old crone that could make even Hedda Gabler look like a saint? Well she keeps phoning. Wants to do a profile on me and the magazine. I've said no, of course. What a cheek she's got!'

With blood draining from her face, Jenny half-choked on her drink, and said nothing.

'Are you alright darling?'

'Yes, just swallowed the wine too quickly.'

Just then the maître d' arrived to show them to their seats.

Thank God, Jenny thought, knowing that she could stave off the time before she told Jo about Anne Richards. After Jo's conversation, she knew that circumstances had overtaken her, and she would have to talk to Jo that evening.

Jo held Jenny's hand in the taxi on the way home. 'Have you enjoyed the evening?'

'Oh yes Jo, the meal was lovely, and I do like Raymond.'

'Yes he is fun. One of these days I'll tell you all about him.'

Jenny squeezed Jo's hand. How she wished that it was only the meal that was lovely. How she wished ... but wishes are obscure things, left to the hapless. Somehow she had to tell Jo about Anne Richards.

Jenny busied herself making coffee, staving off the moment of crisis as long as she could. She placed the tray on the kitchen table, poured the coffee into the cups, and took a deep breath and then ... 'Jo you do know that I will always love you, don't you?'

'Yes of course I do. But what is the matter Jen?'

'I have something to tell you.' And then she did, and once the words were out, they flowed tumultuously from deep inside her, until she became saturated with perspiration. Once finished Jenny grew near to tears. 'Jo, Jo, say something, please!'

Jo couldn't speak. She didn't know whether to be angry with or sorry for Jenny.

Again came those pitiful words. 'Jo, please say something.'

'Well, I don't quite know what to say. Don't suppose there's any point of recriminations, the damage seems to have been done. But there again Jen, is it terminal?'

'What do you mean Jo?' She had expected a different reaction. Expected fury and condemnation. But there again, did she really know Jo?

Jo lit two cigarettes passed one to Jenny, leant back in her chair and inhaled deeply. 'Well Jen, Richards is an inane human being, if she thinks that people would react negatively to such matters. After all, it is the seventies. Will people really be bothered? We know from experience that today's gossip is tomorrow's chip paper. As for giving up the magazine, there is no way I will let that go. Anyway, I can probably pre-empt her disclosure by running a conciliatory article for this quarter's issue. I was toying with the idea anyway, not for quite the same reasons, but that should take the wind out of her sails. Also, I have a strong team behind me and, well, it's stupid to think that they haven't been aware of my … shall we say, difference.'

'Now that's me sorted. How about you? Do you not think that the notoriety might increase the value of your work?'

'Well … well I, I suppose so.'

'So who else has she left to ruin?'

'Josey.'

'Ah yes. Josey. You'll have to talk to her.'

'I can't Jo. I've protected her from this … this secret all her life. How can I tell her now? I know that I would lose her, and I just couldn't bear that.' Jenny started to cry.

Jo took her hand. 'Don't cry darling. You know it's the only way. We can't let that venomous bitch win. Anyway it may not be as difficult as you think. After all, how would you have explained your coming back to live with me in England?'

'I was going to …'

'Lie!'

'Well it wouldn't be a real lie, Jo. Just …'

'Just what Jen? Does she even know who I am?'

'Well yes. Er …vaguely. We were at my studio one weekend, she was quite young then, and she saw your painting, and those of Tom and Doll, when we were sorting items for showing. I said that you were someone I had known at college, and that we spent one Easter holiday at your home in Wales.'

'Um, I see, you really were economical with the truth. But as we all know Jen, truth will out, and sooner or later …'

'Yes I know, I know. I will tell her, I will!'

They left it at that, and Jo left later for her flat.

'You won't stay, Jo?'

'No darling not tonight, I have an early meeting tomorrow, so best get home and prepare.'

They kissed goodnight, and Jo left for home.

As Jenny closed the door behind Jo, she wondered whether there really was a meeting, or whether Jo had used that as an excuse not to stay the night. *Oh well, I expect she'll ring tomorrow.* She sighed and got herself ready for bed.

Chapter Eight

'Then my soul turned inward,- to examine of what stuff
Time's fetters are composed; and life was put,
To inquisition, long and profitless!'
(Wordsworth, 'Bereavement')

Jo, true to her word, did arrive earlier than usual at the office. As sleep the night before had eluded her, she had spent the waking hours assembling and then dismissing plans to thwart Anne Richards. Having decided upon one, she couldn't wait for Sally to arrive. She replenished the coffee pot and put it on to percolate.

'Morning Jo, you're early.'

'Yes, I've made coffee. Can you pop in once you've caught your breath?'

'Yes, about ten minutes, that OK?'

'Yup, fine.'

Knowing Sally's ten minutes would mean five, she poured out the coffee into the mugs, and sat down.

'Well Jo, what can I do for you?'

'Do you still have that friend at Scout International?'

'Yes I do. Funnily enough I had lunch with her last month.'

'Good.'

'Why do you ask?'

'Well,' Jo had to prevaricate, 'Anne Richards –'

'Oh her!'

'Yes, her. Well she's been making loud noises about the magazine.'

'In what way?'

'Not too sure, but the grapevine intimates some sort of scandal. So we have to nip this in the bud.'

'But how, Jo?'

'Well, and this must be just between you and me, Sally. I need as much information on her as you can get.'

'Ah,' Sally smiled. 'I see, that's where my friend comes in.'

'Yes, Sal. I want you to persuade her to turn over every rock she can find, and see what crawls out. Wine and dine her, do whatever it takes, but please come back with something we can get our teeth into.'

Sally grimaced. 'Sounds a bit serious!' And then perceptively, 'I don't suppose this has anything to do with that artist friend of yours?'

Jo smiled with irony and wondered how Sally had made the connection. 'In a way, yes Sally. That is why I need this to be kept between ourselves.'

Sally knew better than to ask further, and replied, 'Of course Jo, my lips are sealed.'

Jo felt a little satisfied, and hoped that Sally's friend might supply the bullets with which Jo could fire the gun. She poured out some more coffee and rang for Brian.

'Yes Jo?' he asked as he entered the office.

'Coffee?'

'No thanks.'

'Sit down Bri. I have an idea to run past you.'

With her thoughts for Brian's happiness, she told him about Raymond's and the article she would like written.

'What do you think, Bri? A good idea? You could take Joan and conjure up something nice for the mag. And,' she added, 'there might be a free meal or two in it!'

They both laughed.

'Right Jo, I'll speak to Joan. Do you have Raymond's number?'

'Yes,' she replied as she handed Brian one of Raymond's menus.

'Um,' he grunted, casting his eye over it, 'a bit pricey.'

'One of the best restaurants in town, Bri.' And then, as a, calculated, afterthought, 'I'm sure you and Raymond will get on very well!'

Brian left, and she wondered what to do now about the rest of it. She knew she couldn't confront Anne Richards without the necessary ammunition, so she had to be patient for a little while longer. After all, she mused, two can play at that game.'

She rang Jenny that afternoon. 'Hello my love, are you OK?'

'Yes, much better now you've rung.'

'I'll be over about eight. I'll bring some Indian. Er, you do like Indian?'

'Oh yes I do,' Jenny answered.

Jo continued, 'I'll bring some wine.' And then, having a little fun at Jenny's expense, added, 'I know how good you are at shopping!'

Jenny laughed. 'Can't wait.'

With that settled, Jo rang Julie. 'Julie, Sal's gone out for a bit. Can you arrange a breakfast meeting for the team, say this Thursday?'

'Yes of course Jo. I'll let everyone know. What, say about ten-ish?'

'Yup, that will be fine.'

Chapter Nine

Raymond was not surprised to hear from Brian. He knew that Jo was a woman of her word. Ever since that first day she walked into his restaurant that late spring evening, fifteen years ago, they had become firm friends.

Jo had wanted to find somewhere nice to eat, instead of going back to her flat, with yet another takeaway. She had been told about the restaurant from the girls at work, and decided to try it.

After she had apologized for not making a reservation, Raymond had asked, 'Table for one, madam?'

'Yes, thank you.'

Both wine and menus where given, and as Raymond watched from the service station he wondered why someone so attractive should be dining alone. Although he didn't feel sorry for her, he felt a certain empathy. *People of his own sexual proclivities,* he thought, *seemed to attract each other with a certain intuition.* Should he make friends with her? He decided he should.

He approached the table. 'Are you ready to order?'

Jo looked up into his grey twinkling eyes. 'Well yes. I'll have the Chardonnay, and the fish with vegetables.'

'Good choice,' he answered. 'Haven't seen you here before.'

'No,' replied Jo. 'I heard so many good things about your restaurant that I decided to check it out.'

Raymond was taken aback, 'Check it out? What, are you a reporter?'

'Oh goodness no, just an editor of a magazine.' She felt his consternation and hurriedly added, 'Oh, please don't think I'm snooping.'

Raymond heaved a sigh of relief. 'I'm Raymond, the owner. And you are?'

'I'm Jo, just Jo.'

'Well I'm very pleased to meet you, and I hope you will find everything to your satisfaction.'

And she did, in fact she became a regular customer.

Secretly they spoke of all things forbidden: Raymond about his partner Steven, and she about Jenny. As the years went by, their friendship grew into a strong bond.

Jo had loved the fact that she could talk about Jenny without raised eyebrows and recriminations, whilst Raymond was glad to have someone to whom he could moan about his beloved Steven. 'One day he'll leave me,' he said to Jo. 'I'm getting too long in the tooth for partying. He loves the underground clubs, and I ... well I am just that old clichéd pipe and slippers man.'

'Surely not,' Jo replied, not wanting to tell him that love can be "labours lost", especially when she had been so long apart from Jenny.

'I suppose,' he had said on one occasion, 'I suppose that one never finds the ultimate in happiness.'

She, although agreeing, had to console him. 'Don't be silly, Raymond. Steven and you are a team. Let's face it, where would the restaurant be without the both of you?'

Raymond poo-pooed the idea. 'Oh well Jo, I hope you're right!'

So, as the years went by, Raymond tried unsuccessfully to fix up double dates for Jo, but she would always decline, and after a while Raymond stopped trying.

'That woman has a lot to answer for,' he angrily remarked. 'Are you really going to spend the rest of your life stuck in the past, with a love that's continuously absent?'

Jo told him that he had said enough on the subject and the matter was permanently dropped.

One could imagine his surprise then, when the day came when Jo introduced him to Jenny. Finally he understood why Jo had disengaged herself from his attempts to fix her up with someone else. He had never seen Jo so radiant, so self-assured. He sighed. If only Steven had felt about him that way.

The meeting with Brian and Joan was arranged for the following Tuesday – the restaurant was usually quiet then – and Raymond busied himself, cogitating on what he should say.

Chapter Ten

Sally arrived at Scout International at about half past twelve. At reception she asked to speak to Angela.

'Hi,' she said, as Angela walked through the entrance hall.

'Hello, this is a nice surprise.'

'Free for lunch? On me of course!'

'Yes, that'll be nice.'

Arm in arm they walked down the High Street towards the Hungry Mouse, a favourite bistro used by many Fleet Street personnel.

They ordered their food, plus a glass each of the house wine.

'Well Sally, as I said before, this is a nice surprise.' She then laughed, 'Can I assume that I will have to pay in kind for this free meal?'

Sally, also laughing, replied, 'Well, how well you know me Angie!'

'Been friends since forever, haven't we? Of course I know you.'

'I'm after some information.'

'Oh yes, on whom?'

'Anne Richards!'

'I see. So she's causing trouble again,' Angela scowled.

'Again? What do you mean?'

'That bitch should have a warning sign pinned on her. She's dangerous, Sally. Are you sure you want to do this?'

'Yes. I need everything you have on her, even what she eats for breakfast.'

'That'll be me if she finds out!'

'Oh sorry, I shouldn't have asked. Forget it, Angie, I'll look for other avenues.'

'How long have we been friends? Don't be silly, I would love to consign that witch back to the gutter where she belongs. You're not the only one with an axe to grind. She's damaged quite a lot of people over the past years. I'll get on it straight away, and ring you when I have something.'

Sally patted Angela's hand. 'I'm so grateful Angie, I don't know how to thank you.'

Angela laughed. 'A few more free lunches would be nice.'

'You've got it!'

They both laughed and carried on with their meal.

Angela did have more than an axe to grind. She had never told Sally that years ago, before she had started at Scout International, she started her apprenticeship on a local paper, of which Anne Richards was the editor. On the pretext of befriending Angela, Anne used her, and gradually stole every article that Angela brought to the paper and bylined it as her own. When Angela remonstrated, and said she would go to the owner of the paper, Anne played her ace card by threatening to disclose Angela's illicit affair with a married man. Knowing what damage this would cause to every one concerned, Angela had no other option but to leave the paper.

If necessity is the mother of invention, then determination, and hate for Anne Richards, were the catalyst upon which Angela built her career. She moved to London, and started out as a runner for Scout International, and very soon moved up to become the present-day director of research, all the time gathering more tit-bits of information on Anne Richards. *One day, yes one day,* she thought, *the day will come...*

And that it had come in the shape of her friend Sally, whom she had befriended some years ago at the Hungry Mouse, was all the more pleasurable.

All the team gathered in the boardroom awaiting Jo to arrive.

'Any idea what's this about?' asked Little Jimmy.

'No,' they all said.

'Must be something important,' Sally mused. 'It's unlike Jo to call a meeting so near to the end of the quarter.'

Just then, as Brian was about to add something, Jo arrived.

'Well troops, I expect you're probably wondering why I called this meeting. Well I've been very disturbed lately about the things I've been reading in the newspapers. It seems that we have become a nation of bigots. *Millennium* has always prided itself on truth and honesty and I think it's about time we stood up for the minority.'

Seeing raised eyebrows, she continued, 'No I don't want us to take the moral high ground, I just want us to be – as we always have been – fair and non-judgemental.'

'What do you mean, Jo?' asked Little Jimmy.

'There is too much prejudice. It needs to be stamped out. And yes,' Jo added, in response to Sally's raised hand, 'I know, we are not the arbiters of morality, but I think our readers need to be given the freedom of choice.'

She turned then to Jimmy. 'Your article on space exploration was brilliant, so I want you to run this – for a better word – campaign. Once we have decided that we are all in agreement with it, then we'll run it as a headline in the next quarter's issue. Any questions?'

'Are we talking about individual discrimination, or discrimination as a whole?' Brian asked.

'As a whole, Brian. Let's say the inequality of women in business, the prejudices of race, creed, colour, people's sexuality and so on.'

'Oh I see, a pretty tall order.' And then turning to Little Jimmy, 'Are you able to cope with all that?'

Yes Jimmy was. He knew all about discrimination. He had found it at school, in his street and in the employment workplace. Born of a Nigerian father and an English mother, he had lived with prejudice all his life.

'Never mind,' his mother would say, when he again returned from school with a torn jacket and a bruised face. 'Don't give into it Jimmy, remember what your father and I have always said, bullies are just ignorant and so know no better.'

Well, he had thought, *you don't have to suffer the humiliation, and dread every day when I go off to school!*

Finally at the age of fifteen Jimmy left school with an RSA in English. His studies had suffered from his bouts of depression and disinterest. He was unsuccessful at every job he went after, until finally he decided not to bother.

It was his father who showed him the advert for a runner at the *Millennium* magazine.

'What about this Jim? Don't say anything about qualifications!'

Well, Jimmy thought, *should be OK, I'm good at running!* 'I'll write off Dad, but don't be surprised if I get no answer.'

He did write off and he did get an answer.

'Well,' Jo had asked as he sat in the chair in front of her desk. 'What makes you think you would be good for this job?'

Jimmy thought a while. 'Well, er ... well, I'm good at running!'

Jo laughed, warming towards this little light brown boy, with his tight-knit curly hair. 'That'll do then.'

'Sorry?' An astonished Jimmy added, 'Do you mean that I've got the job?'

Jo laughed again. 'Well yes, if you want it.'

'But ... but ...'

'But what?'

'I've no qualifications. Surely –'

'Yes you have, you've just said you're a good runner.' Then feeling his consternation, she added, 'Look Jimmy, it's not a prestigious job, but if you are willing you can work from the bottom up. That's of course if you want to?'

'Oh yes, ma'am I do. And' – as he leapt up, knocking over his chair – 'I won't let you down.'

'That's alright then. See you on Monday, and don't be late.'

'Oh, I won't.' And he never was.

Hardly a week had gone by before Sally received the telephone call from Angela. Armed with a folder, Angela met Sally at the Hungry Mouse.

'Well, that was quick,' Sally responded, taking the folder from Angela.

'Didn't take too long Sal. Been collecting these for years. So I hope you can put them to good use.'

Sally's brow furrowed. 'Is there something you're not telling me? I mean, I expected to wait at least a month, before you came up with something.'

'Sal, it's a long story, perhaps I'll tell you someday.'

Sally placed the folder into her briefcase, kissed Angela goodbye and said, 'Well Angie, you know I'll be here whenever you need me.'

'Yes I know.'

Sally arrived at the *Millennium* offices and found Jo in the print room. Bob, the mechanic and handyman, was simultaneously shaking his head, and running his hand over his brow. He carefully stroked the Heidelberg, as if this was not an inanimate object.

'Got a problem Jo!'

'Oh dear! Can it be fixed?'

'Yeh, but it'll need a new part.'

'OK Bob, how long?'

'I'll phone Humphries. Shouldn't be too long.' But Bob was not an optimist. 'That's if they've got it!'

As Jo saw Sally standing in the doorway, she put her arm around Bob's shoulders. 'I'm sure they will. Can I leave you to sort it?'

'Yep,' was the succinct reply.

Bob had been with the magazine since time immemorial. There was nothing he couldn't fix, but like the old artisan he was, complaining always preceded his ingenuity.

Jo gave Bob another pat on his shoulders, turned on her heel and walked back to her office with Sally.

'Well my dear, did your friend come up with anything?'

'Yes,' she replied, placing the folder on Jo's desk.

'Right, let's have a look, shall we?'

Most of the information consisted of news of Anne Richards rise to the echelons of high society. There were a plethora of articles detailing the unfortunates who had had the misfortune to cross her path, but nothing that Jo could get her teeth into.

Finally, feeling a little disappointed, Sally picked up a news cutting, and with a quizzical look passed it to Jo. 'I wonder why Angie put this in here.'

Jo looked at the headline, and had to agree with Sally. 'Yes, I wonder.'

As she looked further at the cutting, she saw that it was an old 1952 headline in the *Bradford Tribune*. 'Baby found in railway station. Mother unknown.' Jo read the rest of the article to Sally:

A two-week-old baby boy was found by a commuter on the Bradford railway station platform. Police were called and the baby was taken to Bradford Infirmary. All efforts to trace the mother have proved fruitless.

The police have strongly requested that the mother get in contact, as she may need medical attention.

'Well!' they both exclaimed in unison.

'Well yes, can you think of any reason why your friend should include this particular article?'

'No Jo, but knowing Angie, she would have had a good reason.'

'1952, eh? Well the boy would be what, twenty-four now.'

'Yes,' added Sally, 'he would be.'

'I think, Sal ...'

'Yes Jo, I know what you are going to say. We need to find out more about this boy.'

'Can you approach Angie again?'

'No, I don't think so. It may open old wounds. I think a trip to Bradford would be profitable.'

'I agree Sal. Would you like to come with me?'

'Yes, I would, there is obviously something here that might help Angie.' And then she tentatively added, 'And you!'

Jo prudently ignored Sally's remark and requested her to organize train fares for the following day. She would need to talk to Jenny, so arranged to leave the office early. She would go home and pack an overnight bag, bathe and change, pick up the promised takeaway, and drive to Flaxman Square.

Jo was in an ebullient mood. She phoned her order through to the Karmar takeaway, to pick up on the way to Jenny's, and regretted how little she knew of Jenny's tastes. Wanting the evening to be special, she had dressed carefully. A light blue shirt, denim trousers and jacket. 'There,' she said looking in the mirror, 'not too bad for your age!'

Jenny had spent her day at the gallery, choosing places where her paintings were to be hung. The paintings of Tom and Doll, and of course Jo, were kept aside, ready for her to take back home.

She had felt so much like a girl again, since returning to Flaxman Square and her beloved Jo. She knew that with Jo's strength of purpose, she would be safe and unafraid, even when it came to confronting Josey.

'After all,' she mused, 'why shouldn't I have a life of my own choosing?'

She bathed and changed into a blue kaftan. She looked in the mirror, and was pleased how well it complemented the blue pendant necklace. She sighed as she put the pendant to her lips. 'Oh Jo I do love you so!' And as she walked into the kitchen, she thought of that old adage, *Today is the first day of the rest of your life.* Yes she thoughtfully reiterated the saying as she filled the coffee percolator.

Jenny, impatient for Jo to arrive, looked out of the bedroom window, leaning as forward as she could to ensure she would see Jo's car. She was a young girl again, impulsive and deliriously happy. When it appeared, she leant precariously on the window ledge, and cried out, 'Hello you!'

Jo looked up, opened the passenger window and shouted, 'Hello yourself, are you going to let me in?'

They both laughed, that giddy youthful laugh full of wonderment and expectation.

Jo put the carrier bags onto the kitchen table. 'Not too sure what you like, so I've got Chicken Korma, Madras and all the trimmings.'

'Ooh lovely,' laughed Jenny.

Was Flaxman Square her second home? *Yes,* Jo thought. Flaxman Square and Pen Marig – in both places she could be herself, uninhibited by social constraints, comfortably aware of her own self.

They ate their Indian, drank their wine and reminisced. 'Do you remember?' Yes they did, and on and on it went throughout the evening.

What bliss true love is when it is unfettered and free to fly without clipped wings.

In bed, Jenny snuggled up against Jo's chest. 'I can do it, you know.'

'Do what?'

'Tell Josey.'

'Are you sure?'

'Yes, quite sure.'

They kissed and Jo stroked Jenny's hair. 'Well my darling, you may not have to.'

'Oh?'

'I have some information that might stop Richards in her tracks.'

'Oh,' Jenny reiterated.

'Yes, but it will mean that I shall have to be away for a couple of days.'

Jenny leaned on her elbow and looked straight at Jo. 'You won't get into any trouble will you?'

'Gosh no. Can't tell you what it is yet, don't really know myself, but ...'

'But what?'

'Well we shall have to wait and see.' Jo kissed Jenny and the moment of fear passed.

Next morning, Jo rose early, made toast and tea and took it up to Jenny. 'Darling, I have to make a phone call. Won't be long, save me some toast.'

Sally woke with a start, as the telephone rang. She looked at the clock. 'Hello?'

'Hi Sal it's me, Jo.'

'Goodness Jo, its only seven o'clock!'

'I know. Did you make the train reservations? And what time do we have to be at the station?'

'Yes I did and the time is eleven forty-five.'

'Good, then I wouldn't bother going into the office this morning. I'll meet you on the platform at say eleven. Is that OK for you?'

'Yes Jo.'

'Right. I've been thinking ...'

'Oh yes?'

'Would it be possible for you to speak to Angela, and find out why she left that article in the Richards folder? Don't want to have a wasted journey if it was an error.'

'OK Jo, I'll ring her this morning, although she may not wish to elaborate. She may have left it in for us to find and investigate further. Anyway I will phone her. Where can I reach you, if I need to. Are you at home?'

Jo hesitated. 'Er no, I'm at a friend's.' She gave Sal the number, and they arranged to meet at the station.

'The toast is cold, Jo. Do you want me to make some more?'

'No, I'll have some later.'

She sat on the bed and took Jenny's hand. 'Sally and I are going to Bradford today, so I'll have to leave about ten-fifteen.'

'Bradford? That's a long way.'

'Yes, but we have a story to follow up.'

'This doesn't involve Richards, does it?'

'Might do, but I'll tell you all about it when I get back.'

'Oh Jo, you will be careful, won't you?'

'Yes of course I will. I'll ring and let you know where we are staying.

'With Sally?'

Jo answered Jenny's quizzical look. 'Don't be daft, Jen, she's my PA and a trusted friend.' She leant over and kissed Jenny on the forehead. 'Only one gal for me!'

Jo got a taxi to the station and met Sally on the platform.

'Did you manage to speak to Angela?'

'Yes I did. She was very reluctant to say much … I think she is still in fear of the "devil on her shoulder".'

'That's a shame Sal, but perhaps if we are successful, we can chase the devil away from her, and put an end to that Richards woman's poison.'

'Oh, I hope so Jo, Angela is such a nice person.'

Jo tried not to be impatient. 'Well, Sal what did she say?'

'It's very vague, but she did intimate that we might find Richards' Achilles heel in Bradford. We should start at the infirmary where the child was taken – that's of course if they still have the records.'

'OK Sal, we'll start there. Does she think the child is Richard's?'

'I don't know, but it does seem to point in that direction.'

As they lay back in their seats, Sally hesitated, then leaned forward. 'I don't like to pry Jo …'

Jo smiled. 'But you are going to.' And then as an afterthought, 'Sal we've been friends for a long time, and –'

'I know Jo, and I wouldn't want to destroy that friendship by … shall we say idle curiosity.'

'It's simple Sal, Anne Richards is threatening to ruin the life of a very dear friend of mine, and –'

Sally interrupted. 'That would be Jennifer Standford?'

'Well, yes it would. We've known each other since college and I owe it to her and our friendship to do all that I can to help.'

Sally grew serious. 'Are you not more than friends, Jo?'

Jo smiled ruefully. 'How long have you known?'

'Oh since the media awards.'

'But you didn't say anything Sal.'

'No, it wasn't my place to say, or my tale to tell. And yes, I still consider you both my boss and my friend. You'll never have to worry about loose tongues as far as I'm concerned.'

Not knowing what to say, Jo could only present a wry smile.

Chapter Eleven

They arrived in Bradford at about three o'clock and took a taxi to their hotel.

'Nothing we can do today Sal, so we might as well make the most of the hotel's hospitality. Let me know when you are settled in your room, and then we'll have tea in the lounge.'

During tea, they formulated a plan for the next day, and then Sally went off to explore the town.

Jo went back to her room and rang Jenny. 'Hello darling.'

'Hello Jo. Is the hotel nice?'

'Yes, quite nice. A bit quaint, but quite nice. What have you been doing?'

'Well I rang George, he'll be over in two weeks' time. The invitations have also arrived so I'm busy writing them up.'

Jo laughed. 'I hope you've kept one for me. Oh and by the way, heard anything from that Richards woman?'

'No, but I expect I will before we open. She's expecting an invitation.'

'Well don't do anything until I get back. Depending upon what we uncover, it may well be that the invitation might not be needed. Anyway dear, I'll ring off now, but will phone again this evening.'

'Lovely. And where's Sally?

'Out shopping.'

'Oh, right.'

Jo laughed. 'Oh you are a silly goose. Love you loads."

'Love you loads too.'

From the mini bar Jo poured out a glass of wine, and settled back to review the folder that Angela had given Sally. She leafed through it, finding nothing new that would take her attention, until she saw an article from the *Leeds Tribune*. As this was also dated 1952, she thought another look might be informative. As she read, the headline seemed to shout out at her: 'Renowned

Judge Graham Carmichael found dead in his hotel room'. She continued to read:

Judge Graham Carmichael was found dead yesterday, by a housemaid as she went to clean the room. First investigations have found nothing suspicious, and it is rumoured that Judge Carmichael took his own life.

A spokesman for the Leeds Judiciary said that they have been very saddened by the news.

Judge Carmichael was a devoted husband and father. His family were not able to comment at this time.

Hmm, Jo thought, *if we draw a blank at the infirmary, perhaps we could explore this further.*

Sally arrived back at six o'clock having overdone her retail therapy. She dumped her bags in her room and then knocked on Jo's door.

'Come in.' She smiled at Sally. 'Good shopping?'

'Well yes,' and blushing slightly, 'overdone it a bit. When do you want dinner? Have I got time to change?'

'Yes, of course, but before you go back to your room, I want you to look at this article and tell me what you think.'

With that Jo showed her the item about Judge Carmichael.

Sally scratched her head. 'Mm, seems odd, perhaps we should pursue it further.'

'That's exactly what I thought,' Jo affirmed. 'What say we kill two birds with one stone. I'll go to the infirmary, and you pop to the *Leeds Tribune* and look through their archives. Say you're researching articles involving quality local papers. That should get you in.'

'OK Jo, I'll do that. What time are we eating?'

'Will eight be alright for you?'

'Yes that's fine.'

They left it at that, and Sally went back to her room to change.

They were both up early the next day. Sally had enquired from the hotel reception as to the whereabouts of the *Leeds Tribune*, and caught a taxi. Jo went off to the Bradford Infirmary.

Expecting to find an old, outdated 1800s building she was pleasantly surprised to see it had been replaced with a modern facade. She hoped it was the same inside, as these buildings always brought a shiver down her spine. But, yes, it had been expertly modernized, with no hint of the workhouse, as most pre-1900 buildings had. She introduced herself at reception, and asked if she could speak to the hospital manager.

This came in the guise of Miss Bright, a woman in her late fifties. *Oh good,* Jo thought. *She must have a lot of knowledge about the hospital.*

Miss Bright walked towards her with arm outstretched. 'Hello Miss Dawson, what can I do for you?'

Jo proceeded to tell her that her magazine wanted to research prestigious hospitals for an article she wanted to write on the changing face of the National Health Service. 'After all,' she emphasized, 'we've heard so many good things about your hospital that we thought this might be a good place to start.'

Miss Bright preened, and Jo knew she had accomplished her objective.

As they walked around the hospital wards, Jo ostentatiously wrote in her notebook, remembering – to ensure authenticity – to ask pertinent questions.

'I expect you have some stories to tell, Miss Bright.'

'Oh yes, I've seen a lot of changes over the past forty years.'

'You were here then, at a very young age?'

'Came here when I was sixteen. Started out as an auxiliary nurse on the maternity ward. Learnt from the bottom up so to speak.'

'Well,' Jo added more flattery, 'you must have really worked hard to end up as hospital manager.'

Once again Miss Bright preened. Now was Jo's chance.

'Oh I bet you've some stories to tell about the babies you looked after.'

'Oh yes. We've had twins, triplets and all sorts – lovely little things.'

Jo winked at her. 'Go on, you must have some memorable ones?'

'Well there was one, handed in by the police. Found in a railway station, poor little mite.'

'When was that, then?'

'Oh about 1952.'

'Did you ever know what became of it?'

Miss Bright hesitated. 'Er, no, not really. He stayed here until he was adopted.'

'Oh, he was a boy then? Well that's good,' and so as not to labour the point any further, 'I expect he is happy now.'

'Yes,' sighed Miss Bright, 'yes I do hope so.'

Knowing that her work was done, Jo turned and shook Miss Bright's hand. 'Thank you so much for all your kind help. Here is my card. Please ring if you have any questions, or if you think of anything else you feel might be of interest to us.'

Miss Bright led Jo back to reception, and just as she was about to leave, called out, 'Oh Miss Dawson, there was one thing I remember. That little mite I was telling you about had a gold chain around his neck.'

Jo quickly walked back, 'Oh really?'

'Yes. And if I remember correctly there was a little engraved heart.'

Could Jo enquire further, or would this be too obvious? 'Perhaps it belonged to the mother. Did the police find out from the engraving?'

'No I don't think so.'

Jo silently screamed. *'Tell me ... tell me what the engraving was!'*

As if to read her mind Miss Bright exclaimed, 'Oh I remember now. Funny how things come back to you, I've not really thought of it since. Yes, the letters AG were inscribed on the heart.'

'Oh well,' Jo said, 'thank you again for your kind help. I'll send you a copy of the article once it's completed.'

Miss Bright smiled, and Jo called a taxi to take her back to her hotel. *Well, that was informative,* she thought, *feeling quite pleased with herself.*

She let herself into her hotel room. Reception had already advised her that Sal had not yet returned. OK, I'll have a glass of wine from the mini bar and ring Jen.

'Jen, it's me.'

'Oh hello darling. Had a good morning?'

'Yes, really good. I think we may be turning a corner as far as Richards is concerned.'

'Oh?' replied Jen, still unconvinced. 'What happens next?'

'Well I'm waiting for Sally to return from her searches, and then we should be further along with our enquiries. Anyway dear, what have you been doing?'

'Not much. I've finished the invitations and am now just waiting for George to arrive the week after next.'

'Good, that means we shall have a few more days before the furore starts.'

'Well yes, that's if you're back in time.'

'Oh don't worry darling, should only take one more day, if that, and I'll be home. Must go now, speak to you tonight, and love you.'

All that was left for Jo was to wait for Sally to return. She rang down to room service and ordered some sandwiches and coffee.

Sally arrived two hours later, ravenously hungry. Jo ordered some more sandwiches and coffee. When it arrived, Sally tucked in and laughed, 'Hungry work, this investigating!'

Once fully satisfied, Sally asked, 'Well Jo, how did you get on?'

'Very well, I think,' and Jo proceeded to tell her about the conversation she had had with Miss Bright.

'Umm, sounds interesting Jo. A and G? Could be Anne and someone else?'

'Yes it could. Anyway, how did you get on?'

Sally then commenced to tell her of her day at the *Leeds Tribune*, and how at first it was difficult to prise out any pertinent information. However, after engaging in flirtatious conversation with Mr Weaver, the man in charge of archiving, she was allowed into the basement where all the back issue microfiches were held. On the pretext of writing an article on 'Local Tabloids Through the Ages', she was given full access. Naturally, after ensuring that Mr Weaver was out of sight, she concentrated on the 1952 back issues.

The microfiches were old and scratched, and her eyes burnt from the constant back and forth movement it took to find the information. Then finally the issue regarding the suicide of Graham Carmichael came up. She looked for more items, and finally found what she was looking for.

She needed to print them off, and looked around for a printer, but there was none. Should she just take the fiches, or would that be stealing? Consoling herself that no one would want to look at these in the future, as most certainly no one had looked at them in the past, she decided to take them.

'I can always take them back,' she excused herself. 'After all this is for a good cause!' Placing them on the table, she said, 'We will need to scan these once we return to the office. However, from what I can remember, Graham Carmichael was not the good husband that everybody thought. It was alleged that he had a proclivity for visiting, shall we say, the most unsavoury quarters of Leeds.'

'Oh, you mean …?'

'Yes Jo, that is exactly what I mean.'

'Do you think Anne Richards …?'

'Could be, Jo. There must be more information we can gather on Richards' early career. I don't think there is anything further we can get from being down here.'

'No you're right, Sal. We'll stay tonight and leave tomorrow. Can you book our seats?'

Jo phoned Jenny that evening. 'Be home tomorrow, lunch time.'

'Oh good Jo, I've missed you.'

'Silly goose, it's only been two days.'

'I know, but I've still missed you.'

On the train it was agreed that Sally would go back to the office to scan and copy the purloined microfiche, and then if needs be talk to Angela again.

'Are you sure, Sal?'

'Yes, I'm quite sure.'

Jenny was thrilled to see Jo. She held her in her arms, not wanting to let her go. 'Are you hungry?'

'No, but a glass of wine would be good.'

Jenny sat at the kitchen table, watching Jo sip the wine. She wanted so much to ask, but remained patient just in case the trip had not borne fruition. Until she couldn't wait any longer.

'How did you get on Jo? I mean, were you successful?'

'I think so Jen, but at the moment it is all supposition. I know there is a link here, but we will need further investigation.'

'Oh I hope it's alright Jo. Josey finishes here tour next month, and then. And then …'

'I know darling. Let's hope we can consolidate our enquiries before then. Sal has been brilliant. She would make an excellent investigative journalist.' She mused, 'I think I may make this another string to her bow.'

'You think a lot of Sally, don't you?'

'Yes I do, and when you meet her, which you will when this is all over, you will think a lot of her too.'

Sally returned to the office, ate the salad she had bought from the deli, and set about scanning the microfiche. It was far too scratchy for her liking, but she persevered until finally she extricated a legible copy.

As Jo had said, the information was full of supposition. It was as if the reporter had been reluctant to taint the memory of the renowned judge. However, in a later article, speculation seemed to take over:

Police investigations continue further, after a tip-off that Judge Carmichael was not alone in his hotel room on the night of his suicide. A spokesman from Police Headquarters has intimated that Judge Carmichael entered the hotel in the company of a 'lady of the night', who was seen leaving alone. So far, tracing this person has proved unsuccessful. In an interview, Mrs Carmichael, who distraught at this time, has refused to comment.

Judge Carmichael leaves two sons, who are currently being cared for by his mother-in-law.

Sally wondered why the police investigations hadn't widened the net further to find this woman. Perhaps, she thought, the old boys' network was at work here.

Another scan of the fiche revealed nothing further.

Time to talk to Angela I think, as she lifted the phone.

'Hi Angela, it's me, Sal. Bit late I know, but can you do dinner?'

'When?'

'Tonight.'

'Yes, OK, what time?'

'I'll meet you outside your offices at say about six.'

'Yes that'll be fine.'

Yes, and it was fine for Angela. She had spent days wondering what would be produced by Sal's investigations. Would she bring Arthur's sword to slay the dragon, or just "the Sword of Damocles"? She awaited Sally's arrival with trepidation.

Outside the office, Sally linked her arm in Angela's. 'We'll go to Raymond's. Jo is thinking of doing an article on fine dining, so I thought we might as well try it before he gets too nervous. I won't tell him I'm from *Millennium*.'

Angela smiled, a weak and kittenish smile. A smile that held no humour, but acknowledged Sally's comment.

After their meal, they ordered coffee and brandy.

Angela took a sip from her glass, looked up at Sally and said, 'Well Sal, did you find anything helpful in the articles I gave you?'

'Yes I did. Jo and I went to Bradford and found it quite interesting. However, there are a lot of gaps we need to fill. Is there, anything, anything you can tell me that would be of more help, than you have given me?'

'Well ... Yes there might be!'

'Come on Angie, you know that anything you say to me will be in confidence.' Angela looked down at her glass. 'Now come on Angie, you know you can trust me.'

'Yes, I do, but this is strictly off the record.'

'Of course, now what can you tell me?'

'Well, when I gave you the 1952 article, I omitted to enclose the 1951 one.'

'Why?'

Angela looked again at her glass. 'I was afraid, Sal. I knew that you and your boss would look into it further, and I didn't want Richards to find out. You and I both know what a vicious woman she can be. She has friends in high places, and I thought ...'

'You thought what?'

'I thought that she would find out the source of this information.'

'Don't be daft Angie, even she is not that telepathic. I promise you nothing will be disclosed about our source. Now tell me what the article said.'

Angela, still unconvinced, asked for another brandy. When it came, she drank it down almost in one gulp. Putting the glass down on the table she looked up at Sally and said, 'Well according to the *Leeds Tribune*, a certain Anne Mary Hayes was convicted for soliciting, but because of her age, she was given a caution, and it wasn't taken any further. There was a note in the *Tribune* of the court proceedings, but they only revealed the same. Now I can't tell you if that person is the same as Anne Richards. All I know is a birthday.'

'Well that's a start. What is it?'

Angela reached into her bag and handed over a document to Sally.

'Here, I don't know if it will help, but I hope it will.'

They left the restaurant, sharing a taxi. Angela, arriving at her home, leaned over and kissed Sally on the cheek. 'Thank you, thank you so much Sal.'

Sally patted her arm, 'Sweet dreams Angie. I'll phone you.'

On the way home Sally thought how fragile her friend was, and resolved to chase away her demons.

She arrived home, bathed and changed for bed, and only when she had settled down on her settee did she open her bag and take out the paper that Angela had given her.

Mm, she thought, holding the copy birth certificate in her hand:

Anne Mary Hayes, born 17.11.1933. Father Gordon John Hayes, carpenter. Mother Elsie Elizabeth Hayes, housewife. Registration of birth 20.11.1933. Town of birth Bradford.

Well, Sally mused, if this is the same Anne, then she must have changed her name. A trip to Somerset House, I think! Feeling quite pleased with herself, Sally retired to bed. She would tell Jo tomorrow.

Chapter Twelve

Jo sat in the lounge drinking her coffee, and wondered whether this would be the day when the nightmare would end. Yes, she felt very satisfied. Soon Jenny's nemesis would be consigned to Dante's Inferno, that dark place where even the angels abandoned all hope. Yes, she was full of conviction: Anne Richards, I think your day has finally come.

Sally walked out of Somerset House full of enthusiasm. *Gotcha!* she thought, holding the copy of the deed poll, changing Anne's name from Hayes to Richards. She caught the bus back to *Millennium*.

'Well Sal,' Jo said 'all we have to do is to link this all together, and then I think we'll confront her.'

'Well if we do Jo, we'll have to be sure of our facts.'

'Yes I know. Do we know what happened to Carmichael's wife and children?'

'No, I could telephone the *Leeds Tribune*, and ask.'

'I doubt whether they will tell you on spec, so we'll have to think up a good story.'

'Yes I know. Could say we want to run an article on how suicides affect the family?'

'Brilliant idea Sal! Can I leave that to you?'

'I'll get right on it.'

Sally left the office, leaving Jo to carry on with *Millennium* business. She phoned Jimmy.

'Jimmy, have you anything to show me on your article?'

'Not yet, Boss. Not quite sure where to start!'

'Go out on the street Jimmy. Canvass people's views on the subjects and see what you come up with. Take Carol with you. She might be able to solicit the feminine point of view.'

Jimmy sighed, still overawed at the prospect of writing such a controversial story. 'Right Jo, I'll do that.'

'Good luck Jimmy. Although I know you won't need it.'

The telephone call from George threw Jenny into a panic. 'Not now,' she breathed when George told her that Anne Richards had telephoned him and advised that she was leaving for London at the end of the week. She would be staying at the Gladstone, and would Jenny ring her!

She rang Jo. 'Jo, oh Jo.'

'What's wrong Jen?'

'Anne Richards will be here this weekend.'

'Don't worry Jen. If she wants to see you, tell her you're too busy with the exhibition. There's nothing she can do about that. She can't force you to see her.'

'Are you sure?'

'Yes of course. Don't worry, I'll see you tonight.'

As she replaced the receiver, Jo wondered whether there would be anything to worry about, and hoped that Sal could come up with some solid evidence that would divert Anne Richards from her destructive course.

Chapter Thirteen

Brian and Joan arrived at Raymond's shortly after the dinner covers were finished.

Raymond flounced from the kitchen, and shook Brian by the hand. 'Hiya, you must be Brian,' he said as more a statement than a question.

'Yes.' And then nodding to Joan, 'This is Joan, she will be taking notes.'

'And what will you be doing?'

'Oh me, I'll be taking the pictures.'

Raymond's eyes sparkled. He was already warming to Brian. 'Ooh good. You'll get my best side I hope?'

Brian laughed, feeling rather charmed at the egotism, and couldn't help having a little fun at Raymond's expense. 'Oh, you do have one, then?'

'Ooh you are awful.' Cloning the catchphrase.

Joan nudged Brian's arm.

'Yes, sorry, we digress.'

Raymond took them to a table at the back of the restaurant and called out, 'Simon, some Chardonnay please.' And then turning to Brian, 'You do like Chardonnay don't you?' without requiring an answer.

Wine was dutifully brought, by a small, pimply faced boy who was obviously unused to serving at table. Raymond, ensuring the wine was properly chilled, dismissed the boy and poured out the wine.

With three glasses filled, he took a sip, and looking straight at Brian, enquired, 'Well, where would you like me to begin?'

'At the beginning of the restaurant, I think, don't you?'

Taking another sip from his glass, Raymond proceeded to tell Brian and Joan, how he and his partner Steven had met at catering college and longed to start a restaurant of their own. After working tirelessly for different catering establishments, refining their skills, they borrowed money from their parents and opened Raymond's.

'Whose idea was it to have just the one name? Surely Steven wouldn't have been happy with that?'

Raymond grimaced. 'Steven was never happy. But to answer your question it was thought that a two-name restaurant would be a little over the top.'

'Oh I see!' answered Brian, not quite seeing at all, and then added, 'Where is Steven? Does he not want to be involved in this article?'

'Oh him! He's flown the coop, so to speak. Gone off to pastures new.' And before Brian could interject, 'Good riddance, that's all I can say.'

Feeling a slight atmosphere, Joan interceded. 'I should imagine that it must be hard running the restaurant on your own?'

'No, not at all, I have three really good sous chefs, who with more training will be able to support me in the kitchen.' Then, turning specifically to Brian, 'You must come and eat one evening.'

'Well, yes, and not wanting to leave Joan out, 'We would like that.'

Feeling Raymond's disappointment, Joan interrupted, 'Oh no not me, I'm a philistine when it comes to fine dining. Meat and two veg, that's me!'

Raymond smiled, and if he could have hugged Joan, he would have. 'Well then Brian, that's a table for one?'

Brian smiled. He too was grateful for Joan's refusal. Reluctantly, he admitted to himself that the meeting with Raymond had stirred a latent possibility within him. He wanted to push it aside, but the feeling of elation kept returning.

Jo, you sly old thing, he thought. *This is a surreptitious blind date!*

They left the restaurant, with Brian arranging to dine there the next evening.

'Dinner on me, of course,' laughed Raymond, adding, 'Only if you give me a good review.'

Brian also laughed. 'Don't worry about that.' And then turning to Joan, 'I think we have everything we need.'

'Yes,' answered Joan, slightly amused by the whole thing. She loved Brian like a brother, and could only be happy for him if he had found a friend with whom he could have a relationship.

Would she ever tell him? No! That would be a betrayal of their friendship.

Brian did dine at the restaurant that next evening, and many evenings after that. Raymond's flamboyance was a breath of fresh air to Brian. He loved the bright blue sparkling eyes that twinkled with fun, and the wavy dyed blond hair that shimmered under the dining room's lights. Could he be falling in love? He didn't know. All he knew was that this man had brought a long lost spring to his step.

Raymond, however, was more certain. It had been a long time since he had felt comfortable in another man's company, His lacklustre life with Steven had revealed cracks in their relationship, and once the rot had set in, every day had become a case of mere cosmetic wallpapering. Although he had been reluctant to admit it, he was glad when Steven finally decided to leave. When he had said 'good riddance', he knew now that he had really meant it.

It took a few weeks before Raymond could coax Brian to a late supper in his flat above the restaurant.

Unlike Raymond's frivolous persona, the flat was remarkably sophisticated. The walls were papered in gold regency stripes, which complemented the black and white furniture. On scarlet lacquered shelves were placed an eclectic array of literature. A black japanned record cabinet held both classical and modern music.

'Goodness me, Raymond,' Brian mused, expecting to find eccentricity to match his restaurant's flamboyance. 'You have surprised me!'

Seeing Brian's amusement, Raymond, appearing from the kitchen, remarked, 'Yes Brian, I'm not all frills and fancies.'

They both laughed and Brian took the tray of nibbles from Raymond and placed them on the glass coffee table.

'Sit down Brian, you look like a spare part standing there!' Brian dutifully sat. 'Thought we might have these with some wine, until the supper is ready.' And not waiting for a reply added, 'I hope you're hungry? It's coq au vin with Mediterranean vegetables.'

'Good Lord,' Brian remarked, 'you didn't have to go to all that trouble!'

'Oh don't worry, it'll be egg and chips next time!'

They laughed, each one hoping there would be a next time.

The evening was a delight. They ate, drank wine and listened to music, and reluctantly, when the hour was late, departed with a tender kiss on the lips.

Would this evening be the special ingredient that would glue their future years together? Yes, they both knew it would.

Sally's research at Companies House bore fruition. Jumping into a taxi, tightly clutching her handbag, into which she had placed her precious cargo, she returned to *Millennium*.

Once there, and eager to show Jo what she had found, she raced into Jo's office. 'Jo, Jo, I've got it!'

Seeing Sally flushed, and out of breath, Jo said, 'Sal, sit down for goodness sake, you'll have a heart attack!'

Once Sally had composed herself Jo asked. 'Well now, what is it you've got?'

Taking the document out of her handbag, Sally replied, 'I've got Anne Richards' change of name. Anne Richards was Anne Mary Hayes! Well Jo, what do you think about that?'

Jo sighed, and hoped the light at the end of the tunnel was finally becoming clearer. 'Right Sal, what we have to do is to connect Anne Richards, or Hayes, with Graham Carmichael, and the boy who was left at the railway station. If we can do that, then I think we've go her. We shall have to be quick, Richards will be in London at the end of the week.'

'Oh Jo, I don't think we will have enough time. It'll take more than five days to uncover the truth. Can't you go to her with what we have? Bluff it out a bit? '

Jo nodded. 'Perhaps, but –'

'In the meantime, I can go back to Bradford, find Carmichael's family, and try to … Well, I don't know what I'll try to do, but hopefully I'll come back with something.'

Sally went off to book her train to Bradford, whilst Jo formulated a plan to persuade Anne Richards that she knew more than she did.

Chapter Fourteen

Allison Carmichael had tried hard to come to terms with her husband's suicide. She had ignored the rumours as petty scare-mongering, and journalistic innuendo. However, after the funeral, logic had become her guardian, and once her grief had assuaged itself, her maternal instincts took over. She knew that she must shield her two sons from malicious gossip, and find her way through the bleakness of it all. With this in mind, and after a reasonable period of mourning, she sold the house and moved to Keighley. Here, she and her boys could live in anonymity.

A pretence was kept up. When asked, she would say her husband died suddenly of a heart attack. Perhaps a little economical with the truth, but the white lie perpetuated itself, when confronted by her son's questions.

Sally arrived at the train station and rang Jo. 'I'm on my way to Leeds. I have an idea, will ring you later, and let you know where I'm staying.'

Sally was good, very good. She seemed to revel in her new-found investigative journalist role. *Going back to the Leeds Tribune,* she thought, *would be over-egging the omelette,* so she decided to trawl the paper's archives in the city's library. Success was hers, when she finally found the item she was looking for:

After a brief period of mourning, Mrs A. Carmichael moved to Keighley, taking both of her sons with her. In a short interview with our reporter, she said that she needed to put all the unhappiness behind, and the only way was to have a new start in another town.

'Ah!' exclaimed Sally. 'So it's off to Keighley is it?'
Once she had found the address from the electoral roll, she

returned to her hotel to consider a plan of action. *Perhaps,* she thought, *Jo might have some suggestions.*

Jo was pleased, very pleased with Sally's news, but where to go from there, she couldn't think. 'It's a difficult one Sal. You can't just turn up at their front door.'

'No, you're right, I should have a good reason for being there. Don't want to chance my arm, and lose the contact.'

'No. Let's think. Who would you open the door to?'

'A charity worker? No, that won't do, I'd need to have identification.'

'How about …' Jo interrupted, 'how about you were looking for a lost cat or something? She might be susceptible to that?'

'Good idea Jo. I'll name it Tiddles. Better still, I'll have some flyers made up at the local printers. That should add authenticity.'

If the matter hadn't been so serious, they would have both laughed at the irony of it.

True to her word, Sally had flyers made up, from a Polaroid she had taken of a cat she had seen in a front garden many streets away, and copied the telephone number of a public telephone box, just in case, and added this to her flyer. So as not to arouse suspicion, she canvassed all the houses before that of the Carmichaels.

When the door was opened, she explained her trauma of the lost cat.

'No dear,' the woman said. 'No, I haven't seen it, but I'll look out for it. Do you have a telephone number I can call?'

'Yes,' she said, and then started to cry.

'Oh dear, you poor soul, please come in and I'll fetch you a drink of water, or would you like a nice cup of tea?'

Although feeling very guilty, Sally could not believe her luck, and sniffing for effect she accepted the invitation.

Alison Carmichael's house was neat and tidy. The living room into which Sally was ushered was warm and cosy. *No sign of children,* Sally thought.

A pot of tea, with all its accompliments was brought on a silver tray.

'How do you like your tea … I'm sorry I didn't catch your name?'

Thinking on her feet Sally answered, 'Oh it's Julie Potter. White with two sugars, please.'

Alison Carmichael poured the tea, passed the cup and saucer to Sally and said, 'I'm very sorry about the cat, how long have you had it?'

Not knowing about cat's ages, Sally improvised. 'Oh for quite a few years.' Prudency prompted her not to enlarge on the subject.

Alison Carmichael sipped her tea and nodded sympathetically. 'Yes, it's really terrible to lose a loved one.'

Sally knew that this opportunity wouldn't come again, and jumped right in. 'Yes it is. Forgive me for my presumption, but you sound like someone who knows what it feels like to lose a precious soul.'

Alison stared out of the window, her eyes glazed with unreleased teardrops. Sally waited, and then with a consoling hand touched Alison's arm. The touch seemed to open the floodgates, and all the heartfelt misery poured out. If Sally had not been there from an ulterior motive, she would have cried with Alison, but she kept hold of her emotions.

After Graham Carmichael's death, all the worms crawled out of the woodwork. The rumours gathered momentum. The boys had adored their father, so there was no reason to enlighten them. 'But,' she added, 'as they grew up, they wanted to know more about their father. But what could I tell them?'

Sally just nodded, her sympathy growing with Alison Carmichael's outburst. Could she have felt sorrier for someone? She didn't know. Finally, after much hesitation she asked 'and what of your sons now?'

'Oh, Gordon's forty-one, and Michael is thirty-six. They're all grown up now.'

Sally had to ask, 'Do they hold any animosity towards their father for what happened?'

'Not really, although Gordon still feels very angry inside. Every time I mention his father, he changes the subject. But ...'

'But what?' Sally asked.

'But I think ... I hope, he'll get over it.'

'Oh that's good. And you, will you get over it?'

'Yes, I have now, it was just ... just ... Your lost cat that brought it all back.'

'Oh I am sorry! I didn't mean ...'

'It's not your fault, and I do hope you will find it.'

Sally realized it was time to go. There was nothing more she could glean from their meeting. She rose up from her chair, stretched out her hand and said, 'I do hope that my visit hasn't made you too sad. Hopefully Tiddles will come home eventually.'

'Oh so do I. Where can I reach you if I find him?'

'You can ring me at the number on the flyer.'

'Oh, please I don't want to trouble you any more. I'm sure he'll come home when he's hungry.' With that she turned quickly towards the front door.

'Oh I do hope so,' Alison sighed. 'Are you sure you'll be alright now?'

'Yes, quite sure, and thank you so much for your kindness.'

Sally walked around the corner, and caught a bus to her hotel. In her room she showered, trying to shake off her guilty feeling at her betrayal of Mrs Carmichael. Having warmed to her, her subterfuge had left her wondering whether all this was worth it. She ordered some food from room service and then rang Jo for some kind of reassurance.

It came. Jo was ecstatic at Sally's revelations.

'Well done Sally, very well done. Now we can progress further.'

'But Jo, I feel so dirty.'

'If you do Sal, don't forget we are fighting to slay that Richards dragon. Surely any amount of, well … shall I say dishonesty, will be worth it?'

Reluctantly Sally had to agree, and advised Jo she would return to London tomorrow.

Alison Carmichael wondered why a lost cat should stir up all her long-buried emotions. She had spent years creating an alternative persona to that of the cuckolded woman. Since moving herself and the boys to Keighley, she had hoped that the nightmares would cease. Primarily they had, until today. A lost cat, a lost husband! Could she endure any more of the terror? Could she suffer any more of the slings and arrows of infidelity?

Damn that woman, she thought, *reopening old wounds.* Wounds that she had kept covered beneath an antiseptic plaster.

Suddenly she had the urge to telephone Gordon.

'Oh, hello Mum. Are you alright?'

'Yes my darling. Just wanted to see how you are.'

'Oh I'm fine. Still working hard as usual, but working from home, as Lydia is away at the moment. How about you?'

Alison hesitated, she didn't want her voice to sound depressed when she answered. 'Oh I'm fine as well, and ... Guess what?'

'What?'

She then went on to relate the story of Sally's visit and the lost cat. Throughout the years, Gordon had learnt to know his mother well. There would be no reason for her to phone about a lost cat. No, it had to be something more.

'Look Mum, Lydia's not back until tomorrow, so why don't I come over and we can have dinner together?' And then as a comforting afterthought, 'I'm sure you can whisk me up one of your lovely omelettes, and perhaps some chips as well.'

Alison, heaved a silent sigh of relief. If it meant she could have Gordon's stalwart presence near her, she would have cooked up a feast.

'Of course Gordon. I'll make a Spanish omelette, just the way you like it. And yes, we can have chips.'

Gordon laughed. 'OK Mum, see you in an hour.'

As Alison replaced the receiver, she began to chastise herself. What a fool she was. How could she be so fragile as to let a stranger's visit upset her so. She would say nothing to Gordon, for knowing him as she did, she knew that only a small spark could ignite his flammable temper. *Yes*, she thought. *Better to let sleeping cats lie.*

And so she did, despite Gordon's subtle prying. It was only after Gordon had left to go home that the tears of frustration cascaded down her face. She knew that she had been right not to mention her anxieties to Gordon, as her equilibrium was not to be regained by fanning the flames of Gordon's intense dislike of his father. *No*, she thought as she finally drifted into sleep, *life has to go on, I must really let go of the past.*

Gordon had that feeling. That feeling that bugs, like a tooth cavity into which one must constantly place one's tongue.

'There's something wrong with Mum,' he confided to Lydia when she returned home. 'Otherwise why should she ring me out of the blue?'

'Well, perhaps she was lonely.' Lydia hesitated. As far as Gordon's mum was involved, she knew to tread carefully.

'No, it's got to be something else.'

Lydia was not about to argue. 'Well,' she answered, 'if you think there is, then you had better go and talk to her.'

The conversation ended with a nod of Gordon's head.

Chapter Fifteen

Brian was curious. It was unlike Jo to keep secrets. Why was Sally away from the office? It seemed to Brian that these days she was never there! Although he knew Jo was a very private person, they had shared deep personal confidences, and yet she seemed to have excluded him these past weeks. She had even forgotten to enquire about his meetings with Raymond. Yes, Brian was not only curious, but perhaps a little disappointed. Making up his mind to confront her, he marched into her office.

'What's up Bri, you seem a little flustered?'

'Well yes I am,' he stammered, brushing his curly hair from his eyes. 'I'd like to know what's going on with you and Sally.'

Jo sat upright in her chair, perturbed by Brian's unusual abruptness. 'Sit down Brian.'

He sat, and sighed, feeling slightly embarrassed by his outburst. 'Sorry Jo, but you have got me really worried. It's not the magazine is it? I mean, it's … it's still viable?'

Jo reached across the desk and patted his hand. 'No Brian, it's not the magazine.'

She then proceeded to tell him about Anne Richards and the reasons for Sally's absences.

'Well!' was all Brian could muster after she had finished.

'So you see Brian, why I couldn't tell you. The less people and all that …'

'Oh Jo,' Brian felt rebuffed, 'surely you know you could trust me. You never know, I could have even helped.'

Jo patted Brian's hand again. 'Yes of course, but I know you. You would have at best gone off on a tangent, and at worst run off to confront her, and … and my dear, I couldn't let you do that.'

An abashed Brian looked down at his hands. 'Well, yes. I suppose you're right. What's going to happen now?'

Jo lit a cigarette, inhaled deeply and answered, 'I'm not too sure. We've nothing concrete about the boy. So I expect I'll have to bluff it out with what we do have. She's due in London the day after tomorrow. I'll take a couple of days' leave, and formulate some sort of game plan. In the meantime, now that you have the full story, perhaps you and Sally can try to find out more. We know he was adopted, and that's about all, really.'

Brian got up from his seat. 'I'll speak to Sally now. And …' A deep frown furrowed his forehead. 'And you will be careful, won't you?'

Jo managed a hollow laugh –yet another person to say this to her! 'Yes of course!'

Sally was pleased to have Brian's help. A fresh perspective on things might aid progress, and lessen the burden upon her shoulders.

Gordon Carmichael could not rest. The more he thought about his mother's conversation – or should he say non-conversation – the more he felt perturbed. He decided to take up his wife's suggestion and speak to her further.

He picked up the telephone. 'Mum, it's me, Gordon. Been thinking about that lost cat. Do you still have the flyer?'

'Well yes son, but why do you want it? Surely the cat wouldn't be in your neck of the woods.'

Gordon smiled at his mother's naivety. 'No Mum, but I have a nagging feeling at the back of my mind that all is not kosher. Anyway I'll pop in on my way home tonight.'

'Alright son, but I'm sure you are wrong, and worrying over nothing.'

Alison Carmichael retrieved the flyer from her kitchen drawer and perused it thoroughly. *Seems genuine enough,* she thought, placing it on the kitchen table for Gordon to look at when he arrived.

Jo photocopied all the information Sally had gathered, together with a front page Sally had mocked up for her. The originals she then placed in the office safe.

There, she thought. *See what you do with this, you old shrew.*

She rang Jenny. 'Hello darling, just tidying up a few bits and pieces and then I'll be home.'

Home to her was now Flaxman Square, as she rarely stayed at

214

her flat, and had considered selling it. However, life with Jenny had its uncertainties, so she had dismissed that thought as soon as it arrived.

Before she left for the day she called Brian and Sally into her office. 'I'll be taking a couple of days' leave, so will you both be OK? You know you can telephone me at any time.'

They nodded. 'Don't worry Jo,' Sally insisted. 'Brian's come up with a few ideas, and Little Jimmy's still out and about, so I don't think he'll have his copy ready before next week.'

'Good. So I'll leave it all in your capable hands, and thank you both for all that you are doing.'

They both gave Jo a kiss on the cheek as they left, and Jo marvelled at the camaraderie they all had. No names, no pack drill, just friendship and deep affection.

Jenny had cooked a chicken and arranged a salad under fly-proof containers to protect it from 'foreigners' arriving through her open windows. She felt hot and sticky from the balmy evening, so showered and changed.

As she looked in the mirror she could see the growing years marching dramatically across her face. *Ugh,* she thought as she hurriedly applied eyeliner and pink lipstick. *Ugh! What does she see in me?* The moment of self-doubt passed as soon as she heard Jo's key in the front door. Jenny need not have had any misgivings as Jo swept her up in her arms. Could she have ever felt more comfortable? Happier?

'Yes Jen, a very good day. I'll tell you all about it once I've showered and changed. God, it's sticky isn't it?'

'Yes it is. Do you want to eat after?'

'No not yet. We'll have a glass of wine, and then I'll show you the papers on that Richards woman.'

Jenny went off to open a bottle as Jo climbed the stairs.

As Jo pulled on her jeans and T-shirt, she marvelled how life had changed. For years she had resigned herself to live without Jenny, and yet now! She daren't think the thought – she sighed – and yet now!

As they sipped their wine, Jo took out the portfolio from her briefcase and showed Jenny the copies of the documents Sally had gathered.

'Oh my goodness!' Jenny exclaimed. 'Is this really true?'

'Yes my darling. so you see, this is goodbye to Anne Richards.'

'Oh I do hope so, Jo!'

Jo lit two cigarettes and handed one to Jenny. 'Darling, there's only one question I need to ask you'

Jenny's brow furrowed. 'And what's that?'

'Do you intend staying with me?'

'Oh Jo my dearest, of course I do. How can you ask me that?'

'I ask, Jen, because if you do, then despite Richards you will have to find some way of telling Josey.'

'Oh I know, Jo. But not now, not now.'

'Alright Jen, but one day you will have to tell her.'

Jenny's eyes glazed over with a threat of imminent tears. 'Yes, yes I know.'

Jo cajoled, trying to break the moment. 'Come darling, one more glass of wine and then we'll eat.'

Once the dinner things had been washed and tidied away, they retired to the living room to listen to music. Jenny snuggled her head in Jo's lap, rising up briefly to kiss her.

If there was a moment to be etched in history this was it. Timeless, without explanation, "when heart with heart in concord beats, and the lover is beloved".

They rose early and ate breakfast.

'Now I think it's time I rang Anne Richards!'

Jo's statement sent a chill down Jenny's spine.

Chapter Sixteen

Gordon arrived at his mothers at six-thirty in the evening. She had made tea and sandwiches.

'You didn't have to do that Mum, you know I'll have dinner when I get home.'

'Yes my dear I know, but old habits and all that!'

They both laughed. Gordon loved his mother, and as he grew up became her keeper of souls. A guardian that would keep her safe from harm.

'Now Mum, let's have a look at that flyer.'

As she handed it to him she remonstrated, 'I really don't know why you're going on about it Son, it's only a lost cat, and the lady was so upset.'

'Well, yes, you may be right Mum, but even so, just humour me on this occasion.'

At first glance nothing appeared out of the ordinary – as it said – a lost cat.

'I don't suppose Mum you thought of ringing the telephone number?'

'Well no. I mean, I didn't find the cat, so why should I ring it?'

'Well let's try it, and see if the woman answers.'

Alison Carmichael still bemused by her son's persistence, nodded, 'Well if you think so, but I'm not sure what you are going to say. After all we haven't found her cat.'

The number was rung, and predictably was not answered.

'I'll phone GPO and see if there's a fault.'

Alison was becoming angry. 'She's probably out, son. Please just let it go.'

'No Mum, you know me, once I've got the bit between my teeth, I can't let it go until I find out.'

Alison was becoming more irritated by the second. 'Find out what? I really don't know why you're keeping on so.'

'As I said, Mum, humour me.'

Reluctantly she remained quiet whilst he telephoned the operator.

'Oh I see,' he said as he placed the telephone back on its receiver. 'There you go Mum!'

'There you go what?'

'It's not a private line at all, but a public telephone box! I knew something smelt funny – now tell me exactly what the woman said.'

To the best of her recollection, Allison Carmichael related their conversation. When she had finished, Gordon spoke softly.

'So you told her about Dad?'

'Well yes, son, we were comparing what it was like to lose someone you loved.'

Gordon mused, 'Perhaps that's what she wanted all along, but why now? Dad's been dead for over twenty-three years. Is there something you're not telling me Mum?'

Alison Carmichael's hands shook as she absently straightened the kitchen tablecloth.

'Mum, what it is?'

As tears began to flow, Gordon rose from his chair and put his arms around his mother.

'Now, now Mum don't cry. Tell me what's upsetting you so. Come on, you know you can tell me. Don't you know I'm a big boy now?'

Through a myriad of tears, she related the whole sorry story until exhaustion overcame her.

Gordon fell into a stunned silence. He could hardly believe that the man he had strived to emulate for all these years had had feet of clay. His whole motivation as a barrister had been founded upon the reputation of his father, now only to find that all he had been, was a tissue of lies, a fake, and a Lothario of the worst kind.

As anger and hatred consumed him, he demanded, 'Do we know who the woman was?'

'No son, and I want to leave it that way.'

'Well I don't, and by God I'm going to find out. How could you have lived with this all these years? It's like you've condoned his actions, it's like –'

'Oh don't son, please don't. All I wanted to do was to shield both you and Michael from the shame of it all.' She grasped her son's hand. 'I beg of you, please let this go, nothing good will come of it.'

'Sorry Mum, but I have to. I'm even more convinced that the lost cat scenario has something to do with Dad. Now I have to go, but I'll see you on the weekend.' And then, as an afterthought, 'Oh I don't suppose Michael knows anything about this?'

'Oh no, and he mustn't. You know how sensitive he is, this would break him. Please, please, Gordon promise me that you won't say anything to Michael.'

Gordon said his goodbyes, satisfying his mother that Michael would not be told.

Chapter Seventeen

Jo's telephone call to Anne Richards was succinct. 'I'll meet you in your hotel lobby in one hour.'

A grin lit up the whole of Anne Richards' face. *Alice in Wonderland*'s Cheshire Cat could not have outsmiled her. *Ah ha!* she thought. *So Jennifer Standford has bottled out, has she? Well, Jo Dawson, let's see what you're made of!*

Jo arrived at the hotel reception at five past ten.

'Yes madam, can I help you?' the manager asked.

'No thank you, I have an appointment with Miss Richards.'

'Shall I ring her room and let her know you're here?'

'No thank you, I'll wait here,' Jo answered pointing to the reception couch.

'Would madam like coffee while you wait?'

Again Jo acknowledged his question with a polite, 'No thank you.'

At twenty to eleven, Anne Richards flounced out of the lift. 'Oh my dear, have I kept you waiting?'

The sickly treacle voice turned Jo's stomach. 'No, I've only just arrived,' she lied.

'Oh good. Come,' she waved to Jo, 'let's have coffee in the arboretum, it's much nicer there, and' – she bent forward – 'quite private.'

Once seated, Anne nodded to the waiter. 'George, coffee for two, and some of those gorgeous amaretti biscuits.' She turned to Jo. 'I do so love those biscuits, don't you?'

God, what an arsehole, Jo thought.

Jo sat down at the table and looked out of the window overlooking the hotel's garden. If she could avoid looking at Anne Richards for a while longer than necessary she would.

Coffee and biscuits arrived. 'One lump or two, or are you sweet enough? I'm sure Jennifer Standford thinks you are!'

Jo, refusing to become drawn into Anne's game, quietly answered, 'None, thanks.'

They drank their coffee in absolute silence, with Jo wishing that Anne Richards would quietly choke on the amaretti biscuits she insatiably devoured. Once she had finished, Anne carefully wiped her mouth with her napkin, selected a purple Russian cigarette from her cigarette case, and lit it, inhaling deeply.

She then looked at Jo and said, 'Well my dear, what have you brought for me? Your *Millennium* holdings?' And without waiting for an answer said, 'I'm sure that it's a small price to pay for anonymity.'

Jo threw back her head and laughed. 'In your dreams, Richards. What I've brought is something you certainly didn't bargain for.'

Anne's eyes formed into slits. 'Oh yes? And what's that?'

Jo, wanting to protract the moment, lit a cigarette, and then slowly drew the specimen front page from her briefcase.

'This,' she said, sliding it towards Anne.

Scandal begets scandal. Renowned gossip columnist hoist by her own petard. See inside for details.

Anne scoffed. 'Well, well, well, we are breaking new ground!'

Jo was not to be put off by the sarcasm. 'Now let me see … ah, what else do I have?' She waited a while, hoping to catch a glimmer of interest, but there was none. *Oh well,* she thought as she slid the copy of the deed poll towards Anne.

'What's this?' Anne retorted. 'Another rabbit out of the hat?' Was she perturbed at the document? She seemed not. 'So what, a change of name. What's that got to do with me?'

Jo, determined to get the upper hand, replied, 'It's your change of name!'

Again Anne seemed unconcerned. 'So what?'

'Well,' replied Jo. 'Why should you do that if you had nothing to hide?' Anne remained unperturbed.

'Perhaps,' Jo went on, 'I can enlighten you.' She carefully took out the police reports, studied them, and said, '1950, Anne Mary Hayes – arrested and cautioned for soliciting. 1951, Anne Mary Hayes arrested for soliciting and fined £100. 1952, Anne Mary Hayes arrested for soliciting, and bailed to appear in Magistrates Court. Sentenced to one month in jail.'

Anne fidgeted a little. Jo waited. *What would she say now?*

Anne, regaining her composure, answered, 'So what! All you have is a name change, and a few misdemeanours that happened over twenty-four years ago. Do you really think my peers will worry about that now?'

Jo sat back in her chair. It seemed that nothing could faze Anne. Could she bluff with her ace?

Well, she thought, *it's now or never.* 'And what about the baby? Was that another misdemeanour?'

Did Anne's face pale, or was that just wishful thinking? From the silence that prevailed it would seem so.

Anne leant towards Jo, and fixing her with steely threatening eyes said, 'It is obvious Miss Dawson that you seem incapable of seeing the logic in this matter. You come to me with this … this flimsy attempt at blackmail, which I might add has no substance in reality, and you expect me to walk away with my tail between my legs. Well my dear Dawson, I have met greater adversaries than you, and if you think this is your "get out of jail free card" then you are totally misguided. What you don't seem to realize is that I have concrete proof of your … shall we say, perverted liaisons?'

With that Anne Richards got up from the table and stormed out of the arboretum.

Jo smiled a faint smile. She knew that the mention of the baby had hit a nerve. Now all she needed to do was to prove it. Had Brian and Sally come up with something? She really hoped they had.

It was Tuesday, and Alison Carmichael went as usual to her hairdressers. Walking into the salon she was greeted by Ingrid.

'Hello Alison, are we feeling adventurous today? Or is it the usual?'

'Oh the usual, I'm afraid.'

'Shampoo and set then?'

'Yes please.'

'We're a bit behind Alison, do you mind?'

Alison sat down on the chair in reception, 'No of course not.'

Alison's Tuesday outing to Ingrid's Salon was the highlight of her week. She loved the cosy conversations of housewives' frivolities, holiday escapades and harmless gossip.

'Would you like a magazine while you wait?'

'Oh yes, thank you Ingrid.'

Alison never minded waiting. This was her time, her space, where she could sit and listen to chatter and imagine what each individual's life was like. She retrieved her spectacles from her handbag and flicked through the magazine, not realizing that such a flippant act would have so many consequences.

As she glanced through the pages, a headline caught her eye.

Finally, after much deliberation and on our Accountant's advice, Millennium is to become a limited company. We are therefore pleased to announce, that the magazine will be held in the capable hands of the following directors:
Jo Dawson, founder and Managing Director/Chairman.
Sally Bishop, News Director.
Brian Cooper, Art Director
James Watson, Topical Affairs Director.

Alison looked at the photographs that accompanied each name, then she screamed. 'Oh my God, that's her! That's the woman!'

Ingrid rushed over to Alison. 'What's the matter? Are you alright? Do you feel ill?'

'No. No, but I have to go. I'm sorry, so sorry!'

Ingrid stood and stared in amazement as the salon door closed behind Alison. She pushed her hand through her hair. 'Well I never,' was all she could say, as she walked towards Mrs Jones, who was patiently waiting for her curlers to be unwound.

Alison, with the magazine she had purloined from the salon, could hardly get the key in her front door. She had to ring Gordon. But what if he was in court? What if …

Now woman, calm down, get yourself together, she cajoled herself as she rang Lydia.

'Hello.'

'Hello is that you, Lydia?'

'Yes it is. Is that you Alison?'

'Yes it is. Is Gordon there?'

'No, he's in court,' answered Lydia, wondering what new trauma had beset her mother-in-law.

Both Lydia and Alison tolerated each other because of Gordon. Long since, Lydia had grown to know the various foibles that Alison had accumulated in order to keep her son close.

Lydia repeated again that Gordon was in court and asked if there was anything she could do to help.

'No,' replied Alison, 'I need to speak to Gordon.'

Lydia sighed, knowing her offer would fall on sterile ground, but decided to ask anyway, and waited to hear the usual rebuff. 'He'll be home about eight. Are you sure I can't help?'

'No. No, I'll ring him tonight.'

Lydia replaced the receiver. She was used to her mother-in-law's indifference towards her. After all these years, her attempts to engage with her, hoping she would accept Gordon's marriage, had only resulted in monosyllabic responses. Alison could not accept Lydia's role in Gordon's life.

Gordon was tired, very tired. He had finally left his chambers after dictating his summation, ready for his secretary to type up the next morning. It was a difficult trial and left him with minimal energy resources. What he didn't need was Lydia complaining, yet again, about his mother.

'She's phoned in a stew, wants you to ring her.'

'Did she say what it's about?'

Lydia laughed. 'Does she ever?'

'Alright, alright,' he answered, thoroughly exasperated. He had hoped for – no wished for – a little compassionate patience from his wife. Will they always be at odds with one another? 'I'll change and then ring her. Can dinner wait a while?'

'Yes, I suppose so,' Lydia retorted as she flounced into the kitchen.

Gordon showered and changed. He felt older than his years. He loved his mother, but sometimes the "piggy in the middle" role became tiresome. Sometimes he wished he could be more like his brother Michael, a traveller with nothing but his dreams to sustain him. He would wander through life oblivious of its shortcomings, and see only beauty. Yet he could not be like Michael. He carried his father's mantle, and yet sometimes, yes sometimes, he just wondered.

Yes, he thought, *how lucky you are Michael!*

Having had enough of his regrets he heaved a sigh and went downstairs to the dining room to call his mother. 'Some fortification,' he murmured, as he poured out a gin and tonic. His sip was satisfactory, and as it trickled down his throat he dialled Alison's number.

'Hello Mum. What's up?'

'I know who she is!' Alison blurted out.

'Who's what?'

'The lost cat woman. I've seen her in a magazine.'

'What magazine?'

'Something called *Millennium*!'

'Are you sure?'

Alison was beginning to feel irritated, and retorted, 'Of course I'm sure, do you think I would ring you if I wasn't?'

'Er, well, no Mum.'

'Can you come over?'

That was the last thing Gordon wanted to do. 'Can it wait Mum?'

Alison was adamant. She had had the bit between her teeth all day. 'No it can't.'

'Alright Mum, give me half an hour.'

Lydia marched back into the dining room. 'Another dinner spoiled, I suppose!'

Gordon was in no mood for another row. 'Oh put it in the oven, I'll warm it up when I get back.'

Lydia knew there was no room for argument, and pointing to Gordon's glass, grumbled, 'Might as well have one of those then!'

Alison was waiting at the front door as Gordon's car drove up. If she had felt remorse at calling him out so late in the evening, this was diluted by her naiveness at being led astray by the 'lost cat' woman. Her 'Sorry Gordon' was a formality.

'Well Mum, what's this all about?'

Alison handed the magazine to Gordon. 'This, this!'

As Gordon read the article, his face paled, as he wondered why this Sally Bishop should be visiting his mother. Surely after all these years there was no mileage to be gained out of his father's death.

'Um …' was all he could say.

'Um what, Gordon? What are you going to do about it?'

'Don't know at the moment Mum. I'm tied up in court all week.' Seeing his mother's dismayed look he added, 'I suppose I could ring her.'

Alison had to be satisfied with that.

Gordon took the magazine with him, and left for home, leaving Alison to ponder the outcome of Gordon's telephone conversation with Sally Bishop.

'Well?' asked Lydia. 'Another storm in a tea cup I suppose.'

Gordon was in no mood to placate his wife. He walked straight into the dining room and poured another gin and tonic. Placing the magazine onto the coffee table, he sat down and began to flick through the pages. He realized from first glance that this was an extremely sophisticated set-up. So why the subterfuge? He took another sip from his glass and decided to ring before he was due in court.

'Shall I warm up your dinner now?' Lydia asked, as Gordon poured out a third gin and tonic. He nodded and Lydia went back into the kitchen.

He lit his pipe, took another sip from his glass and re-thought his strategy. No, he wouldn't ring in the morning. As soon as the trial was over, he would catch the train to London and confront Miss Sally Bishop. This way she would have no opportunity for manoeuvre. He knew from experience that lies come easily over the telephone.

Jenny was subdued during Jo's telling of her meeting with Anne Richards. She had hoped for finality, whereas all she had was a continuance of the ongoing nightmare.

'It's not as bad as it seems,' Jo said, trying a semblance of consolation.

'I know from the way she behaved that the child was hers. We just need to prove it.'

'But how?' queried Jenny.

'You never know, perhaps Brian and Sally will come up with something. Anyway let's not dwell on it now. How has your day been?'

'I've had a telegram from Josey.'

'Oh that's nice, how is she?'

'Very happy by all accounts. She has a surprise for me. She'll be back from New York the week after next.'

'Oh!' exclaimed Jo. 'I thought she was there for another month.'

'Well yes, so did I, but it seems that she's cancelled the rest of her performances.'

'Got to be a big surprise then, if she's done that.' This was more of a statement from Jo than a question, although it seemed that matters were about to come to a head. Which came first, the chicken or the egg? Could Jenny pre-empt Anne Richards' exposé? She had to ask her.

'Yes, I know what you're thinking. And yes I realize that it has to be done now.'

'I know darling how difficult this will be for you, but if we can't find anything concrete to stop Richards in her tracks, we must –'

'I know, Jo. It has to be done. I've put it off long enough now. Cowardice I suppose. But don't they say that fortune favours the brave?'

'Yes, but that doesn't make it any easier. Would you like me to be with you when you tell her?'

'No, I don't think so. She may feel intimidated and that would make it worse. No dearest, I have to do this alone.'

They spent the rest of the evening in quiet communion, neither of them wanting to add more fuel to the fire. Jo secretly hoped that Jenny would not renege on her decision, fearing the loss of her daughter's respect. Whilst Jenny was secretly hoping that she would not let Jo down by avoiding, once again, the inevitable.

Chapter Eighteen

This was the second time Anne Richards had felt scared and out of control. The first time had been when she suffered her father's abuse. And now came Jo Dawson's revelations. She had denied all knowledge, and counteracted with denial. But this, she knew, despite all efforts to the contrary, would not die even if she put a salvo across Dawson's bows.

She had thought with the adoption that the child would have become an irrelevance, a suppressed memory, and that she would suffer no consequence for her actions. She had fallen into prostitution out of necessity, rather than a career choice. But whilst men were prepared to pay for her services, she thought this was also her way of retaliation for her past abuse.

However, Graham Carmichael was not the normal "wham bang, thank you ma'am". He treated her with kindness and consideration, and soon he became her only "man of the night". The relationship, if one could call it such, lasted for over a year, during which gradually Anne hoped the promises he had made her would culminate in her eventual escape from the sordidness of her life.

However, when Graham Carmichael refused to believe that the child was his, and terminated the affair, Anne's world fell apart. Incensed with the desire to become his nemesis, she hounded him to distraction, leaving him with copies of the letters he had written to her, that she threatened to send not only to his wife but to the judiciary.

'There you are Graham!' she had said. 'What do you think they will feel about their sanctimonious judge then?' And sensing the hypothetical noose drawing ever closer around the judge's neck, added, 'I'll get rid of it and stay quiet, but it will cost you.'

Graham, who had always managed to keep to the moral high ground, now felt his personal and legal life slipping away. His weakness for covert sexual gratification had left him between a rock and a hard place. He could neither admit responsibility for the pregnancy, nor give way to financial blackmail as a means to eradicate it from his life. He had only one way out, and his desperation and depression left him no other choice.

He left no note, for this would serve no purpose. There should be no explanations, of 'I can't go on'. He would leave the earth quietly, hoping to find forgiveness on the other side.

When Anne learnt of Graham Carmichael's death she knew her ace in the hole had turned out to be the joker in the pack. She had no further hands to show, and conceded her luck had really run out this time.

The baby was born on the 12th January 1953, in the spare room of one of Anne's "ladies of the night".

'What will you do now?' the friend asked.

'Don't know, but I can't keep it.'

'Well you can't just leave it here. I mean, what will my men friends say?'

'Don't worry, give me a couple of days to recover, and then I'll leave it somewhere it will be found.'

'Are you sure? Don't you want to keep it?'

'Oh yes, I'm sure. And what would I do with a baby?'

'Well,' her friend replied, 'I suppose it would be difficult, in our profession!'

Anne laughed quietly to herself. No way would she end up like her friend. One day she would be someone to be feared. She still had this thought in her mind when she left the baby, wrapped in a blanket, at Bradford Station. Shortly afterwards, with a change of name she began her new life.

She knew the child had been adopted, but not by whom. Information on adoptive parents, because of their personal nature, was sacrosanct. There was no way that the Dawson woman could have found out about the baby, or his whereabouts.

No, she thought, *there is no way.* And yet that tiny doubt irritated the back of her mind, like a piece of grit one can never remove from the eye.

Right, she decided, *I'll have to bring matters forward. I said two weeks. Well she'll have ten days. See what she does with that!*

Gordon booked a first-class seat on the train to London. He was thankful for the peace and quiet of the compartment. The trial had ended, and although he was successful, it seemed to him a hollow victory. He knew within his heart that the man he had defended so expertly was guilty, but he had to do right by the law and present an absolute case that the jury would find irrefutable. *Justice however oblique,* he thought, *had to be done.* He settled back in his seat, closed his eyes and hummed an inconsequential tune to the clatter of the train wheels.

His secretary had booked a room at the Savoy, into which the hotel porter carried his overnight case. Gordon withdrew £1 from his pocket and dropped it into a gratefully extended hand.

'Thank you sir, will there be anything else?'

'No thank you.'

He unzipped the case he had lifted onto the bed and unpacked. He placed his suit trousers into the trouser press and hung his jacket in the wardrobe, putting the rest of his clothes into the neatly lined chest of drawers. After taking his toiletries into the bathroom he took the room service menu from the mahogany desk in the bedroom and carefully perused each item. He was surprised how hungry he felt, and ordered a club sandwich and a pot of tea.

This came with expert promptness, together with another outstretched hand, into which Gordon placed another £1, thinking that this short visit was proving to be quite expensive.

Sally's call from reception stunned her, and she had to ask the receptionist to repeat the name.

'Gordon Carmichael.'

'Er ... er ... Can you tell him to wait?'

'Yes.'

Jo was busily proofreading Little Jimmy's article when Sally burst into her office.

'Oh my God, my God!'

Jo looked up, startled by Sally's outburst. 'Goodness Sal, what ever is the matter?'

'It's Gordon Carmichael! He's ... he's ...'

'He's what?'

'He's in reception!'

'I don't understand Sal, how can he be in reception?'

Sally was beginning to become exasperated. 'I don't know, but he is! What are we going to do?'

'Nothing we can do. He's here, so we will have to see him. You'd better ask him up.' And then seeing Sally's nervousness she added, 'Don't worry, Sal, we'll see him together.'

Feeling quite anxious, Sally went down to reception, and with an outstretched hand walked towards Gordon Carmichael.

'Mr Carmichael, I'm Sally Bishop.' And feigning ignorance, 'How can I help you?'

Gordon scoffed. 'Found your lost cat yet?'

Knowing there was no escape without sounding ridiculous, Sally answered, 'Well no, but if you come with me, I am sure we can explain the subterfuge.'

'You'd better,' Gordon grunted. He was in no mood for fabrications.

Joyce was requested to get coffee, as Sally led Gordon into Jo's office, and pointed towards a chair.

Gordon sat with his arms folded, and faced them with a steely glare that could have frozen boiling water.

'Well,' he demanded, 'I think you owe me an explanation.'

'Of course,' answered Jo, 'that's the least we can do.'

Once the story had been told, Gordon, still glaring, responded, 'So. Now let me see. You created a drama, a subterfuge, a whim, on the assumption that this woman, this Anne Richards, had a baby by my father, which was later left at a train station and then adopted by who knows who?'

'Well, er, yes,' stammered Sally.

'But you don't know?'

'Well no, but the times and dates do seem to match.' Again, a stammered answer from Sally.

'I see,' Gordon said, like someone who didn't see at all. 'So you decided to visit my mother on a pretext of a lost cat, for what?'

Jo interrupted. 'For a little piece of the puzzle that might add up to the whole picture. And,' she added, seeing Gordon's anger, 'We had no intention of upsetting your mother. That was why we invented the lost cat scenario.'

'I see,' he said again but with a little more conviction. 'It seems that you had your reasons, so I'll accept you meant no harm to my mother. So what do you propose to do now? I mean, if you are right, then I have a half-brother somewhere.'

'Well yes,' replied Jo, feeling a sudden relief at Gordon's more conciliatory words.

Gordon leant back in his chair, and pulled out his pipe from his jacket pocket. 'Do you mind?'

'No,' they replied.

Gordon carefully patted the tobacco into the pipe's bowl, took out his lighter, and having confirmed ignition, puffed deeply from the stem.

'Well, it seems that we have no other alternative but to pursue this matter, if only to satisfy myself that my father had nothing to do with this Anne Richards.'

Sally interrupted. 'But what if he did?'

'Then,' answered Gordon, taking another puff from his pipe, 'then we'll have to draw this ugly mess to its rightful conclusion, and confine this woman back to the gutter from whence she came. I'll need all the documentary evidence you have and I'll get my people on to it. Just one more thing. There is no way that you will ever contact my mother again.'

'Of course not. You must believe that we are sorry we had to, but there didn't seem to be any other way.'

'Right. You'll find me in room 204 at the Savoy. Perhaps you can arrange to have the documents brought to me by this evening.'

'Yes of course,' Jo replied, as Gordon got up from his chair. With no cordiality of hand-shaking, he walked out of Jo's office.

'Well!' Sally exclaimed. 'That went better than I thought it would.'

'Yes,' replied Jo. 'Perhaps he may be able to get further than we did.'

'Well let's hope so. How long have we got?'

Jo felt no longer alone, and heartened by the 'we', smiled at Sally. 'Well my dear, we have ten days.'

Now she was faced with the problem of telling Jenny!

Gordon sat in the lounge bar of the Savoy, having downed two gin and tonics in quick succession. Puffing ferociously on his pipe, he couldn't shake off the disgust he felt at his father's promiscuity. If it had been only that, he might have had some semblance of forgiveness, but a child! If this was true ... Gordon couldn't contemplate the matter further. He would draw comfort from another gin and tonic.

When Gordon had left, Jo called Brian into her office, and told him of Gordon Carmichael's visit.

'I suppose,' – Brian was stating the obvious – 'I suppose it could have been worse. An astute barrister such as him could have sued the pants off all of us.'

'Well yes, but at least he seems to be on our side now. Did you and Joan manage to come up with anything more?'

'Well something. From searching the church records, it seems that two babies were christened during that month. Both boys, but one – and I suppose this sounds odd – but one with the middle name of Graham. Do you think that Richards had the last laugh by insisting that the adoptive parents kept the name of Graham?'

'Could be,' Jo mused. 'Do you have the certificate of baptism?'

'Yes, I was going to show it to you today, but you had that meeting.'

'Right, take two copies and leave me with one. This could be another small piece of the puzzle that we need. I'll make certain this is passed to Mr Carmichael with the other documents we have. And' – she smiled at Brian – 'jolly well done. Thank you so much.'

She then turned to Sally. 'Best not keep Carmichael waiting. Will you take the documents over to him? Take a taxi, and then call it a day. I'm sure you'll want to relax after all this!'

'Yes Jo, I think I will. Don't you leave it too late either.'

Jo kissed Sally on the cheek. 'No pet, I won't. I'll just finish proofreading Jimmy's copy and then I'll head for home.'

'Good,' replied Sally as she left the office.

Jimmy's article was amazing, specific and yet unintrusive. He had caught all sides of the variable minority spectrum. His insight was compassionate, non-judgemental, and above all truthful. Jo felt proud that her Little Jimmy could show so much humility towards the differing aspects of human nature. *Yes,* she thought, *Little Jimmy has done well.* She left him a memo to that effect, pinned to his copy, and placed it on his desk as she left the office.

Jenny, however, would need a lot more convincing. Quietly Jo put the key in the front door still dreading the prospect of telling Jenny that she now had only ten more days left to talk to Josey.

'Is that you Jo?' Jenny called from the kitchen.

'Yes my darling.'

'Come into the kitchen, I can't wait to tell you my news!'

Jo did as she was asked and before she could sit down, Jenny spluttered, 'Josey is coming home!'

'Well yes,' Jo answered. 'Yes, you told me, the week after next.'

'No, no, Jo, she'll be here in two days' time! Apparently she can't wait to tell me her news, and has cancelled the rest of her engagements. Oh, isn't it lovely? Oh Jo, I can't wait, I've missed her so.'

Jo was less enthused. She could see her future with Jenny hanging on the slender thread of Jenny's ability to disclose their relationship to Josey.

'You don't seem happy for me Jo. What's the matter?'

Jo answered carefully. 'I don't want to pour cold water on your happiness Jen, but time is running out now.'

'What do you mean Jo?'

Jo related her meeting with Anne Richards, and then her meeting with Gordon Carmichael. 'So you see, Jen, if we don't find any additional information within the next ten days then you will have to tell Josey. And my dearest, the sooner the better.' Jenny remained silent. 'Well say something. Anything!'

'I can't, I don't know what to say!'

Jo had had enough of Jenny's back-tracking. She had had an exhausting day. She was tired and frustrated with Jenny's non-committal stance. It was time to face facts. 'Well, let's put it this way Jen. Either you tell Josey or you don't, but I'll not hang around any longer with this pretence. I am what I am. You are ... well, what are you? Hopefully my lover and partner, but if you can't own up to that, then we can't go on with this, this ... well, I don't know what you would call it – behind closed doors.' Jo got up from her chair. 'I'm going to change. I'll leave it for you to decide what you are going to do.'

Jenny had only once before seen Jo so angry, and that was when she first came to London with the letters. Whilst secretly she could understand it, she was also aghast. Surely Jo knew how difficult this was for her? Surely a little support was needed?

She lifted the blue pendant to her lips, and as if a sign realized that the small blue token of love was all the answer she needed. Yes, she would tell Josey, yes she would be satisfied with either acceptance or dismissal. She had wasted most of her life protecting

Josey from the reality that she loved another woman, but she would do this no longer. She became resolute. As Josey had her own life, so should she. As she kissed the blue pendant again, she felt a weight was lifting from her shoulders, and she knew then what she had to do.

She went up to the bedroom, and stood in the doorway watching Jo dress. How she loved this woman! How could she ever lose her? They had sailed the oceanic divides of long absences, scaled the heights of passion and cultured the pearls of friendship. No, there was no greater love than that she had for Jo. As she had loved her all those many years ago, so would she love her always. She moved quietly into the room so as not to startle Jo, placed her arms around her waist, turned her around and kissed her.

'To lose you, Jo, would break my heart into tiny pieces, and I will not let that happen. I know now that as long as I have you beside me, I can do anything. Josey will be told when she arrives, and if ... and if ...'

'And if what, my darling?'

'And if she won't accept my love for you, then that will be that!'

'Are you sure darling?'

'Yes I am. I have loved you all my life. I was afraid once, but you have taught me "to your own self be true", and my own self is you. I will never, ever live without you again.'

'Well my darling,' Jo replied, 'we must formulate a plan. If Josey is to be told, then we should do it together.'

'Perhaps ...' responded Jenny, 'perhaps I should do this alone.'

'Well if you think so.'

'Yes I do. It has to be between me and Josey, I have to make her understand. Make her realize that no matter how much I love you, this could never, ever detract from the love that I have for her. It's just a different kind of love.'

Jo sighed. 'Well if that's what you want to do, I'll not interfere. When will you tell her?'

'I'll wait a couple of days, and then I'll tell her. Telling her before she has told me her news might prove to be counterproductive.'

'Yes you're probably right Jen. I don't think she would take very kindly to you raining on her parade.'

Having finally found the courage to confront Josey, Jenny felt unafraid. For the first time in her life she realized the truth in Jo's wish for openness. If life was merely a mountain to climb, then her love for Jo would be the ladder.

She ate with a hunger she had never felt before, and as Jo smiled she answered the smile with a reminiscence. 'Do you remember our song?'

'Yes. Good Lord, we haven't played it for years.'

'Let's play it now.'

Jo pulled the album from its sleeve and placed it on the record player. 'There you are. Might be a bit scratchy.'

'Not to worry Jo,' and as the strains of Shirley Bassey's voice rang out the first lines of 'It's yourself', Jen added, 'Doesn't sound too bad.'

They both laughed at the words being constantly interrupted with missed lines as the stylus found its way between the dented grooves. They spent the rest of the evening in fond remembrance giggling at silly things that only related to them. Finally, with great contentment they retired to bed.

Chapter Nineteen

Josey had fallen in love with Richard G. Lewis, the first violinist. He was a handsome youth, whose genius belied his humble background. He had joined the Philharmonic in New York, having been headhunted by Jacques Duval, the orchestra's conductor. This, to him, was indeed the highest accolade that could be bestowed upon him, especially as he was to accompany Josey St Clair, the renowned concert pianist.

Their first introduction was a brief one, with just a shake of hands, although Richard had to admit to a shy liking for the pianist. During the next weeks, the friendship grew through their shared love for music, and during the intervals they could be found eating doughnuts and sipping coffee.

'You play beautifully,' Josey commented. 'It's like the birds sing when you bow the strings.'

Richard's face reddened. 'Yes, but –'

'Yes but nothing! The Maestro knew what he was doing when he chose you. You have added another dimension to the concerts. You are wonderful.'

Could Richard tell her how he felt? He thought not. She was far above his class. Better to remain just friends, he had decided. As time went on, Richard wondered whether it was him or his violin with which Josey seemed infatuated. All he knew was that he had fallen head over heels in love with her, but she was out of his reach.

A glimmer of hope shone through when Josey announced, 'Richard, when the tour is over, would you come back with me to London and meet my mother?'

'Oh my gosh, do you really mean it? I mean, meet your mother! Oh my gosh ...'

'Is that a yes then?'

His answer came in a tumult of nervous laughter and acquiescent humility. 'Are you sure, Josey? I mean your mother is ...'

'My mother is what?' Josey was becoming slightly exasperated.
'Well she's …'

'She's lovely, flamboyant and talented, just like you. So there. Will you come?'

He had no more excuses. 'Yes of course I'll come.'

Although he had agreed to Josey's request, in the stillness of his room he wondered where he would fit into Josey's family. He thought then of his father, who he knew would be shaking his head and saying that "oil and water don't mix".

Herbert Lewis was a cobbler by profession. He had wanted his son to carry on the family tradition, and vehemently disagreed with his wife's insistence that they should engage a music teacher for Richard.

'Don't know why, just throwing good money after bad,' Herbert had remonstrated. 'Why can't you leave well alone? A son should follow in his father's footsteps! Where's playing a fiddle gonna get him?'

'It's not a fiddle, it's a violin.'

'Whatever it is, just sounds like cats to me. And I'm telling you there's no money in it.'

Mary was not amused. 'Oh yeah, and you'd have him mending shoes for the rest of his life. Coming home with blackened hands from the heel ball and clothes reeking of leather and dubbin.'

'Didn't do me any harm!'

Mary softened. 'No my dear, but haven't you heard him? He plays beautifully.'

Herbert grunted, not wanting to lose the upper hand. 'Still sounds like a lot of cats to me. But whatever. If your heart's set on it, who am I to disagree, you'd never let me hear the end of it if I did.'

Mary had to be satisfied with that. At least it wasn't an outright no. So, with the money she saved from her housekeeping, Richard was sent to Professor Flowers.

On Richard's sixteenth birthday, Professor Flowers made a visit to Mary and Herbert. After being ushered into the front room, used only for "best", the Professor placed a sheet of paper onto the living room table.

'Well, Mr and Mrs Lewis, I can't go any further with Richard.'

Mary raised her eyebrows. Herbert gave an ironic cough, thinking, all that money for nothing, then?

'Is it the money?' asked Mary. 'Do you want more?'

'No Mrs Lewis, it's not the money. Richard needs to go to music college. He has a very rare talent for the violin, and it would be a disservice to him if we stopped now.' He passed the sheet of paper to Mary.

'I've brought the entrance application form. I've ascertained that there would be a place for him, if he passes the audition. All you need to do is to fill it in and I'll do the rest.'

'Oh yes,' rebuked Herbert, 'and how much is that going to cost?'

'Nothing. If he passes he'll get a grant to study at the London College of Music. Now Mr Lewis, all you need to do is to give your consent.'

Mary glared at Herbert, daring him to decline the offer. Herbert knew better than to reap the wrath of his wife, and bleakly nodded his head.

Richard knew he had been caught up in a whirlwind. First the London College of Music, then New York, and now...! What of now? London and a meeting with Josey St Clair's mother. It all seemed to go too fast for him. Would he be able to hold on tight to this merry-go-round? Or would he lose his grip and fall flat on his back? He sighed. *Well, if I fall I fall, but I would have had a jolly good ride.*

Chapter Twenty

Anne Richards was not her usual self. She had been disconcerted by Jo's visit. Was she about to reap what she had sown? Was her pernicious desire for power about to destroy her? She felt so vulnerable, so out of control. How much did Dawson know about the child she had abandoned? Was it just an enormous bluff, or did she really have something that could send her spiralling back to the depths from which she had worked so hard to rise?

She had to think, had to hold her nerve. She would sit tight. She had given ten days grace before she would show her hand, and publish her article and the accompanying damning letters. Her mind ran rampant. Ten days ... did she promise ten days? Well, she could change her mind, after all that was a woman's prerogative. She rang Jo.

'Dawson.'

'Yes.'

'Darling, I've changed my mind. Got a wee bit fed up with prolonging this matter. I want your share of *Millennium* by noon tomorrow, otherwise my dear ... Well you know the saying, "publish and be damned".' Not waiting for an answer, Anne Richards replaced the receiver and snorted, 'Now my dear, see what you do with that!'

Jo called Brian and Sally into her office. Even before they had sat down she blurted out, 'Tell me you have something new?'

They looked at each other, dismayed. Brian spoke first. 'Well no, Jo. I thought we had a few more days.'

'Well we don't!' retorted Jo. 'Like the perverse woman she is, we have only until noon tomorrow.'

'We'll never have anything by then!' exclaimed Sally.

Jo ignored her. 'Have we heard from Carmichael?'

'No,' they both replied.

Ignoring them again, she picked up the phone and dialled. 'Jimmy. My office please.'

Jimmy was astounded. He had never heard Jo speak so abruptly. 'Well, yes. OK.'

Jimmy entered, red-faced and somewhat abashed.

Without waiting for him to sit down, Jo said, 'Your article.'

'Yes Jo.' No longer the familiar "Yes Boss."

'I want it on my desk tonight, before I leave with the amendments I've made and ready to go to print.'

'OK Jo,' stammered Jimmy. 'Er, what time will you be leaving tonight?'

'As soon as I have your finished copy.'

Looking back at the papers on her desk Jo mumbled, 'Now you can all go, I have things to do.'

Sally and Jimmy left the office quicker than any scalded cat. They had never seen Jo like this.

Brian decided to stay. 'Well Jo! That went down well. What's wrong with you? I've never seen you like this before? Whatever it is, I think it very bad form that you should take it out on all of us. I would have thought better of you than that!'

Jo grimaced, she had let her fear overwhelm her. 'I'm sorry Brian, can you give my apologies to both Sally and Jimmy.'

Brian grunted. 'I think you should do that yourself.'

For the first time Jo felt her strength and resourcefulness abandon her. She was tired; weary of it all. Nothing she attempted to do could assuage the relentless onslaught brought about by the prejudices that pursued her. Seeing Brian was awaiting an explanation, she related the imminence of Josey's return and the demands set by Anne Richards.

Placing her head in her hands she whispered, 'I really don't know what to do now, Bri. It all seems pointless. How can I tell Anne Richards to go to hell, and yet still keep Jenny safe? It's all such a horrible mess. Is love really worth this price?'

Brian looked straight at Jo. 'How long have you known, or shall I say loved, Jennifer?'

'Since 1962.'

'Well it's 1985 now. Are you really going to waste all those years with capitulation? You've always told me to hang on to what I know is right.' He laughed. 'Even to pairing me up with Raymond. So Jo, don't ask me if it's worth it. You go and tell that Richards person to go hang herself, and no matter what, we will always support you.' Again he laughed. 'Even if it means taking that woman to a dark place and shooting her.'

'Oh Bri,' Jenny sighed, 'what would I do without you.'

'Well, you just go there tomorrow, show her Jimmy's article.'

'Oh my God, Bri. Jimmy. How could I have treated him so? I must speak to him.'

'Good,' Brian stated as he left the office.

Jimmy worked furiously to finish the amendments to his article. He felt disappointed and rebuffed by Jo's abruptness. He had adored her from the very moment she had taken him under her wing and offered him the job on the magazine. All through his school days, and then in later years, people had made him the butt of every 'short' joke, and yet when Jo called him "Little Jimmy" he had accepted the affection with which it had been given.

As Brian approached him, he tried to hide his face, conscious of its embarrassed redness. He finally looked up. 'What do you want?'

'Just to say, Jimmy, that at the moment you must pay no mind to Jo's outburst. She really has a lot on her plate, I know she didn't mean to upset you. But ...'

'But what?'

'She's very stressed and unfortunately you bore the brunt of it.'

Before Jimmy could retort, his phone rang.

'Jimmy, it's me, Jo. Can you come in for a moment?'

Jimmy remembering the previous encounter hurriedly answered, 'It's not quite ready yet!'

'Never mind about that, can you come in, please.'

'Right,' Jimmy answered still angry about Jo's former abruptness. He got up from his desk and walked towards Jo's office.

Jo realized that she had been dreadfully wrong in her attitude towards Jimmy, and hoped that she could make amends. Jimmy stood in front of her desk, declining Jo's invitation to sit down. This time it was Jo's turn to capitulate.

She walked towards Jimmy and whispered, 'I am so sorry, Jimmy. Will you forgive me?' She waited. Jimmy said nothing. Jo hurried on, 'I should not have spoken to you like that, and I am really truly sorry Jimmy. I had no right to take my stresses out on you. Please forgive me.'

Jimmy weakened. 'Well yes, I will, but it seems to me Jo, if I may say this, it seems to me that these days I am a director in name only.'

Jo placed her arm around Jimmy's shoulders. 'Of course you're not. You must know you're a valued member of this team.'

'Then, Jo, why all the secret squirel stuff? You must surely know by now that you have my complete loyalty and, if needed, my support.'

'Yes I do Jimmy, and this is no reflection on your friendship, but ...'

'But what Jo, do you think I'm unaware of what's going on? Remember, you taught me how to think, act and be a reporter. How to sift the wheat from the chaff. Well I learnt your lessons well. I know your relationship with Miss Standford is ... well, shall we say, a little ambiguous, and something that should be kept away from pernicious gossips like Anne Richards.'

Jo was incredulous. Her Little Jimmy, with so much insight. She gasped. 'Well, Jimmy, how did you know?'

'Remember the article we did on Jennifer Standford?'

'Yes.'

'Brian showed me the roughs of the photos he had taken. Well,' he paused. 'Well, my favourite painting was the *Welsh Metaphor*. It was so like the views you had described about your home in Wales, and there would be no way that Miss Standford could have painted that from imagination. Only a philistine could not see that this was painted out of love. It was your place Jo, so Jennifer Standford had to have been there at some time.'

Jo laughed. 'Goodness me, Jimmy, I have really taught you well. You really do have the reporter's nose!'

Jimmy sniffed. 'Well Boss' – the familiar term was back – 'how can I help?'

There was nothing more Jo could do but to tell him all about Anne Richards.

'I see,' he said, as she finished. 'So my article is really important then?'

'Yes Jimmy, if we are to stop her. So, you see, that's why I really need the copy today.'

'Why yes, of course. And do you think confronting her will make a difference?'

'I hope so Jimmy, I do hope so. I'm gambling on the fact that by bringing alternative lifestyles into the spotlight, we may, just may, steal a march on her vindictiveness.'

Jimmy went back to his desk, his outrage at Anne Richard's villainy catapulted him into frantic industry. His article had to be more than good, it had to be the catalyst for a defence of human rights. 'How dare she, how dare she,' he muttered to himself as he set about completion.

Down in the print room the Heidelberg clattered as Jimmy's article was fed through its rollers.

'Bit controversial,' Simon said, as he lifted the pages from the belt.

'Never mind that,' stated Jimmy. 'That red's too glary, it needs to be toned down.'

Simon doffed an imaginary cap. 'Yes sir.' And then barked up the line, 'Boss wants less red!'

'OK,' a voice acknowledged.

When the final pages were pulled off and handed to Jimmy, Simon asked 'Will that do?'

'Yes that's fine. Good work Simon. Thank the men for me, will you.'

'Yes Boss. Only one article is it? Or shall we go for a full run?'

'No just the one at the moment, we'll go for a full run next week, ready for the quarter issue.'

Simon nodded, not quite sure why the premature print-off, but there again, "ask not want not", as his mother would say.

Jo read Jimmy's copy. 'Well my dear, you have really excelled yourself this time.'

'I hope so Boss. Can you do anything with it?'

'Oh yes, this should take the wind out of Richards' sails.'

'Might do,' mused Jimmy. 'But let's hope not at the cost of our readers.'

Jo sighed. Not Jimmy as well! She had had enough of prejudices. 'If we lose circulation Jimmy, so be it. But our magazine has always stood up for the truth. If our readers find this unpalatable then all these years have been for nothing. No Jimmy, I credit our readers with more intelligence than that.'

Taking his foot very quickly out of his mouth, he nodded in agreement. 'What will you do now?'

'Meet Richards tomorrow, as requested. Show her the article, and hope for the best. So my dear Jimmy, keep all your fingers crossed. Now I must speak to Brian and Sally.'

'I'll get them for you,' Jimmy said, walking towards the door, pausing briefly to look back at Jo.

'Good luck, Boss.'

Brian winked at Jo. 'Everything alright with Jimmy?'

'Yes,' answered Jo. 'Now, have you got anything new?'

'Carmichael rang,' answered Sally. 'He thinks he's found the adoptive parents.'

'Thinks! Only thinks?' exclaimed an exasperated Jo.

'Well yes. I don't know anything more than that he will ring me once he has completed his enquiries.'

'Did he say when he'll ring you?'

'Probably tonight, but he wasn't sure.'

'Well,' sighed Jo, 'I suppose that's the best we can hope for.'

'Yes,' answered Sally, 'at the moment it is.'

'Well I'll be home at Jenny's. Ring me, Sally, as soon as you have anything from Carmichael. I'll go straight to Richards' hotel tomorrow, so I won't be back in the office until, hopefully, this matter is settled.'

'All right Jo,' Brian answered. 'But please be careful, you know what a conniving witch she is.'

'Yes I know Brian. I will be careful. I'll ring you. Oh and by the way, Little Jimmy is aware of what's going on. After all, I should have given him more credit than I did.'

'Oh right,' Brian answered. 'And is he OK with it?'

Jo smiled. 'Oh yes Brian he's OK. In fact he's more than OK.'

With that, Brian and Sally left, leaving Jo to assimilate all the information with which she would confront Anne Richards.

Jo had hardly opened the door when Jenny greeted her. 'Oh Jo, Jo!' she burst out with excitement. 'Josey's here!'

'What you mean here, in the house?'

'No, no, silly. Here in London. She's staying at the Marlborough, and ... and has asked me there for dinner. You don't mind do you?' Jo frowned. 'Yes I know, but she couldn't wait to tell me her surprise, so arrived two days earlier. You don't mind if I go?'

Jo hid her consternation. 'No, of course not. Anyway I have some office work to be getting on with. No, you go and enjoy yourself.'

Jenny bounced into the living room, like a teenager going out on her first date. 'What should I wear?'

'Darling, it's only Josey. I shouldn't think she'll worry too much, after all it's her mother she's come to see.'

'Yes I know, but –'

'But nothing Jen, you'll look lovely in anything.'

Satisfied with that, Jenny ran up to the bathroom.

Jo poured herself a Scotch and soda. There was no way she could tell Jen about her meeting with Anne Richards, as much as she wanted to.

She sat down in the living room and took Jimmy's article out of her briefcase. Its title engendered curiosity: 'Are They Wrong?' She read it through. It was good. No, it was excellent. She found it neither judgemental nor voyeuristic. It discussed all spectrums of the minorities and of sexuality, prostitution, heterosexuality and single-gender relationships. If Jo could run this before Richards could galvanize her gutter press into action, that should nullify any media free-for-all. Yes, Jo hoped that this would pre-empt any fallout from Anne Richards' venom.

She felt anxious. If she could not outsmart Richards this way, then she really needed another broadside in her artillery. Would Sally ring? She hoped above hope that she would.

Jenny, walking into the living room, interrupted her thoughts.

'How do I look?'

'Darling you look ... you look breathtaking.'

'I've phoned for a taxi, it should be here soon. Are you sure I look alright?'

'Of course my darling.'

The door bell rang.

'I have to go.'

'Yes I know. have a wonderful time. And don't worry, you look amazing.'

'Will you wait up?'

'Of course I will.'

Chapter Twenty-One

Josey strolled up and down in the hotel's reception, impatient and excited at seeing her mother.

'Oh Mama!' she shouted as she ran towards the revolving doors. 'I'm here! I'm here.'

Jenny smiled. 'Hello my darling, you look … you look beautiful.'

'Do I Mama?'

'Oh yes.'

Josey took Jenny by the arm. 'Come Mama, let's have wine. Lots of wine.'

Again Jenny laughed. 'Not lots, my darling.'

'Oh alright, a glass then.'

They sat in the lounge bar. Josey ordered two glasses of red and turned towards her mother.

'I've got such wonderful news Mama, such wonderful news.'

'Alright darling, slow down. Now tell me calmly what this wonderful news is.'

'I'm in love, Mama! He's wonderful, you'll simply love him.'

Jenny sat with her mouth slightly open. 'In love? You can't be, you're just a child!'

'Ugh,' scoffed Josey. 'I'm twenty-two! Go on Mama, ask me what he's like.'

Jenny couldn't but be engaged by Josey's excitement. 'Oh go on then, what is he like? I mean, apart from being wonderful.'

Josey grimaced. 'Now you're making fun.'

'No. No, I'm not, really I'm not.'

'Well Mama,' replied Josey, taking a large gulp of wine. 'He's twenty-four, his name is Richard G. Lewis. He's our first violinist, and he makes me cry.'

Jenny glared. 'What do you mean? He hurts you?'

'Oh no, don't be silly Mama. It's when he plays, it is so beautiful.'

'Am I going to see this Richard?'

'Yes Mama, he'll be joining us for dinner.'

'Oh, right.' Jenny felt a little disappointed. She had hoped to have Josey all to herself. 'Perhaps I will have another glass of wine.'

'I'll go and get him. There really is no need to be nervous Mama, I know you'll just adore him.'

Josey left the bar, and Jenny went back to her wine, wondering how anything could get any worse. Now there was another person in the equation. How could she say something now? Oh what a tangled web we weave.

A light tap on her shoulder interrupted her thoughts. 'Mama, I'd like you to meet Richard.'

Jenny turned around and understood why Josey was so enamoured. Standing before her was a slim, blue-eyed, dark-haired young man, slightly taller than Josey, and extremely well turned out in a dark blue pinstriped suit, white shirt and dark blue tie.

As he took her hand, Jenny found it to be firm and strong. *Must be from all that playing,* she thought.

'I'm very pleased to meet you, Miss Standford. Josey has told me so much about you. I'd love to see some of your paintings. I understand that you'll be exhibiting at the Whitechapel Gallery Perhaps … perhaps Josey could bring me.'

They all fell silent after the introductory words.

'Come,' Josey said. 'Let's eat, I'm famished.

Richard smiled, touched Josey gently on the arm and said, 'Yes, let's.'

They were escorted to a corner table by the maître d', who handed them a wine list.

'Shall we have a bottle?' asked Josey.

'More wine, Josey? Are you trying to get me squiffy?' enquired Jenny.

They all laughed, the embarrassment of the initial meeting dispersed amidst their laughter. The wine was ordered, dispensed into glasses, and the menus handed out.

Jenny did not want to appear like an overanxious parent, but it was hard. 'Now, Richard, so you play the violin?'

'Yes ma'am.'

'For goodness' sake,' Jenny cajoled, 'I'm not the Queen Mother, please call me Jennifer.'

Josey kissed Richard on the cheek. 'There you are, darling, didn't I tell you my Mama was a bit of a radical?'

'Yes, so I see.'

Jenny, not to lose momentum, continued. 'And what do your parents do?'

'Mama,' grumbled Josey, 'this is not the Spanish Inquisition you know.'

'Well yes, darling, but I'm sure Richard will appreciate my interest.'

Richard gallantly interceded, 'Josey, I really don't mind. It's only natural that your mother should want to know all about me. After all, Jo' – Jenny gasped, how odd that name should sound on someone else's lips – 'you have rather sprung me on her!'

'Well, er ... Jennifer. My father has his own cobbler's shop, it's an inheritance thing handed down from his father. My mum, she was a nurse up until the time she had me.'

'Are there any other children? I mean, brothers and sisters?'

'No just me I'm afraid.'

'Just like Josey then, an only child.'

'Yes,' he answered.

'So what started you on the violin?'

'Mama!' exclaimed Josey.

Richard patted Josey's hand. 'Now, now, Jo. Your mother has a right to ask.' And answering Jenny's question he replied, 'The school orchestra really, and then my mother, much to my father's horror. Unfortunately my father is quite Victorian in his outlook, and couldn't understand why I did not want to follow in his footsteps.' He grimaced and added, 'I really don't think he has accepted it at all.'

'It's a shame you had to postpone the tour, Josey. I expect the organizers and your agent weren't happy about it. Will they not lose money or something?'

'Oh don't worry Mother, we have said that we will do the next one for free.'

Jenny said, 'Well, that's alright then. And oh, it is so lovely to see you, Josey, and even earlier than expected.'

With enquiries exhausted they turned their attention to ordering dinner.

With main course and dessert eaten, Jenny looked at her watch and turned to Josey. 'Well my darling, it's getting late, so I really must be going. Do you have anything arranged for tomorrow?'

'Well no, Mama. Richard is going to Bradford to see his parents, and I shall be phoning Papa to see if we can go over to France at the weekend.'

'Oh good,' replied Jenny, 'I'll have you to myself for a couple of more days.' And then, as she saw Josey's quizzical frown, 'It's no reflection on you, Richard, just a mother and daughter thing.'

Richard smiled.

'Very well Mama, do you want to meet here or at Flaxman Square?'

'Flaxman Square, I think. Say about lunch time. I'll cook something nice.'

With arrangements made, Jenny bade farewell to both Josey and Richard. 'It was very nice to meet you Richard, I'm sure we'll be seeing more of each other.'

Richard nodded, took Jenny's hand, shook it gently and replied, 'Yes, I'm sure we will.'

Jenny couldn't wait to get back to Flaxman Square and was grateful that Jo had been true to her word and stayed up.

'Well darling, how did it go? What was her surprise?'

'She's in love. His name's Richard. It's obvious that they are both head over heels with each other.'

'Well, that's good, isn't it?'

'Oh yes,' Jenny answered bitterly, 'just another person to worry about.'

'What do you mean, another person?'

'Do you think he'll still be in love with her when he knows about me?'

'Hmm, I see. But surely if he loves her …?'

'His father has Victorian ideals, how do you think he'll react?'

'Not really his business, surely?'

'Oh I don't know Jo. What a mess, what a God-awful mess.'

Jo was worried. 'You're not going to back out on me over this are you?'

'Of course not, I just hope I can live with the consequences.'

They had very little sleep that night, talking well into the small hours. There had been no salvation of a telephone call from Sally. No silver lining to the cloud hanging over them. Therefore there was nothing they could do, but to leave their fate in the hands of the gods. Now it seemed with the addition of Richard, another mountain to climb was added to Jenny's task.

Finally, morning came and they got up, made tea, and sat quietly in the kitchen.

As Jo got ready for her meeting with Anne Richards, Jenny busied herself with cooking some chicken to have with the salad she would give Josey for lunch. It seemed that their continued future together hung on the unrealistic idea of Anne Richards' capitulation and Josey's ability to accept their relationship. If neither could be achieved then would it mean they would be confined to obscurity, where unlike fairy stories, there would be no happy ever after?

As Jo collected her things to leave, Jenny rushed up to her. 'Jo, I'm so scared.'

Jo held her close. 'Yes I know dearest. I'll stay if you want.'

'No, as much as I want you to, you can't. You must meet Richards, and I must be alone to talk to Josey, but Jo, what if ...?'

'Don't say any more Jen. Whatever happens, you must know that I will always love you, and if it means that I need to go out of your life to protect Josey, then I will. But darling let's see what happens.'

'Don't say that, Jo!' Jenny cried in terror. 'Please don't say that! I couldn't live without you now.'

'Then my darling you must make Josey understand. It's a good thing she's fallen in love. Perhaps you could capitalize on that. What do you think?'

'Well yes, I suppose so,' a hesitant Jenny replied.

'Now darling, I must go.'

'Yes I know.'

Jo, reluctant to let Jenny out of her arms, kissed her passionately.

Jenny watched the door close and with a deep sigh returned to the kitchen. She had two hours before Josey would arrive. She had to gather her wits. She must not be found stumbling before she had even reached the first hurdle.

Unlike her waiting for Jo, there was no hanging out of the window to greet Josey. She would wait in the living room, calming herself with a cigarette and a large glass of wine.

The door bell rang. She had not anticipated it: Josey was early, it was only half past eleven. She stubbed out her cigarette and replaced the wine glass on the table. Breathing deeply, she walked towards the door.

'You're early!'

'Yes Mama, I've left Richard at the train station, and came straight over.'

'Well come in, come in. Lunch is not quite ready. Shall we have a glass of wine while we wait, and then you can tell me all about the concerts?'

'Isn't it a bit early for wine, Mama?'

'Perhaps, but let's pretend we're still in France.'

Josey giggled, 'Oh yes, Mama.'

As they sipped their wine, Josey regaled Jenny with her descriptions of the concerts. 'They loved me Mama, they really loved me.'

'I'm sure they did, you are a wonderful pianist. I've got all your recordings.'

'Have you, Mama?'

'Of course I have, you must know how very proud I am of you.'

'Anyway, Mama, what did you think of Richard?'

'I thought he was very nice. I can see why you fell for him.'

'Can you Mama? Can you really?'

'Yes of course.' Now was now her chance. 'There is always that certain something you feel, when you know it's love.'

'What, you mean just like you and Papa?'

The ground was becoming harder to tread. Was she digging a deeper hole? Hurriedly she diverted the conversation. 'Josey, do you remember Anne Richards?'

'Oh yes, you mean that horrible woman that Papa went out with?'

'Well, yes. Well do you remember that time when you all came to my house, and I went to my studio, while you Papa and Anne Richards were at the cottage having coffee?'

'Oh yes, I remember, well I think I do. Was she meant to come to the studio? But didn't and left early saying she had a headache or something?'

'Well ...' Jenny took a deep breath. 'Well, while I was away in my studio, she stole something from my house.'

'What? Oh don't say she stole a painting!'

'No, it wasn't a painting. It was some letters.'

'Some letters? But I don't understand Mama. What letters?'

'Some love letters.'

'To Papa you mean?'

Jenny took a long, deep breath. 'No not to your father, but to someone else.'

'Oh, I never knew you had someone else. Was that why you and Papa never married? Well, you are a secretive one, who was he?'

Now the moment had come! Could she go on with yet another lie?

'Well Josey …' she hesitated, her words becoming stuck deep within her throat, making her mouth dry and uncompromising. She took a deep breath. 'Well no, Josey, it wasn't a man. It was … er, it was a woman.'

'A woman, Mama? I don't understand'

'I know you don't, Josey, and it's very hard for me to tell you this, and I wouldn't have done if it weren't for Anne Richards.'

Josey still confused, unable to take it all in, asked, 'What has Anne Richards to do with all this?'

'She has threatened to use those letters to ruin your career. If I could not satisfy her demands, she would use them to besmirch my name, and consequently yours.'

'But Mama, I still don't understand. Surely you loved Papa, otherwise you wouldn't have had me. The whole thing is monstrous! I really don't understand. How could you love a woman? I mean, you do hear about these women who frequent underground dives … but you, Mama! Surely you must have had a brainstorm or something?'

'Well, I suppose you could class me as one of those women. It was, and is, no brainstorm.'

'What do you mean, "is"?'

'The woman is called Jo. We met at college. We fell in love.'

'Fell in love? Fell in love! It's horrible. How could you? What about Papa?'

'He was a consequence I suppose of my denial.'

Josey interrupted before Jenny could finish. 'Oh I see, then I was just a consequence?'

'Oh no, darling, no. I have never regretted having you, you are the love of my life.'

'Well that's a lie,' Josey retorted. 'Surely the love of your life is this ... this woman. God, I can hardly get the word out. How could you, Mama?'

Jenny knew if she was to win this battle, she needed to think fast. 'How could I, Josey? How could you?'

'I don't understand.'

'How could you know that you were in love with Richard? Was it written, did someone tell you, or did you just feel it?'

'I felt it Mama, but that is different, he's a man and that's normal!'

'Yes I know, Josey. But in the broad scheme of things, what is normal? Does love discriminate?' Taking the bull by the horns, Jenny continued, 'Does class discriminate? You have expected me to accept your love for Richard, irrespective of his humble beginnings. You have not even thought of what your father may think. You're in love, and that's all that matters.'

And then, softly, 'Do you think this was easy for me? Not knowing whether at best you would disown me, and at worst even hate me? I have brought you up to be a free thinker, to your own self be true, and yet if you denounce me now, then all my teaching has been in vain.'

Josey stood up. 'I really don't know what to think, Mama. My head's all over the place. I have to go, I don't think I can bear this!' With that, Josey picked up her handbag and walked out of the front door.

It was done, and now all Jenny could do was to wait for the fallout.

Anne Richards sat in the hotel lobby drinking coffee and staring at the revolving doors. *Soon,* she thought, *very soon I'll have Millennium.* She slowly licked her lips, removing the froth from the coffee.

She had obtained a substantial commission from the *Sunday Enquirer* on the promise of producing something to feed the insatiability of its readers.

She greeted Jo like a long lost sheep, but without the fatted calf. That would remain her trump card. 'Oh my dear, how lovely to see you.'

The approaching waiter smiled and asked, 'Can I get you and your guest anything?'

'Oh yes please, a brandy for me.' And then turning to Jo, 'And what would you like my dear?' Bitter-sweet honey dripped from Anne's lips.

Jo nodded towards the waiter. 'Nothing, thanks.'

'Oh my dear, you must have something.'

'I said no thank you,' Jo retorted.

'Very well then, just one large brandy for me.'

The waiter nodded and walked towards the hotel bar.

'Well Dawson.' All familiarity was suspended in the absence of the waiter. 'What have you got for me?'

Jo folded her arms, presenting a defensive posture. 'Nothing that you'd want.'

'Oh dear, aren't we the defiant one! Are you really going to be difficult? Well let's see if I can change your mind.' Anne said, withdrawing some papers from her briefcase. 'Will this do?' she asked, sarcasm dripping from her tongue.

Jo took the papers and read the headline: 'Famous artist has illicit affair.'

'So what?' Jo said, shrugging her shoulders.

'Oh my dear, that's only the appetiser. Read on. And I think I've worded it very well, certainly up to *Millennium* standards.'

The words seemed to jump from the page:

Famous artist Jennifer Standford reveals in recently obtained love letters that her daughter was just an aberration. A denial of the perversity of her love for a woman. Josey St Clair, the renowned concert pianist, born out of wedlock we might add, has yet to comment. See next Sunday's issue as the letters expose Jennifer Standford's depravity.

Heads turned as Jo stood up and shouted, 'Publish and be damned! You're just a malevolent woman who should be disposed of like the vermin you are!'

Jo realized that Anne Richards had the upper hand. There was no way in which she could pre-empt the Sunday publication with her own article, and she knew that Richards had banked on that possibility.

She had to go. But before she did, she would fire a warning shot across Richards' bows. Leaning over the table, pushing her face into Anne's, she whispered, 'We've found your son. Now add that to your article.'

With that, Jo marched angrily out of reception towards the exit.

Anne froze, her whole body set rigid with fear. Was it a lie, or had her past really come back to haunt her? Either way she had to find out.

Fortunately for Anne, Jo was still waiting for a taxi. Anne ran down the hotel steps and grabbed Jo by the arm.

'Oh no you don't, my lady, we still have things to discuss.'

'I don't think so,' Jo replied as the taxi drew up.

'Well I do,' insisted Anne, still clutching Jo's arm.

'Do you want this taxi or not?' the driver asked, slightly irritated.

'Not,' Anne replied.

The taxi drew off, leaving Jo and Anne on the pavement competing in what seemed to the onlookers to be a tug of war.

'Let me go!' Jo shouted.

'No I won't. You're coming with me.'

With that Anne pulled Jo up the hotel steps. Without letting go of Jo's arm, she marched to reception and demanded her key. Still arguing, and much to the amusement of the receptionist, they got into the lift, their shouting still to be heard after the doors had closed.

Once inside her hotel room, she pushed Jo onto the settee.

'Now, you little worm. I want to know what you mean. You've found my son?'

Jo smiled with a sense of satisfaction. Had her passing shot placed Anne on the back foot? 'That's for me to know and for you to find out. Other than that I am saying nothing further.'

Anne glared. 'Well of course not. It's all a fabrication, an attempt to deflate the balloon that is about to blow up in your paramour's face.'

Jo, feeling that she had the upper hand now, taunted Anne with another, 'Well, we shall see shan't we? Now if you don't mind, another minute in your company would be slightly overkill, don't you think? Publish your damn article, but be warned, it might prove more expensive than you think.' Jo then added with a hollow laugh, 'You might have to go to your gutter press and ask for more money!'

With that Jo got up from the settee and walked towards the door. Feeling she wanted to have the last word she shouted, 'See you in hell, you malicious bitch.'

Brian had felt jittery all that morning. His nerves set him pacing from one room to another.

'Oh for goodness' sake Brian, do sit down.'

'I can't Sally, I'm so nervous.'

'Yes Brian, so am I, but you know Jo, she'll be OK.'

'Hmm, I hope so. Heard anything from Gordon Carmichael yet?'

'No, but he did say he would ring. Perhaps he's held up in court or something.'

'Well, yes, perhaps. Nothing to do then but to wait to hear from Jo.'

'No, nothing to do. Now let's get this magazine ready for next week's quarterly issue.'

'Yes of course, no point sitting here wondering. I'll go and see Jimmy, there may be some final adjustments to his article. Or not,' he added sighing.

'Oh for goodness' sake, Brian, stop your bothering, we can best serve Jo by getting on with things.'

Brian walked up to Sally and kissed her on the forehead. 'You're right, my dear, but then you always are.'

The affection of their friendship diffused the tension, and they went back to their work.

Chapter Twenty-Two

Gordon was not an impulsive man, but after his wife's, "You're never at home any more", and his client's pleading guilty, he felt that this time, perhaps impulse was what he needed. With the information he had discovered on the child's adoptive parents, he decided that rather than telephone, he would catch a train to London and talk to Sally personally.

Lydia was her usual unhappy self. 'Oh I see, yet another night alone. I really don't know why you wanted a wife Gordon, you never seem to want to be with me.'

'You knew what my life was like when you married me,' he retorted. 'So please let's not do this all over again. Go shopping, that's usually your solution.'

Lydia retaliated, 'Well you're certainly not.'

Gordon packed an overnight bag and drove his car to the train station. Parking it up in a satisfactory spot, away from opportunist carjackers, he bought his ticket and waited for the London train to arrive.

Jenny was inconsolable when Jo arrived back from Anne Richards. No amount of persuasion could alleviate her depression. She felt her whole world had fallen apart, and even her Jo represented the source of her heartache.

Jo held Jenny in her arms until the tears had subsided, but her compassion could not assuage the terror that gripped Jenny's heart. She felt abandoned, strangled by the love that had now become her nemesis. Could she ever love Jo in the same way again? Was it really monstrous, as Josey had claimed? Could she ever feel clean again?

Still holding on to Jenny, Jo guided her slowly on to the living room settee. Once they had sat, she asked, 'Was it really bad, darling?'

'Yes Jo, it was. She hates me.'

'How do you know that? Did she say so?'

'Well no, but she did say that it was monstrous. Surely that's a kind of hate, isn't it?'

'No darling it's not. It's just a big shock for her. Once she's had time to assimilate it, she'll come round.'

'But what if she doesn't Jo? I couldn't bear it.'

'Then my darling, we will have to part. There is no way that I would want you to chose.'

Jenny's tears were heart-rending and she was inconsolable. Jo could do nothing but hold her until the deluge subsided, knowing that this may be the last time she would hold Jenny close. She felt anguish, but couldn't show it. It would be the last thing that Jenny wanted at this time.

Perhaps, she hoped, Josey was more grown up than Jenny thought. Only time would tell, and time was all they had.

Dinner was nibbled at and then discarded.

'I think I might have a lie down, if you don't mind Jo.'

'Of course not.'

Jo tidied up and sat quietly in the living room. She lit a cigarette and tried not to contemplate the inevitable. The ring of the telephone startled her. God, who's this now?

Not wanting to speak to anyone, she lifted the receiver and barked, 'Yes?'

'It's Brian, Jo.'

'Oh hello.'

'Didn't go well, then?' Brian replied sensing Jo's reluctance to make conversation.

'No.'

'OK. Jo, talk to me!'

Jo then related both her meeting with Anne Richards, and Jenny's visit by Josey.

Once she had finished Brian was silent. Then, 'Well my dear, we can't let it stay like this can we? Where is Josey staying?'

'At the Marlborough. But Bri, please don't think of going to see her, it can only make matters worse.'

'Could they be any worse?'

'Well, no, not really.'

'Well then, trust me Jo. Perhaps I may be able to present a different impartial aspect, and if not? No harm done. So do you trust me in this?'

'Of course Brian, I'd trust you with my life, you know that.'

'Right then, I'll say *au revoir* then.'

It was after six in the evening when Brian turned up at the Marlborough.

'Miss St Clair, please.'

The receptionist rang Josey's room.

'Miss St Clair, you have a visitor.'

'Who is it?'

He turned to Brian. 'Your name. please.'

'Brian Cooper.'

The receptionist relayed the name.

'Who is he?'

'Who are you?'

'I'm a friend of her mother's.'

'He says he's a friend of your mothers.'

'I really don't want to see anyone.'

'She doesn't want to see you.'

By now Brian was becoming irritated by the go-between conversation, and grabbed the receiver out of the receptionist's hand.

'Whether or not you wish to see me Miss St Clair is immaterial. I am going to see you, and will stay here in reception until I do.'

'Well then, I suppose you had better come up. I'm in room 203.'

Brian took the lift to the second floor, and gave a sharp rap on the door.

His first reaction to seeing Josey was shocked surprise. How much she resembled her mother. Blonde wavy hair, chiselled features that framed the pale blue eyes. Josey was indeed her mother's daughter.

'Well, what do you want?' Josey asked, as she ushered Brian into the room. 'If it's an interview, then you are wasting your time.'

'No Miss St Clair, it's not an interview.'

'Then again, I ask, what do you want?'

Brian smiled. 'I wonder if you realize how much like your mother you are.'

Josey was taken aback, she hadn't expected the answer to be so personal.

Brian continued. 'I expect you're feeling extremely outraged by now, like your whole world has fallen apart. Well I'm here to tell you it hasn't.'

Josey was angry. 'What on earth has my life got to do with you? I don't even know you.'

Brian gestured towards a chair. 'Oh for goodness' sake sit down, Josey, and stop acting like a spoilt child.'

Josey did as she was told, but still remained defiant. 'As I said, Mr Cooper, what has this got to do with you? Or did my mother send you? In any case it won't make any difference. I can't bear to even think about my mother and this other woman.'

'Hmm,' Brian quietly murmured. 'So at the age of twenty-two you feel able to make an informed decision that will affect the rest of your mother's life. Well let me tell you, my dear, you cannot. Do you really think it has been easy for Jennifer? Well it hasn't.'

Before Josey could interrupt, he related Jo and Jennifer's story, going right back to when they were eighteen. If he had hoped to see a glimmer of remorse from Josey he was disappointed. There was nothing but steely defiance.

He would try another tack. 'So Josey, when your father decides that you must desist from your relationship with ... what's his name?'

'Richard.'

'Oh yes, Richard. Well when your father expresses his opposition to your relationship, advising you that this Richard is not good enough for you, I assume that you will wave goodbye to Richard and acquiesce to your father's wishes. No harm done then, surely there are plenty more fish in the sea, especially those of which your father approves.' Josey went to stand up. 'Oh sit down, I haven't finished yet.'

'Well I have!' shouted Josey. 'You're completely wrong. There is no way that I would let anyone come between Richard and me. We're soul mates. Never, ever would I leave him.'

'What, even against the wishes of your father?'

'Yes, even then. Richard and I are in love and that's that!'

Brian felt quite pleased with himself. He had opened the door and Josey had walked straight in. 'So, let me be clear about this. Your father's prejudices are of no consequence, whereas yours are.'

'That's different.'

'How so?'

'My relationship is normal. But those people ...!'

'Well, good for you to take the moral high ground. There's a saying in this life, "Normality is a state of the mind. Love is a state of the heart". So think on, Josey. You may keep hold of Richard's love, but lose the most precious gift of all, your mother's.' Josey didn't answer. 'Well I said what I came to say, so I'll bid you goodbye. Oh and by the way, Josey, I'm one of those people!'

Josey sat staring at the door that had closed behind Brian. She felt lonely and insecure, and if she could had admitted to it, guilty. Yet, despite all these emotions, she just could not seem to reconcile the mother she knew with the woman she had seen just hours ago.

Should she telephone? Should she go round? And if so, what would she say? Had that Brian person been right? She picked up the telephone and rang Jenny's number.

Hearing a stranger's voice at the end of the phone, she asked for her mother.

'I'm sorry, but your mother's sleeping.'

'Who's that?'

'Jo.'

She hesitated, and then replied, 'Oh yes, you're my mother's friend.' The ambiguity of the word stuck in her throat. 'I would like to come over, if that's alright.'

'Well yes, I'll fetch Jenny for you.'

Jo fetched Jenny, and told her that Josey was on the phone and wanted to come over. 'You must speak to her,' Jo told Jenny, who was insistent that she wouldn't.

But finally Jenny agreed, and she picked up the phone and said, 'What is it?'

'I'd like to come and see you.'

'Oh yes, so not afraid of being contaminated by your monstrous mother, then?'

After Jenny had agreed to see Josey, Jo picked up her coat.

'And where do you think you are going?'

'Back to my flat. Jen, this needs to be settled one way or another, and I don't think it will if I am here.'

When Josey arrived, Jenny beckoned her to the sofa, saying, 'Well, you'd better sit down.' Josey did and fidgeted with her handbag. 'Oh stop fidgeting, and say what you've come to say.'

'Just one question.'

'Oh just the one?' Jenny waited. 'Well?'

'If you hadn't been pregnant, would you have come back to England to be with that woman?'

Angrily Jenny shouted, 'That woman is called Jo, and yes, I would have. Instead I spent over twenty-three years lonely and unhappy.'

'So, I was an inconvenience then?'

Jenny had had enough of Josey's sarcasm. 'You know, Josey, you say you're in love with Richard. Well I do hope that you never have to feel the pain of being without him. You will have children someday, but when they grow up and leave home, how empty do you think your life will be, without him?'

'But you are two women!'

'So what! If you can't support me in this then so be it. I am not, not giving Jo up. She is the guardian of my heart, so if you don't like it, hard luck! Now go, Josey, I'm tired of this conversation.'

After Josey had left, Jenny realized that instead of feeling devastated, she felt a kind of liberation. All those pent-up emotions, all those closeted secrets, unashamedly revealed. She had opened Pandora's box and found Hope inside.

She raced to the phone. 'Jo, darling Jo, come home!'

> *Serene will be our days and bright,*
> *And happy will our nature be,*
> *When love is an unerring light,*
> *And joy its own security.'*
> (Wordsworth, 'Ode to Duty')

After she had put the phone down, she ran upstairs to the bedroom window to look for Jo's car arriving. When it came she almost fell down the stairs in her haste to reach the front door. She grabbed Jo's hand and pulled her inside. 'Sit, Jo, sit!'

Jo could do nothing but sit as she was told. She had never seen Jenny so forceful. Jenny placed her hands each side of Jo's face and pulled it towards her. With lips almost touching, she whispered, 'You can sell your flat now!'

Not waiting for any questions, she kissed her without inhibition.

After a while, and when Jo could finally catch her breath she said, 'So, she's come round to us then?'

'No.' Jenny replied.

'But ... but ...'

'I told her. I told her, Jo, that if she didn't like it, well ...'

'Well what?'

'Well,' Jenny laughed, 'I said "hard luck".'

'You said that?'

'Yes I did, and I'm not sorry, not sorry one bit!'

Jo hugged Jenny. 'But what if you never see her again?'

'Then so be it. I'm weary of it all, weary of all the secrets and lies.'

'But what about your letters?'

'Let them be published. I don't care any more. Although I do care that people will read my personal thoughts, but ...'

'But what?'

'I've sacrificed too much of my life without you. I'll not do it any more!'

Jo sighed deep within her soul. She could finally open that box she had kept locked inside her heart all these years.

Jenny stood up and took Jo by the hand. 'Come my darling, I want to make love to you!'

There was no longer any need for those furtive snatched moments of passion. Tenderly Jenny's lips kissed Jo's body, as her brushes had kissed her canvases. She traced every outline with her hands, and felt an abandon she had never felt before. This was her Jo, her love, and as if wanting to melt within her, she drew Jo's body close, imprinting every part upon hers. Now, there was no more leaving, no more lost years, and as they consummated their love, as if for the first time, they lay together tenderly touching every part of their bodies. They held each other and whispered, 'and the lover is beloved'.

Had Brian managed to convince Jenny's daughter? He hoped so. If he had been too hard on her, there was no taking back the words. He hoped that Jo would forgive his intrusion.

It was about nine o'clock when he arrived at Raymond's.

'My goodness sweetie, you look really frazzled. What have you been doing?'

Brian grimaced. 'Just been one of those days, some of your pasta would go down very well.'

No sooner had Brian spoken, than Raymond disappeared into the kitchen, calling, 'One Cannelloni, lots of sauce.'

'Yes Chef,' came the obedient reply.

Raymond took the plate from the service, and placed it on the table – especially reserved for Brian – poured out a glass of wine, then demanded, 'Eat, eat. You'll feel better after you've eaten. Just one last cover and I'll be right with you.'

Brian smiled as he took a sip of wine, after which he paid his attention to the plate of cannelloni.

Raymond was true to his word, and within half an hour was seated beside Brian. 'Now sweetie, tell me all about it.'

Could Brian disclose where he had been, without betraying a confidence? Although their relationship had grown from strength to strength, Brian was still a little unsure of what he could or could not disclose to Raymond. 'Just a God-awful day, love. Had to point out some home truths to someone, and now with hindsight I feel that I might have overdone it a bit.'

'Did the person warrant it?'

'I think so.'

'Well then, no harm done. Someone at work, was it?'

Brian prevaricated. 'Yes, it had to do with work.'

'Oh well I expect it'll be all forgotten tomorrow. I hope you haven't been worrying about it all this time. What have you been doing, anyway?'

'Just drove around a bit, didn't realize it was so late. You don't mind, do you?'

'Darling' – this time the carefully chosen endearment – 'of course not, you should know by now I love to see you, whatever the time is.' Raymond winked at Brian. 'Want some dessert?'

'No thank you love, but I will have some more wine.'

With that Raymond fetched a bottle from the bar, together with a second glass. 'Shouldn't be too long before they've finished in the kitchen, and then we can go up.'

Gordon Carmichael settled himself into the Savoy, and went to the bar for a drink.

'Yes, sir?'

'Gin and tonic please, and make it a large one.'

He had felt for some time that his life was abseiling down a precipice, with no safety net to stop him falling into the abyss. Lydia … well, Lydia was Lydia, with her insatiable desire to be the centre of his attention. With this, and his high-maintenance mother, life seemed to have taken its toll. He had become a man older than his years, tired and without enthusiasm. Even his professional life no longer held its initial excitement. He should leave, that's what he should do. Be more like his brother, travel and find new experiences, leave the drudgery of respectability behind, become an explorer …

Yet another pipe dream, he thought, as he downed his drink and asked for another. With obligations weighing heavily upon his shoulders, he knew that he would have neither the temerity nor the courage to unlock the chains that held him captive.

He would visit *Millennium* tomorrow and present the evidence he had obtained by overstepping his legal authority. Although he knew this to be wrong, in a way he found a kind of excitement to stray from his normal path of righteousness. *What would Lydia say?* he thought, chuckling to himself. But stray he had, and he had found the names of the family who had adopted the child who, he was almost certain, was his half-brother.

He called for yet another gin and tonic, still not quite satisfied that a little discretionary diversion from the law was justified. After his fourth glass he called for the menu, and walked into the dining room. He felt adventurous. No usual meat and vegetables for him. He would try something exotic. *A curry,* he thought.

After drinking gallons of water to cool his mouth, he thought perhaps he might have been a little too adventurous, but persisted in his new found freedom, and ordered a large brandy and coffee to round off the meal. Fully sated, if not a little uncomfortable, he returned to his room and retired to bed.

With the morning came the hangover and the upset stomach. *Was it worth it?* he wondered, as he swilled mouthwash around his mouth for the third time. Perhaps, but he still remained to be convinced.

Sally was there to greet him as he sat in reception.

'Mr Carmichael, it's good to see you, but I thought you were going to ring.'

'Yes, but I couldn't show you the documents over the telephone, so here I am.'

Sally, feeling rather that the horse had bolted, answered, 'Never mind, we'll go to my office.'

She led the way, quickly followed by Gordon.

'Would you like a coffee?'

'Yes I would thanks. Black – very black!'

Sally laughed, feeling herself warming to Gordon's boyish embarrassment. 'A late night was it, Mr Carmichael?'

'Yes, well I think so. But please call me Gordon.'

'Then,' she smiled, 'you must call me Sally. Now Mr ... er ... Gordon, what can you tell me?'

Gordon handed Sally the copy of the adoption certificate.

'How did you possibly get this?'

'Don't ask,' replied Gordon.

Sally smiled. 'Has its usefulness, being a barrister, then?'

Gordon left the question unanswered.

'So the child was a boy. But can you be sure that this is the child we have been looking for?'

'Yes, I'm entirely sure. Born the same time as the baby left at the train station. The adoptive mother worked as a nurse at the Bradford infirmary. She would have seen the baby. The date of the adoption coincides with the date she resigned from the hospital. Having searched the registry, no birth has ever been registered to her. It must be her.'

'I see, well if you're sure, what do we do now?'

'I don't know, what would you like to do?'

'Go and see Richards, tell her what we know, and see what happens.'

'Well, if you're sure?'

Somehow Gordon's presence seemed to empower her. 'Yes I'm sure, I'll just let Brian know.'

Sally, feeling heroic, and Gordon marched into the hotel.

'Miss Richards' room number please!'

'And you are?'

Gordon thought quickly. 'I'm her barrister.'

'Oh, right. Its number 410. Shall I ring to let her know you've arrived?'

'No need for that,' replied Gordon, 'she will be expecting me.'

Taking Sally by the arm they marched towards the lift.

Anne Richards was not in a receptive mood. Jo's parting shot had left her vulnerable, a condition she did not like to countenance. For the first time she wondered why she had ever embarked on this course of destruction. Could this be a major bluff on Dawson's part, or was she finally to reap the harvest of her own treachery?

'No!' she exclaimed, as she opened the door. 'Not another lot from Dawson's fan club. Well, what have we now? Snow White and one of her seven dwarfs?' Then looking at Gordon she remarked, 'Well, you can't be Grumpy, I've already seen her. I know, you must be Dopey.'

Gordon, not waiting for an invitation, stepped inside the room. 'Well Miss Richards, by the time I've done with you, you'll wish I was.'

Anne grunted. 'Well, now you're here, what do you want?'

Gordon smirked. 'Well surely, Miss Richards you must recognize me?' And after seeing the blank look on Anne's face added, 'No? Well you definitely knew my father.'

Still the blank look confronted him.

'Judge Carmichael!'

If astonishment had crossed Anne's mind you would never have seen it, but for the faint pallor on her face. As was her way, she kept her composure and answered, 'No, doesn't ring a bell.'

Gordon was becoming extremely angry at her non-committal attitude. 'Well let me enlighten you further.' He then commenced, in his usual eloquent fashion, to relate his father's demise and subsequent discovery of the boy that had been born.

'So Miss Richards,' he said. 'I'll ask you again, did you know my father?'

Anne blustered, 'It's all a bit of hearsay, don't you think? What proof do you have? I mean, a bit of paper won't hold much sway.'

Gordon was beginning to despise this woman even more than he could have imagined. 'It may be just a bit of paper to you, Miss Richards, but somewhere I have a half-brother, and I can promise you now, I intend to find him.'

'So?' demanded Anne.

'So, if you want to retain both your anonymity and keep your reputation intact you will, firstly, return the letters you stole, and secondly, cancel all publications pertaining to Miss Dawson and Miss Standford.' He drew a deep breath. 'So – and I won't ask you again – are you going to do this, or shall I ring my friend at *The Guardian*?'

Anne knew there was no way in which she could bluff this through. 'I suppose I have no choice, then. So yes, you can have the letters, but they are not here.'

'Well where are they?'

'In my safety deposit box.'

Gordon leant forward and grabbed Anne by the elbow. 'Right, no time like the present, get your coat.'

Anne stood back not used to being handled roughly. 'I don't think so,' she spat, disdainfully.

'Well I do, so I'll not ask you again!'

As Anne walked towards her dressing room, Gordon nodded. 'Sally, go with her, don't let her out of your sight.'

Sally complied.

With a firm grip on Anne's elbow, Gordon marched to the lift. On the ground floor a taxi was called and the driver given the name of the bank.

Anne's hands shook as she opened her box.

'Why Miss Richards,' Gordon scoffed. 'I do believe that you are worried that there are more than letters in here!'

Anne did not reply, her silence an admission of guilt.

Gordon took out the letters, turned to Anne and barked, 'Is this all of them?' Anne nodded. 'It had better be, but just in case, we'll take everything in the box as insurance.'

Anne was now beside herself, no composure left. 'You can't do that!' she yelled. 'They are my own personal papers.'

'Oh yes, not nice to have the boot on the other foot for a change.' Gordon laughed, a rather hollow laugh, as he put the contents of the box in his briefcase and took Sally by the arm. 'Well Miss Richards, that concludes our business, don't you think?'

Anne's incoherent reply was lost amidst the laughter as Gordon and Sally walked out of the bank.

Sally beamed at Gordon. 'You were wonderful.'

'Years of practice, my dear,' Gordon answered, then hesitated before asking, 'Can I be presumptuous and ask you to have dinner with me tonight?'

Sally beamed again. 'Yes, that would be very nice.'

'Very well, shall we meet at my hotel, say about seven-thirty?

I'll reserve a table for later, and we can have an aperitif before we eat.'

Sally, beginning to more than warm to Gordon Carmichael, repeated, 'Yes, that would be very nice.'

'Great. Now, Sally, can I escort you back to your office?'

Sally smiled. 'No thank you, I'll get a cab from here.'

'Very well, I'll meet you in the lounge bar at seven-thirty.'

Sally was overwhelmed with joy at the prospect of having dinner with Gordon, and by being able to give Jo those infamous letters. Gordon had left them with Sally, keeping the rest of the box's contents safely tucked into his briefcase.

Sally raced into Jo's office. 'Jo, Jo, oh Jo! I've got them!'

Jo looked up from her desk. 'Oh do calm down Sally. What have you got?'

'The letters Jo, I've got the letters!'

'But how ... what? How?'

Sally, breathless from her run, could not get her words out.

'Oh Sally sit down, breathe deeply, and then tell me.'

Sally did as she was asked, and as she related the story, Jo's eyes grew wider and wider at every sentence. 'Oh my God Sally, this means ...'

'Yes dear Jo' – this was the first time she had used the "dear" word – 'this means it's all over.'

Jo took up the letters Sally had placed in front of her. 'I must ring Jenny. No, better still, I'll go home.'

'Yes, yes, do!' cried Sally. 'I'll tell the others.'

> *'While here I stand, not only with the sense*
> *Of present pleasure, but with pleasing thoughts*
> *That in this moment there is life and food For future years'*
> (Wordsworth, 'Lines Composed a Few Miles above Tintern Abbey,
> on Revisiting the Banks of the Wye during a Tour. July 13, 1798.')

Jenny was surprised to hear Jo's key in the door. It was unexpected, so it could only mean bad news. 'Darling, why are you here. Oh God Jo something's wrong!'

Laughing, and remembering the day before, Jo said, 'Now Jen, I want you to sit down.'

'You're frightening me now!'

'Nothing to be frightened about. Just sit down, I have something for you.' Whilst Jo felt a wee bit guilty to be toying with Jenny, she wanted to savour the moment when she placed the letters into Jenny's hands. 'Now sit down, close your eyes and hold out your hands.'

'It's nothing nasty is it?' Jenny replied, wincing.

When Jenny sat down with her eyes dutifully closed and her hands held out, Jo placed the letters in them.

'Right my darling, you can open your eyes.'

Jenny carefully opened one eye, then the other, and looked at her open hands. Staring down, with eyes now wide open, she gasped. 'Jo, Jo, they can't be … they just can't be!'

'They are, my dearest. Now we have nothing to worry about.'

If Jenny had felt like fainting, now was not the time. 'But how? Why? What!?'

'I asked the same thing when Sally placed them on my desk. so I'll tell you what she told me.' And so she did, savouring every tiny morsel, as if tasting food for the first time.

Now it was time for Jenny to collapse into Jo's arms. Relief chose to send waterfalls cascading down her cheeks. Relief that defined a watershed, that imaginary line over which she and Jo could now cross. Nothing was now left to chance. No more was that unpredictable ball spinning round a roulette wheel in the hope that it would land fortuitously.

Jo held her close, catching Jenny's relief and tucking it deeply into the safety of her heart. It seemed they sat there for hours, although only minutes passed.

'Let's celebrate Jen, let's, let's –'

'You mean go out?'

'No my darling, we now have two things to celebrate.'

Jo giggled. 'Didn't we do that yesterday?'

Jenny also giggled, and jumped up from the sofa. 'I think I have some champagne in the fridge. I was saving it for after the exhibition, but this is more important. I'll get it, you get the glasses Jo.' And then, as an afterthought, 'Oh I forgot to ask. Did you read the letters?'

Jo laughed. 'No darling, I thought we would read them together.'

'Oh yes!' Jenny cried. 'Oh yes, let's.'

And so they sat on the floor, backs against the sofa, a thing they often did when they wanted to feel close to each other.

One by one, in between sips of champagne, they took the letters from their envelopes.

'Goodness,' Jo laughed, 'this one's a bit racy!'

'Oh I know, must have had a glass of wine.'

'Or two!' Jo replied.

'Or three,' Jenny confirmed, laughing out loud. A laugh Jo had not heard for a very long time, and she remarked upon it.

Jenny nodded, turned and held Jo's face in her hands. 'Oh I do so love you Jo.'

Jo took her hands and kissed them. 'Oh and how I love you.'

As Jo leaned back into Jenny's arms a thought suddenly occurred to her. 'Of course Jen, you do realize that this might make a difference to Josey. If she knows there will be no scandal after all, she may, just may, come around to the situation.'

'Oh Jo, does it really matter now?'

'Well, if you're sure?'

'Yes my darling, I'm sure.'

Chapter Twenty-Three

After Jo had left, Sally didn't know whether to laugh or cry. Yet she did know that if it wasn't for this sorry business she would never have met Gordon.

When foolish fantasies threatened to consume her she steadied herself and went to find Brian and Jimmy. They were both ecstatic at the news.

'Let's give everyone the rest of the day off!' a cavalier Brian shouted.

At Sally and Jimmy's frowning faces he exclaimed, 'Well come on, we can all work late tomorrow.'

Together they said, 'OK, you go and tell everyone.'

Brian pushed his hand through his hair. 'Phew,' he laughed, 'what a day this has turned out to be.' And went off to tell the rest of the workforce.

There was no hesitation as they all made a quick exodus from the building.

'We'll go to Raymond's, Brian stated as he put his arms around Sally and Jimmy's shoulders.

Raymond was bemused; he had just started the lunchtime service.

Brian patted his arm and laughed, 'You get on with it Ray, don't mind us, we'll sit at my usual table. We'll be as quiet as church mice, promise. Can William bring the wine list?'

Raymond gave a haughty shrug of his shoulders and went off to fetch William.

As promised they tried to keep quiet, although an intermittent laugh brought a scowl from Raymond.

Anne Richards, however, had nothing to celebrate. Her anger and frustration took its toll out on the hotel minibar. Downing the fourth miniature bottle of gin, and throwing the empty bottle onto the floor, she slumped into an armchair.

She felt powerless, like a car that had unexpectedly run out of gas. No AA to come to her aid with a replenishing can of petrol. All she could do was to start walking.

But where? She had put all her eggs into one basket, and they were left cracked and scrambled. She had to think.

More gin, she thought, but the mini bar was empty. Room service dutifully brought a bottle of gin and some tonic.

'Will that be all, madam, or would madam like to order from the menu?'

'No madam wouldn't,' she barked as she ushered him out of the door.

Drinking herself into a stupor, she finally fell into an alcohol-induced sleep.

After the lunchtime service had ended, Raymond joined Brian and his friends at their table, who after another bottle of wine were giggling like mischievous school children.

'OK, OK, you lot, I suppose you're gonna tell me what this is all about?'

Sally looked at Jimmy, Jimmy looked at Brian, and they all burst out laughing.

'What's so funny?' Raymond was now becoming irritated.

It had not been long since Brian had confided in Raymond about Jo and Jenny's situation. He reached out and gently touched Raymond's hand and smiled. 'Laughing with happiness, Ray. it's all over.'

Raymond frowned. 'What's all over?'

'Can I tell you later? Have a glass of wine, and then Sally and Jimmy have to be off.' The last sentence was said with a wink to his friends.

Sally nudged Jimmy's arm. 'Yes, Jimmy, we ought to go now. I'm sure you have something to do, and I ... and I have to get ready for my dinner with Gordon.'

On hearing this Brian and Jimmy burst into hilarity, nudging and winking at each other amidst bouts of laughter.

'Oh shut up you two,' Sally laughed. 'It's not like that, it's only a dinner.'

Unconvinced, their laughter grew louder.

'Come now you two!' Raymond barked. 'Leave the poor girl

alone. Now Brian dearie, I have to tidy up, so you two go home!'

After they had left, Raymond told Brian to go up to the flat. He would join him as soon as he had finished in the restaurant.

Brian had almost finished his brandy when he heard Raymond's key in the door.

'Thank goodness, all done. Now dearie, where's my G and T?'

'All ready for you,' Brian replied as he stood up to kiss Raymond.

'Oh God Bri, I'm full of sweat.'

'No matter, I'll kiss you anyway.' And he did. A long, lingering kiss, just to prove he loved Raymond sweat and all.

'Right now my chickadee, I'm off to pour another brandy. Want another G and T?' Brian asked.

He mused to himself how he could ever begin to thank Jo for engineering his meeting with Raymond. As he poured the tonic into Raymond's glass he sighed, knowing that Raymond and Jo were the two people he loved most in the world.

Raymond had already departed to the bathroom. 'Leave my drink on the table, I'll have it when I come out.'

'Want me to scrub your back?' Brian yelled.

'Later, dearie,' Raymond laughed.

Gordon felt a tinge of excitement as he plugged in his electric razor, and began to shave. Perhaps it was adolescent of him to think that Sally could countenance sharing such a feeling of anticipation. He chastised himself for such thoughts. *What would she see in a 42-year-old married man?*

Duplicity was something he had defended in the courts, excusing it for the vagaries of human fallibility. However, he consoled himself with pragmatism. After all, it's just a dinner.

When Sally arrived promptly at half past seven, she saw Gordon waiting in the lounge bar.

On seeing her he smiled and walked quickly towards her. 'Well my dear, what shall you have?'

'A glass of wine I think.'

He ordered two glasses, and cupping her elbow with his hand, gently led her to a vacant table. 'We'll sit here, if that's alright by you?'

Sally smiled, thinking – quite shamelessly – that anywhere with Gordon would be nice.

They chatted very briefly about that morning's triumph, and

then, as if Gordon had only just realized, he said, 'Do you know Sally, we really should be thankful to Richards.'

Sally frowned.

'Why? Well if it hadn't been for her, we would never have met!'

Sally began to laugh, but didn't admit that she had earlier had the same thought. Instead she said, 'Well yes, Gordon, but aren't you forgetting something?'

'What?'

'The lost cat!'

With that they both burst out laughing, so loudly that people began to stare at them.

Gordon leaned over the table and placed his hand over Sally's. 'You know, my dear, that was such an ingenious thing to do. Never in a hundred years would I have thought of a lost cat.'

Sally blushed, but had to own up and tell him it was really Jo's idea.

'Never mind,' he answered, 'it was still a brilliant idea!'

Over dinner, they shared little confidences, which seemed a natural development to their conversation.

When, finally, the dinner was over and it was time to go, Gordon leaned forward to brush a hair that had fallen over Sally's eye, and whispered, 'Can I see you tomorrow?'

Sally having no relish in seeing the evening end, lowered her eyes and said, 'If you want to, that would be very nice.' There, she had said it again, that 'nice' word which could not convey the way she really felt.

'I don't have to go back home until the day after tomorrow, so I thought it would be nice to spend a day out with you, that's if you can get time off?'

Sally would have called in sick if she hadn't known that Jo would be happy for her, so there was no need for subterfuge. 'What time shall we meet?'

'Well, I'll pick you up from your home about ten 'o' clock.'

'But you don't know where I live.'

'If you think I'm letting you go home on your own at this late hour ...'

'But I can get a taxi.'

'We'll both get the taxi, I can drop you off, and then come back in the taxi to the hotel.'

'Well, if you're sure ...'

'Of course I'm sure.'

As agreed, he dropped Sally off at her home, kissed her on the cheek, and confirmed their arrangement for that following day.

True to his word, Gordon picked Sally up at ten 'o' clock the following morning. What a delight she was in her pink pleated skirt and white silk blouse. Her pale face had just a hint of blusher, gently framed by her long auburn hair that had been swept back with two silver clips. Again Gordon felt his heart race, and knew how easy it would be to fall in love with her. He wanted to tell her how lovely she looked, but instead related his plans for the day.

'I thought Sally, if it's alright with you, that we'd take a trip into the country. Find a nice spot to have lunch, and then decide what to do afterwards. What do you think?'

Sally looked up and smiled. 'Oh yes that sounds lovely.'

Her smile disarmed him, and for a brief moment he forgot what car he had hired. 'Blue Escort I think!'

'Sorry, Gordon?'

He hadn't realized he had spoken out loud, and laughed. 'Just remembered what car I'd hired.'

They giggled like children sharing a secret.

Gordon drove slowly through the Kent countryside. As they passed the oast houses standing stately on the hills overlooking the hop gardens, they marvelled at the way the hops used to be picked manually by families who spent their holidays in the fields.

'Yes quite an industry in those days, now a lot of it is done by machinery.'

'Oh what a shame.'

Gordon sighed. 'Yes it is.'

They found a small country pub in a village called Seal, just outside Sevenoaks. It was quaint, with the traditional oak beams festooned with horse brasses. Refurbished oak chairs with spindle legs and carved backs were placed uniformly around oak tables covered with Irish linen tablecloths. They chose a table by the window, and ordered two glasses of wine, which were brought accompanied by the menu.

'This is lovely,' Sally whispered.

'Yes it is,' Gordon whispered his reply. And then, 'Why are we whispering?'

Again they giggled, their eyes meeting in that singular glance of recognition. *Yes,* Gordon thought, *I could fall in love with this woman.* Sally, however, was certain. She knew she had fallen in love with Gordon. She felt herself blush at the thought, and hid behind the menu to avoid detection. Too late, Gordon had seen it.

He leant over and gently touched her arm. 'Well Sally, what shall we have?'

They chose an avocado starter, and then roast lamb followed by a lemon sorbet. The food was as tasteful as their surroundings. They ate leisurely, savouring their meal and their time together. Over coffee, they decided to pootle around the countryside, find a quiet spot, park and enjoy the view.

The quiet spot was a small river with ducks, swans and the occasional angler. Gordon fetched a blanket from the boot of the car, and laid it on the ground. They sat in comfortable silence. Gordon lit his pipe, first asking if Sally minded, but of course she didn't. He drew on the tobacco and watched the pale blue smoke disappear into the sky.

'Sally,' he turned to her as he spoke.

'Yes, Gordon.'

'This has been a most wonderful day. Which, if I can hope, could be one of many.'

'Oh yes, Gordon, so do I, but that's not possible. I mean, you are married, Gordon, and I would hate to come between you and your family.' She did not want to say "wife" as this would have brought home the absurdity of it all.

Gordon put his arm around Sally's shoulders, and quietly said, 'You do know what is happening, don't you?'

Sally blushed and gave a little shiver. 'Yes Gordon, I think I do!'

He raised her face to meet his, and kissed her gently on the lips. 'So, my dearest.' This was the first time he had dared to call her that, and the joy of it hung delightfully upon his lips.

'But can it be that simple, Gordon?'

'Well dearest ...' The sound of it for the second time reaffirmed his growing love for her. '... well Lydia will get over it as long as she is still able to surround herself with material things.' At that he laughed. 'Well, she may need to cut down a bit. That will be more of a shock to her than any divorce.'

Anne Richards woke the next morning, and for a brief moment wondered where she was. Looking down, and realizing that she was still fully dressed, the nightmare of yesterday came flooding back to her. If her head wasn't pounding so much, maybe she could make more sense of it. However, Gordon's words, "You have now reaped what you have sown", hung heavily upon her.

As she undressed and showered, she felt depressed and powerless. Not an emotion she was used to.

After dressing, she rang room service and ordered a pot of black coffee and some buttered toast, thinking this would quell the nausea threatening to rise up from her stomach.

She mused over the third cup of coffee that the only thing she could do was to leave London, return to her home in the Cotswolds, and then decide where to go from there. Losing the letters was, she thought, an inconvenience, but the loss of her other personal items traumatized her more than she, in another time, would have allowed.

She packed, paid her account, and drove slowly to her home. The mind that was before yesterday as sharp as a knife, was now a blunted, redundant utensil.

Chapter Twenty-Four

Jenny and Jo woke early that morning, and unlike Anne Richards they were happy to greet the new dawn. Over breakfast, interspersed with giggles, they decided they should ring Josey. At least, if nothing else, to tell her she didn't have to worry about any disclosures.

A very curt voice answered the phone.

'Josey is that you?

'Yes Mother, it is.'

Ignoring her curtness, Jenny told Josey about the letters, but if she had expected any softening in Josey's demeanour, she was disappointed.

'Well Mother, I'm happy for you. Now I have to pack for my visit to see Papa.'

'Very well, perhaps you can give him my regards.' And as an afterthought, 'And to Richard of course.'

As Jenny replaced the receiver, she turned to Jo. 'Well my darling it's time we both got on with our own lives.'

Chapter Twenty-Five

Gordon sat in the train, humming softly to himself. Before he had met Sally, he hadn't fully realized how empty his marriage was, and how his work had filled the void of the day-to-day routine he had become used to in his home life. Was he just a meal ticket? A paymaster for the insatiable spending which his wife had taken for granted?

Again he thought, *yes I will tell her tonight. I want this fruitless coupling ended. Yes,* he thought, with a determination that lifted his soul, he would waste no more time, he would tell her tonight.

After putting his briefcase into the boot of his car, which he had left at the station car park, he turned on the ignition, and still humming to himself, drove home.

He had not looked at the rest of Richards' paraphernalia, as he wanted to have a clear mind. Time for that later.

Lydia was in the kitchen, when Gordon turned his key in the lock.

'Oh so you're back?' came the terse greeting. 'Thought you might have rung at least.'

Oh shut up, he thought. And then, *nothing changes, does it.* He placed his coat on the rack in the hall and put his briefcase in his study. Pouring himself a G & T, he slowly walked into the kitchen.

'Dinner's not ready,' Lydia stated. 'I wasn't sure when you would be home. You didn't bother to phone and let me know.'

Again Gordon thought, *oh shut up,* but instead replied, 'Leave dinner, come and sit down in the lounge, I want to talk to you.'

'Oh yes, what has your mother done now?' The usual sarcasm dripped from Lydia's lips.

'Nothing to do with my mother.'

'Well what is it then?'

'It's us.'

'What about us?'

'I want a divorce.' There, it was out.

'A divorce? Whatever for?'

'Come now Lydia, you know this marriage is a sham. There's no love in it. I'm just your paymaster, and you ... well you're so wrapped up in your high society friends – and I use the term loosely – that you really don't care whether I'm here or not, just as long as the money keeps you in the comfort to which you have made yourself accustomed. Well it's over, Lydia. I'll see Stephen tomorrow and he can get the ball rolling.' Fortunately although they had never been able to have children, he now felt it a blessing. No reasons or excuses to confront them with.

For the very first time Lydia could not speak, not even to spit bile from her mouth.

'Good then.' And not waiting for a reply, 'That's settled. And don't worry you'll get your fair share of the spoils.' He laughed humourlessly at that final word. 'Now, I have work to do, I'm in court tomorrow. I'll not be needing any dinner, I'll get a takeaway later.'

With that he turned on his heel and walked into his study, closing the door behind him.

Lydia, with all the wind taken out of her sails, just stood looking at the closed door. If she had been honest with herself, she would have realized that this was a long time coming.

But her thoughts were not on the man she had married, but on what this would mean to her income. She was used to luxury, used to competing with her wealthy friends. But now, would they leave her like rats from a sinking ship? No she was not going to have that, she would obtain her own solicitor, and make sure she got that to which she firmly believed she was entitled.

Sally sounded overjoyed to hear Gordon's voice on the telephone.

'I've done it Sally, I've told her.'

'Told her what?' Feigning ignorance.

'Told her I want a divorce, and as quickly as possible. I'm sorting it with Stephen tomorrow before I appear in court. Stephen and I have been friends since law school.'

'Oh,' was all Sally could reply, beside herself with happiness.

'Must go now, my darling. I'll speak to you tomorrow. Will you be at the office?'

'Yes,' she answered, and then whispered softly, 'Goodnight my love.'

It was only after Gordon had put the telephone down that he focused his attention on the contents of his briefcase. It seemed that Anne Richards had collected an eclectic array of slanderous documents pertaining to the higher echelons of society, judges, politicians, police commanders and the like. *Well,* he thought, *these can go in the shredder'.*

Sorting them through and placing them into a pile ready to be destroyed, he noticed an old black and white photograph of a small baby. Could this be her son? And then this suddenly reminded him that he had a half-brother somewhere. Should he look further into it? Yet, thinking it through he knew that if he did, this would mean bitter ramifications for his mother. Could he put her through all that heartache again?

No, he decided, he would wait until his mother had passed away. And with that thought he locked the photograph and all the papers relating to the adoption into his bureau drawer, and shredded the rest.

Sally was beside herself with happiness. So much so, that she couldn't sleep. She wanted to tell someone, but she knew that whoever she rang would not be pleased at being woken up in the middle of the night, even if it was good news. So, she made herself a cup of hot chocolate and sat down in her living room. I'll ring Jo tomorrow, she consoled herself.

And she did, at half past six the following morning.

'Who's that?' Jo asked.

'It's me Jo, Sally.'

'What on earth? Do you know what time it is?'

'Yes, but I couldn't wait to tell you.'

'Tell me what?' Although Jo loved Sally, she felt a little irritated at the early intrusion.

'Gordon and me.'

'Yes, what about it?'

'He's getting a divorce!'

'Look Sally, I know this is exciting for you, but can't it wait until later?' And without waiting for a reply she added, 'Look come round say at about nine, we'll both be *compos mentis* by then.'

Ignoring Jo's lack of enthusiasm, Sally said she would call round then.

Jo got back into bed, and snuggled into Jenny's arms.

'What was that all about Jo?'

'Oh, it's Sally being her usual excitable self. Something about Gordon. I've told her to come at about nine, if that's OK with you, but knowing Sally she'll be here about eight-thirty.'

Jenny grinned. 'Poor girl, she must have it bad.'

'Mm,' was all Jo could respond.

'Now come on Jo, don't be a wet blanket, you must remember how we were when we first fell in love!'

Jo leaned forward and kissed Jenny on the forehead. 'Yes of course, it's just that at this time of the morning ...'

'Oh shut up you, come and kiss me.'

Sally was true to Jo's prediction and arrived at Flaxman Square at eight thirty-five, full of profuse apologies.

With the cup of coffee drunk, which Jo had given her, Sally related her day out with Gordon, how they both felt the same about each other, and the essence of Gordon's telephone call that evening.

'Phew, Sally,' Jo exclaimed. 'Are you sure? I mean, he is a bit older than you.'

'No he's not, only two years,' Sally remonstrated.

'Well he looks older than that,' Jo retorted.

Jenny prodded Jo's foot underneath the kitchen table.

'Well, I mean, it's a bit sudden, don't you think?'

Sally shrugged her shoulders and bravely said, 'Well, that's a bit like pot and kettle don't you think? How long was it before you two knew you loved each other?'

At that they all laughed, and Jenny touched Sally's hand. 'Of course, Sally. Don't mind Jo. She's bound to act like a mother hen, after all she's only got your well-being at heart.' And then, turning to Jo, 'Isn't that right Jo?'

Lightening the mood, Jo said loudly, 'Well don't think I shall be wearing a hat when you two get married. You will be getting married, won't you?'

Sally laughed and replied, 'Yes of course Jo, Gordon is a very honourable person.'

The conversation was ended with Jo stating, 'Right Sal, off to work you go, I'll follow later. Oh, and can you have Brian, Little Jimmy and yourself in my office about eleven-ish.'

Sally frowned, 'OK Jo. Nothing wrong is there?'

'No sweetie, just need to talk to you all.'

After Anne Richards arrived back home, she unpacked and poured a G&T, thinking hair of a dog and all that, and sat down in her lounge. Bereft of all the aces she had kept up her sleeve, she had no column to write, no poison to spread, no power left to wield. With this in mind she telephoned her friend and confidante Suzanne.

'Hello Anne, what a lovely surprise. I do love a bit of gossip.'

Anne dismissed the last part of Suzanne's sentence. 'Thought I might come over for a visit, if that's alright by you. Of course, unless you are doing anything ...'

'Of course not darlink, I'd love to see you, and we can catch up on all the things you have been doing. I must say, my gossip has been a little threadbare recently. When do you think you'll be over?'

'Well,' Anne breathed a sigh of relief, 'in the next couple of days if that's OK with you.'

'Of course, let me know when you will be arriving and I'll meet you at the airport.'

Anne replaced the receiver, thanking God that she had at least one friend left.

Chapter Twenty-Six

That previous night, Jenny and Jo had discussed moving to Pen Marig permanently. Jenny would keep Flaxman Square, for George, and if it were to be, for Josey. Jo would leave the magazine and write the book she had always wanted to. Although Jenny had tried to dissuade her from leaving *Millennium*, Jo was adamant, so Jenny gave into Jo's wishes.

As asked, Sally, Brian and Little Jimmy were sitting in Jo's office when she arrived. All three of them looked perturbed and a little uneasy. Brian was picking at his fingers nervously, Little Jimmy was fidgeting in his chair, and Sally was attempting to pour coffee into four mugs.

Jo laughed. 'Oh for goodness' sake you lot, you're not about to be hanged.' And then, laughing out loud, 'Although it may be a life sentence without parole.'

Jo's humour was lost on them, as they stared at her open-mouthed.

Jo sat down in her chair, took a sip of coffee and said, 'First of all, I want you to know how much I care for each and everyone of you. You have been my staunch friends for all these years. You have proved to me how lucky I have been to have had your friendship and loyalty.' She took another sip of her coffee, and continued, 'Well as you were all instrumental in ending the Richards debacle, you have made it possible for Jenny and me to have a future together. So ...' – she breathed deeply – 'so I'm leaving *Millennium*.'

At this they all gasped.

'But you can't,' stated Brian. '*Millennium* is you, it's Jo Dawson.'

'No my dearest Brian, it's not, it's you three, and so I'm transferring my shares to the three of you.' Jo waved her hand as Brian was about to interrupt. 'This will mean that you will not only run the magazine, but you will own it as well.'

Their silence was broken by a string of questions. Finally, Brian asked what Jo was going to do.

'Me? Well folks, Jenny and I are going to live at Pen Marig. Jenny will continue with her painting, and I will finally have time to write the book I always wanted to write.'

After another load of questions, Jo finished the meeting with, 'Now you lot, I'll only be in Wales, not Australia. If you need (and I don't think you will) if you need advice etcetera then I will be at the end of a phone. But,' she added, 'there will be neither interference nor judgement from me. It is your magazine, and you can do what you would like to do with it. Now that's all, so I'm off to see the accountants, and you lot, well you lot, take the rest of the day off.' Then with a friendly wink and giggle, 'That's my last order as your boss.'

They spent their day off in the Pressman's, toasting each other, toasting Jo, and toasting *Millennium*. After yet another bottle of wine, Sally began to cry. Brian put his arm around her shoulders, and Little Jimmy passed her a handkerchief.

'Don't cry Sal, we'll still have Jo, and we'll make *Millennium* a magazine she will always be proud of. As she said, she'll only be at the end of a phone, and anyway we can always visit her en masse.'

Feeling a little comforted, Sally wiped her tears with Jimmy's handkerchief, saying, 'I'll wash it Jimmy, and then give it back.'

'No worries Sal, I've plenty more.'

As Jo left the accountants, having organized the share transfers, she couldn't help the tinge of sadness that crept through her. She knew that she had done the right thing, but leaving *Millennium* was harder than she thought it would be. But after all, children grow up and leave home, to be loved by a new family.

As she sat in the taxi taking her back to Flaxman Square, she thought of all the possibilities she had to look forward to, now with Jenny and Pen Marig, and thought of the book she would write. She would call it *The Blue Pendant* and dedicate it to Jenny and her beloved friends.

Gordon had been right to ask Stephen to arrange his divorce. He, like Gordon, was an astute and clever practitioner of his craft. The hearing was quick, as were the financial arrangements, and within two months, Gordon was free to be with Sally.

As Sally had stated, Gordon was an honourable man, and he

and Sally did not consummate their love for each other until the divorce had become final. As Sally lay in his arms, they discussed their wedding. It wasn't to be a big affair: registry office and a small reception.

Mrs Carmichael was overjoyed. Whilst she had tried over the years to tolerate Lydia, she always knew in her heart of hearts that she was not the one for Gordon. Having met Sally for the second time, she knew instinctively that this was the right one for Gordon. She began to take Sally to her heart, as Sally took Mrs Carmichael to hers.

Lydia, on the other hand, saw her entourage of friends diminish, until finally she left for New York to live with her sister.

The wedding, as they had both wanted, was a small affair. Brian was to give Sally away, and Jo and Jenny were to be their witnesses. As Gordon's brother Michael was still abroad, Stephen was to be his best man, but no – and he was adamant about it – no stag night.

Jenny had asked Josey if she and Richard would like to attend the wedding, but their engagements precluded that. However, Josey did agree to meet Gordon and Sally on another occasion, and left a cut glass vase for their wedding present. Gradually, Jenny and Josey's relationship had become better, especially after Josey's thwarted trip to France, and the animosity she had suffered when telling her father about Richard. She had cancelled his visit, as she in no way needed him to suffer the wrath of her father.

Brian was magnificent in his dark blue tuxedo with pastel blue tie, and walked Sally down the aisle like an emblazoned peacock. Jo wore a grey pinstriped suit with a white silk blouse, and Jenny wore a green dress that flared out under her breasts, and flowed down to her ankles. Arm in arm they walked to their seats, amidst smiles and claps from their friends.

Sally, however, stole the show as she walked with her arm entwined in Brian's. Her silver-grey dress with matching headdress, which framed her face, brought out the radiant colour of her eyes.

Gordon's breath was taken away as he saw her walking towards him. *No,* he thought, *he would never let any harm come to this woman,* and promised silently to care for her, and to love her every single day.

Mrs Carmichael, Jenny, Raymond and Brian were crying as

the vows were said, and Jo almost, but not quite, felt a tear drop from her eye onto her cheek.

The reception was a lively affair. Raymond had closed the restaurant for the day, and although agonizing over the menu the day before, excelled himself with the food. When the food was eaten, and more drink ordered, it was time for laughter and more dancing.

Gordon danced with Sally. Jo danced with Jenny. Brian danced with Raymond, and even Little Jimmy danced with Celia, a girlfriend about whom he had kept very quiet. Mrs Carmichael was happy to sit on the sidelines with Stephen, smiling like a Cheshire cat.

As the night drew on it was time for Gordon and Sally to head off on their honeymoon. They were to spend the night at the Savoy and from there leave for their trip the following morning. Gordon would not disclose the destination beforehand, and it transpired that it was to be Venice.

After Gordon and Sally left, there was more wine drunk, until well-inebriated Brian suggested that they help Raymond by washing up. Amidst raucous laughter, Brian filled the sinks and nominated himself and Jimmy to wash up, whilst Jo, Jenny and Celia wiped. As Brian poured more and more washing up liquid into the sinks, bubbles floated over the drainers. Like children they picked up the suds and started throwing them at each other. This was too much for Raymond, who stood in the kitchen door, hands raised high above his head, shrieking, 'What are you doing to my kitchen? Stop it all of you!'

At this more laughter resounded, and Brian picked up a handful of suds, walked over to Raymond and patted these onto Raymond's head. 'Oh shut up you silly old queen. Loves yer, don't I?' After which he planted a long kiss on Raymond's lips.

At this there was more raucous laughter, even from Raymond. 'OK, OK. You load of monkeys, haven't you got any homes to go to? Be off! Brian and I will sort this out. I'll call for a taxi. And no, you can't have another drink while you wait.' The latter sentence said with laughter and a twinkle in his eye.

As they all tottered to the door to await the taxi, Brian asked if he and Jo could have a chat later, and it was left that he would phone her tomorrow. Jo was to drop Jimmy and Celia off and then go on to Flaxman Square. Stephen was to take Mrs Carmichael back to their hotel.

'One address is it?' Jo whispered in Jimmy's ear.

'No,' grimaced Jimmy, 'not at that stage yet!'

'Oh,' Jo replied, and patted his shoulder. And then as if to console him added, 'Plenty of time yet, eh?'

Jimmy shrugged.

After they had dropped both Jimmy and Celia off, they nestled down in the back seat of the taxi.

'Gosh darling,' Jenny said, 'I bet we'll have a headache tomorrow.'

'Yes I bet we will, but what a lovely day it's been. Although I don't envy Brian having to clear up all the mess.'

'No, but I bet Raymond will make it worth his while.' At this they both shouted with laughter.

A brusque voice came from the front of the taxi. 'Are you alright back there? You're not going to be sick in my cab are you?'

Jo put up her finger to her mouth, and whispered 'Shh', which led to a more subdued laughter.

The meeting that Brian had requested at the wedding revealed that they wanted to add a publishing company to the magazine's portfolio. Jo was enthused at the idea, and realized that she had left her legacy in very careful hands. And so the company was formed, and it wasn't long before they were attracting new writers.

Life was wonderful for Jo and Jenny. Jo had a contractor build a studio on the back of the farmhouse which Jenny could use for her painting. While Jenny painted, Jo roamed the hills with Mattie, her new collie, stopping to sit at Marling Rock and contemplate the beauty of the valley and her life with Jenny.

She had made one of the spare rooms into a study, where she would write furiously, ideas flowing unhindered and profusely.

'I want to read it!' Jenny had exclaimed, but this was denied. 'No my darling, not until it's finished. You don't know, it could be rubbish.'

Jenny had poo-pooed the idea, knowing how clever Jo was.

It was just a couple of weeks after Sally and Gordon's wedding that Jo and Jenny went shopping in Aberystwyth. As they stopped by a jewellers, Jenny yelled, 'Oh Jo, let's get married!'

'But how?'

'Well we could buy rings and have our own private ceremony.'

'Do you think so?'

'Oh yes, I do. Come, let's go in and buy the rings.'

'Well, if you're sure …'

And so they did. With rings chosen and engravings requested, they walked out of the shop like children who had just stolen a sweet.

Jo giggled at Jenny. 'I think he thought we were mad! Well, what could he say when we told him what engraving we wanted?'

Jenny tucked her arm in Jo's. 'Doesn't matter, darling, he's got our money, what more does he want?'

Jo laughed. How she loved this woman. 'Well yes, what does it matter? I'll pick up the rings next week, and we can have our own ceremony.'

The next week Jo went back to the jewellers and fetched the rings.

'I hope,' he said, 'that the engraving is alright.'

'Oh I'm sure it will be,' answered Jo.

He placed the two gold rings in separate boxes and handed them to Jo.

'Thank you,' she said, wanting so much to look at the engravings. As she looked she saw what they had requested 'J & J Alpha Omega 1962'. *Yes,* she thought, *that'll do very nicely.*

That evening, they lit the stove and sat on the floor their backs against the sofa. On the record player they put their special song on, and listened to the words as they exchanged rings.

Chapter Twenty-Seven

Josey and Richard had visited Pen Marig on two occasions, when their concerts would allow, and it seemed that a little more warmth was creeping into the mother-and-daughter relationship.

Richard was a delight and he and Jo became firm friends, walking the valleys with Jo's collie Mattie.

'You know what, Jo,' he said, 'I could easily give up all that travelling and live here.'

'Well you never know what the future will bring.'

The future brought the secret wedding of Josey and Richard when in La Vegas, much to Henri's disapproval. And soon after, the birth of Josey's baby Sarah, and with it a greater understanding of what motherhood meant.

Richard, coming from a humble background, couldn't understand Josey's reluctance to build bridges, and said so on many occasions. However, with the birth of Sarah, Josey began to realize that in life there were very many different avenues to walk, and that love in itself guided the way. And very soon they became more frequent visitors to Pen Marig.

On one of these occasions, whilst Richard, Jo and Sarah were out walking, Josey sat down at the kitchen table drinking tea with Jenny. It seemed a long time before she spoke, and Jenny asked her if something was wrong.

'No Mama' – the familiarity was back – 'No Mama, nothing wrong. I just want to ask your advice.'

'Well yes dear,' Jenny said, not quite knowing what was to come.

Josey put down her cup, looked straight into Jenny's eyes and said, 'I want to give up the concert tours. I've had enough of them Mama. I want to spend my time with Sarah.'

Jenny interrupted, 'What does Richard say?'

'Well Mama, you know Richard, he's happy whatever I do.'

'So what will you do, if you stop playing?'

'Well Mama, my agent has been talking about my making more records, and … and Richard wants to give it up too.'

'But my darling, what will he do?'

'What will he do? Well Mama, I think that is Jo's fault!'

Jenny began to feel a little uncomfortable. 'What has my Jo got to do with it?'

'He wants to buy a small farm or something like that.'

'But I don't understand, Josey, he knows nothing about the country ways.'

'Well Mama, he didn't until he found Pen Marig.'

Jenny, perturbed, continued, 'But what about his playing? He is dedicated to his violin. Surely he'll never be able to play with calloused hands, which is all you get when working on the land.'

'He, like me, has had enough of touring. He wants to settle down. Don't forget, Mama, his father was an artisan and I think he has realized that this is where his roots lie, and anyway he'll probably get a farm manager or somebody who will help with the labouring.' Josey was at full steam and wouldn't be interrupted. 'He loves it here, and so does Sarah. I can't, and I won't take that away from him. I can continue with my music, and he can continue to be happy.' She sighed then. 'Mama, that's all I want is for him to be happy, and for Sarah to grow up with true values.'

As there was no shaking Josey from her course, Jenny only smiled. She could have been bitter, thrown up the past, but Josey's happiness gave no reason for it.

'Well if that's what you both want to do, then let Jo help Richard find somewhere.'

Red-faced, Josey looked down at the table cloth. 'I think, Mama, she already has!'

Jenny laughed. 'She has, has she? Well she kept that very quiet.'

'Don't be cross Mama. She wanted me to talk to you first.'

'Well that's alright then.' And then, very quietly, 'So Josey, now you can see why I love her so much.'

'Yes Mama I do, and I don't think I shall ever stop feeling guilty about my shameless attitude towards you. I … I am so sorry!'

Jenny lifted her hand up to stop Josey from saying any more. The next few weeks were a hive of industry. Richard and Jo went again to visit the small abandoned farm they had found, ten miles from Pen Marig.

'Best thing, Richard, is to start small. As my uncle used to say, nice things come from small packages. You'll of course need someone to help you, and if I can, I would like to suggest a retired farmer. You could advertise, but Francie at the post office will probably know who would be suitable.' And then laughing, 'The bush telegraph has nothing on what Francie knows.'

This was done and very soon the small farm became a viable entity. They started small with a dozen sheep, and a very large vegetable plot. Richard rejoiced at his new-found freedom, and with Bert, the retired farmer who became the farm manager, enlisted some of the boys from the village to help with the heavy work. Richard soon became quite proficient in the ways of the land.

Josey had made their little cottage homely, and added a music room where she could play and practice for her records. Sarah, however, had no interest in music, and took more pleasure in her first pair of dungarees, and Wellington boots.

Chapter Twenty-Eight

Gordon and Sally, together with Brian and Jimmy, were frequent visitors to Pen Marig, and all was idyllic until Jo noticed that Jenny was beginning to have more frequent headaches, and seemed to feel constantly unwell.

'We need to take you to the doctor,' Jo said.

'Oh Jo, don't worry, it's probably working too hard and not having enough fresh air.'

'I don't care,' Jo adamantly replied, 'I'm going to make an appointment, whether you like it or not.'

Doctor Mushlin, although hiding it, was a little anxious. 'I think Miss Standford that you ought to see a consultant.' And as Jenny raised her hand, 'Just to make sure that these headaches could just be migraine.'

The consultant ordered an MRI scan, and the appointment was made for the following week. Jo was worried. *So soon,* she thought.

After the scan, Jenny and Jo were taken into the consultant's room, and told to wait.

'Oh I don't believe this Jo, this is stupid, and it's just a headache.'

Jo was not convinced and patiently waited for the consultant to appear. And appear he did, a stocky grey-haired man, with kind eyes.

'Well Miss Standford,' he said, folding his arms, 'It's not good news. It seems that you have a small brain tumour.'

Jo was aghast. 'How small? Surely you can operate and get rid of it!'

'Well, we could, but it is right behind the eye, and we would only have a fifty-fifty chance of removing it without dire consequences.'

Jenny hadn't spoken a word.

'What dire consequences?' Jo asked.

'Well, because of the position and of course your age, Miss Standford, there is a chance that you could have a major stroke, or …' and he hesitated, 'or could die on the operating table.'

'I see,' replied Jo, with Jenny still silent.

'So if we don't have the operation, what then?'

'Well, as the tumour grows and begins to put pressure on the brain, there will be the incidence of seizures. Which,' he added, 'can be contained with medication.'

'I see, so now what?'

'I will be writing to Miss Standford's doctor, and he will prescribe the medication. However, an MRI scan will be needed in the next six months, to see how fast the tumour is growing.'

With that he rose from his chair, shook Jenny and Jo by the hand, and said, 'I am so sorry.'

Jo, with her book almost finished, moved her desk into the studio, where she could keep a watchful eye on Jenny. Gradually Jenny began to have more and more vacant episodes, where she would stare into space. After six months, Jo took her back to the hospital for another scan. The news was not good: the tumour had grown, and the consultant advised that there would be the likelihood of the vacant moments turning into seizures. Stronger medication was given, and Jo and Jenny returned to Pen Marig. If Jo was terrified, she did not disclose it. Breaking down would be of no help to Jenny. No, she would remain strong, and care for her twenty-four hours a day.

She sat Jenny down in the kitchen and made a pot of tea. Turning away from the stove she said, 'Jenny, you will have to tell Josey you know. You'll not be able to keep it from her forever.'

'I know, but I don't know how to.'

'Would you like me to tell her?'

'Well yes, my darling, you remember everything, whereas these days my memory is deteriorating.'

Jo poured the tea, and agreed to tell Josey on her next visit to Pen Marig.

The weeks went by and as the seizures became more and more frequent, a lot of Jenny's memory was lost. Josey was told, and became desperate at the thought of losing her mother, and although Jo tried to console her, Josey's devastation was complete.

'Look Josey, you know I will look after your mother, and you … well you have Richard and Sarah to help you through this.'

Promising to keep Josey informed, Jo hugged her and reiterated that she would keep Josey up to date on the situation.

Chapter Twenty-Nine

2004

'Let me not to the marriage of true minds
Admit impediments. Love is not love
Which alters when it alteration finds.
Or bends with the remover to remove:.
O, no, it is an ever-fixed mark
That looks on tempests, and is never shaken:

Love alters not with his brief hours and weeks,
But bears it out even to the edge of doom.'
(Shakespeare, 'Sonnet 116')

It was the day after Jenny's sixty-first birthday when she took Jo by the hand, and requested that they walk up to Marling Rock. Whilst Jo was unsure whether Jenny could walk up the hill, she agreed.

As they sat down under the tree, Jenny laughed. 'Remember, Jo, the first time you brought me here? How wonderful it was?'

'I know sweetheart, we were so much in love.'

'We still are Jo, aren't we?' Jenny interrupted.

'Yes we are,' she quietly answered.

Holding Jo's hand, Jenny leaned her head against Jo's shoulder. 'I want to talk to you very seriously Jo. I know, and you know that every time I have one of those turns, as you call them, I lose more and more of my memory, and I am so afraid that one day I will wake from them, and forget who you are, and I can't have that Jo, I can't.'

Jo took Jenny in her arms and held her tight.

'No Jo, let me finish please. I don't want that day to happen. I need to end this before it does.'

Jo couldn't believe what she was hearing. 'That won't happen my darling, I'll keep reminding you who I am.'

'But Jo, my Jo, it may be too late, so …'

'So what?' Jo was becoming scared.

'So, I need to end this, whilst I can still know the person I have loved all these years, and …' She started to cry. 'And you must let me go in my own way.'

Jo held Jenny tightly, and said nothing.

'Say something Jo, please.'

Jo inhaled deeply. 'I see, so you are firmly set on this, then?'

'Yes I am, Jo!'

'In that case we shall go together!'

'But I don't understand, Jo!'

'It's very simple my darling. I have loved you all my life, keeping my heart just for you. With you I am a whole person, without you … well, I dare not think of it. So we shall go together.'

'Oh Jo, I can't let you do this!' Jenny cried.

'Sorry dearest, it's not your choice to make. As you don't want a day to come when you can't remember who I am, well I don't want a day to come when I wake up and you are no longer there.'

'But darling, what about our family and friends? What will they think?'

Jo leaned her head against Jenny's. 'Don't you think that after all these years they would know that this could be the only inevitable end to our love story?'

'Oh Jo, yes it is, isn't it. Our love story, that began forty years ago.'

Jo gently kissed Jenny and sighed. 'Yes my darling, our love story.'

For a long time they sat under Jo's tree, holding and kissing each other, without words, without remonstrations, and for a brief moment the valley surrounded these two people in a blanket of warmth and affection. Even the breeze seemed to hum a soft lullaby.

They decided that they would not tell Josey and Brian until they had put all their affairs in order. Mr Jones, the village solicitor, was called for, and together they made their last will and testaments.

Pen Marig was to go to Brian, who on his demise would leave

it to Sarah. Josey and Richard would have half of Jenny's estate, with the residue left in trust for Sarah. Jo's estate would be divided between Brian, Sally and Jimmy. Mattie, Jo's collie, would be entrusted to Richard. Once Mr Jones had completed his task, both wills were executed, and witnessed.

'There that's done,' Jo sighed. 'Now I think we'll have a party. I'll get everyone together, and we can drink, dance and laugh like we did when Sally got married. What do you think?'

'Yes that would be lovely, and we'll tell Josey after the party.'

As Jenny's headaches became more severe the doctor had prescribed an increased dose of the morphine tablets, and after their conversation at Marling Rock, Jenny had reduced the dose and stockpiled tablets, ready for when she and Jo would choose their time.

The party was arranged, and life at Pen Marig was happy again. As Jo had said, they ate, drank, danced and laughed outrageously.

'Brian,' Jo stated, 'you are not going anywhere near my sink?' Again, the laughter followed recollections of Sally's wedding and Raymond's consternation at seeing his kitchen drenched with soap suds.

At the end of the party, taxis were rung for, to take all but Josey and Richard, who would follow later, to their rooms in the village pub.

After kisses all round, and Brian whispering to Jo, 'I'll be back tomorrow', they left; their laughter resounding over the valley as they got into their taxis.

Josey and Jo (without the abundance of soap suds) washed the dishes and tidied up. When the last glass was put away on the Welsh dresser, Josey turned to Jo and said, 'I think you have something to tell me, don't you?'

Richard, Jenny and Sarah were sitting in the parlour, leaving Josey and Jo alone in the kitchen. Jo poured out two glasses of wine, lit a cigarette and sat Josey down at the table. Although this conversation had been turned over in her mind, now that the time had come, Jo was at a loss as to how to start.

Josey sipped her wine and looked straight at Jo. 'Mama's dying isn't she?'

'Yes,' sighed Jo, and then related what was happening with the tumour, and how it would only get worse.

'I see, so this was a goodbye party, then?'

Jo had never realized how astute Josey had become. Perhaps it was motherhood, she mused. 'Yes,' she said, and then took Josey's hand in hers. 'Yes, and it's all arranged now.'

'But how?'

'Oh Josey, do I really need to spell it out? Jenny will go peacefully, before the very essence of her no longer exists.'

'And you Jo, what about you?'

'I will go with her.' She lifted up her hand to stop Josey from saying anything. 'This is how I want it, I cannot bear the thought of living without her. Don't you see, Josey, she has been my love, my life. I cannot, will not exist in this place without her.'

Josey was crying then.

'Shh,' Jo said, taking her hand. 'Shh, you can't let her see you like this, you have to be happy for us.'

'I'll try,' was all Josey could say.

'Good, I'll tell you when.'

'Will it be soon?'

'Yes quite soon.'

With that they left the kitchen and joined Jenny, Richard and Sarah in the parlour.

'Come on now you three, I think it's time you went home,' Jo smiled. 'I'll call a taxi.' And then, 'Oh Richard, could you take Mattie with you, I'm sure she will love to show you how to herd those sheep of yours.'

Richard laughed. 'What you mean all thirty of them?'

'It will give her practice, won't it?'

'Of course, if you are sure.'

Jo said she was, and Mattie was called for. It was a new adventure for her, as she walked behind Richard, after having hugs and kisses from Jo.

Walking back into the house, Jo finally let the tears flow. There was no sleep for either of them that night. Sitting up in bed, they remembered all those years they had together.

'Do you remember Jo, when you gave me the necklace, and I kissed the pendant and told you that I would wear it forever. Well, I'll tell you a secret now, what I really meant to say was that I would love you forever.'

'Well you did, didn't you? As I did, my darling.'

Looking down at her hand, Jenny said, 'What will we do with our wedding rings Jo?'

Jo thought for a moment. 'Well, I would like to give mine to Brian.'

'Oh yes, yes, he can have mine as well. After all Jo, he has been the one constant in our lives.'

Jo was happy with that.

Leaving Jenny in bed, Jo rose early next morning and Brian, true to his word, arrived at ten-thirty.

'Too early for a drink I suppose,' he asked.

'Why not Bri, it must be twelve o'clock somewhere in the world.'

'Right then Jo, no messing about, tell me straight.'

'I don't know what you mean Bri.'

'Oh yes you do, so come on, tell me.'

Jo did, amidst frequent nods of the head from Brian. 'And when is this to happen?'

'Probably tomorrow Brian.'

'Does Josey know?'

'Yes.'

'So, my dear Jo, what can I do?'

'Aren't you going to try to stop me?'

'Good Lord no Jo, I think I know you well enough to realize that that would be futile. Anyway your life has always been with Jenny, and your love for her. It would be churlish of me to try to dissuade you.'

'Thank you dear,' was all Jo could say.

'So what is going to happen?'

Jo told him then of her and Jenny's plans, and how he should get in touch with Mr Jones when it was all over.

He agreed, and with heavy heart took Jo in his arms and held her close to him. 'Will this be the last time I shall see you?'

'I think so Brian.'

'Then I must tell you that, apart from losing Raymond, the loss of you in my life will be a devastation that I can hardly bear. And yet I am so proud of you Jo, so comforted that I have had you in my life, and yes my dear, my very dear friend, I will never forget you.'

Jo unfolded herself from his arms. 'Can I leave it to you to tell Sally and Jimmy? I really don't think that I could face them.' And then she said, 'Brian, I don't want you to forget that all through these years you have been the safety pin that has held me together, and I will leave being forever thankful that I had you as my dearest friend.'

As tears began to well up in their eyes, they said their goodbyes. Jo watched him as he walked down the path to the bottom gate, and silently thanked him from the bottom of her heart, for the friendship they had shared together.

The rest of the day they spent together in Jenny's studio. Feverishly she painted, needing to finish the canvas she had started two months ago.

'Must get this done, must get this done!' she cried. 'Jo, I must get this done.'

Jo brought her tea and put her arms around Jenny's shoulders. 'You will my darling, you will. Now is there anything I can help you with? Do you want me to bring your pills?'

'No, no, they will hinder my progress. It has to be finished today.'

'Alright my darling, but tell me if the pain gets worse.'

'I will, I will,' Jenny replied knowing she wouldn't.

The painting was a montage of her and Jo, from when they first met to when they lived together at Pen Marig, and this (she had written down) was to hang at Pen Marig, so that no one would forget them.

At about four-thirty she put down her brushes and slumped into a chair. 'There, my darling it's all finished.'

Jo was astounded. this was surely Jenny's best work. 'It's, it's … Well, words fail me Jenny.'

'It's our legacy,' Jenny answered. And then, 'I don't want anyone to forget who we were, who we are. It is to go in the parlour, beside those of your Aunty Doll and Uncle Tom, and that of Pen Marig.'

'Oh my dearest, I don't think they will forget.'

That night they prepared themselves for the next day.

Jenny lay in the bed, while Jo went down to the kitchen to phone Josey. 'It's today, Josey.'

'Right, I'll be straight up.'

Josey had previously told Richard of her mother's and Jo's plans. They left Sarah at home, while he and Josey drove up to Pen Marig. No tears from Josey on the way, just stunned silence.

Jo was busy in the kitchen when they arrived. She had made tea and buttered scones, reminiscence of Aunt Doll, who would do this to alleviate any crisis.

'Where's Mama?' Josey asked.

'She's in bed.'

'Can I go up?'

'Of course,' replied Jo.

It seemed ages before Josey returned to the kitchen. Tears cascaded down her face, and as Richard reached her she fell into his arms.

Jo sat quietly at the kitchen table, lit a cigarette and gazed out of the window, imprinting the picture of Marling Rock on her mind. After a while, Josey, still crying, sat down at the table and took Jo's hands in hers.

'Jo, is there nothing I can say to stop all this?'

'No Josey, it is what your mother and I want. You see, we have loved each other for a very long time, meeting when prudence permitted, but loving always. So no, there is nothing to do now. Fate decreed we should meet and be together, so as we said when we exchanged rings, till death do us part. And Josey, please let us do this.'

'When will it be?'

'This morning, so you will need to come here later in the afternoon. I have spoken to Richard and he will telephone the doctor when it is all over. Don't be sad Josey, all our years together have led us to this day.'

Josey nodded and got up from the table. Richard placed his arm around her shoulders as they left Pen Marig.

Jo busied herself washing up and tidying Jenny's brushes and paints in the studio. Then she went back to the kitchen and placed two slices of bread in the toaster, opening a small can of baked beans whilst the bread was being toasted.

There, she thought to herself, when she placed the beans on toast on a tray. *There, as it began, so it shall end.*

'Oh darling, beans on toast, how lovely.'

'Yes my darling, this is what you called a meal, when I first stayed with you at Flaxman Square.'

'Oh I know Jo, but I was so excited, I didn't think to go out shopping.'